DRAGON SCRIPT

K.N. NGUYEN

DEDICATION

To my friends near and far who've inspired me to follow my
passion
You are my strength
You are my future

PROLOGUE: A HAIL OF FIRE

A hail of fire spewed from the clouds above, quickly followed by a crack of flaming lightning. Ashen meteors screamed as they fell from the black clouds of soot and cinders. One, roughly the size of a goblet, hissed as it thudded through the stone parapet beside a lone figure. Aiken stopped, skidding to a halt behind the merlons of the castle to look out over the hills beyond the moat. The wind ripped at his long, silver beard and pulled at his dark purple cloak. Taking the moment it took for the stone to turn from a glowing orange back to its slate gray, Aiken turned to check behind him. A zip of blue light showed where his loyal familiar flew down an adjacent hallway behind the ciborium to his left. His eyes darted back to his destination, and he regripped the massive tome in his hands, pulling it to his chest.

"Can you see them?" he shouted to his familiar.

Only the sound of his echo reverberated through the stonework towards him. Sweat made the ash from the falling stars stick to his unlined face. Despite his beard, Aiken showed few signs of age. A few creases around his eyes turned black as the soot gathered there—the only indicator of the decades he'd walked the earth.

"They are going north," the lilting voice of his dragon-shaped familiar replied. The small being flashed past him, diving over the quickly disintegrating battlements. "The well. They are heading for the well!"

Aiken snapped his head back around to look into the now dark castle. So he had been wrong. The last talisman hadn't been in the cloisters. The well waited hundreds of feet under the foundation of the ancient castle. A beautiful, turquoise pool, it glowed in the darkness, lighting up the crystalline caves that spidered out underneath. It was the perfect hiding place: it was forbidden to go into the water save for a certain rite. The talisman has to be in the well.

With a grunt of distress, Aiken turned and dashed back into the castle. Three talismans clinked on his wrist as he ran. One more to go. His order had unleashed three of the dragons on the unsuspecting pastoral land they were tasked with over-seeing. Instead of saving the people, leading the way, teaching them—they had destroyed them. This was why he turned against the order. Why he had to betray them all. Why he had to lock away the dragons one last time, destroying millennia of tradition and magic.

His feet slipped on blood and rubble as he spun down a spiral staircase to a large painting of the last Vedic: the one who could unleash or subdue the dragons. The painting showed a man reaching his hand to the sky, the four talismans wrapped around his arm in all their golden glory. In the sky above, four dragons glared down, waiting to be commanded. Aiken flung the painting open and slid into the hidden passageway.

Master! his familiar called into his mind. The blue gem that represented his dragon-shaped familiar on his wrist glowed. It's Edward. He's gone.

Rage filled Aiken. The order had poisoned the boy's mind, forced him into being the next Vedic. Unknowingly, the young ward had unleashed hell onto earth, all in the name of righteousness and power. He had trained Edward ever since he came to the order. The boy had been quiet, reserved, but a promising enchanter. Perhaps he should have tried harder to build a real relationship with him. But it was too late now. The beasts soared through the skies. Burned the fields. With only one talisman still locked, there might be a chance to…

"I'm going to the well," Aiken panted. He stopped and looked over a dark, deep drop. These stairs led underneath the castle, built in case a quick, secret escape was needed. His order, The Future, had a way with secret escapes. This one would lead him right to where he needed to go. "Get the others," he said, his chest suddenly growing heavy with understanding. "It's too late to save everything. But we can save them. They're not all lost causes."

Master? his familiar asked. What are you doing?

"Don't mind me." He lashed the tome to his belt, fixing it so he could run. "I know what I have to do."

Above him, something rocked the earth and what sounded like an avalanche crashed over his head. The castle would fall. The Future had dug their own grave and even they couldn't escape their grand scheme. He slid into the dark tunnels, holding up his hand after a quick incantation to cast light into the sparkling network. The alcoves were quiet. Frowning, Aiken walked quickly.

"Edward!" he chanced, calling the boy's name.

"Aiken," a smooth, low voice whispered.

The wizard spun, his other hand poised to attack. He knew that voice. Down a large tunnel, the shapely silhouette of a woman turned to face him. He couldn't see her creamy skin, her blood-red lips, or long rose-gold hair, but knew beyond a doubt the first in command, the high enchantress, spoke from the shadows. Her voice, though she spoke just the one word, dripped with poisoned honey.

"Where is the boy, trickster?" Aiken growled.

The woman tilted her head at the insulting word. "You know me better than that, dear friend. But perhaps I overestimated you." She turned, sauntering down the tunnel. "There is only one monument left, old man." She raised a hand. With a flash of red sparks, three of her henchmen appeared from seemingly nowhere.

Aiken dropped his orb of light. It vanished before it hit the stone ground. Using both his hands, he conjured a sword of white-steel to face the brutes. One ran headlong at him. He easily parried the clumsy attack and spun to face a more methodical one who sashayed to his left. Aiken flung the full folds of his purple cloak into the man's face before releasing the clasp. The man spun, confused and wrapped in the heavy fabric. Turning quickly, Aiken kicked the first man down and stabbed him hard in the shoulder to incapacitate him. Using the butt of his blade, he rendered the second unconscious. The third, seeing his fellows so easily dispatched, ran to follow the woman.

Aiken gnashed his teeth in determination and gave chase.

The blue-green light from the well splashed onto the walls of the last few yards of the tunnel. Cries of hurried incantations rang up to meet him. He recognized Edward's high, terrified voice as he spoke the words to wake the last dragon.

"Edward, stop!" he shouted, bursting into the cavern.

The woman loomed over Edward, her hand firmly gripping the back of his neck. She held him at arm's length, facing a monolith with an ancient carving covering the entire front. The elements had smoothed out most of the detail, but the mysterious light from the blue well cast shadows on what remained, outlining a four-legged, winged dragon on the face of the monolith.

"Traitor!" the woman snapped, leaping between Aiken and the boy. "Catál is waiting. The last dragon. You cannot stop it, no matter your convictions. I grow weary of trying to convince you that the magic in our veins was given to us to use. To wield!"

"This is not what we do," Aiken called. He stopped his chase, concerned she might harm Edward if he came closer. "This is not what they do!" He thrust his hand towards the relief of the ancient dragon Catál.

"They do as I say," the woman murmured back, narrowing her eyes and lifting her head.

Edward gave a small cry and stumbled back a few paces. "It's asking me a question," he moaned, eyes fixed on the monolith. "I-I don't know the answer."

"Don't do this, Edward," Aiken tried again. "Catál will destroy you if you do not pass his test! And you can't, Edward. There's no way for you to wake him and live."

Above them, the castle rumbled one last time. A cacophony of thunder, meteors, and the roar of the other three dragons signaled the final blow above.

"Then we best just fetch the damn thing," the woman screeched. With a savage cry, she flung Edward into the blue pool. The surface cracked as if it were ice and the small child sunk beneath. The sound of his splashing cut off as the surface once again turned to hard, blue crystal.

"What have you done?" Aiken cried, rushing to the edge. Pressing his hand against the hard crystal, he watched helplessly as Edward's eyes drifted closed.

The woman screamed and hammered her fists against the monolith. "Catál waits for me. We must awaken all four. This is your doing, old man." She turned on Aiken.

His heart broken, like his world above, the wizard stilled. Once Edward's body vanished into the green darkness of the well, he took a deep breath. His hand went to the tome on his hip that he had prepared.

"There is not one creature who can waken the dragons," he whispered. A single tear rolled down into his white beard. "The magic is not reserved for one chosen child. Edward was just like any other ward of The Future, my friend."

"You're wrong," the woman moaned, pressing her forehead against the cold, stone monolith. "I made sure he was strong. They should have awakened for him." With a final growl, she slammed her fist into the dragon's likeness. Then she pushed off to face him. "It's not over for me."

A whistling, zipping sound alerted Aiken to what he'd been waiting for. His familiar cut past him in a blur of blue light and slung a powerful spike of his own magic at the woman. She screamed, not seeing the tiny, lightning fast dragon, and jumped away.

"Little devil!" she cried, swatting at him wildly.

With the tiny distraction, Aiken ripped the tome from his belt and threw it to the stone floor. The spine cracked open, and the pages flapped in the magic wind from Aiken's incantation. They were blank. Calling on all his power, Aiken shouted out to the three dragons above. Even they submitted to some old magics. But it cost him. It had cost the others who guarded the dragons. It had cost the world.

His familiar roared, reared his head back, and bit deep into the woman's face. She reeled back, blood splashing down her neck. She tore at the little dragon, but he held fast.

A surge of power shot through Aiken as he connected with the three dragons above. They fought his tether, but he held on with every last drop of his essence.

"Sleep!" he commanded, slamming his palm onto the tome. "I have destroyed the Codex of Quezacotl, the Tablet of Mehen, and the Scroll of Tianlong and now the Tome of Catál.

Here in this Script I hide you. Only answer to one who doesn't understand. Who doesn't know. Who will not take your power for themselves. None other ever again!" A dark red ink spread from where his palm hit the tome, scribing a looping script that squirmed and danced from one language to another. Glyphs, runes, and lettering seeped into the pages, always changing. Looking down, Aiken watched the Script's words come to life. The thick pages blotted with a dark red ink not even he could read. "I know who I am," he whispered as the spell sapped his strength. "Thus shall I not have the sight to read this."

With those last words, the tome's edges turned to bright embers. The fire of the dragons crawled over the edges of the page to where his hand pressed into it. The heat burned him, but he held on.

A blast of red lightning shot through the ceiling above, striking the tome before spidering out onto the ground. A roar sounded, confirming the dragon was bound.

The second strike came yellow and loud, nearly shoving him off the tome. But the third eluded him. He didn't have enough strength.

"Give me your essence!" he called, reaching his other hand to his familiar.

With a final snarl, the small blue dragon released himself from the tussle with the woman and shot to his master's outstretched hand.

"Hurry!" the familiar called, understanding the sacrifice he was about to make.

Destroying his old friend and taking his magical essence into him, Aiken called down the final beast. The woman teetered on her feet, hand clasped to her bloodied face.

"Why?" she screamed, tears and blood soaking her cheeks. "Aiken, tell me why! You were one of us."

The final crack of lightning struck the tome. The smoldering pages extinguished, but the magic still rushed around them, tossing his beard and the pages in a mysterious gale.

He raised his eyes, hardly seeing her through the glow of the magic. "If you don't know, old friend, then I cannot tell you."

Reaching down, he slammed the Script shut. In a flash, the wizard and the torrents of magic vanished. The cave went perfectly silent, not even the trickling of the rivulets of spring water making a sound. The woman's good eye bulged, landing on the Script. She lunged for it, knowing this would hold the answers to what the old man had done.

Just as her fingers grazed the leather binding, a flash of white, red, and yellow blinded her. The colors shone so brightly that her eyes stung and she had to look away, covering them. Snapping back, she found only the empty cave. The tome, the wizard, and his dragon were gone.

CHAPTER 1: THE ROOK

The heat and humidity of the Connecticut summer hadn't touched the asphalt yet. The hinges clicked, and the rack roared as Cass opened the huge, metal warehouse door. She stood in the opening, scanning the foggy street for the truck that should be delivering a shipment of new baubles, books, and pretty trinkets. Working at The Witch's Bones hardly ever required 6:00 a.m.deliveries, but when it did, she volunteered to take care of it. Felicity and Everly had finally let her.

"That's bold, really, for a college student," Felicity, one of the owners, had said the night before. Felicity had a way of drawing her black and silver shawls tightly around her too-thin body and looking at Cass with wide, concerned eyes under a wild pixie cut that made her feel bad. Even if she had been trying to do them a service.

"I told you," Cass had said, "I want to prove I can take on more responsibility."

"We know you can," Everly, Felicity's pointy-toed-shoe-wearing husband had added. "But your studies come first."

Cass thought Everly looked like an old sage. With his

Albert Einstein salt and pepper hair and his huge, round glasses, he looked like a dusty old librarian in an ancient monastery who would yell at you for touching a book. But on the contrary, Everly smiled often.

"I can do this," Cass said out loud through a huge yawn that closed her eyes. Above the store, a rook flapped down and landed on the W of the old wooden sign. It deposited a leaky, white gift to Cass below. "Gross!" she shouted at it, jumping out of the way just in time. "Is that how you ask for water?"

The rook had been coming to greet her for some time and she'd always filled the decorative bird bath out front for it. With the summer heat in the aptly named city of Rookwind, Connecticut the water dried up fast. The bird landed outside the front window first, panting. That had been enough to melt Cass's heart and offer it some water. Now, she filled the stone bath every morning.

"What have you got for me today?" she asked the bird. "Maybe a quest that will show me my true inner strength?"

Just then, a piece of crumpled up paper blew past her on the street. She watched it, imagining it was a map to a hidden treasure, or genie in a bottle that would grant her wish to pass her classes. She didn't chase it, watching it vanish instead. The rook cawed.

She ran inside the store from the back warehouse to the bathroom to fetch a pitcher of water. As she filled it, she looked up at her reflection in the ornate mirror. Everything about Witch's Bones was elaborate, Salem-styled decor—even the bathroom the customers never saw. Cass took in her auburn hair and noted the flyaways. A single dark circle had appeared under her right eye, dulling the green of it. She'd never loved her red hair or green eyes, but Felicity said she had the eyes of a witch and that a witch's power came from their hair. She'd not cut in some time thinking about that.

"I need all the help I can get," she sighed, marching out

front to fill the bath. Classes at Weathermoore College were not a drag. She loved studying anthropology, but she felt unprepared for the workload. The classes and projects in her third year intensified just as she had adjusted to life alone, with a job, and taking care of her own life.

"All right, you chalk-turd," she said with a smile to the rook. "Come and get it."

Just as she poured the water into the stone bath, pretending she was the lily maid from the poem, the truck rumbled up the hill towards the back.

A man hopped out and asked if everything should go in the warehouse. She nodded, then pulled a pen out of her long, messy hair. She signed for the delivery, her hand shaking a little, and fumbled with the pen, handing it to the man.

"Yours," he grunted.

"Oh, right," she laughed nervously, tucking it behind her ear. It fell loudly to the concrete behind her, but she dare not bend to pick it up after that. Her face burned, and she held her breath. Well done, she thought to herself. Look at you, big delivery taker, pen dropper.

Cass didn't move until the man left. Then she picked up a medium-sized, heavy box into the store for cataloguing. The Witch's Bones was an everything-you-need dream shop for the alternative crowd in the small town. Every dark corner was filled from nice things like fairy statues with glitter to a room in the back where darker curiosities lay. Incense, brooms made of lavender, glittering statues of Vishnu with his beautiful blue skin, little golden buddhas, some bloody crosses, racks of jewelry, and books filled the store's floor. There was even a narrow, tall, turquoise bookshelf with tea pots and loose leaf. The store smelled amazing to Cass. Sure, it was crowded, but she loved the closeness of it. It made her feel safe.

She slammed the heavy box down onto the counter, then turned on the store speakers to blare Eddy Grant's Romancing the Stone. Then she went to work, making several trips to get the boxes. Her rook watched her go back and forth, singing with the music, until the last box was safely inside.

"See?" she panted to herself, checking her watch. "I can take care of business."

Just as she declared her victory, the bottom of the first box gave away, ripping and spewing the contents all over the rug behind the counter. Cass stood, taking the barrage of heavy books against her knees, grimacing.

"Spoke too soon," she sighed, bending down to pick them up. They were all books like "Cocktail Witchcraft" and "Yoga for the Egyptian Gods" and other weird mishmashes. One caught her eye amongst the glossy and matte covers. A simple, large, leather-bound journal with a blue stone on the front. She'd seen dozens like it before come through the shop. This one was larger, and the leather was soft, like suede. She hummed, amused, and flipped through the blotchy, blank pages. "Used journals, Felicity? Really?" She dropped it on the counter with the rest, shut the warehouse up, locked the store, and waved goodbye to her rook friend.

She looked longingly at the small coffee shop across the street that was just opening. Biting her bottom lip, she thought about her drive to the college and the line already outside the shop. She deserved a muffin and coffee, right?

Her phone vibrated madly. Almost angrily. Looking down, the unflattering picture of her best friend Vamshi—the only goth Indian in the entire state (her words)—winced up at her.

"Oh, my god, girl!" Vamshi shouted when Cass picked up. "We have an 8:00 a.m.class with a group project presentation and you're not here!"

Cass looked down at her watch. "Seven thirty?" she shouted. With a sad, coffee-less groan, she slammed her car door and flew down the street to her twenty minute commute.

Cass glared hard at the long, glossy brown hair of her absent project mate. Vamshi stood next to her, seething through lips covered in matte black lipstick and eyes surrounded by the darkness of black eyeshadow.

"This is why group projects are the worst," Vamshi growled, unable to uncross her arms. "All she had to do was make one slide. One damn slide."

Cass sighed, picking up the fake Egyptian artifacts she'd borrowed from The Witch's Bones and placing them gently back in the box. "It's not fair that even though we did our part—more than our part—we get Cs because she can't make a slide."

She watched their other partner, Cathy, hang off her boyfriend's neck. Cathy smiled and giggled, no doubt enjoying her effortless C. "Maybe having a hunk like that makes everything not matter," she groaned.

Vamshi rolled her dark brown eyes. "Trust me, guys suck too."

Cass winced, picking up the box and her crossbody bag. "No luck with Advik?"

"Do you know his name means 'unique'?" Vamshi asked, slinging her own bag over her shoulders as they marched out to their next class.

"No, Vam," Cass laughed. "No one knows what the color orange represents, no one knows what it means when you dream of gold coins, no one knows name meanings but you."

Her friend let the sideways compliment go. "He is anything but unique. And he's such a mommy's boy." Vamshi elbowed her when she didn't reply.

Cass'd been trying to set Cathy's hair on fire by mere

thought as the girl sauntered away with her boyfriend's arm over her shoulder. "Sorry, was watching Derek's ass," she lied, inclining her head to the couple.

"He's a mommy's boy, too," Vamshi laughed. "I saw him carrying his laundry basket out to his car Friday afternoon."

"So?" Cass asked.

"He takes it home on the weekends." This news brought a deep, diabolical laugh from her friend. "For his mom to clean."

Cass couldn't help but smile. "Isn't he a senior?"

Vamshi nodded. Changing the subject, she said, "So, Hanging Gardens for lunch?"

The Mediterranean restaurant waited just across from the student parking lot, wafting its savory cooking over all day, making Cass's stomach growl. "Of course," she replied.

The girls parted ways then. Vamshi to her pre-colonial Indian literature class and Cass to art history. They had just started to study Mesoamerican art and folktales and Cass loved it. Her professor, Ms. Dawnstride, had worked at a huge historical art museum before turning to teaching. She often told stories about her time there and the exhibits that came and went.

Ms. Dawnstride pushed through some old slides on a carousel, making a clacking sound that made Cass imagine she was in a tent on safari in the 1920s. She rested her chin in her hand, completely taken in by the wild depiction of a man and a kind of feathered serpent on the screen when a soft, smacking sound reached her ear. Sighing in frustration, she realized Cathy and her boyfriend had started to make out in the dimly lit room. Why Cathy was in the anthropology program baffled Cass. She bet her scholarships that the boyfriend was even more in the wrong career.

"Miss Mills?" Ms. Dawnstride said suddenly, drawing

everyone's attention from the feathery dragon on screen to the couple in the back.

Cathy gasped and looked up, shoving her boyfriend off. "I wasn't ignoring you again, Ms. Dawnstride," she said in a simpering way.

"That's great," Ms. Dawnstride said with a knowing smile. "Then maybe you can tell me why the Aztecs believed such a thing."

Cass froze. She had to admit she hadn't really heard the words Ms. Dawnstride had said either. She'd been distracted by the creature on the screen. Its green and blue coloring and the strange shape of the Aztec art had captivated her.

But Cathy was quick on her feet. Or so she thought. "Well, Ms. Dawnstride, the fact is," Cathy began, smirking so smugly Cass thought it must be hurting her lips, "they were ignorant."

"How so?" the professor said, deadpan.

The girl shrugged. "It's all bullshit. Serpents. Hero twins. Virgin birth."

Her boyfriend laughed.

Cass looked down at the page in her textbook and remembered reading the story of the feathered serpent and one of the modes of its birth. The story said a woman swallowed an emerald. A similar one said a god had appeared to her, telling her she should conceive the creature that would become a hero of mankind.

"Well," Cass said, slowly raising her hand. "Sometimes, people need to believe in something."

Looking relieved, Ms. Dawnstride signaled for her to go on, smiling.

"Is it so hard to decide that you think something so fantastic could have been true?"

Cathy made a disgusted face and rolled her eyes. "You believe this?"

"No, what I mean is: Why couldn't Chimalman—the woman—believe it? Maye she needed to. Maybe she was pregnant and needed to know that something fantastic had happened to her."

At this, Cathy's boyfriend laughed and made an obscene gesture by thrusting in his seat. "Hell yeah, something happened to her."

A few of the other kids, most likely just here for an elective, laughed. Cass's face burned, and she hunkered back down in the dark classroom. This was why she never spoke up. A few people in life liked her point of view, supported her. She'd studied anthropology to take in the fantastic in other cultures. But most people around her just thought she was desperate for a thrill. And had a wild imagination.

"Also," Cass said to Ms. Dawnstride, shaking from the burn she was about to inflict on Cathy, "that's Mayan culture she brought up. Not the Aztecs. We're in the Aztec unit now. Mayans were last month."

Cathy glared, mouth open. Ms. Dawnstride smiled again and shook her head.

Cass shrugged and murmured an apology to Ms. Dawnstride. But the professor smiled at her before going back to the slides.

Vamshi allowed Cass to vent on their walk from the college to Hanging Gardens.

"I just don't understand why they're in the program," Cass groaned, scanning the menu above them while the Greek owner, a mother, shouted at her son over the sounds of sizzling meat in the back to get off his phone. "I see them at mixers, at departmental meetings. I'm so afraid they're going to end up being peer reviewers on my capstone project that I may just drop before my final project."

Vamshi closed her eyes and raised her hand up, hovering it just inches before Cass's face. "Your aura is way off. You need to chill." She fluttered her fingers as if she could pluck Cass's frustration right out of her soul.

"Hello?" Cass quipped. "I'm genuinely concerned here. What if they screw me over on purpose? On my final!"

"First," Vamshi said sternly, "you need to order your same old order and stop pretending like you're actually looking at this menu."

She was right, of course. Cass always ordered the same weird gyro: everything was normal on it except she asked them to add jalapenos and mayo. She couldn't remember when she'd first ordered it, but had for the last couple of years.

"Second," Vamshi went on, "I kyped a pic of the grade book."

Cass groaned and massaged her temples hard, eyes closed. "I thought your sleight of hand, petty theft days were behind you?"

Vamshi smirked. "I'm going to be an archeologist. A literal professional thief." She pulled her phone out. "Want to see?"

She did, but that was like cheating. Or was it? It was her grade, after all.

Wincing, she asked, "Is it good or bad?"

Vamshi smiled and said, "Well, Cathy's is—"

"Vam!" Cass cried, smacking her friend. "You can't look at other people's grades. That's cheating." She dropped her head into her hands. "No. As punishment, I don't want to see my grade, you pickpocket."

Insulted, Vamshi blew a sigh through her lips and deleted the photo. "Order your gross gyro, damn it."

Begrudgingly admitting Vamshi was right, she ordered the

thing they decided to call the New England Special, and moved down the counter to wait to pick up her food. As Vamshi ordered, Cass absentmindedly scanned the other patrons. Most were college students or businessmen out of the office from work. But one stuck out. A boy about her age, maybe a year younger, who stood alone. His arms were crossed and the hood of his faded black hoodie was pulled up over his head. A few strands of jaw-length blond hair stuck out. His blue eyes steadily moved from person to person as he waited for his order. He almost looked sad.

The man behind the grill shouted, "New England Special!"

Cass moved to grab her tray and the mystery boy did too. She thought he must be going for the drink station next to the counter, but he reached out for the tray. She stopped and so did he.

"Sorry," he mumbled, backing away.

"Did..." Cass tried not to stare at him. "Did you order the New England Special, too?"

He nodded, averting his eyes.

"Wow," she smiled, taken in by his shyness. No one was ever shy around her. She didn't have that strong enough of a presence. "I thought no one else got this gross thing but me."

He shoved his hands deep into his pockets and took a step back, not looking her in the eyes.

"I'm Cass," she tried. "I study anthropology at Weathermoore."

Now his eyes snapped up to hers. "Charlie," he said. He stepped around her, grabbed the tray and slithered around her and a few other patrons. He took the gyro off the tray, tossed the tray aside, and exited the restaurant. Cass watched him go.

"Sad boy alert!"

Cass jumped as Vamshi shouted in her ear. Her best friend

laughed and led them to a booth. "What?" she snapped, sitting down and taking her order from Vamshi.

"You just like him because he's all hood-wearing and pouty-lipped," Vamshi jibed. "You cannot help yourself when something a little mysterious, a little attractive waltzes into your life. But it's fine," she added, dropping her straw into her cup. "He is very cute."

"He's not a sad boy," Cass defended. "Maybe he needs a friend. He almost smiled."

"Almost," Vamshi repeated, mockingly.

"Vam," Cass said, unwrapping her unique gyro, "not all of us are lucky enough to have an Advik in our lives."

"Hah," Vamshi said through a mouthful of food. "One day, you will wish you had a boring-ass man your too-traditional mum wanted you to marry."

That was, of course, a lie. Vamshi knew better than anyone how much Cass craved the fantastic. The adventures she'd read about. She wanted to take pictures in the wilds of Africa, to explore a lost temple...but, no. That would never happen to her. Not boring, Connecticut Cass, and her normal, cookie-cutter, future laid out by well-meaning parents.

That night, Cass went back to work at Witch's Bones. Felicity was there when she arrived and praised her for her work that morning.

"I think you are more than ready to close on your own, too," Felicity said from the book section of the store.

"I appreciate that," Cass called from where she had to reorganize the incense from a pack of wild teens who had left it in shambles. "But really, I'm not sure how well I'd do in a position of authority."

"Cass," Felicity cooed, coming around the corner with an armful of books. "Don't doubt your authority." She smiled, making her dark eyes sparkle. "You said you wanted to be a closer. Have you changed your mind?"

"No, it's not that." Cass picked up a stick of Egyptian Musk and inhaled the delightful aroma. "What if I do something wrong?"

Felicity smiled and shrugged. "Unless you die, burn down the building, or rob us blind—everything should be okay."

"That's a low bar, boss," she smiled, but laughed, appreciating her long-time boss's candor.

Felicity smiled, handed her the books, and moved to the stockroom. "Put these in the system on hold for a Miss Meredith Smith. She called today and will be in sometime this week to pick them up."

"Will do."

Cass took the books and set them down by the computer to make a customer profile and get the books on hold. None of them stood out until she picked up the soft, brown leather of the journal from that morning. The blue gem sparkled in the shop's light. Something in her jumped when she picked it up, almost like she had been waiting all day to get back to it. The beautiful simplicity of the large journal enchanted her. She ran her hands over the woven spine. Glancing around to make sure Felicity wasn't looking, she held the book up just below her nose and flipped the pages. The dusty, leathery scent of the book wafted up to her, and she smiled, taking it in. Book sniffing was a thing people did, right?

Smiling down at the book, she stopped.

Someone had written in the book. "What the hell?" she sighed, flipping through the pages. Had someone come into the store and scribbled nonsense in the journal? Every page had something on it. The images didn't appear whole. The writing was in a different language, almost every word, making it look like a jumble of runes, sigils, letters, and other symbols. Aggravated, she flipped through, page by page.

Then, she caught a sentence she understood. Stopping, she flipped one page back. Yes, she hadn't imagined it. She understood the page. Blinking, she realized it hadn't changed script: it was still an odd mishmash of languages, but...

"I can read that?" she whispered. She stared at the one sentence. No, she couldn't read read it. She just understood it. It was about a creature of lightning and fire. It rested... somewhere. It waited to be awakened.

A spark from the blue gem on the cover that rested in her palm zapped her. She gasped and dropped the journal.

"You all right?" Felicity asked, looking at her from around a display shelf.

Cass nodded. When Felicity disappeared to finish closing up the back, Cass grabbed the book, looked around quickly, and shoved it into her leather bag before she knew what she was doing.

CHAPTER 2: PAKHBA

The next morning, Cass caught the sun coming up from her east-facing window. She'd been staring at her leather crossbody bag for a long time, she guessed. When the sun finally splashed over the bag in an amber beam of end-of-summer warmth, she took a deep breath.

Great, she thought. I've been up all night just waiting for that book to spring out and scare me.

Perhaps not exactly "scare," but she did expect something. Or that the book expected something of her. Especially after the way the blotchy ink writing had writhed and twisted so she could understand it the night before. No, she hadn't even been drinking. She was in her right mind and saw the text appear and move.

Right?

She'd skip class. She had to. One, she was tired. Two, she wanted to look at the book again. Maybe more writing appeared over night? She looked up at the mattress above her own cramped bunkbed. No downward arch showed where Vamshi lay, so she was up already. Cass checked her watched:

7:00 a.m.. Vamshi was an early riser and would usually start the coffee for her.

Just as she thought about it, the sweet, warm aroma wafted into the tiny bedroom they shared in the dorm from the common area outside. They weren't allowed to have coffee pots, hot plates, or burn candles and incense in the dorms, but that never stopped Vamshi. She knew the RA and could probably have gotten away with a full-on kitchen if she'd tried hard enough. She'd really shown her ingenuity when she offered to help Cass secure a small cooler to the windowsill, hanging out the window against the brick on her twenty-first birthday. They hid beer in it and were able to close the window if anyone untrustworthy came by, giving the image of a beer-less celebration. Vamshi was clever and brought out the cleverness in Cass.

So she needed Vamshi to leave. She'd know Cass was up to something.

Cass picked up her duvet and prepared to grab her bag off the laundry chair when the door opened and Vamshi sang a high, piercing note.

"It's daytime, sleepyhead, and I have coffee." Vamshi set it down on the night table and moved to the laundry chair to plant herself.

Cass gasped when she grabbed the bag and moved it to the floor.

"Calm down," Vamshi said, sipping her coffee. "Why aren't you up yet?"

Her heart raced. "I'm sick," she shouted a little too loud.

Vamshi locked her black-lined, dark brown eyes on Cass and slowly raised a single brow. "Of course you are."

"No, really," Cass doubled down. "I was up all night. Headache, the chills. I think I feel nausea coming on."

A sudden concerned look pulled at Vamshi's face. "Are you skipping because you don't have all your text books yet?"

Cass frowned, confused. "I told you I could lend you money to get them and you can pay me back later. Come on, girl, this is your future we're talking about."

"Oh, Vam, no," she laughed. "I got my books. Everly and Felicity paid me a week early last month. I'm fine."

Her best friend's eyes lit up as she smiled over the rim of her cup. "Please tell me you are not sneaking off to spend all day in the Hanging Gardens hoping Sad Boy comes around again."

Confused at first, Cass frowned. Then she remembered him and his—true—sad, pouting lips. She almost smiled. "No. I almost forgot about him. I really do feel unwell." Lying always made her heart race and her head spin, so she hunkered down into the over-stuffed duvet. "I swear, Vam."

The other girl clicked her tongue. "Okay. So you won't be wanting this." She picked up the mug of coffee and dumped it into her own to refill it.

Cass's heart sank a little. No, that she wanted.

"Yeah, knock yourself out," she lied again.

"All right, then." Promising to take notes for her, Vamshi picked up her leather bag. "Can I borrow your text book? I never did buy mine..." She stuck her hand into the bag and yanked out the leather-bound book.

"Don't!" Cass shouted, reaching up for it.

Laughing, Vamshi spun out of the way, gripping the book. "When did you start keeping a journal?" Eagerly, she whipped it open, eyes scanning the pages.

Cass's heart hammered hard. She'd explain. Vamshi would understand. She'd take the book back. The conflicting fear wrestled in her heart.

"Haven't started yet?" Vamshi asked.

"What?"

Her friend closed it, apologized for trying to snoop, and pulled out the test book for the cultural studies class they shared. "It's empty still," she said. "Waiting to be filled with your unique and quirky thoughts," she mocked.

Empty? Cass's eyes darted to the bag as Vamshi put it back on the laundry chair. Vamshi couldn't see the words.

"Uh, yeah. Empty," Cass stammered. "Have a good day," she added as Vamshi hurried out the dorm room door.

Taking no chances, Cass set up a circle of five white candles the way Vamshi had shown her a million times. A magic circle was supposed to protect one from weird hocus-pocus.

"I'm ready for something amazing," Cass told herself out loud. She'd eaten up ideas of magic, stories of monsters and fairies all her life. She'd run over the scenario a million times in her head what she'd do if she found a magic book that could transport her away to a hidden kingdom. Those plans had slowly dwindled as she finished high school and started college, though. But the feelings came back fresh now.

"I want something fantastic," she whispered, lighting the last candle behind her. "I wanted this."

Her hands moved steadily as she picked up the book. Inside the blue gem on the front, it almost looked like the smokey veins and lines of sparkling element moved as she picked it up. She opened it to find the blotchy ink script alive and coming into focus just like the night before. A sudden feeling of "you sure you know what you want?" filled her.

"No," she confessed. "I just know I want something. Something bigger than me. Something chimerical," she finished, using a word she learned from Ms. Dawnstride's art history class.

Your wish is your commandment, the script in the book suddenly read.

Cass gasped and clutched the sides, realizing she could read it, feel the words. Her eyes locked on to the yellow pages so much she didn't notice the blue, pearlescent smoke rising from underneath the book until it covered her crossed legs.

With a cry, Cass dropped the book and rolled to the side, outside the protective circle. Realizing her mistake, she grunted, crawling back into it and tossing the book to the outside of it. As she chucked it, the smoke spiraled with the front cover, showing it came from the gem on the front. The book landed under the window, the smoke blacking out the rising rays of the sun. The room grew dark, only the light from the candles glowing.

A deep, gravelly rumble rippled out from the smoke. A sort of small, serpentine shape appeared in the midst of the smoke, hovering just a few feet off the ground. Cass blinked, thinking the smoke must have made her hallucinate because she swore the thing was in the shape of a long, lithe dragon. She froze, holding her breath as the smoke quickly dissipated. Her eyes watered since she didn't blink.

The eyes of the summoned creature pinned her down before the smoke finished clearing. She locked onto them. They were blue, with smokey veins and a sort of gold glitter under the irises. Just like the stone on the front of the book. They were indeed set in a serpentine face of shimmering blue-green scales. The creature's long body was covered in them with tiny tendril yellow accents softly moving in the air like the whiskers of a catfish. It also had four sets of long claws at the end of each scaly foot.

It furrowed its brow, looking down at her seriously. Cass finally breathed, gasping for air and blinked, releasing the tears down her cheeks.

Do not weep, child, it said without moving its draconic jaw.

"I'm not a child," Cass said. Her voice came from her throat, but it sounded like someone else said it. She felt as if she were outside her own body, dizzy, confused.

"If you are less than a century old, you are," the creature replied, finally moving its maw. It slowly coiled into an arch and flew towards her. "You seem undisturbed by my speech."

She slowly curled away from the approaching thing. "You appeared out of smoke. From a book I stole. The fact that you speak is the least of my concerns," she replied.

"So it must seem," the creature replied. "You now have many concerns, reader."

Cass swallowed hard. Vamshi had always joked about accidentally summoning a demon if one wasn't careful with magic. And now she had.

"What do you want?" she asked when the creature finally hovered just outside the candle circle, still glaring down at her.

"It is not what I want," the thing's deep voice replied. "It is what you want. Your wish is your commandment."

She frowned. "It's 'your wish is my command.'"

A sort of deep, chuckle rolled up the creature's long throat. "For a lesser magic, yes. But not this." He gestured slowly with his foreclaw to the tome.

"Okay," Cass breathed, still unable to move. "Magic. Sure."

"Fear not," the creature said. Its brow smoothed now, and it looked much friendlier. "I am Pakhba, the keeper of the Script and am tasked with guiding, protecting, and counseling the one who reads the Dragon Script."

It clicked in her head so suddenly that she thought she felt it tick against her skull. "Yeah, I read it. It was an accident, though! It was just mumbo jumbo, then suddenly it made sense. I didn't do it on purpose."

"If you had," the dragon called Pakhba said steadily, "I wouldn't have been released from my prison."

Cass's eyes shot to the book. "Were you locked inside?"

"Alas." The dragon slowly coiled into a turn and sailed to where the book lay under the window. It touched the blue gem on the cover and closed its bright eyes. "My master Aiken locked me away, true. But only so I could one day awaken to the next Vedic and guide them to their calling."

Cass took a deep breath and uncurled her body, pushing up to her feet. She looked around to see if maybe she had inhaled too much smoke from the candles somehow. Passed out? Eaten a pot brownie by mistake? Was this a really bad hangover from some frat house part she couldn't remember going to?

"You asked for something bigger than yourself." Pakhba's voice intruded into her chaotic thoughts. "You wanted this. Wished for this. Thus, it was commanded."

Her eyes flew open, latching onto the small blue dragon. "How do you know what I want?"

He slowly gestured to the book with his clawed forepaw. "If you didn't, I wouldn't be here. If you understood what it was you wanted, I wouldn't have been released. As it were, all you knew is that you desired something bigger than yourself. This is it. As you have summoned me, you shall summon the others."

"Others?" she cried, quickly wrapping her arms around herself. She snapped her head around, expecting something like the cheshire cat, a leprechaun, and a magical cat to emerge from the corners of her dorm.

"The four dragons," Pakhba said to clarify. "The four seasons. The four winds. The corners of the earth. Whatever you want to call them."

Her jaw popped open purely against her will. She tried to

pull her lips together to ask him to elaborate when the door burst open behind her.

"Ah-ha!" Vamshi shouted triumphantly. "I knew you were lying about being sick. I caught you in... the... act?" Her voice petered out into a question as she took in the book, the candles, and Cass's pale, tear-stained face. "What the hell are you trying to do?" She closed the dorm room door. "I told you magic won't make you pass speech class."

For the first time in her life, Cass's breath came in ragged gasps. "D-dragon," she stammered, pointing to Pakhba.

"Dragon?" Vamshi cautiously watched Cass and skirted around her magic circle to pick up the book. Her nose came within a few inches of Pakhba, but she didn't say anything. She flipped the book over in her hands.

Cass stutter-stepped a bit closer to Vamshi. "Don't you see him?"

Vamshi looked up. "What are you on about, girl?"

Cass whipped around to look at Pakhba. "She cannot see me unless you command it," he offered simply.

"Well, I command it!" she shouted. She refused to get on this crazy, dragon-hallucinating trip herself.

Her best friend's eyes widened at her sudden shout. "Maybe you do have a fever." She crossed the room and placed the back of her hand against Cass's head.

Cass smacked her hand away. "I am not feverish. Show yourself!" she shouted at the little dragon.

Pakhba's judgmental eyes shifted to Vamshi. Cass didn't notice anything change. She grabbed Vamshi's arm and turned her back to the window where Pakhba hovered.

"Great Braham!" Vamshi cried, stumbling back, pulling Cass into the candle circle as well. "I knew you'd be the death of me, Cassandra Warren! If anyone would summon a demon for a pact, it would be you."

"I assure you, I am no demon," Pakhba said softly. "I am nothing so base as a hellion."

Vamshi gasped and opened her mouth wide to scream. Cass grunted, smacking her hand over Vamshi's black-covered lips. Her friend screamed into her palm anyway. Cass winced, wondering if she did the right thing.

"Vam, stop," she begged. "I'm so glad you came back. I need you to listen."

Under her palm, Vamshi stopped screaming and took a deep, smothered breath. Her eye whipped to Cass's. She nodded.

"Thank you," Cass sighed. Somehow, having Vamshi freak out put her at ease. As if she'd had her experience and now could calmly help Vamshi have hers. She removed her hand. "Shall we sit down?" she asked the dragon, gesturing to the two dish chairs she and Vamshi had bought during their freshmen year.

"If you so desire," Pakhba replied gently.

Vamshi grabbed her chair and loudly dragged it across the floor closer to Cass. "What the hell did you do?" she hissed.

Cass took a deep breath and pointed to the book. She told Vamshi how she'd found it that early morning in Witch's Bones, how it had been blank then. "Then it appeared in blotches," she said. A strange excitement rose in her as she explained it. The more she talked about it, with Pakhba's eyes on her, the more it felt real. Vamshi's calm demeanor and steady gaze always grounded Cass, made her feel sane. She finished telling her tale and gestured to the dragon. "That's when he said his name was Pakhba and I was some chosen one to waken four other dragons."

"Chosen only by yourself," Pakhba correct. "Alas, the dragons do not choose their Vedic."

"Vedic?" Vamshi repeated, frowning.

"You know that word?" Cass asked. This is why she loved Vamshi. She was a living encyclopedia of the strangest things.

"It's one of the oldest kinds of Hinduism that has actual written documents," she started. "Remember how Ms. Dawnstride said that most history in ancient times was oral?"

Cass nodded. Her mind suddenly cleared. She'd never felt this alert before.

"Well, Vedism used written materials. It's how we know some ancient rites of old Hinduism today. Some that we still practice."

"So a writer?" Cass asked.

"A scribe," Pakhba interrupted softly. "A writer of scripts. A sacred honor."

"Pakhba?" Vamshi asked. The dragon raised his head to her. "As in Pakhangba, the dragon god of the Meitei people? Northern India," she added to Cass, who felt more lost every minute.

For the first time, the blue dragon's arrogant head dropped a little. "Only in bearing the honor of his name and his shape," he replied. "I am a herald, but I am not The Herald."

"Aren't dragons always depictions of evil?" Cass asked, finally feeling like she could contribute something to the conversation.

"Those who are victorious write history," Pakhba said steadily. "There are a people who have long told mankind the dragons of the four seasons are monsters to be tamed. In a way, they were right. But they would never bring hale of fire down on your kind without a Vedic who commanded them."

Cass glanced over at Vamshi, who now leaned forward with her elbows on her knees. "A chosen one?"

"Not chosen by the dragons," Pakhba reiterated, his tone turning stoney, tired of the questions.

"Unchosen one," Cass offered. She almost smiled, but the unusual situation still filled her with fear and uncertainty. "So, what about these four dragons?" She suspected it might be metaphorical. But the literal floating dragon in her dorm room made her doubt it.

Pakhba's eyes snapped to the dorm room door behind them. "Another time, Vedic. It is enough that you have awakened me for now. I shall be with you and you shall know your fate in time."

"Oh, no you don't," Cass shouted, jumping up from the chair. "You are not vanishing on me with that cryptic talk. You are going to tell me—"

The blue dragon shot towards her in a flash of gold and blue light. She screamed and covered her face. A single blast of warm wind shoved her hair back over her shoulders and the light vanished. When she opened her eyes, she discovered a thick, golden bangle around her wrist. It was in the shape of a long, thin dragon. She turned it over and recognized Pakhba's face.

"Jerk," she grumbled, tweaking the nose of the golden dragon. Outside, the dorm hall started to make noise. He must have wanted to hide before she showed him to more people.

Vamshi puffed out her cheeks and sighed dramatically, collapsing back into the chair. "Oh, my god, girl," she said far less dramatically than she used to.

A little lost, let down, and feeling like the wind had been stolen from her proverbial sails, she matched Vamshi's sigh. "I don't know what I'm supposed to do." She tried to not sound desperate.

Vamshi pushed up from the dish chair and snatched up the book from where it had been laying. She flipped through the pages and checked the soft, leather binding.

"You sure you cannot see the writing—the Dragon Script?" Cass asked, her heart falling.

Vamshi shook her head, a slight melancholy slackening her shoulders. "No, Cass. It looks blank to me. I guess you really are the unchosen one." She held it out to her. "It sounds like you don't have to know what to do."

She took the book, and Vamshi offered a smile that slowly grew in excitement. "What are you smiling about?" Cass asked.

"Four dragons?" Vamshi started. "Four corners of the world? Sounds like an anthropologist's wet dream."

Cass allowed herself to laugh a little at this, but it came out as a nervous exhale. Yes, she'd always wanted some huge adventure like Joan Wilder from "Romancing the Stone" but never thought it would actually happen. And worse, she had to wait to see what the little dragon would say next. For now, she just had to wait. And keep her grades up.

CHAPTER 3: THE FUTURE

Cass poked at the blue gem eye of the golden bracelet around her wrist, but nothing disturbed the dragon. The wet kissing sounds of Kathy and Derek behind her in the dark class room scratched through Ms. Dawnstride's sweet voice to claw at her ears. She rubbed at the bracelet, hoping maybe Pakhba would slither out of it in a poof of glittering blue smoke like a genie. Nothing happened.

I'd wish for Kathy's and Derek's lips to meld together, she thought, absentmindedly flipping the pages of her text book. *That way, they never have to suck on each other again.*

The carousel clacked loudly as Ms. Dawnstride switched slides. She kept talking, pointing to the stone carving on the slide. Cass stopped to look at a picture in her textbook when a lithe, serpentine body caught her sight. A plumed dragon coiled around an Aztec pyramid, like it wanted to protect it. She snapped her head up and realized a similar dragon glowed on the white board.

"Really, to understand our great, feathery dragon here," Ms. Dawnstride went on, "it might behoove us to go all the way back to the Olmec civilization. They existed between

1200 to 400 B.C. And produced this." She gestured to the slide. It depicted a man sitting on a stone throne with a long, coiling feathery serpent behind it. "This is La Venta Monument. Clearly, it's the same dragon diety. But the time between this and the next sighting of the dragon was several hundred years. No one can say why since clearly the people had the means to carve the likeness and the desire to do so."

Cass turned back to the book, checked the image and raised her hand. "Is the feathered serpent Quezacotl?"

Ms. Dawnstride smiled and nodded. "And this next slide is the perfect segue into our next section." She clicked the carousel and it changed to the one in the book: the dragon on the pyramid. "Can anyone tell me what kind of structure this is?" she asked.

"Oh, me!" Kathy piped from behind Cass, waving her hand eagerly.

Cass rolled her eyes. Yes, of course Kathy was sure what a pyramid was: it was probably the only thing she knew. Shapes weren't hard.

"Those are the Pyramids of Egypt," Kathy stated stoutly, confidently, and with a huge smile bending her words.

Cass slapped her hand over her mouth to stop from laughing. So life could hand her a win every now and then.

"Well, they are pyramids," Ms Dawnstride went on. She stammered a bit, taken aback by Kathy's ignorance.

Cass went back to poking at Pakhba's blue eye, wondering how she could summon him again. He had a lot of explaining to do. He'd deliberately told her he wasn't going to divulge much last night. He'd also said that if she knew what she wanted, she wouldn't have been able to read the book. So apparently keeping her ignorant was part of his plan. Though, he'd sworn he wasn't a demon. She'd been so nervous about the bracelet that she'd put it in her closet. Could he see through the gem-like eyes on the bracelet? Was he watching her now? Should she call a witch or a psychic or something? A priest?

Class let out and she jealously watched Kathy strut away. She'd made a big blunder in class but it didn't matter when she could swing her arm around Derek's shoulders and still hold her head up high. It must be nice to have someone love her despite her nasty personality and head full of pudding. That would make Cass feel invincible too.

Rain came down gently outside on her way to work, softly washing away the last heat of summer. The sidewalk steamed as she ran to her car to text Vamshi that she had work. She stalled just one minute, wondering if she should go get the dragon book and return it. After all, it had been on special order for someone, right?

"What good would that do?" she sighed. Besides, it almost felt like the book came to her. Chose her. Well...unchose her.

Felicity and Everly were in the store when she arrived and Felicity called her from the front the minute she entered the back room. Cass thought about removing Pakhba from her wrist and tossing him into her backpack. He didn't need to see her working a cash wrap for four and a half hours. It seemed unworthy for someone who could read a magical script.

Am I trying to prove myself to a tiny dragon? she wondered, deciding to keep the bracelet on. She grabbed her name tag and hurried out to the counter. At the same time, she didn't want to squander her chances of...of what?

Felicity's eyes glittered round and suppressed a grin as she clutched her black shawl.

"What's got you all twitterpated?" Cass laughed, speaking softly when Felicity leaned in to whisper.

"Your mother sent us a picture of Ella," Everly said over his wife, hushing her with a playful swipe of his hand. At the mention of her super-talented, energetic, younger sister, Cass glowed with pride and whinged at the same time. "She took home silver in rapier. She's still fencing?"

Cass nodded. "She'll tell you silver in rapier isn't as good as bronze in epee, though." Cass had been forced to practice fencing with Ella for most of her life and knew far too much about the names of swords, old, French fencers, and how to duel. She never minded too much, but it was Ella who took home the trophies.

"Not that!" Felicity hissed, playfully glaring up at her husband. "A young man came here asking about you," she whispered. "Everly is my one and only, but this boy was..." She squinted and twisted her chin to find the right words. "Melancholy. Mysterious."

Cass laughed at the older woman and followed her to the register. "Never have you ever played matchmaker," Cass giggled. "Please don't start now."

"And I'll never do it again," her boss said, still unable to control her smile. "But, so mote it be, he's just...there's something about him." She grinned wildly and nodded with her head to the back where Everly showed a boy to the shelves of books.

Cass's heart involuntarily beat twice then held still. It was the boy from the Hanging Gardens. She recognized his pouting lips, tasseled dirty blond hair, and—as Felicity had mentioned—the mysterious melancholy that lurked behind his round, blue eyes.

"Ah," Felicity hummed, gently placing her hand on Cass's shoulder. "You've met before?"

Wiping the smile off her face, Cass half shrugged. "Once. At Hanging Gardens. Vamshi said I only liked him because he was a 'sad boy.'"

Felicity placed her hand over her heart and sighed longingly. "The damaged ones do attracted the strong ones." She winked at Cass. "Don't miss this opportunity, sweetness."

The witchy woman swooped away from her and floated to the back, calling her husband to take care of the person who just walked in. She glanced over her shoulder and winked at Cass before they both disappeared into the back room. Glaring playfully after them, Cass nervously started to sort some essential oils in a box on the counter while Everly chatted with the customer. She took a few playful glances up. Recalling his name was Charlie, she watched him gently run his hand down the spines of the books, carefully reading their titles. A warm beam of sunlight cut through the front window and splashed over his long fingers. Dust particles sparkled around him.

Cass grunted and shook her head. Yes, Vamshi was right. She had a habit of going after "damaged" people. Her last relationship had been a disaster.

"Excuse me?"

She gasped and looked up. Charlie stood not two feet from her. He gently raised his brows at her sudden start. He didn't smile. Just watched her with his large eyes and down-turned lips.

"Sorry," she smiled, giggling. "I was in my own head. Thinking about my ex." A nervous laugh forced its way out of her throat. "Not that you needed to know or asked. Sometimes people just say stupid stuff because they have a lot on their minds, right?"

Charlie's impassive face didn't change.

Her cheeks seared red with embarrassment. "Anyway, what can I help you find?"

Suddenly, a tiny crease appeared between Charlie's brows showing he frowned, but only a little. "We met at the restaurant," he said, not asking.

"Yup," Cass nodded. "I remember you."

"Once is an accident," he mumbled like he quoted something. "Twice is a coincidence, thrice is purpose." He glanced around. Then, he finally showed some emotion on his face. He thought, pressing his full lips together. Then, he frowned determinately. "I never got your name."

A little butterfly appeared in her stomach. "Cass," she said, smiling. "Sorry, by the way, I talk nonsense when I'm nervous."

Charlie looked down at his hands and smiled weakly. "That why your ex left you?" he asked, bringing up one of the things she'd said in panic.

"Ugh," she sighed, feeling a little more at ease. "No. He met my ex best friend Kathy. Long and gross history." She smiled at him, searching his face. "So what were you looking for?" she asked, eagerly coming around the counter so nothing separated them. She led him back to the books, aware of her backside as she pulled out in front. Thank goodness I wore the good jeans, she thought. It had been too long since she'd tried flirting.

"A book," he started, his voice turning gentle and deep. "Well, a journal actually. But not one of these small ones." He pointed to the regular Moleskin journals. "And not these." He poked at one of the hard-cover witch's calendar-journals.

"I know just what you might like," she said, flashing another grin to him. "These back here are my favorite." She gestured to a wall of shelves near the back where they kept the more ornate journals; leather bound, handmade, some with decorative gems on the outside. She'd thought the dragon script had been one of these.

Charlie's large eyes scanned the shelves quickly, almost like he knew exactly what he wanted. She watched him look, admiring the sharp cut of his jaw and the way his yellow hair brushed it. He turned to face her.

"Thanks," he murmured.

She gulped. He wanted her to go. She opened her mouth and started to stammer when the bell on the front door rang again. "Excuse me," she whispered in agony. The carpet caught her heel as she turned hard on it and headed to the front to greet the customers that just came in. Smooth, you klutz, she thought bitterly.

"Welcome to Witch's Bone, what can I help you find today?" she chipped, seeing three people meandering around the front. Her steps slowed a little as she took them in.

A blonde woman, maybe mid thirties, led a slightly younger bald man in sunglasses, and a man near her age with messy brown hair. All three wore black suits with matching pants and shiny dress shoes. They would have looked extremely sharp if not for the worn out fade of the suits and the disheveled hair. The blonde woman looked sharpest with fresh lipstick and nails that Cass could only describe as manicured to death. Their heads tossed this way and that, scouting for something, until she appeared. All three sets of eyes landed on her.

"I stopped seeding my illegal downloads years ago," she joked to them as she slid behind the counter. They didn't move. "You look like CIA or feds," she apologized. "It was a torrent joke."

Their impassive masks didn't shift at all. They didn't find her joke funny.

She cleared her throat again, unsure how much more she could embarrass herself in one evening before it consumed her to a horrid death. "What can I help you find?"

The bald man, taller than the other two, craned around to sweep the store. The brown-haired younger man smirked at her and smiled licentiously and raised his brows suggestively. An instant wave of caution crashed through her.

The blonde woman leaned heavily on one palm on the counter. "You got a shipment in not two days ago." It wasn't a question.

Cass frowned. "Yeah. We get new merchandise all the

time. You looking for something in particular? Did we order something for you?" She leaned back to check the chest under the counter where Everly put things customers had ordered special. Only a small cauldron, a smudge stick, a few books, and a desk-size Anubis waited in it. Of course the Dragon Script had been in that box of books...

"You did," the woman said quickly. "A book."

The hair on the back of Cass's neck stood up. "The books are back there." She pointed. Her heart fell a little. If the creepy feds were going back there, she might not be able to go back to trying to look like an ass in front of Charlie.

The woman nodded, grabbed the younger man's arm, and marched to the back. The bald man turned, sunglasses fixed on her until he broke from the other two and walked directly down the isle Charlie was in. Cass watched the three of them part. She noted their tired faces hidden behind curt tones. They'd come a long way recently. They were tired.

Even more weird, they knew about the shipment. Not even regular customers knew when the trucks would come in because it was so random. Were they ones who had ordered the books that the Dragon Script came with?

Curious, she ducked and ran down a row of shelves of nicknacks behind the blonde woman. She shot up, realizing the round, security mirror above, made her visible to them on the other side. She pretended to be dusting the incense dispensers.

"We tracked it to the border," the woman hissed to the younger man. Her nails clicked on the spines of the books. "What does it look like? It has to be here. We checked the stupid shop with the crows, the one near New Haven, and the cheap place in the mall. There are only so many stores like this." The woman sounded exhausted.

"This state is only so big," the younger man countered. "Maybe it went somewhere else."

"No," the woman growled. "The manifest said that truck was coming here!" Her voice creaked as her emotions got the better of her. "Look for anything with a dragon on the cover."

Dragon? Cass wondered. The script, Pakhba, and the blue gem on the cover floated up into her mind. No way they are looking for that. No, she was being silly. They might be collectors, not magic-book-hunters. She found a dragon-genie, she couldn't be this lucky twice a week. Nothing like this happened to her.

"Hey," someone hissed in a panic a few rows down.

Cass spun to see the Charlie duck around a shelf full of Buddhas and striking, blue Krishnas. He pulled his hood up and slinked towards the front door. Cass glanced back at the mysterious suits and realized he was hiding from them. Maybe, like her, he thought they were feds?

Damn, she thought. Vamshi was right. I would fall for a guy with some kind of legal record. She sighed inwardly, sad that she hadn't been smoother when talking to him.

"Can you help us find something?"

Cass jumped, spinning to face the blonde woman. "Uh, yeah. A book?" She nervously tucked her hair behind one ear. The dim light above caught the golden bracelet around her wrist.

"Nice flare you got there," the younger man said, suddenly alert. His bright as emerald eyes tracked it as she clasped her hands behind her back.

"Thanks," she quipped. "My grandmother gave it to me last Christmas." The lie slipped out easily as buttered noodles.

The blonde woman smiled. "Of course she did." She took a step towards Cass then froze. Her brows shot up and wrinkled as she caught sight of the mirror and security camerasHer eyes traveled down the wire then to the counter.

Cass's heart hammered in her chest. The woman was checking to see who might be watching.

"Thank you for your help." The woman smiled, turned, gestured for her lackies to follow and slipped out the front door.

Cass released a huge breath she'd been holding. She watched them leave. Facing the counter now, she realized the woman had been looking for a computer that might monitor the security system. It wasn't here at the store. Felicity and Everly backed all their video surveillance to a system at their house. Clutching the counter top, Cass panted, realizing how close she'd come to...something terrible, maybe.

She wrenched the bracelet off and shoved it in her pocket. "What the hell have I gotten myself into." She touched the lump in her pocket. "You are telling me everything I want to know the instant we get home, understand?"

A light drizzle fogged the yellow light from the street lamps as Cass locked the door to Witch's Bones. Vamshi would be getting off from the coffee shop a few minutes later and would meet her back at the dorm. Cass inhaled the cooling air, loving that she could sense the last bits of summer dissipate. She'd be wet through by the time she made it back to the dorms, having not taken her car.

"You just had to walk home in the cooling night air," she chided herself. She slung her crossbody leather bag over her shoulder, pulled her hood up and ducked into the street to head back to campus.

She'd only gone two streets down when she stopped. Rookwind was a small town, only booming as much as it was thanks to the university. The streets were generally quiet around 9PM on a weekday. So why did she hear the shuffling of rubber on pavement behind her? She held her breath and turned. A car zoomed past on the cross street, splashing some water up.

Had she imagined it? She shook her head and walked on. Not a minute later, the unmistakable sound of someone running over the puddles splashed towards her. Unwilling to be a victim in a dark city, she threw her head down and ran. The bag on her hip flailed merciless against her body as she charged. One hand gripped it while the other pumped. The phone in her pocket flew around, slowly bouncing to the edge. Realizing it would tumble out, she grabbed it and sharply cut down a side ally behind a street of restaurants. Steam filled the air and an army of dumpsters offered hiding places. Choosing the third dumpster down, Cass slid into a crouch, ripping her jeans, and threw herself against the smelly side.

Taking a deep breath, she clamped her hand over her mouth and clamped her hand over her mouth to muffle her ragged gasps. In her pocket, the bracelet felt warm against her skin. She fought the urge to grab it, demand Pakhba come out and defend her. What if it was just a regular street mugger?

Because their safety is so important, she thought bitterly. But then she gasped in fright as a man dashed past her. He stopped at the next dumpster. His head whipped back and forth, looking for her.

Shit, she squeaked in her head. Her mind went into overdrive. He would turn, he would see her. She had to move now. The wet street would make her slip if she pushed against it too hard. She had to hit him.

Grasping the strap around her shoulder, she pulled it tighter. The bag rose up until it almost pressed against the underside of her shoulder. She spun it behind her so it rode high on her back. Her feet buzzed as she pressed them into the pavement, eyes locked onto her prey. Slowly rising, she stalked closer to the man. Just a few inches taller than her, she aimed for his knees as he walked down the street, still checking behind the dumpsters. She couldn't believe what she was about to do.

With a high-pitched grunt, she positioned her feet like her sister showed her how, used her torso to cock her elbow and punched the man in the side of his temple with all her strength. She grunted so hard, she choked and coughed. Her knuckles exploded with pain but surely not as much as the man's head. He didn't even cry out. He crumpled, flailing once, as he hit the ground.

With the chance of his whited-out vision, Cass dashed back the way she came. She ran straight down the street, leaping into traffic over a crosswalk much to the horror of a woman no doubt just trying to get home after a long day of work.

"Sorry!" she screamed when the woman popped out her driver side window to shout curses at her.

The arch of Weathermoore University glowed ahead of her. Once inside, she dove at the softly glowing blue emergency post and smashed the button twelve times until a security guard answered. She waited, shaking for campus security to arrive in their black and blue cruiser and drive her back to her dorm. No one appeared in the archway. The man must not have followed her after the punch. Looking down at her knuckles, they already swelled painfully.

She leaned against the post, panting. "Holy shit," she sighed.

CHAPTER 4: THE QUEST

"Wake up!" Cass shouted. She threw the golden dragon bracelet across the dorm room, where it plunked against the back of the couch, and rolled onto the cushion. "You have a lot of explaining to do."

After the security guard showed up and gave her a ride, she expected her nerves to calm down, but they hadn't. She still shook, and her breath came in ragged gasps. Cold sweat sent shivers through her body. And she swore she could smell the fear rippling off herself.

"Good god, girl, I'm sorry." Vamshi appeared in their bedroom doorway, rubbing her eyes. She wore her silky black pajama pants and a cut-off black tank top. She hadn't been sleeping, but looked like she was on the edge of it. "What did I do?"

"Not you," Cass snapped. "Dragon, wake up. Talk to me. Explain what just happened!"

Vamshi finally rubbed the sleep out of her eyes and took in Cass. "Are you okay? What happened? You look pissed and completely freaked out."

"I am," Cass growled, turning back to the bracelet.

At last, a zip of blue light shot out of the eye of the golden dragon. It cut across the room once, then came to a stop above the bracelet. Pakhba materialized in his long, serpentine form. He hovered over the bracelet. Cass thought she saw a bit of righteous indignation in his little sapphire eyes.

"You summoned me?" he said steadily.

Cass launched into a quick explanation about being at work, how the trio in suits showed up, asked some questions, then her chased on her way home.

"Someone attacked you?" Vamshi gasped. She strode across the room to Cass and threw her arms around her.

"Would have if I gave them the chance," Cass cut back. "I know they were looking for the script," she said to Pakhba. "So you are going to spill everything you know. Tell me exactly what I have gotten myself in to and how I can get out."

Both girls glared across at the familiar.

Pakhba's little scaled chest rose as he took a deep breath. "You found the Dragon Script because your mind was open. It came out to you no doubt because of how close The Future came to finding it."

Cass made a face and shared her confusion with Vamshi. Her friend had the same confused look on her face.

"A long-standing organization," Pakhba went on.

"Not good guys, I take it?" Cass snapped.

The dragon tilted his head, the long wisps on his face gently undulating in the motion. "Everyone is a hero in their hearts. The Future have sought out the dragons for time immemorial. It has been centuries since I have opened my eyes..." His eyes glassed over, looking like they went back thousands of years.

A strange calm steadily filled Cass like a warm fizz. It both made her uncomfortable and curious. She pulled up Vamshi's beanbag chair and sat down.

"Go on," she said. Vamshi sat next to her.

"My master, Aiken, was a sage of The Future," he began. "Easily the wisest in the magical arts, he saw the greed of his syndicate long before anyone else. He used to believe in their creed, thinking the dragons were to be taken, claimed, and used to benefit of those who controlled them. But that is not the nature of even such as I."

A small rivulet of sympathy helped keep Cass seated. If the story hadn't been coming from the mouth of a literal dragon, she'd have thought it was a plot to a movie. Maybe a fairytale. A faint sense of wonder joined the other weave of emotions in her spinning head.

"I believe it was with the imprisoning of the four dragons this last time that shut the doors on the world's magic," Pakhba went on. "Aiken knew magic. Strong magic. Those who can weave it are called enchanters. He is the one who locked me away in the Script, sacrificing himself to bind them and hide their reins behind the Dragon Script."

"Wait," Cass cut in. "What happened?"

"Meredith Navarre," Pakhba said, his voice deepening to a rumbling whisper. "An enchantress. Long-time friend of Aiken. They learned together for decades. Both members of The Future. Navarre's grasp and ambition outreached her ability. But... she woke the dragons. An enchanter is not to posses that which gives them their power. That is the duty of the Vedic."

"Meredith Smith," Cass whispered, frowning. "That's the name of the person who ordered the books the Script came with." A chill shot through her chest.

Cass slowly pushed herself up and went into her room to fetch the Script. She'd hid it like a child under her pillow, thinking it would be safe. After being chased through the rain, she wasn't so sure even the campus security could protect her. To her delight, it remained there. She came back and saw

Vamshi had taken her seat in the beanbag chair. She sat beside her on the floor and opened the Script.

"How did she wake these four dragons?" she asked. "I can hardly understand this. Oh, but I'm not an enchantress."

"If you were, you would not be able to read it," Pakhba said sternly.

Cass frowned up at him, even more confused.

"Your mind is open, Cassandra," the dragon explained. "Only those who are not blinded by who they think they are can read the Script."

"I know who I am!" she cut back. "You're making me sound stupid."

"Not unintelligent," the dragon confirmed. "Like a child, perhaps."

This was even more insulting. She scoffed and glared hard, her mouth dropping open.

"This is a good thing," Pakhba replied. He drifted slowly down to her so they were at eye level. "An open mind sees what others do not. An open mind is constantly moving, looking for wonders. Eager to be led into adventure. Willing to learn."

This made her relax a little. "Anyone who has a dragon talking to them should be 'eager for adventure,'" she said, mimicking his rich timber.

"Not all," Pakhba contradicted sadly.

Cass ran her hand over the Script again. "So this Meredith person couldn't read the Script? But this other guy, this wizard-ish guy, locked them away?"

"Aiken," Pakhba said. For the first time, a kind of fondness glowed in the dragon's eye. "A true enchanter. Navarre did not read the Script because Aiken created it the night she released Catál from his slumber to join his brethren Tianlong. But enchanters cannot read the Tome of Catál, either."

"How many tome things are there?" Cass asked.

"One now," Pakhba said. "Before, each dragon had their artifact.

"Navarre traveled far over years to find Tianlong in the east. She sacrificed many others to waken the Coiled One. Once she traveled back to us, she used a young ward of The Future to waken Catál. She thought an eager learner would be the one to waken them." Pakhba's scaly face drooped a little more. "Edward. Aiken's apprentice. He unwittingly woke Catál, and Navarre used the two dragons to nearly raze our home to the ground. Aiken tried to save Edward. To save us all from the misuse of the dragons.

"He wrote the tome from the very fiber of his being. The magic in those pages is pure. He placed a labyrinth of spells on it so no one could read it, so no one could awaken the dragons again. But, alas, my kin cannot and will not stay dormant forever. The weave of your world is wefted with the existence of dragons. They are part of it just as you are, holding together parts of the universe you cannot even fathom. Mehen and Quezecotle have not stirred in thousands of years. They are restless. Navarre does not know where they are and thus cannot awaken them."

"Catál, Tianlong, Mehen, and Quezecotle," Cass recited. "Are Catál and Tianlong safe?"

Pakhba nodded. "They may sleep for some time yet. When Aiken sequestered them, he removed that which can summon them. Navarre would have had to start over in her search. But she is close to finding the location of Mehen and Quezecotle. She may find them. Unchecked, they would bring unfathomable destruction to your world. Once awakened, they may be controlled and put to rest again."

Vamshi frowned. "But it sounds like you want Cass to wake them."

Again, the small blue dragon nodded. "Those who can

read the Dragon Script will not use the dragons for their own gain."

"How do you know?" Cass asked. Somehow, his indirect insults were grinding on her. She wasn't sure she wouldn't use the dragons' magic. But at the same time, the mere thought of unleashing dragon power into the world she lived in sounded terrifying.

Pakhba granted her a small—slightly condescending—smile. "Because while you do not know who you are, I do."

Cass raised a single brow. She'd read about wise, all-knowing dragons, but never imagined one would be so insufferable. "Of course you do."

"Mehen and Quezacotl have slept longer than the others," he went on. "They may burst free on their own, but that leaves them open to binding by The Future." He raised his head, the yellow wisps hanging off his face danced again. "You want to lead, but are afraid to. You think you might do well in authority, which is why you asked your masters at the merchant to be given the keys."

"Witch's Bones?" she asked.

"But you are afraid to be in control," he went on. "You are desperate to try, but afraid you will fail. And so you do not move. This ebbing and flowing power pulls in you, keeping you set in one place, neither moving forward nor backward. This is why you sigh in sad longing while watching the woman in the dark speak of ancient civilizations."

Cass tilted her head.

"Ms. Dawnstride?" Vamshi asked.

"Oh." Cass sank a little where she sat. "Have you been spying on me all day?"

"I have ears, Cassandra," the dragon said stoically.

"Still," she whined, leaning against Vamshi. "You do realize that most of what you say comes across like an insult, right? A real blow to my apparently non-existent moral fiber."

"Hardly." The dragon floated the rest of the way to the floor and crawled to Cass. He placed his clawed forepaw on her knee. "You were not chosen by the stars or blessed by an ancient god. But you can do what needs to be done."

His unexpected praise steadied her mind. "So," she said slowly, "I—or someone—needs to read the Dragon Script, find these two dragons the psycho lady is after, waken them, then... hide them somewhere safe so they can continue to weave the magic of our world?"

Pakhba nodded solemnly. "If we can preserve them in their material form," he indicated the bracelet on Cass's arm, "they may be safe."

"Are you not sure?" Vamshi asked.

The dragon shook his head once in each direction. "It was what Aiken hoped to find out. Call them up and let their magic stay, controlled, safe on this earth."

Cass blanched, rubbing the bridge of her nose with her fingers. "So you're not even sure this will work? And what if it doesn't? What if they eat me or torch the city?"

Pakhba smiled with only one side of his thin, dragon lips. "You can read the Script. You are the only one who can find them. It is written there. She who wakes them shall reign over them. I trust you, Cassandra."

Holding in a long sigh, Cass blew it out through her tight lips. "I'm not sure."

"And that," Pakhba said simply, "is the best thing of all."

Vamshi handed her a hot chocolate despite the end of summer warmth still clinging to the dorm. Cass hadn't moved from the spot on the floor. The Dragon Script lay open over her crossed legs, large enough to prop up on her knees when opened. Vamshi's black laptop sat next to her, open to an interactive map of the world.

"So tell me what you see," Vamshi asked, tapping the leather cover of the Script and sitting back down next to her.

Cass looked back at it. "It moves. At first, it looks like maps with tons of lay lines and symbols. Right when I think I understand what I'm looking at, it shifts into these circles and lines. Like the orientation lines and rose on a compass."

Vamshi pulled back, smiling in surprise.

"I looked up the terms," Cass said with a smile, unable to lie and to say she always knew the names of the lines on a compass. "Then, it turns into this really ornate writing and that's when I start to understand."

Just then, something in the hall fell hard, banging into a door. Cass and Vamshi froze, mouths full of hot chocolate. Cass gulped.

"No way they followed me here," she whispered.

Vamshi's eyes went even wider, then tracked to their dorm door. "Are you serious?"

Cass swallowed again. "We can check the hall?" But she was glued to the spot. The fresh fear paralyzed her. They were on the second floor. There was no escape if her stalkers were in that hall. "Vam?" she whispered.

Taking the hint, Vamshi took a deep breath, held it, and stood up. On tiptoe, she crept towards the dorm door. Pakhba hovered perfectly still. Vamshi's black-nailed hand shook as she reached towards the door. She pressed herself up against the door frame and slowly turned the handle. With one eye, she peeked out and down the hall.

"Oh, my god," she whispered.

"What?" Cass cried, gathering the book in her arms, fear making her skin damp.

Vamshi slowly turned her head to Cass, mouth open. "It's —it's the maintenance guy!"

Cass deflated instantly, sinking into the ground. "I swear, Vam!" she growled, smacking her hard when she sat back down.

"You made me go look out the door," she protested. "For some evil, ancient organization. I think that deserves a good friend award."

Even Pakhba gave the girls a doleful, and somehow chiding, look.

"So you can see letters?" Vamshi said, going back to the original conversation.

Cass shook her head. "It's more like hearing. When I see the lines, the meaning just," she opened her palm quickly, making a clicking sound. "I just understand what it says. Which is why..." She reached over to the laptop and clicked to move the digital globe until Africa faced them. "I need to go to Egypt. I saw it on a page. I know that shape."

"Oh, my god, girl!" Vamshi gasped, her eyes going wide. She wheeled around to stand on her knees, gripping Cass's shoulders tight. "You are not going on your own. Do you have any idea how dangerous it is? Haven't you seen 'Taken'? And you were attacked tonight. In Connecticut! What do you think Egypt will be like?"

"Well," Cass sighed, "here's the other thought I had. If The Future is this close to the Script, they may have been looking for it. Maybe hoping someone would find it. Then... they follow that person to the dragons."

Vamshi made a high-pitched sound somewhere between a gasp and a whale. "You think they will be following you? And you're okay with that?"

"No." She sighed, picking at the corner of the Script. "But I was thinking if I find one, ideally before them since I'm the only one who can find them, that we figure out where to keep them safe. Then we split them up. Or... I don't know. I haven't thought that far ahead yet. But I was hoping... You'd come with me?" She looked up, biting her lip. "You're really smart, and I always think better when I talk out loud to you. You'd be able to help me figure things out. I really really don't want to go it alone."

Her best friend's mouth dropped and her deep, brown eyes widened.

"I know it's dangerous," she went on, taking Vamshi's hand. "But—"

"But what?" Vamshi cut in. "No, 'Oh, it's my quest, I must do this alone, I don't want to put you in danger,'" she rattled off fast.

The words cut through to a part Cass hasn't thought of. She'd thought Vamshi would want to go. She dropped her head. "You're right. I'm sorry—"

"Of course!" her best friend cut in again. Vamshi lurched towards her, crushing her in a hug. "Dragon quests and in foreign lands? Oh, my god I'm so there."

Cass growled playfully, returning the hug. "You could have just said that. I am sorry I didn't think of your safety, though."

"Screw my safety," Vamshi laughed. "Let's figure out how to get to Egypt."

CHAPTER 5: BUS RIDE TO MYSTIC

Despite dragons, potential travel, evil organizations, and enchanters, Cass found herself washing dishes after class, rushing to the dorm hall's laundry room to put her clothes in the one dryer that worked before anyone else, and frantically trying to get homework done on time. She looked over her shoulder for days after the incident downtown. Every sudden movement and every shadow she caught out of the corner of her eye reminded her of the man who chased her. She even mentioned it to Felicity and Everly who took the security recording to the police. That ended up being a dead end since nothing actually happened. Cass took screen shots of the bald man, the younger man, and the blonde woman and hid them in the Script. At first, she didn't want to look at them, knowing they probably sent that mad man after her. But soon, she started to look at them every day to memorize their faces.

She also sneaked a screen shot of Charlie while he spoke to her in the book section. Vamshi had been right: she loved his mysteriously sad eyes. It didn't hurt that he was tall and had that thick, wavy blond hair, either. She'd seen him twice. He had to live in town somewhere. Or at least work in town. She tried some social media stalking but found nothing before chickening out and locking her phone.

The weekend loomed before her and she hadn't made any more plans for hunting the dragons. I know what I need to do, she told herself. Isn't that enough for right now?

The dryer rumbled its last few minutes when her phone buzzed in her pocket. A text from Ella, her younger sister, brought a smile to her face.

Tournament this weekend. Please come. Mom crazy.

Cass smiled and laughed at her younger sister's SOS. Ella had been into fencing since she could walk. She'd won every local tournament New England offered. Some state-wide tournament had decided to host in Connecticut and Ella could talk about nothing else for the last three months. "This is a big one!" she'd cried before Cass left for college. "This will make or break my career." Ella was dramatic, for sure. She got it from her mother.

Cass texted back that she'd be there. Weathermoore University was only a two-hour drive from her parents' house in a small town outside Mystic. The tournament was taking place in the rec center in the middle of the small, posh town. She could make it there and back in a day if she wanted. Part of her wanted to stay the weekend, soak up the last of the summer sun, and maybe watch the boats for a little while.

Deciding to take the bus, she packed a few things in what she called her adventure backpack (a retro 1920s leather pack with brass buckles) and boarded a bus in Danbury to head east. Vamshi agreed to check on the Dragon Script every day and send her pictures that it was safe where they'd hidden it in her junk tote under her bed.

She just settled onto the bus and picked up her headphones to drown out the sound of the road when she spotted someone boarding. His wavy, shoulder-length blond hair caught the early morning sun as it cut across the bus. Her heart fluttered just enough to make her cheeks flush. Charlie didn't see her, his eyes downcast, as he pushed his way to a seat just two in front of hers and sat down.

Don't even think about it, Cass, she growled to herself. No one wants a creepy stalker girl to appear next to them and start to chat when they have no way of escaping you.

The bus pulled away from the stop with a familiar lurch, shoving her against the backrest. She watched the back of Charlie's head, wondering where he was going. What was he doing on a bus to Mystic? Probably something nice and normal, unencumbered by wondering if he should track down two ancient dragons. She unlocked her phone and looked over the maps and articles she'd taken screenshots of about Egypt. That was all she'd gotten from the damned Script. She thought that once she started to read it, it would all come into focus. Instead, every word, every thought from the pages had to be gleaned one at a time. Trying to guess exactly what part of the far-away country the dragon might be in started to look hopeless. Would it be somewhere familiar, like the sphinx? Maybe in a pyramid? Or was that too cliche?

"Hey."

Cass jumped at the deep, gentle voice. She slammed the screen of her phone down onto her thigh and looked up. Charlie's pale blue eyes looked back down at her. He chewed on his bottom lip and looked around at the few curious eyes that craned to see what Cass had exclaimed at.

"Sorry," he mumbled. He shoved his hands deep into the pockets of his gray jacket and turned to leave.

"Wait, wait," Cass stuttered. She half-heartedly reached a hand out, stopping herself before she touched his. "I'm sorry. I was super into research and I didn't see you approach." She tried to smile kindly, but the strain of her face told her it looked more like a grimace. Her heart raced as he tried to be bold. "I was actually going to come and say hi. I mean, I saw you board the buss and thought, well, wondered, what you were doing. Not that you're not allowed to be on a city buss. Because you are."

Charlie's large eyes flicked nervously between her hands, her face, the front of the bus, then back to her eyes. She cringed. She'd made him uncomfortable. Her rambling, inability to get a hold of herself in stressful situations... this was why she would make a terrible manager for Witch's Bones, and the sooner Felicity and Everly saw that, the better. Even if she wanted to be.

"I'm... so sorry," she finally said with a strong exhale. She scooted over to the window seat so that the two seats to her left were open, giving him the option to sit down if he wanted, and offering a courtesy seat as a buffer. To her delight, he sat down. He perched on the very edge of the seat and pushed his palms into his knees. At least he sat down. She smiled inwardly.

Her hand shot out almost on its own. "I'm Cass, by the way. A fellow enjoyer of the mayonnaise gyro. That's where we met the first time?" she added when he didn't say anything. But he took her hand in a polite shake.

"Yeah," he said, finally smiling a little. "I wanted to kind of explain the other day."

Surprise filled her. Of course, she wanted to ask about his sudden, mysterious disappearance, but didn't have the guts to bring it up. Glad he brought it up, she nodded, encouraging him to go on. "Yeah, I thought maybe the weirdos in the suits scared you off."

He searched her face, making her cheeks flush again. "A little," he said nervously. "I thought maybe they were feds. So I booked it."

She laughed, easing the tension in her chest a little. "Me too, honestly. But, uh..." How much should she tell him?

"Well, they weren't, so that's good." She smiled. "So, what do you do? Do you live in Rookwind?"

He chewed on his lip again before answering. "Almost. I'm... looking for work there. I have this crazy, pushy family."

"Ah," she said, nodding. "They really want you to get a good job, make something of yourself?" She lowered her voice to comically mock a man's timber. "I won't have a layabout as a son. Buy a house. Blah blah blah."

A true smile finally cracked his guarded face. It infected her, making her smile even harder.

"Pretty much," he said, easing back into the seat a little more. "It's like they want me to do one thing. Dead set on it. I never had a choice. Not in school, not in any pastimes or hobbies. I thought that if I did everything right, my life would be set, you know?"

Cass suddenly felt as if a tirade of blocked up words were about to spill from Charlie. She turned to face him, leaning into the seat with her shoulder, and cocked her head sympathetically. She'd always been a good listener. "Yeah," she confirmed. "Like, that if we did everything we were supposed to, life would just work itself out in a natural order. But there's nothing natural about human life, I guess. Until a few days ago, I thought I knew what I wanted to do. Where I needed to be." She sighed. "But I'm wondering if I actually knew."

"Do you get to choose?" he asked.

She narrowed her eyes, thinking. "I'm not sure. It's like I made a choice that I didn't know about. I was told I wasn't chosen," she laughed. "I'm not special."

"Lucky," Charlie sighed, completely relaxing into the seat now. He didn't elaborate.

Taking a chance, Cass touched his shoulder. Electricity shot through her, thrilling her. She suddenly wanted to touch him again. "Go on?" she asked.

He squinted, finding the right words. "I've been molded

ever since I was born. They told me what to do, what to eat, how to think. I was told over and over again that I was made for a purpose and if I just did what I was told, then life would be exactly as it should be. I thought I'd be happy."

Pressing his lips together, he suddenly stopped and looked down at his hands. He clasped them together tight.

"Do you have any friends?" she asked. "When I met Vamshi in our first semester, I hadn't had a good friend in years. I just spilled my guts to her one day. There was no going back after that," she laughed nervously. "Talking to someone, even a stranger, felt amazing. She's my best friend now. Girl couldn't leave me if she wanted to."

Charlie continued to look at his hands, his hair obscuring his face. Quietly, he shook his head. "Never had time for them. I was too weird for most kids in high school. Never started college. I was just kind of thrown into my job."

Taking the given opportunity to keep him talking, Cass asked, "What do you do? I just work at Witch's Bones right now. Super glamorous."

He turned his head towards her, but still didn't look up. "I do research for people, mostly. They want to find collectible things like paintings, family heirlooms, museum pieces—that kind of thing. I hunt them down. I end up at a lot of estate sales and auctions. I may have a lead here in Rookwind."

"That's so cool!" Cass exclaimed. "I study anthropology, so I love that."

Her excitement finally drew his eyes up.

Seeing he wasn't going to initiate any kind of continued conversation, Cass launched into telling him everything about her passion for art, history, folklore, and world religions. How she'd always wanted to go to museums as a kid and loved the dark, mysterious glow of the displays.

"I'd always imagine the lady giving the tours was in a secret society or something," she said. "That she knew which artifacts were the magic ones and that she was a guardian of their secrets. I imagined finding out which one had the best secrets, and stealing it like in the movies. Or going to far-off lands and running into a smart-mouthed adventurer before getting tangled up in a wild heist."

"Like 'Romancing the Stone'?" he asked.

A sheepish grin made her blush. "Actually, yeah. Embarrassing, I know."

He allowed another genuine smile onto his face. "Not really," he offered lightly. "It's kind of..." He stopped himself. "You seem really passionate," he said instead.

Damn, she thought, was he about to say 'It's kind of cute?' He'd guarded himself again, but at least he smiled. She'd made some progress.

She went on for some time, telling him about her family near Mystic, her big-time, award-winning sister, and even Vamshi. She was thirsty from talking when the bus slowed to its first stop off the highway. Charlie stood up.

"Your stop?" she asked, her heart falling a little. About a dozen other people stood up, pressing forward.

"Yeah," Charlie said, grabbing his backpack. Cass noted how it almost looked exactly like her adventure pack. Only it was made of black leather and had silver buckles.

He moved down the aisle.

"Wait!" she tired, trapped by the mob moving to exit. But he didn't hear over the brakes and the driver loudly droning the name of the stop. Can I have your number or something? she thought sadly, watching his very attractive wavy hair disembark.

"Damn it," she sighed, leaning back into the seat. "Cass, grow a spine." She smacked her cheek three times. "How the hell do you intend to hunt down dragons if you can't ask a super cute guy for his number?"

She didn't have an answer for herself.

CHAPTER 6: A SPINE

The gymnasium roared and rang with that familiar buzz of dozens of voices echoing off pale blue stone walls. The vinyl floor bounced the sound around up to the bright lights and exposed steel rafters above. Banners from past championships in karate, tennis, fencing, and other sports hung down the walls in mismatched colors that stood out against the powdery color of every other surface.

Shiny metal bleachers hosted dozens of eager, shouting fencing parents. Several long, narrow mats lined the converted area with body cords swinging from both fencers on the mats. The white-clad bodies moved expertly around, the narrow swords hanging limp until a sudden, timed, planned movement and a lightning quick reaction from an opponent threw the stillness into what Cass thought looked like utter chaos.

"Which one is Ella?" she asked her mother, craning to look around at the dozens of fencers.

Overjoyed at them all being together, her mother had been holding her hand most of the day. "There, mat three," she said pointing. "Where your father is filming."

"Umm," Cass squinted. Both fencers were tall, leggy

duelists in white, faces covered in a stainless steel mesh mask. "Which tall, skinny, sword-wielding mummy?"

Laughing and shaking her head, Mom pointed to the one on the left. "With the long red hair. Like yours." She reached up and pet Cass's hair affectionally.

Ella, Cass's younger sister, stood lean and tall on her mat, her epee poised gently low. Now that she knew which one was her younger sister, she recognized her fighting style. Epee was slow and boring to watch, but she knew the numbers, patterns, tells, and other hints from her opponent made this Ella's favorite class of fencing. Ella loved the mind games, the timing, the watching for an opening.

"It's precise and tactical!" Ella always said when Cass complained about the slow, boring bouts. "You just want to see scenes like in an action movie. Not everything is Errol Flynn."

Cass knew a little about sword play. Ella forced her to practice with her. The hours of getting jabbed with the blunt but still steel-tip of a sword had encouraged Cass to learn quick. She'd get heated though, the gear making her hot and the pain and easy losses pushing her into a frenzy.

Once the epee bouts were over and Ella—unsurprisingly—won the local rounds, the groups moved to sabre. This one Cass enjoyed. It was, as Ella put it, a spectator's sport. This was the fencing she liked to see. The quick, long combat, the dancing around one's opponent. She could cheer with this one because she understood what was going on.

After the tournament, and Ella taking gold and silver, she ran to meet her little sister on the floor.

A few of the other fencers shook Ella's hand and nodded to her, praising her form and congratulating her. Others snubbed her as was often the case with Ella's talent. Cass thought sports moms were too stuck up in this part of the world. Wasn't sportsmanlike conduct supposed to be a thing?

"Look at all that scrap metal," Cass called to her sister.

Ella turned, face red and beaming. "You came!" She tucked her helmet under one arm and ran to Cass, her other arm flung wide to hug her.

Cass hugged her sister then made an exaggerated grossed out sound. "You are drenched in sweat. Ew."

"I work hard," Ella smiled. Her blue eyes sparkled extra bright after her victories. "Are you staying for dinner?"

She nodded. "I have a buss late tonight." She swung around her sister and reached down for the massive duffle bag that held her other swords and extra gear. "I have no idea what you did that first half, but you won so that's good right?"

Ella rolled her eyes. "You have got to learn the rules for epee. It's so much more fun than you think."

"Of course it is."

They joined their parents, loaded up Ella's gear and headed to their home. The house was more beautiful than Cass remembered it. Painted a fresh white and nestled on the edge of a peninsula and a nature preserve, it was one of the quietest places outside Mystic. The bigger neighborhood and more busy docks lined the shores farther away.

"Dinner on the boat?" Dad asked once they were home.

"I'd love that," Cass said, smiling. She hadn't been on the water in almost a year. School had been so hectic and work took up most of her weekends over the last year.

Ella and Cass helped their mother carry groceries down the dock and onto the boat. Cass took in the salt water and the wind blowing the scent of the bay up to her. The sun hit her just right, warming her from the sea breeze. Nostalgia and emotion always overtook her when she visited her family and their home. She hadn't appreciated it enough as a child.

"So, Cass," Mom started as she opened homemade jars of cucumber salad, "have you discussed your promotion with your bosses yet?"

Of course Mom would start in with that right away.

She looked up, sheepish. Ella saw the look and laughed off the question.

"As if Cass has time for more work," she said supportively. "Mom, she's working really hard on these research assignments. She has to have them done this year so she can apply for those digs the grad students are doing."

Enormous gratitude for her sister washed over her. But guilt prevailed. "I have not," she confessed to her mom.

Ella widened her eyes at Cass. "I was trying to help you, silly goose."

"Yeah, I know," she mumbled, tearing up some lettuce for a salad and tossing it into a white bowl. The gentle sway of the boat eased the tension only a little.

"Why haven't you asked for the promotion?" Mom pressed. "They make you close. They have you do all the work that comes with the job title. Is it that they can't afford to?"

Mom had jabbed at the weird little store ever since Cass started work there. She didn't like the dark corners, the scary decor, the weird books and everything else about it that Cass loved.

"No," she shot back, defending Witch's Bones. "I just... haven't asked."

Ella met her eyes over the meal prep, waiting. She looked sympathetic but curious at the same time. When Cass didn't defend herself, Ella asked, "What the hell, Cass?"

"Ella!" Mom snapped.

"No, now I'm on your side," Ella cut in. "Cass, grow a spine. Ask for what you deserve!"

Ella knew more than Mom. Cass had been struggling to pay for things like laundry and three meals in the same day. Living downtown was expensive.

"I moved back into the dorms because they're cheaper," she reasoned. "I don't have to drive almost anywhere."

"Do you need money?" Mom asked over her.

"Mooom," Cass whined, rubbing the bridge of her nose. "I'm fine. Why do I have to always push and fight?"

"Because you're worth more than this," Mom shouted at the same time Ella said, "because you've worked hard to get it!"

The pressure smothered Cass. Her hands went limp in the piles of green leaves and she zoned out in defense. Why did everyone want her to always fight, to push, to climb? What was wrong with coasting by as best she could?

Mom and Ella dropped the subject when Dad boarded the boat with candles and a small radio. They finished making dinner in jovial conversation and enjoyed one another's company. They praised Ella's performance at her tournament and joked about needing more wall space for her medals.

Once the meal was over, Cass took a moment to walk down the pier and look at the water. Being inland so long had made her miss the salty air. Taking in the bright red and pink sunset made her stop to think. The bright orange light reflected off the gold dragon bangle when she crossed her arms against the chilling air. Would all this be affected by the whole waking the dragons thing? She looked down the shore at the other homes. Some backyards wafted barbecue out from family gatherings. Kids squealed as they ran into the water to hunt for shells.

"Ugh," she sighed. She sniffled, realizing tears had unknowingly filled her eyes. When she blinked, one fell down her cheek.

"Sorry about Mom," Ella said, coming up behind her.

Cass quickly wiped away the tear. "It's okay. I'm used to it. I've never been a trophy-winner."

Ella pushed her shoulder playfully. "Cut that out. But I meant what I said." Her voice softened.

Cass hated this. She was the older sister. Ella shouldn't be consoling her. She should be giving Ella advice, helping her overcome life's trials.

"Look," Ella started. "Those two kooks, Everly and Felicity, they like you, right?"

Cass nodded.

"Then just ask to be paid for the work you're doing." Ella frowned sternly. "You come in early, you close for them, you make orders. You can't work more and get this internship."

"Those internships are for grad students," Cass objected. "They'd never give it to me. I don't have the experience."

"But you need it to apply for the dig if you get into the master's program. Turn your passion into work," Ella ordered. "Take what you love and make something to show them. Everyone goes into interviews saying how passionate they are, how much they love this or that. Everyone, Cass. That's not what makes you stick out. What makes you stick it out is saying how much you love this anthropology stuff and then showing them something they can touch and see that proves it. Do you think I beat all those other fencers today because I told them how badly I wanted to win? No. I beat them. I beat them by doing the work: studying them, the craft, practicing with goals in mind. Don't convince them with words. Show them what you've done."

Annoyance, sadness, and love at Ella's words roiled up in Cass all at once. She was right, and she knew it. But that didn't make it easier.

"I don't even know where to start," she said, the tears filling her eyes again. But didn't she? Egypt. Somewhere. The book wouldn't tell her where. Or was she just not looking hard enough? Was she scared to find the answer because then she'd have to do something about it?

"I think you do," Ella said for her. "I see it in your face right this instant. Spine, Cass. Strong as a serpent."

"Or a dragon," she sighed.

"I'll give you no more than ten," a woman snapped at Cass from across the counter.

This old lady had been into Witch's Bones many, many times. Every time she came in, she haggled prices, told Cass how ignorant she was—always something. One time, the lady had asked for a triskelion and Cass had, not knowing what that was, nervously shown her to the pentacles. Ever since then, she'd studied every ancient symbol she could find. Still, she could never satisfy this snotty, bargain-hunting old lady.

"Ma'am, I'm sorry," Cass stuttered. "We're not a pawn-shop or a thrift store. The prices are marked as is. I can't—"

"What about this?" the woman shot her gnarled hand across the counter, clamping Cass's wrist in her talons. She turned her wrist over to look at the golden dragon bracelet. "Looks cheap. I'll give you twelve dollars for it."

"Umm," Cass stammered, trying to pull her arm away. "No, this isn't—" Her heart hammered in her head, her anxiety nearly bursting her skull.

She gasped as the woman slipped it off her wrist.

"Wait, no!" she cried, reached out for it. The woman moved suddenly like a ninja, dodging her flailing hands.

The old lady squinted with one eye at the sapphire that was Pakhba's eye. Cass wished he'd appear in a puff of blue smoke and yellow lightning. Could he breathe fire? She'd order him to torch this woman. Burn her purple wig right off her head.

"I think this is real," the woman mumbled, tapping the sapphire. "Where'd you get this? Where do you keep the good stuff like this?"

Cass hurried around the counter, tears stinging her eyes. "Please give it back, you don't know what that is."

"What's going on up here?" Everly's deep, stern but calm voice asked as he came around the corner. He was even more flamboyantly clad today in a tail suit and faded top hat. Felicity appeared behind him, the fringes of her long black shawl blowing in a threatening breeze as she glared at the purple-haired woman.

The woman, seeing Everly's tall glower and Felicity's mysterious warning eyes, stopped. "It's junk, anyway. All of it," she snapped. She threw Pakhba down onto the counter and hurried out the door into the setting sun.

Cass struggledto catch her breath, her chest aching, and scooped up the bracelet. She held it to her chest. Not expecting to have that much fear of losing the little dragon, she took another deep breath.

"Cassandra," Everly said gently, "don't let her bully you like that."

Felicity came to her side, petting her shoulder to soothe her. "Ev, can't you see she's shaken up." She took Cass's hand and led her back behind the counter. "Why don't you close up early. Go home and relax a little for the rest of the weekend."

"Thanks, guys," Cass said, sighing . She couldn't seem to catch her breath. "And I'm sorry."

The eccentric couple gave her kind glances before heading out the back to let her close up. Aggressively rubbing the bridge of her nose, she thought about how if she did ask for that promotion, they might not be here to save her from rabid customers. Help her if she got the math wrong on the register. Why did these things drive her mad so easily?

She flipped the sign to closed, locked the doors, turned down the lights and went to work on the register, carefully counting, and taking out the deposit. For once, she'd get done before Vamshi and could pick her up from the coffee shop and they could walk home together. She'd seen Vamshi for a few minutes when she got home Saturday night, but hadn't had a chance to talk her thoughts out with her.

After Witch's Bones was closed, she left out the back and headed down the cobbled road to the coffeehouse. It perched on a hill with a river literally right out back. A back deck attached to the coffee house overlooked it, facing a tall, thin waterfall behind it. Vamshi came running out the front door to her, arms thrown wide.

"Aww, are you going to walk me home?" she cooed, smothering Cass in a hug.

"No, smother mother, you are walking me home," Cass corrected. They trotted down the hill into the more modern downtown area as the streetlights started to blink on. "I was hoping you'd maybe have some words of wisdom for me," Cass sighed. "Ella kind of gave me an earful while I visited."

Vamshi pressed her black-coated lips together and twisted her face. "I'm not going to discourage you from doing one of the single greatest things I've ever heard in my life. Especially if I can go with you."

Cass moaned, genuinely upset. "Have you ever traveled like that before?"

"While escaping the British," she joked. Then she turned serious. "You wanted to do something like this."

"Yeah, like with the Peace Corps or something," Cass shot back.

Her best friend gave her a condescending, doubtful brow raise. "How safe and organized."

Exactly, she thought dolefully.

They made it home without Vamshi pressing the subject Cass had brought up. Knowing each liked their quiet time before Monday, they split up into their separate rooms and shut their doors to give the other some peace. Cass flopped onto her bed, which took up exactly half of her bedroom, and turned on her overhead lamp. The familiar lump under her pillow that was the Dragon Script pressed into the side of her head.

She didn't pull it out, unwilling to open herself up to the idea that it might show her exactly where to go now that she was even more doubtful. Instead, she scrolled on her phone, looking up various Charlies in the area. She scrolled through hundreds of profile pictures. None of them were a blond, melancholy boy who looked like he could be a poet.

Until one zipped past. Gasping, she sat up and quickly used her thumb to scroll back up. A single picture of a shaggy-haired boy with wide, blue eyes looked up at her. He wore a loose black sweater and stood in some sort of rocky ruins with mist all around. Cass breathed out loud at the pure mystery and romance of it. She clicked on the profile.

Pictures of him in other similar, old looking places peppered throughout weird things like screenshots of internet maps, pieces of paper that had scribbles on them, and what looked like English cities every once in a while. The license plates were black and white and the cars drove down the left side of the street in those pictures.

"Wait a minute," she laughed, going back to his main page. It didn't say where he lived, but his profile picture was geotagged in Dorset, England. "He travels?" she whispered, smiling. Her heart fluttered and she couldn't stop the happiness that filled her.

She laid back down, looking at his picture. It wasn't a selfie, someone had taken the picture. He was looking past the camera at whoever took it. Vamshi was right; he looked sad.

Thinking up silly scenarios about asking him to go with her on her dragon hunt, she smiled and closed her eyes to dream them up more vividly. She didn't have a guarantee about finding the dragons. Or even what to do when she did. In her imagination, she did. She held the book open, a trilby pushed low over her eyes, a leather satchel at her side and a belt with rope, a lantern, and every other thing she'd need for adventuring. Charlie would be there, helping her read the maps and compass.

The images filtered into her dreams as she drifted off to sleep, filled with wild—though tepid—anticipation.

CHAPTER 7: THE SIGNS

ass gripped the straps of her backpack, waiting for the last student to file out of the still dark classroom where Ms. Dawnstride packed up her artifacts. She looked up when Cass moved through the desks.

"You look very worried," she said, her brown eyes sparkling in the projector light. "I did do a grade check for you. You're doing great in this class. Making me proud as your advisor."

"Thanks, Ms. Dawnstride." Cass flushed a little at the praise. "But that makes my question suck that much more."

"Eleanor," she offered, tossing her thick coils of cold-clasped braids over her shoulder as she heaved up her old carousel. "We're all adults."

Cass had never gotten used to professors and other adults letting her call them by their first names. It made her shiver every time she did. "Well, I was wondering... Is there time to...?" She stopped. A sudden headache ran up her skull as she tried to formulate at least one coherent question. She needed to find a way to ask about dragons in Egypt that wouldn't sound crazy, needed to ask if it was okay to take a trip in the middle of the semester, how could she do that, and where might an ancient dragon even be hidden in Egypt?

Her mouth went dry, hanging open. It was all too crazy.

"Cass," Eleanor said softly, logging out of the campus computer, "what is it? It looks important. Just ask."

"It's going to sound crazy," she sighed, letting out some anxiety. "But I have nowhere else to turn to besides my insane roommate and best friend. And she's being dangerously encouraging."

Eleanor smiled. "I like it so far. Go on."

Deciding it was better to do this sitting, Cass nearly fell into a front row desk and dropped her pack onto the floor. She griped the edges of the desk, not looking Eleanor in the eyes.

"I need to take a trip to Egypt. Sometime. Soon maybe. I'm not sure."

The anthropology professor stopped, her text book halfway into her own ornate leather pack. "As in the next year or so?" She narrowed her brown eyes. "You mean as in this semester? I don't think we have a study abroad in Egypt this year."

"I know." Cass's throat closed up. This was crazy. It was all crazy. But Pakhba hadn't said anything about not telling anyone. He hadn't mentioned a rule or anything that she'd be struck down dead if she let others in on the secret. But she'd already been attacked once. She couldn't do that to Eleanor. To Vamshi.

She calmed down, a sudden peace filling her brain. She knew what she needed to do. "I'm going for a personal research project," she started again. "I can't tell you about it."

To her surprise, Eleanor smiled. It spread slowly and mischievously across her face. "Students make discoveries all the time, Cass. I understand you wanting to protect your find."

"Oh, no, it's not like that!" she cried. "I just don't want to say I'm on to something and then... not be."

"Fear of failure?" Eleanor asked, gently crossing her arms and looking down at Cass. "Do you know what you're looking for?"

Cass shook her head, her heart falling. "I don't even know where." She perked up. "Do you know about Egyptian dragons?"

"Oh, yes." Eleanor smiled again. More knowingly this time. "The Coiled One. Mehen. She who guides Ra through the underworld."

This was news to her. "Underworld?"

"Tuat." Eleanor nodded. "She is a guardian. She watched over other gods but was not necessarily worshiped herself." She pulled another book out of her bag and started to flip through it. "I loved that about her. She is there to protect, not to be venerated. She protected Ra's boat from Apophis, the enemy of the very sun and thus Ra. There is a proverb the ancient Egyptians said that goes, 'One should welcome the ureas and spit upon Apophis.' It means welcome the serpent—the dragon—and defy the dark god. Ah, here."

She set the huge book down before Cass and pointed to a full-page illustration. It depicted a great, coiling, white dragon around a slim Egyptian boat with the falcon god Ra standing in aboard, safe behind the coils. Behind the dragon and Ra, a deep dark cavern loomed opened with evil eyes looking out. It gave Cass a chill to look into the monster's eyes. Like it saw her through the painting. It looked back.

Cass gasped as the hairs on the back of her neck stood up. "Freaky," she mused.

Eleanor nodded. "I'm surprised you know about her. Mehen, not being a god, isn't very well known. Or talked about. Outside academic circles, I suppose." She took the book back. When she did, Cass felt immediately warmer. "Does your adventure have something to do with Mehen?"

Eleanor was safe. Cass nodded. "But I have no idea where to start. I have a source, but it's being difficult."

"Have you spent much time studying it?"

Conviction landed in her chest. "No. You'd think I would, though, considering how interesting it is."

The older woman nodded slowly, frowning down at her student. "Are you afraid once you solve the riddle, you will be unable to stop yourself from going?"

Lightning struck through Cass. That was it. She thought she wanted to go, but now that Eleanor had said it, that was the issue. Why was she hesitating?

"I don't know what will happen if I go," she confessed.

Eleanor smiled, taking up her bag to end the discussion. "It sounds like you are close, Cass. Very close. You might be wrong about your expedition. I won't pretend going to a foreign land with no direction isn't dangerous. Scary, even. You can prepare, plan out the trip. You can take a friend to be safe. You might not find what you're looking for. But do you know a surefire way to not find what you seek?"

A deep breath escaped Cass. "Yeah. Not go."

Her professor nodded. "Are you willing to make sure you lose out on this adventure? Or risk taking a look?"

"**S**he's supposed to be an adult," Cass panted as she hurried down the street towards a coffee shop. One Vamshi didn't work at. Pakhba hovered just above her, invisible to everyone else.

"You must find your courage, Cassandra," he chided. "Already The Future watches from within your city. They tracked the Script. They know you have it. I am surprised you are still unharmed."

"Gee, thanks," she said sarcastically, rolling her eyes so hard it hurt. She turned to take a shortcut down an ally to Main Street on the other side.

"I am in earnest," the little dragon replied. "Never have I seen The Future wait so long to strike. Meredith Navarre is not known for her patience."

She heard his alternate concern in his tone. "Go on."

He floated down to her arm, landing near the bracelet and turning to look at the museum as they passed. "She must have another move to make. Some other plan. She's not behaving in fear or out of desperation. This tells me she has control. I don't like that."

"I appreciate your concern," she said. "But I'm not sure what to do. I need a sign or some kind of flag waving and saying 'Hey, Cass, come here! This is the way.'"

"Ah, if only," Pakhba sighed.

Cass followed his eyes across the street as they exited the alley. They lighted on the museum's massive Grecian front. Hanging from the pillars were banners advertising the new Egyptian exhibit.

"No way," Cass cried. She turned and ran towards the coffee shop. "No, I mean from the Script. I need to read the Script. You said it would let me read it if I was meant to find the dragons."

"And it has," Pakhba insisted. "You cannot read a book you will not open!"

Growling, Cass raised her hand, signalling Pakhba to get back into the bangle. He did with a final glare at her, vanishing into a stream of blue and yellow smoke. She knew no one else had seen him, but still pulled her sleeve down over the bangle and swatted at the dissipating smoke.

She slid up to the counter once inside the coffee shop; the

lobby was packed with university students in mid-afternoon caffeine deprivation. She opened her mouth to order when...

"One black coffee with honey and a sprinkle of cinnamon," the barista at the end of the counter called.

Cass smiled, hearing someone else order her drink. "That's what I'll have, too," she told the cashier with a grin. "Can't believe someone else gets that." She craned her neck as the cashier ran her card to see her coffee twin. A black jacket and wavy blond hair came into view.

"Charlie!" she called before she could stop herself.

He turned around, coffee in hand, and met her eyes. He almost smiled at her, nodding in her direction. Forgetting her card, she pushed past a businessman in a disheveled suit and two moaning students. He didn't move, blue eyes trained on her.

"Hey, how was your trip?" she asked, smiling. "Did you find the lead you were looking for?"

A quick confusion passed over Charlie's face, making his cute, pouting lips part. Cass almost sighed out loud. Then, his eyes suddenly lit up.

"Oh, the conversation on the bus," he said jovially. "Actually no. May have been a dead end, honestly. I'm back to square one. Thinking I might have to look into something else. How's school?"

"Actually," Cass said, picking up her coffee and smiling at the cashier as he returned her card to her, "I'm going on a trip now. Maybe."

He led her to a small table and pulled a chair out for her. "Sounds mysterious. You're leaving in the middle of the semester?"

Her heart skipped joyfully when he pushed the chair in under her and took the seat on the other side. "I'm feeling a little pressured," she confessed. "I'm hesitant, but my sister told me to grow a spine and be brave."

Charlie narrowed his eyes playfully and smiled. "You seem pretty gutsy. Or at least like there's a strength in you just waiting to burst out. You don't talk like a person afraid."

His praise melted her insides. His gentle smile didn't fade, and he kept eye contact. Could she ask for his number now? Just as the thought crossed her mind, she swore the golden dragon bangle on her wrist twisted and slithered in a circle around her arm. She jerked her head down to look, but Pakhba hadn't budged.

Seeing her sister and family made her rethink defying the little dragon and the Dragon Script. And Pakhba was right: she hadn't exactly tried to read it again. Her phone buzzed with a text, but she ignored it. Why was Charlie being so interested in her and cute *now*? Now that she had almost decided to leave?

"Listen," she started. "I hope this trip to Egypt only takes me a couple of weeks."

His pale brows shot up at the mention of the faraway country.

"Yeah," she laughed nervously. "But I was thinking I'd give you my number?" *And you'd give me yours?* she thought hopefully.

Charlie's eyes almost instantly returned to their steely, caged off version. He opened his mouth to reply when his phone rang loudly. They both jumped at the sudden sound and he answered it quickly. He didn't speak, just listened. He hummed a single, deep acquiesce, then stopped the call.

"I have to go," he said, tossing his untouched coffee into the trash. He avoided her eyes, quickly dodging between the next wave of patrons and vanishing out the side door.

Cass watched him go. He didn't turn around to glance back, didn't say goodbye, didn't ask when she'd leave or come back.

"Cut it out, Cass," she chided herself. "This is what you

get for turning down Damien Dorian in eighth grade. And for not being clever enough to see your best friend was into your boyfriend. And for being boring."

The mean thoughts made her angry. She crossed her arms, no longer interested in her coffee, and glared at her reflection in the glass tabletop. Would she not ever have someone to smother in affection? Would she ever feel involved in someone else's life? What was the point of her if she couldn't even figure out how to flirt and keep a man around? Yeah, there was more to life than that, but she hadn't been this close since senior year. It was just something nice to think about. Life would be easier if she had a teammate, someone always on her side.

She looked up, but Charlie had long since vanished into the streets. These feelings of lacking hadn't hit her in a long time. Something about being able to read a magic, ancient dragon text and having a dragon familiar on her arm suddenly put her hopes and dreams of being an anthropologist into perspective.

"Ugh, fine," she sighed, taking a long drink and burning her throat. "I'll read it."

CHAPTER 8: THE DRAGON SCRIPT

"Mom, dad. I'm going to Egypt to hunt down some ancient—hopefully sleeping dragons—and potentially save the world from burning in a fiery hail of brimstone and blood if they awaken and are not controlled. Or worse, an evil enchantress wakes them and takes control over them, doing god knows what." Cass gripped her hands together behind her back, bouncing on the balls of her feet.

"I don't think so," Vamshi said, frowning with a critical eye.

The girls stood in the middle portion of their dorm, practicing what to say to their families and the university. Pakhba hovered nearby, investigating the mini fridge.

"I don't see what's so wrong with the idea I gave you two nights ago," Vamshi whined. She took the chocolate syrup bottle from Pakhba, opened it, and drizzled some on a paper plate on the desk. "Tell them it's a study abroad program and that you're going on the school's dime. It's for work, it's for a project. Hell, tell them it's for credit and will look great on your resume. They'll love that."

Cass watched the little dragon ignoring them, indulging in the sweet, thick liquid. "What if they call the school? What if The Future follows me there and kills me? Kills us," she reminded her best friend. "Then they'll get the school in trouble."

Vamshi made a bizarre face, widening her eyes and pressing her lips together. "You're worried about the school?"

Cass winced.

"No, you're not," Vamshi said triumphantly, pushing away from the desk. "Stop stalling!" She shoved past Cass and into her room.

"Vam, it's not that," Cass begged in vain. She chased after her friend, stumbling over a duffle bag she had half inspected for a potentially long journey.

Her friend blended into the darkness with her all black clothing and re-emerged holding the Dragon Script. Vamshi shoved it so hard into Cass she fell into the beanbag chair.

"How are you not excited?" she asked. "What is this pathetic, reluctant hero facade you're putting on?"

"For once, it's not a facade," Cass cried. Real tears pricked at her eyes as Pakhba's and Vamshi's landed on her. "You have no idea what this could mean. I'm past doubt. I believe everything the talking, floating dragon eating ice cream in my fridge has said."

Both girls glanced quickly at Pakhba.

"Then what is it?" Vamshi asked savagely. "Why won't you dive into this?"

"Because—!" Cass started, clutching the Script hard against her chest. She found herself hugging it like a protective barrier between her and Vamshi. Her breath hitched, and the tears fell. "Because I never do anything right! I'm a fraud! Why do I think I can be a leader, be in charge, take command? I can't even act like a big sister to Ella. My parents constantly want to bail me out of car payments, groceries, pay for tuition.

I've never done anything!" The quivering took her over, and the sobbing started. "I can't do anything on my own. I'm just Cassandra from Connecticut. I study anthropology because I was too scared to ever leave and actually see the world." She gasped, sniffling. "I'm afraid that if I choose to go this one time, that's it. My life will change forever. I won't be Cass Warren anymore. I'll be something I have no idea how to control, no idea how to be. No one can help me with this. I'd have to do it alone. Alone!"

Her emotion leaked across the room to Vamshi. Black tracks already spread down her best friend's face. Vamshi didn't move or speak, simply glaring through her own tears. Cass glanced at Pakhba where he hovered. His yellow eyes glowed in his blue face, impassive. He had to think she was weak now. The wrong choice.

"Vedic," Pakhba spoke softly, steadily, "are ones not in touch with their atman."

Cass sniffled and shook her head, not understanding.

"The spiritual life of the universe," Vamshi supplied through a stuffy nose. She took a deep breath and moved across the room to sit next to Cass. She flicked her hands, signaling Cass to move over on the fluffy chair.

Cass obliged, still tense, but willing to indulge in a calm moment. "My atman? My divine universe inside me?" She didn't mean to sound mocking, but it did.

The dragon tossed the tiny carton of ice cream back into the mini fridge, finally closing the door. He hovered closer to Cass. "Yes. A Vedic is not in touch with their atman. This was by design. If you were, you could not read the Dragon Script. If you knew you wanted to be master of the four dragons, it would not reveal itself. I have told you this."

Cass's breath caught in her throat. "That's not comforting. It just confirms what I said. I'm-I'm not the one for the job." She gently rubbed her thumb over the blue gem on the front of the soft leather book.

Pakhba narrowed his eyes, seemingly stealing himself. "But you are, Cassandra. I promise you. No, you are not a prophesied hero. Only fools believe in prophecies. Your humankind has free will. Do not let it go on the whim of mysticism."

An unbelieving frown pulled at Cass's face. Somehow, getting a pep talk about not believing in mysticism from a dragon didn't feel right. Pakhba reached down and pulled the book open. The partially blank pages waited for her to look at them.

"Open your mind, Vedic," Pakhba instructed. "The Script and the dragons will give you their strength. You will not be alone."

"Hell no, not alone," Vamshi chimed in.

Cass held up her hand to make them both be quiet. "Okay," she sighed. "Give me a second."

Taking a deep breath, she opened the book and laid it across her lap. Trying her best to ignore the two sets of eyes on her, she glared down at the pages of the Dragon Script. She honed in on the few lines of symbols and lettering that she could see. Chiding it in her mind, she imagined she could see how one particular looping symbol would curl, then flash across the page in its design.

That one means location, she thought. Gasping, she realized what had happened. "No way," she whispered. Feeling Vamshi was about to speak, she raised her hand to shut her up. She tracked the swooping line with her eyes.

Then, everything that was not the pages of the Dragon Script vanished into blackness. The pages didn't glow but rather radiated a warm, canvas-colored light. The black symbols grew bold. The more Cass focused on one, the more it spread across the page. A sensation overtook her mind the more she understood. Like being submerged in a warm pool. Eventually, even the book disappeared.

Cass stood in a single spot of that warm canvas light coming from above. A hazy, golden light lit the ground under her feet. It was some sort of stonework. The words of the Dragon Script floated in a solid, golden circle around her, shimmering and twinkling. She swore a humming came from them.

"Holy shit," she gasped.. Gentle drops of water on rocks echoed around her. The damp earthy musk of petrichor hit her nose. Somehow, she was in a cave. . "Where...?" She took a step.

"I'd remain still." Pakhba's deep, melodious voice reverberated pleasantly around her.

"Where are you?" she asked, squinting through the glimmering letters, maps, and symbols. Nothing appeared on the other side.

"I'm your familiar," he said simply. "I see what you see unless you don't want me to."

A blue hue lightened the golden tones of her bracelet. The eyes shimmered.

"Can you read this?" she asked, blood still hot and pumping through her tingling limbs.

"No. Of course not. That is your job, Vedic."

But she couldn't read it. At least, not in the sense she read her textbooks. The information was there in the words and symbols, but she didn't read them. She simply understood them. The likeness of a map formed in the air around her in glittering, golden sand. A hawk crowed, catching a scarab in its mouth, and a blue river cut through her mind's eye.

"Egypt," she gasped. "I was right. But where?"

"Just wait," Pakhba advised.

She was glad he did because she was about to step out of the golden circle. Trying to focus on the map like she had the initial Script, she let her mind sink into the warm, welcoming sand. The pyramids came to mind, then burned away into an orange cinder. Then the Sphinx rose from a sandy blackness before it too smoldered away. At last, a huge obelisk pierced up from the shifting sands. It rushed towards her, growing in height and magnificence, until it cast a solid black shadow over her.

Her neck craned to look up. A symbol of a sun ringed in fire waited, etched into the top. It wavered in and out of view of her mind's eye, never solid. She couldn't be sure what she saw.

"How can I find a single obelisk—" she began before a hot wind tore the words from her throat. Moaning, she shielded her eyes from the cutting sand.

A soft, feminine voice cut through the gale force. Squinting, Cass looked up. A woman warbled before her, almost like she stood behind a wall of vapors. Cass squinted hard, trying to make out the details.

"A guide?" she asked, realizing the words being given to her.

Then a final, deep, male voice from every direction of the circle said one word: Atminadab.

Last, a name came to her: Rana Saad.

Just as Cass wrapped her brain around the imagery of a small city and the names, everything melted away in a rush of golden, glittering sand. She covered her face with her hands and panted as every sound and the hot wind faded.

Silence filled her ears until they rang.

The cold of the dorm room touched her skin, making her look up over her arms. Vamshi's wide, brown eyes locked on to her, mouth open. She was halfway between sitting on the beanbag chair and fleeing from it.

"I know where we have to go," Cass said.

Vamshi swallowed, lips still parted. "Good, because you were speaking in tongues, girl."

"It's a place called Atminadab," Cass whispered. "I think." Doubt crept in when a singular word didn't appear on the pages now. "And I have to find a guide named Rana Saad."

"Wow," Vamshi breathed, lowering herself back onto the chair. "So... when do we start?"

Cass held her breath. "If I do this, can I be in touch with my atman?"

"Beyond a shadow of doubt, Vedic," the dragon replied. He'd landed and stood on the floor for the first time.

Was she the kind of girl to never rise to the occasion? To take danger by the horns? To try? "I'm not going to spend my whole life not being in touch with my atman," she murmured, glowering at her reflection. "I won't be Cass the coward forever. I refuse."

The dragon lifted his blue head, the whip-like whiskers on his face floating gently around him. "But you do not refuse the Dragon Script."

"Hell, no," Cass promised. She turned to open the window. The heat from the vision still lingered in her body. With a grunt, she threw open the dorm room window. She took a deep breath, drinking the cooling Connecticut air into her lungs.

Below, her eyes caught a strange posse. A bald man and a messy-haired man in black suits with red ties stood together. They didn't look up, simply leaned against the bus stop, eyes cast down each side of the street.

The danger was closer than she'd thought. Did they know what room she was in? No, surely they would have come up already.

The bald man flicked his head to the younger man, signalling him to follow. The duo walked down the street and turned towards the main downtown area. If she left, they might not know. She could leave them far behind. After all, they had no idea where to begin to look for the dragons. This was her chance.

"We start tomorrow, Vam," Cass said sternly. "We're skipping class."

CHAPTER 9: PLANS

Cass spent two days panicking about telling her parents she was going out of the country. Off the continent. She'd never traveled farther than to Maine to see some distant relative on her mother's side. Vamshi had helped by ordering an array of travel garb online.

"We can't travel and not look like adventurers," she said, unpacking probably the third box of wide-brimmed hats, scarves, and ornate backpacks. The most recent box held a "survival kit" with oddities in it like flint and steel, and a tiny, rolled up thermal blanket. The last box held a first aid bag.

Seeing Pakhba eager to get started and Vamshi excited did help, Cass took the plunge. She called her mother and sister to tell them the news.

"I knew you'd get that chance!" Ella cheered in the background. "Dad will be so psyched and freak out."

I'm freaking out, Cass thought. "I'm hoping it's just for a couple weeks," she said to Mom and Ella. "Ms. Dawnstride is helping me to contact my other professors for the time off. I'll make it up when I get back."

"You'll put yourself behind for midterms," Mom said

cautiously. "This is your pivotal year. Are you sure you want to risk your grades?"

Of course Mom would worry about grades. "I'll be fine," she lied.

"Well, at least let me help pay for the ticket," Mom countered.

Her heart dropped. Too bad magical familiars didn't have bank accounts. This last-minute plane ticket, finding a place to stay, and no doubt paying for access to ancient ruins, would cost her. She had savings, but using it on a wild dragon hunt wasn't how she intended to use it.

"I'll be fine, Mom," she sighed. After stopping the call, she sat on the floor and watched Vamshi move between their bedrooms. "Is that my rain jacket?" she asked when Vamshi hurried across with a bright red, plastic jacket in hand.

"Does it rain over there?" Vamshi called. "Get on that computer and start looking, girl."

Sighing heavily, Cass crawled over to the computer where Pakhba hovered above the desk, looking out the window.

"They've passed by twice today," he said steadily. "They know something."

Cass leaned over to look out but didn't spot any suit-clad freaks. "I should leave at night to the airport. Just in case."

The little dragon nodded soundlessly.

Opening a browser, Cass searched for travel agencies. Cheap ones.

"Why plan thusly?" Pakhba asked, a slight scold in his tone. "Can these agencies not be monitored? Hacked,f as you say? What if The Future finds out, follows you?"

She bit the inside of her mouth. "I cannot go over there alone. Have you seen what happens to American females when they travel alone?"

"I have not," he replied simply.

"It's dangerous, Pakh," she sighed. "I'm not some magical

warrior wizard like your last guy. I'm a college student from New England." She stopped herself before she said, I am a bad choice, but remembered it was because she was a bad choice of a hero that she was, in fact, the hero.

Unable to get details on websites, Cass realized she'd have to actually call a few places. Every time she did, she asked if they had a guide in Egypt named Rana Saad, since that was the name the Script gave her. After an hour, none of them did. Deciding to go about it the old-fashioned way, she put the name into a search engine, followed by the location. Only five pages of results showed up.

"Promising," she mumbled, clicking through the results. At last, she found one on an old GeoCities hosted website. "Not promising."

She clicked. The website was black with gold details and held very little information. A picture of the pyramids greeted her, as well as some outdated graphics. She scrolled further down until a huge image of a woman rolled up the page.

The woman looked young, but had gentle smile lines. Thick, black hair tumbled over one shoulder in a hairdo of half a dozen puffballs. The amber color of her skin complimented the large, wide, brown eyes smiling out at her. She wore a trilby over her hair and a military green jacket over a black top. She looked like she knew what she was doing. Underneath, the text read, "Hi, I'm Rana Saad, your local and freelance guide to the northern side of Egypt. I specialize in finding the little hidden places off the beaten path. I also have a don't ask, don't tell policy..."

It went on.

"Wow," Cass breathed, finally finding her breath back. "She exists. Vam!" she called. Once her best friend hung over her shoulder, examining the page with her, she explained. "I heard her name while I was reading the Script. And look." She jabbed her finger at the map on the next page of Rana's website. "She mentions a riverboat to take us through to Atminadab." For the first time, a light, excited feeling erupted in her chest.

Vamshi pressed her black-coated lips together and frowned. "True. She says she doesn't go there, though." She scrolled down to point to the area where Rana mentioned having only gone to Atminadab once and was not eager to go back.

"Yeah, but if we pay her?" she asked Vamshi. "She said she won't ask. I could use that kind of security."

"Ghawazi," Pakhba murmured, looking over Cass's other shoulder. "A people banished from Cairo hundreds of years ago."

"How do you know?" Cass asked, looking back at Rana's picture. "Is that bad?"

"Not for what you need," he mused. "She may be of use. She will know the streets, taverns, and shops."

"We call them hotels now," Cass corrected the ancient dragon. "Well, she sounds great. If not a little risky."

"With no paper trail, they'll need to find us if we get eaten by an alligator," Vamshi sighed.

"Crocodile," Pakhba corrected.

"We can't do this the entire trip," Cass cut in, tired of the correcting and small talk. "I'm going to email her. The sooner I leave, the sooner I can come back and make sure I finish this semester strong."

"I'll order sunblock," Vamshi smiled.

Forty-eight hours later, Cass stood in line at airport security with only a small leather pack on her back and what Vamshi called "an adventurer's hat" on her head. She shook as she felt at her backside through her jeans for the millionth time that day to make sure she had her passport and hadn't lost it. Vamshi stood next to her, humming the lyrical theme from Indiana Jones.

"I really need you to stop," Cass hissed, taking her shoes off and tossing them in a tub on the conveyer belt.

"Sorry," Vamshi smiled, following suit. "Do you think we can write a paper about our trip or something and get extra credit? I mean, it's pretty amazing."

She'd been hoping the same thing, but hadn't thought too seriously about it. She laughed and stepped through the metal detector when, suddenly, her spine tingled. Someone had moved just out of the corner of her eye. They'd been standing so still she hadn't noticed them. Then when they moved, she caught them. In her periphery, she noted a dark face looking her direction. She froze, the people behind her starting to complain.

"What is it?" Vamshi asked, pushing her along and guiding her since her eyes still fixed on the spot.

"Pakhba was right," Cass whispered. "Someone is following us. How did they know?"

She glanced around and found a women's restroom not too far off. She could see from the way it sat in the wall near the food court that it had a backside exit. "Come on," she hissed, gathering her things. She dragged Vamshi, their shoes, and packs across the cold marble floor into the restroom. She tried to discreetly check around for her pursuer, but didn't see anyone.

"I'll check out front," Vamshi whispered, dodging around a pack of old women all wearing the same label.

Cass inched to the other exit, peeking out. Huge floor to ceiling windows looked out onto the tarmac. Sunlight splashed into the waiting areas. Fewer people marched back and forth on this side. Every man and woman in a suit made her gasp and hone in on them.

Vamshi appeared behind her. "I didn't see anyone like you described. Let's hurry."

Not believing her bad luck, Cass followed Vamshi closely. "How could they know?" she repeated.

"We don't know it was them," Vamshi replied. "You could be paranoid."

It was a sixteen hour flight from Connecticut to Cairo. She couldn't be this stressed for that long. It was just after noon, her time. They'd land in Cairo at one in the afternoon due to the time difference and the length of the flight. Cass clutched per pack where the Dragon Script lay hidden.

"Can you steal one of those little bottles of vodka off a cart when we sit down?" she asked.

"Easily," Vamshi smiled.

CHAPTER 10:
RANA SAAD

Once they boarded and took off, Cass felt better. No one could possibly follow them on a huge passenger jet unless they were already on the plane. They had seats at the very back and could see the entire aisle up to where the curtain cut off first class. Vamshi had kept her word and stolen two bottles off the stewardess' cart before Cass could even see her do it.

The nonstop flight seemed to take days rather than just hours. Cass got anxious, constantly got up to get the circulation back into her legs, and at one point, thought she might actually rather throw herself out the window than wait another eight hours. Her cell phone battery got low, but Vamshi had packed a portable battery. She checked out the window every hour or so, thinking she'd see the pyramids on the horizon. She knew that was silly, but couldn't stop.

Several times she gasped, gripping her hair and asking, "I shouldn't have done this, should I?"

If Vamshi hadn't been there to hug her, hold her hand, tell her stupid jokes, and assure her she was doing the right thing,

Cass might have asked for an emergency landing and walked back to Connecticut if she had to.

"Look at this way," Vamshi said. "School doesn't matter compared to this. Even if you somehow mess this up, at least you went. Girl, you went to Egypt! I mean, how did you even get this far?"

Cass loosened her arms around her pack and stared ahead. "When I visited Ella and Mom and Dad, I saw them..." She twisted her lips, trying to find the words. "I saw the life they lead. It's so pure. So simple. I mean, mine is too, don't get me wrong. But knowing that something much bigger—far much bigger things—are out there just made me stop and look harder." Sadness welled up in her like a mist. "It's not that simple life is bad. It's that someone has to protect it from all the other shit. So that those people living that life can keep on doing it. It's okay if I know there are dragons and ancient evil organizations. But not them. I don't want them to know."

Tears prickled the corners of her eyes.

Vamshi put her arm around her and pulled her close. "Thanks for letting me on the other shit, then. I was born for adventure."

Cass laughed, sniffling. "Hell yeah, you were."

What felt like ages later, long after the jitters and the vodka wore off, an accented voice came over the coms, saying they would start their descent. This news sent Cass's gut flipping all over again. They'd drifted off and gotten about four hours of sleep between dreams of the Sphinx charging at her, maw open, and the Scales of Ma'at dropping her into the darkness, a light of light striking the Feather of Truth. Checking her phone, she saw she still had no service from the flight and it showed Connecticut time. It would change once they descended.

"What do we do?" she asked, panicked.

"Put your tray table up and your seat back in the upright position," Vamshi laughed. "And buckle up."

Cass griped the arms and her mind went blank from then until she stood in one of the largest, echoing airports of Cairo.

"I have no idea where to go," she gulped.

Not a single sign was in English. Every announcement over the speakers was in Arabic or something that sounded like it to Cass. Even Vamshi stood paralyzed. Seeing her brave, bold friend wide-eyed, she took out her phone. She'd texted Rana Saad before, after they'd bought her services as a guid and the local had given them her number. Cass grabbed Vamshi's arm and steered her away from the hordes disembarking. They didn't check any luggage for this very reason and marched away from the main terminals.

Rana Saad replied quickly, asking if they had tourists visas.

"Visas?" Cass gasped. She didn't know they needed one. "How do we do that?"

"Follow me," a voice like milk and honey said behind them.

The girls spun to come face to face with their mysterious guid. The woman stood taller than both of them, and was the fittest human Cass had ever seen, and looked just as bright and energetic as her picture on her old website.

"Rana Saad?" Cass asked cautiously.

"At your service," she smiled, hands on her hips. "Glad I found you first. I can brief you on all things inner-city while we find a cab and get your visas."

"Brief us?" Cass asked, her nerves coming back anew.

Rana nodded. "Watch out for street peddlers, handsome men in white shirts, and worst of all: the adorable little children."

Confused, amused, and terrified, Cass only nodded. She introduced Vamshi and together, the three of them made their way towards the immigration kiosk. With Rana guiding them, speaking rapidly in the local dialect, it only took a few minutes to get the girls their visas.

"I came down from Alexandria for you," Rana said in her rapid, perky tone. "Just got done with some sort of ambassador tour." She shivered. "Rich people, am I right? We'll need to get a ride up to Atminadab. Where are you staying?"

Cass's heart fell again. It must have shown on her face because Rana smiled kindly, taking their packs for them, and leading them outside. "Now worries. Rana has you covered. If you don't mind humble digs."

"No," Cass said quickly. "I'd really appreciate it. If it's not too much—"

"Nothing is too much for Rana," the woman beamed. "Truly. Are you familiar with Mossad?"

They both shook their heads.

Rana shrugged, still grinning. "No worries. Stay close, say no as often as you can, and don't look them in the eye. Yala, habibi."

Rana's warnings had been well-founded. When the girls attained their visas and got out onto the streets of the large city, Cass felt immediately overwhelmed. Thoughts of magic, dragons, and evil, ancient organizations got pushed from her mind by the loud ruckus and quick pace of the Egyptian streets. Modern buildings towered over her, hazed in dry, hot dust. Cars and buggies drawn by horses alike moved around her in a deafening clatter. Cass found herself clinging to Vamshi as eyes turned to them. She took out her phone and snapped a few pictures.

"You look like tourists," Rana called over the noise of a passing truck. "Stay close."

Cass quickly learned what Rana meant about saying no. Men and children alike approached them, asking if they needed help, were they lost, what were they looking for. At first, Cass stopped when a man appeared in front of her, speaking in broken English and smiling.

"No, thank you," she stammered, not sure what he wanted. He moved closer with every sentence. "I don't—I'm sorry—I don't understand," she coughed. The man grabbed her upper arm and started to pull her away from Vamshi, who was struck just as mute as her.

"Hey!" Rana shouted, turning around. With two long-legged strides, she marched up to the man and hissed at him in quick Arabic.

The man blanched and turned to look at Cass, then laughed. He raised his hand again towards her. Rana hissed. She shoved one hand out towards the man and the other hovered mysteriously over her right hip. Her brown eyes flashed. The man mumbled an apology in English, shrugged, and turned back down the alley.

"Holy shit!" Vamshi gushed, shaking Rana's arm. "You totally freaked that guy out!"

But Cass's eyes were trained on Rana's hip. She couldn't be sure since she wore a long khaki jacket, but she swore she noted a thick black belt hidden underneath. Did Rana have a gun? Cass had checked, just in case, and remembered reading that only security and other such people were allowed to carry in public. Rana was either a bad ass or totally crazy.

They wound their way through more downtown streets before Rana turned to them. "Stay here. Do. Not. Move. I'm going to get us a cab to take us to out of town. The outer city of Atminadab is a little..." She winced, thinking. "Poor? But they are kind and it will be a safe place to stay. The inner city is dangerous."

Bracing herself, Cass watched their guid vanish into a stall. The sun beat down, but the air blew cool with a gentle breeze. She looked around, astounded at the city.

"For some reason, I expected it to be like all the paintings," she confessed. As she spoke, a deep purple Ferrari drove past, revving its engine. Several people leapt out of the way as it turned down an alley. She smiled. "I remember when you used to joke about how you wanted to marry a rich oil sheikh."

Vamshi rolled her black-rimmed eyes. "I just want out of this heat."

"At least it's not humid like in Connecticut," Cass offered. She turned and looked up, taking in the architecture. Through one gap in the cars and buildings, she caught a golden wall lining what must have been the coast. "Oh, we're so close to the sea!" she called to Vamshi, taking a few steps down the sidewalk.

"The Citadel of Qaitbay," a small, sweet voice said.

The girls turned. A small boy with large, round, brown eyes looked up at them. He smiled, showing a few missing teeth. His brown hair was stringy and long, falling in front of his eyes at an adorable angle.

"What's that?" Cass asked, entirely drawn in by his innocent face.

"The Citadel," the boy repeated in a gentle accent. "Built in the fifteenth century to protect the coast."

Cass looked around. Rana wasn't on her way back yet. "Do you know a lot about the old places around here?"

The boy winked. "Of course I do. I live here. What are you looking for?"

Unsure, Cass shared a nervous look with Vamshi. Her friend's face tightened in disquiet. To the boy, Cass said, "We're looking for a few things, I guess. Not sure. Do you have a map?"

He smiled. "I have a map." He called behind him to two men who casually walked forward. "They need a map," he said.

Immediately, Cass's flesh crawled. "No, it's okay, we have a guid."

One of the older man tried to give an alluring grin. "It's no problem. What are you looking for?" He motioned to his companion, who produced a well-worn, wrinkled map of the coast. He leaned over it and so did Cass, following his lead. He started to point out historical sites and roads. Cass felt even more lost looking at the blue and red lines of the city map. This wasn't helpful at all.

"Hey!" Vamshi shouted, turning and smacking the boy across his face.

"What the hell?" Cass asked, stepping away. Vamshi clutched her wallet in her hand, shoving the kid once more.

"He was going for our wallets," Vamshi hissed.

Enraged, Cass turned and glared at the men. One held her backpack. With the Dragon Script inside. "Give that back," she commanded, holding her hand out. "You have no idea—"

"How much it's worth?" the older man asked, leering at her. "Tell me. And that's how much it will cost to get it back."

Emotions welled up in Cass. Tears pricked at her eyes and she started to gasp.

The purple Ferrari from before appeared around the corner, revving its engine again. The windows were tinted so black, Cass couldn't even see silhouettes inside. Rana appeared then too, calling out to them. Cass turned to her, begging with her eyes for her to do something.

Rana's eyes snapped from Cass to the bag, to the purple car. "Don't," she said to the men. She flicked her chin towards the car. "The baltagiya are here."

The men turned to take in the idling car. Silently communicating with their eyes, they threw Cass's bag back at her. She caught it, pressing it against her chest, feeling the tome inside.

"Lucky once," the man growled to Cass. "Not again."

The three of them disappeared like shadows into the streets. Cass sighed audibly and turned to Rana. "Thank you," she cried, a single tear releasing down her cheek. It felt hot against her skin despite the warm sun.

"You don't seem to understand," Rana said, taking her hand and leading them to a cab she'd procured. "This may be an adventure to you, but you are prey to them. Not all are like them, but you have to watch your back. You have to assert yourself. Do not show fear. They can smell it a block away. They will take everything from you if you let them."

The guide's words hit Cass hard. She didn't need this conviction right now. Being far from home, far from everything familiar, made it ten times worse. She gasped, sniffling, and simply nodded. Vamshi took her hand and the three of them cut through the people to the waiting cab.

The hotel Rana found for them was indeed small. Being one floor and made of a soft, white sandstone, it looked shadier to Cass than any of the buildings in the big city. The hotel rested between a more provincial looking part of Atminadab and a few streets down, the larger, more modern looking structures took over. It took about an hour of city travel to get there from where they had the run-in with the street hustlers. When they unloaded their few bags and walked them in, Cass could smell the salt from the Mediterranean and hear the waves now that the city was quieter.

Rana locked her and Vamshi in the room to find food and instructed them to not leave. Having no intention of ignoring her rules this time, Cass settled on to the creaky bed and opened the Dragon Script. Vamshi showered with the bathroom door open for safety, giving Cass had some privacy to work with the Script.

"All right," she said to the Script, touching Pakhba on her wrist as she did. "I'm here. What's next?"

Gently running her fingers over the rough edges of the book, she waited. Familiar symbols came to her the more she looked. The circles, lines cutting across them, and swooping script appeared in patches. Like the last time, the more she read, the more she understood, and the pages filled. Until, with two pages half covered in Script, it stopped. The blotching stopped seeping. The lines filled out, solid and unmoving.

"What?" she cried. She shook it like an Etch-a-Sketch. Nothing changed. "There are words missing," she moaned. Shaking her arm, she released Pakhba. The golden bangle circled on the creaky bed, then came to a rest before the small dragon appeared in a burst of blue and yellow light.

"Your command?" he asked, before his eyes fixed on the script. "What do you see?"

"That's the issue," Cass sighed. "I see the Script like I did before on the other pages. But this new one is... half missing or something. Like if I wrote out every other letter to abracadabra. It's not whole."

"It's not whole," Pakhba repeated, his eyes narrowing. He slowly descended onto the bed and curled up to think. "Like a puzzle," he offered. "Pieces are missing."

She nodded. "Look, I came here. This is the farthest away from home I've ever been. I'm freaking out. I'm losing out on school, I lied to my family. I need more help."

The dragon hummed deeply. "If there is a whole and we have one part, there must be another part."

Dumbstruck and agitated, Cass shouted to the ceiling. "Of course! Is this what's next? The words won't come to me if they're not whole. This is just jumbled symbols now."

Outside, someone started to shout a lyrical prayer. Glancing to the window, she looked out over the thinner part of the city. Orange lights dotted the blue darkness, and the dunes turned white in the distance.

"I'm going out," she said with finality. "Just to see things on my own without Rana breathing down my neck."

Pakhba floated towards her to return to her wrist.

"No," she snapped. "You stay here. I need to be alone."

Atminadab at night came to life in a way Cass and never dreamed. Street lights beamed down in blues and yellows, highlighting community art on sandy stone walls. Bars opened their entire fronts to the streets so the music, chatter, and smell wafted out to her. Old men stood on corners chatting with one another. Young girls ran giggling from older women, scolding them.

Cass found one smaller pub with open windows lined with hookahs and music blaring from the inside. Traditional dancers roamed between the tables, laughing and clapping to the music that vibrated the walls. They demurely took bills from the patrons and shimmied their way to the next donation. Curious, Cass watched them for some time. She glanced around, wondering if she could slip in. She was thirsty, but had no idea how or what to order. Hopefully, Rana returned with food and drink soon. The smell of the kitchen hit her hard in the face as a young server burst through with trays piled high with hummus, vegetables, and some kind of leaf wrapped around rice. The smell reminded Cass she hadn't eaten in a day.

Deciding she'd try something, she slipped out to a small store on the other side of the wall. She hoped they could help her exchange some currency. She dug in her wallet for some American bills and was just about to go into the shop when a hand grabbed her shoulder and pulled her so hard she spun, lost her balance, and fell.

"Hey, habibi," the man leered at her. He had ill intent written in every crease of his face. He couldn't stop grinning.

"Yala!" a young woman cried from the other side of the street. Cass snapped her head over to see a gaggle of clubbing Egyptian women point at the man and start a barrage of curses. Some of them started to run across the street to her defense.

"Wait, no," Cass cried, realizing the women were going to get into a physical altercation with the man. She scrambled to her feet and moved to intervene, but another man cut her off.

"Don't," he hissed. "Let's go this way. They're a distraction. They'll be fine."

"But," Cass started, but the man grabbed her hand and dashed away. She caught his American accent and followed without question. She looked back and saw the women laughing at the man as he whipped his head back and forth looking for her.

One block later, Cass stopped and jerked her hand out of

her savior's. She could see the door to her hotel now. "Stop," she cried. "Who are you?"

The man held his back to her for a beat before turning around. Familiar, sad, blue eyes, and wavy, shoulder-length blond hair greeted her under the dark hood.

"Charlie?" she gasped.

CHAPTER II: STREETS OF ATMINADAB

The overwhelming feelings of her pumping heart, surging adrenaline, left over fear, and sheer confusion and delight at seeing Charlie came down in an avalanche onto Cass all at once. Crying out and exclaiming in shock, she leapt onto Charlie in a sudden embrace. He stiffened under her hug, but only for a moment. She felt his hands drop onto her shoulders. Then they slid down to her waist and squeezed.

Cass buried her face in his shoulder, standing on her tiptoes. The ends of his hair were soft and smelled like amber. She clutched his neck and held on, letting out a relieved sob. She took a few calming breaths in his safe embrace before lowering herself back onto her heels and pulling away. Tears made a few golden strands of his hair stick to her face.

"I'm sorry," she sighed, rubbing her palms into her eyes. "I'm tired, hungry, and scared." She sniffled once, then looked into his face. "What the hell are you doing here?"

"Working," he said simply. He scanned both ends of the alley before putting his arm around her shoulders and steering her towards the opposite street. "I have a contact here who I meet with for business. Really boring stuff, actually."

She laughed dryly, hoping he didn't feel her lean more into him as they walked. Suddenly, the golden and blue streets seemed more sinister. She gently touched Pakhba on her wrist and wondered: if he was her familiar, could he grant her magic? Or help her cast a spell or something in case an attack like that happened again? That'd be useful.

You'll see, Pakhba's voice trilled in her head. *We haven't gotten there yet. Don't know how much I can trust you with that.*

Are you kidding me? she thought angrily. *You're telling me there is a chance I could be a wizard or something?*

Pakhba waited a moment before humming a note she couldn't decipher as a yes or a no.

"Can I buy you something?" Charlie asked.

Her head shot up, his voice cutting through her thoughts. "I'm actually starving," she agreed. "And thirsty."

"I know a place," he smiled.

This bolder Charlie could be something Cass got used to. She smiled and said, "You weren't like this back home. You were so quiet. Mysterious."

He offered her a shy smile and looked away in a way Cass thought was adorable.

"I like to be left alone. But you needed help. So I intervened. Here." He pointed to a more quiet restaurant that also had open air seating.

She let him lead as he found a table and ordered drinks in broken Arabic. She watched his ears turn red as the server asked him to repeat himself a couple of times. He blew out an anxious breath when the man finally understood and left to get their beverages.

"Still better than what I can do," Cass laughed. "I only know the words Rana said." She placed her chin in her palm and let her eyes roam over Charlie's face without fear. He notice and tensed.

"What?" he asked.

"I'm just curious about you," she said. Her toes curled in her travel boots and her cheeks flamed red. Her crush quickly smoldered in her. "What else can you do?"

He nervously ran his long fingers through his tasseled hair. "Well, I travel for a living, so I try to speak as many languages as I can. I have to learn a lot about the places I go, so I know weird facts. For example, I know that Egyptian regulations don't allow opposite sexes to room together. Unless you're foreign." He gave her a shy, slightly playful grin. "Drones are totally illegal unless you have permission from the Egyptian Civil Aviation Authority."

"Huh," she interrupted. "I never thought about a drone. Damn, that would have been a good idea."

Now he looked intrigued. "Why are *you* here? Are you stalking me?"

"No!" she giggled and playfully smacked his arm. The golden bangle hit him as it slid down to her palm.

He took her hand and admired the golden circle. He traced the details, touching Pakhba's sapphire eye. His gentle touch sent instant tingles up her arm, to her skull, and down her spine. She wondered if he had done that on purpose. Did he know she had a crush on him? Was he playing in to that?

"I'm not stalking you," she finally said. Her throat went dry. Where was the water they ordered? "You are stalking me. You knew where I was on the street back there. You have to have been following me."

His blue eyes turned back to their standard sad, far off look. "This is beautiful. What is it?"

Her eyes went to the dragon bracelet. "Uh," she stammered. A lie came to mind, but so did the urge to not lie to him. Besides, travel was his thing. He might be able to help. "It's complicated," she said instead, cringing at her own words.

Not letting go of her hand, he moved his fingers to her palm and gently touched the sensitive skin there. He tilted his head to the side. "I'm a puzzle solver. I'm pretty good at complicated."

"Are you?" she choked. His fingers moved their gentle caress from her palm to the soft skin on the underside of her arm. Something deep in her belly ignited, and she almost reached across the table to grab him and kiss him. The room seemed to heat up, scorching her face.

"Yeah," he nodded. "I grew up pretty alone. Going from one place to the next. Everything was always changing: the people who were supposed to take care of me, the place I lived, the training I got."

Cass frowned and finally tore her eyes away from his hand on her arm. "Were you in the system? Sorry," she blurted, realizing how callous it sounded.

He shook his head. "No need. Yeah, something like that. I guess all the moving around gave me a taste for it. I tried to stay in one place once, put down roots, get a life that could grow. But..." He winced sadly and his eyes turned empty. "That's not the life I was meant to lead. You know when you try to get out of something, leave stuff behind, but it's just so ingrained in you, you don't know how to live without it?"

Guilt churned the heat still simmering in her. "A little. But I don't know why I'm this way."

He tilted his head again, listening.

"I've always known I'd be a good leader if I got the chance," she started. "I'm good at figuring things out on the go. People have a tendency to follow my lead. I don't exactly ooze confidence."

Charlie shook his head. "On the contrary. You feel like someone with a plan."

"That's just because I want to do *anything*, you know?" Something cooled her inside. Put her at ease. Talking about her mixed-up, heated feelings to Charlie soothed her. "I know I want to go out, explore, take charge. But whenever I get the chance, I freak out and collapse in on myself. Almost like getting what I want scares me. I know it makes no sense."

She sat back in the chair as the server brought them their drinks and Charlie haphazardly ordered some appetizers for them. Cass watched him stumble around the words when her phone suddenly vibrated in her pocket. Realizing she didn't tell Vamshi or Rana she was going out, she panicked and picked up the phone.

A waterfall of feminine babble, cursing, and shouting erupted from her phone. Vamshi seemed to have the thing on speaker and both she and Rana were chiding her. Rana not entirely in English, hitting Arabic every other word or so, making it even harder to understand her.

"Guys, clam down!" Cass called, half laughing as Charlie's blue eyes went wide at the noise from her phone. "I'm fine. I am so sorry I didn't tell you I was going out."

"Where the hell are you, girl?" Vamshi said, sounding like she walked far enough from Rana to get in a full sentence. "Special Agent Saad is blowing her top and wouldn't let me out to look for you."

Cass laughed genuinely.

"Laugh all you want while the baltagiya comes and kidnaps you," Rana shouted from the other side of the room. "And sells you to some drug dealer."

"Funny she should mention that word," Cass said, enjoying the energy. She was safe. More than safe. They were over reacting. "I did see one."

Rana exploded into a fresh wave of curses, and Vamshi joined her.

"Where are you?" she shouted. "Don't move. We'll come and get you."

"No, no," Cass sighed. "I'm fine. I'm with a friend. Who happened to be here."

"Friend?" Vamshi asked, drawing out the word. She waited a beat, then gasped. "No way. Is he stalking you?"

"She's stalking me," Charlie called so Vamshi could hear him over the phone.

"Oh, my god, girl!" Vamshi hissed. "How?"

"What is it?" Rana asked.

"Nothing," Vamshi called back to her. "I have way more questions now. But you need to come back. Rana has a lead for us in a secluded village not far from the city limits. There's a folklorist who lives there, and she says will be able to tell us some interesting places to visit."

Cass didn't miss Charlie's eyes light up in interest, though he tried to hide it behind a passive mask. She frowned slightly. He caught her expression change and licked his lips, looking away, guilty.

"Vam, I gotta go," she said more flatly. Her laughter died a bit. "I'll have him walk me back to the hotel in an hour, okay?"

Rana protested, but Vamshi agreed and hung up, cutting off the argument.

Charlie cleared his throat and looked Cass right in her eyes. "So you're here for research? For what?"

Feeling like she had done something wrong, she fiddled with a piece of flat bread he'd ordered for them. "School?" she tried.

Charlie's face fell, saddened by her lie. "This place doesn't need more digs. More tourism."

Understanding dawned. "Oh, no, no! I'm not here for that kind of thing. Just personal research. I'm not bringing colonizers and thieves to Atminadab's doorstep." She laughed nervously. It would be awesome if she discovered something that could warrant a dig, though. Then she could get it funded and never have to worry about getting a job again. Surely, anything in this remote part of Egypt would be a legendary find.

The thought of using this adventure for school never occurred to her. She'd no doubt be rewarded for her work. Get offers, scholarships, never have to worry about her family again about whether or not she'd make it.

"I wonder," she mused out loud. "But, no," she said to Charlie. "Just personal interest."

He shifted his seat and took a grape-leaf from their shared tray and bit half of it off, chewing the soft rice inside. "In that case, do you mind if I come with you tomorrow?"

She couldn't hide her face lighting up at that. He grinned. "You might be useful," she said. "You know more about this place than I do. I'm sure Rana would like having someone not totally worthless with her to talk shop with."

"Rana?" he asked.

She nodded. "I brought my friend—"

"The loud one," he inserted.

"Yes, the loud one. And we hired a guid. To help us find the interesting places." She took a bite of flat bread and hummus.

"And dragons?" he asked.

Cass choked instantly on the entire mouthful, spewing it in a powerful cough all over Charlie. She hacked for another solid minute, chugging water. Her eyes teared up and her nose ran as she finally cleared her throat.

"D-dragons?" she wheezed, pounding her chest.

He pointed to the golden bangle, and her heart stopped. "Atminadab has local folklore about a dragon master. It's just about the only story local to this place. I figured that's why you were here."

"Is it?" she asked, wiping tears away. Of course it was. The

Dragon Script had told her to come here. She had her doubts, but now she knew for sure. "To be honest, I am interested in anything like that. Do... you know anything about dragons?"

Charlie nodded, but before he could reply, his phone buzzed. He looked down at the screen that lit up his face. Cass watched his demeanor crumble. His face returned to that sad, far-off look.

"I... I have to go," he murmured.

"Tomorrow?" she asked, panic and sadness replacing the warm glow his presence had put there.

He shook his head. "I have to meet with my sponsor. About work." He stood up, looking forlornly down at her. "Sorry." He took one more drink and prepared to step away.

"Wait!" she cried so loud a couple tables turned to look at her. "Can... I have your number? Or something? Please?" She sounded desperate, but she supposed she was. She couldn't let him leave again without having a way to find him.

That sweet, shy smile took over his face again. "Yeah," he said.

They swapped numbers and texted each other. She sent him a pyramid emoji and laughed when he sent her a dragon one in reply.

"There," she said, saving his number. "Now I won't lose you again."

"Lose me?" he joked, moving towards the exit after dropping some currency on the table. "You're the one who flew off to Egypt on a whim."

He waved and turned to vanish into the street. Cass watched him go until his black hoodie made him into an invisible shadow. She stuffed a few more grape-leaves into her mouth and headed back to the hotel.

CHAPTER 12: MADI SAGHIRA

The sun heated Cass's face through the open window to wake her the next morning. She'd taken a verbal lashing from Vamshi and Rana, but they tired out after a few minutes. They spent the night flipping the strange channels on the TV before boredom put them to sleep.

Rana woke early, appeared with coffee from a Turkish-owned shop around the corner, and launched into her findings.

Their guid slapped down a well-worn map and pointed to a few roads lined by gray boxes. "Madi Saghira," she said, pointing to the boxes. "A tiny village outside the main city but still within the civil boundaries of Atminadab. However, they are something of a sovereign village."

"What does that mean?" Cass asked, sipping on the too-strong coffee.

"They—as a village—have taken a vow of poverty and minimalism," Rana explained. "Like the Amish in the U.S. They follow their own culture, civilities, and have a very rich and old history. Mostly because they live very much now like they did when they first broke from the rule of the ancient pharaohs and founded their own monarchy."

Vamshi stuffed a biscuit in her mouth and took a long drink of her coffee before saying, "Never heard of it," and pulled out her phone to do a quick internet search.

"You won't find anything," Rana said. She sat up and began to braid her hair to prepare for travel. "Cameras are forbidden within Madi Saghira's borders. They will take them if you pull them out. Respect them and don't."

Cass nodded. "Of course. What drew you to it?" she asked. "If we can't document, I'm not sure what good it will do us."

Their guid smiled politely, if not a little condescendingly. "Listen. They have very strong oral traditions. Not much is written down. They speak to each other and that's how they pass on their history, traditions, and stories."

Curious, Cass nodded again. "We're going to meet with one of these historians?"

"Exactly." Rana stood up, picked up her sand-colored trilby, and put it low on her head. "I think from there, your real adventure will start." She smiled knowingly. "You will be inspired by the lore teller. You might have more to look into once they tell their legends than you imagine."

This actually sounded exactly like what she wanted. "I hope so," she confessed. Her stomach flipped. Looking up, she caught Vamshi watching her with concern. "This is it," she said. "Finally, something to go on. I'm... I'm nervous."

Vamshi took her hand and handed her a biscuit. "Eat something. Even if you puke it up in five minutes."

Rana looked between the girls, hands on her khaki-clad hips. "With Rana, you will find exactly what are you looking for."

Cass dressed in her best adventure gear: she packed her leather bag with some dried fruit and nuts, a tightly folded rain poncho, a first aid kit, and Rana insisted on giving them nylon rope, carabiners, something she called a belay device and a few other rock climbing tools as well as a wool blanket.

"Are we planning on going up a sheer rock face?" Vamshi asked after Rana gave them a quick lesson on how all the scaling gear worked.

"You never know," Rana said. "You'll thank me one day while you're hanging off the side of the Marco Caldera in Scotland."

Cass laughed but frowned as she heaved her pack out of the trunk of the cab. "That's very specific," she noted.

Rana nodded. For the first time, her face darkened. "Be ready for specific situations, Cass, and you will never be wrong."

The cab had stopped out in what Cass would call the middle of nowhere. Or a desert wasteland. With the city behind them, what lay before them were huge, golden dunes, blue sky and, somewhere beyond, the Mediterranean roared softly. A small sand-blasted settlement boasted a shop, a run-down gas station, a sort of post office or delivery spot, and a shack that rented out camels, horses, and mules. Cass wrapped her scarf around her neck and tightened the strap on her hat to keep it from blowing off in the hot desert wind.

Vamshi hid her face behind huge, bug-eyed sunglasses and a long-sleeved jacket. "I'm grinding sand in my molars," she hissed as Rana led them to the camel shack.

Cass nodded, pressing her lips together and breathing carefully so as to not inhale sand up her nose. "No wonder people don't visit Atminadab." She scanned the distance where a man-made forest loomed closer to the rivers. She bet that Madi Saghira and its mysterious people lived under those trees.

"No way!" Vamshi protested when Rana approached with three camels following her.

Their guid held the thick, red and gold rope-like reins of the desert mounts easily. The creatures stood far taller than Cass had ever imagined. Their fur was coarse but soft nearer their skin. Their giant lips turned down but also looked like they smiled mischievously. Thick rugs padded them between the saddle and their hump backs. Tassels hung down in red, green, and blue designs. Cass's heart spun in thrilled anticipation.

"Yes," she said, pushing past Vamshi. "Hell, yes."

"Hell, no," her friend protested again. "You know they bite? And spit?"

"Then it's a good thing you'll be riding on their back," Rana called as she stood in the bowl-like stirrup and swung her long legs over the saddle. "They can't spit on you from there." She smiled.

Vamshi quickly realized she stood in front of the three of them and slid to the side. Cass mounted hers with some difficulty. Rana reached over and grabbed the horn of the saddle so Cass could use it as leverage to haul herself up onto the creature's back. Once on top and situated, she looked around her. The ground looked farther away than on any horse she'd ridden.

"Direct them with the reins," Rana instructed as she expertly moved hers closer to Vamshi to help her up. "They are well watered and will take us all the way to Madi Saghira."

"Couldn't we take a dune buggy or something?" Vamshi grunted, finally topping her camel. Her sunglasses slipped askew on her face, and her hat fell sideways by the time she was on top.

"No," Rana answered, beginning to lead them out towards the desert and the forest beyond. "They do not want the sounds of motors near their homes. It disturbs the song of Ra."

Vamshi rolled her eyes, but a thrill went through Cass. It would be like stepping back in time. Finding an ancient people, hearing their stories, and getting her first clue on where Mehen, the dragon of Egypt, slept, waiting for her to wake it.

As Cass had imagined, the village of Madi Saghira lay quietly inside what was obviously a man-made forest. Rana explained how the trees were planted some one hundred years ago to help shelter the Madi Saghira people and contributed to their thriving food source and keep the river filled. The river flowed from some invisible source, winding through the entire village. Irrigation ditches branched off, feeding homes along the shore.

Tiny huts made of mud and brick popped up out of the sand here and there. Raised gardens overflowing with scented herbs, vegetables, and edible plants made the air spicy and fragrant. Women along the shore of the river stopped filling buckets and washing clothing to watch the three women pass. A small crowd surrounded them the deeper they went into the village. A few people in blue and gold robes touched their shins as they passed, whispering in something akin to Arabic.

"They speak a rare dialect," Rana supplied. "Like the tribes on your continent, they are not permitted to teach their language to outsiders."

A huge circular structure came into view around the next bend. Like a cobbled patio, stones lay in the dirt, making a clear space for a huge triangle—almost like a pyramid. Fire burned inside it. An old man with leathery skin stood before it, smiling down at a group of young teenagers who just left for chores. An older woman appeared behind him in a modern skirt and shawl, but with a beautiful golden necklace twinkling underneath. She tossed a bundle of fragrant herbs into the fire and turned to face them.

"Habdul," she said in an aged by lyrical voice, "we have guests."

The man, who looked important by his gold and blue robes and humble, gold circlet on his head, turned to face them. His brown eyes darkened as he took them in.

"They have come far," the woman added when Rana signaled the others to dismount.

"We have," Cass agreed, impressed by the woman's guess. She led the way towards the cobbled pavement and fire. She couldn't get close, the heat was too intense, and the smell filled her nose. When she drew close enough, she realized the woman was blind: her eyes were misty white.

The man, Habdul, held his hand up to them to stop her approach. Cass looked down and realized she was about to set foot on the stone surrounding the fire. She guessed it wasn't her place. The man's lined face fell stern on his sharp bones. But the old woman smiled.

"They come from American, Habdul," she said joyfully. "Students."

Impressed again, Cass smiled. "Yeah. You're good."

The woman took her compliment with a grin. "I should be after ninety years."

"What is it you want, foreigner?" Habdul asked, gently clasping his hands in front. His eye flicked to Rana and Vamshi in turn before landing hard back on Cass. He had a way of making her feel like she was trespassing on something very private.

"Uh," she stammered. "I heard that the people of Madi Saghira tell stories. That your history is oral. I'm looking for a very specific story."

The tall man raised his head, almost looking like a pharaoh of old to Cass. "There are ways to hear our stories," he said stiffly. "But we no longer tell them to strangers. Not since the man from New York tried to write them into a book. We took what you would call legal action." He glared hard.

"You speak English really well," Cass said as an aside. She couldn't keep the shock out of her voice.

"Only because you English insist on coming here," Habdul sighed. "I also speak Mandarin and Spanish." He stepped off the cobbles and led the trio into the heart of the village with a sweep of his robed arm.

"Those are oddly specific languages," Cass mused. Her guard dropped a little when the blind woman came up alongside her and took her arm. She guessed the woman didn't need leading, but that the blind woman was leading her.

"When I took the burden of leadership onto myself as a young man," Habdul said, quickly blessing a woman who brought what looked like a newborn baby up to him, "I was told to learn those three in addition to our own Madi Saghira words."

The blind woman sniffed the air and frowned. She turned her white eyes to Cass. Cass wasn't sure what she was sniffing for. A little self-conscious, she pulled her jacket open and discreetly sniffed. She didn't smell anything unnatural.

"I smell fire," the woman whispered to Habdul.

"Well." Vamshi waved her hand to the monstrous blaze behind them now and the small fires here and there near homes.

"Not that fire," the woman said. She stopped and ran her

hand down Cass's arm to the dragon bangle. "I smell brimstone in her veins," she whispered.

Cass's mouth popped open in shock, and her chest tightened. The woman smiled.

"My name is Imani," she said. "I am the keeper of the lore. Perhaps I can tell you what you seek?"

"Imani," Habdul said in a deep, warning tone. A few more women lined up with their new babes to be blessed by their leader.

"You are busy, Habdul," Imani said with a grin. She motioned the new mothers forward. "He will bless them all." She took Habdul's hand and moved him before the waiting women, signaling them all to kneel and form a line.

Cass watched in amazement as a small, seemingly common, village rite played out before her eyes. A few monks in matching gold and blue robes joined Habdul as he said prayers, took a strange, rubbery leaf full of scented oil and dribbled it over the babies' heads.

"He anoints every child," Imani said, beaming at the sight she could not see. "For every babe has the chance to lead the Madi Saghira people. So all are royalty." She took Cass's hand and Vamshi's and led them to a beautiful grove. Rana came in behind them.

The grove was a genuine oasis. A small creek trickled joyfully down silver rocks covered in orange flowers Cass couldn't name. The pool fed by the waterfall glittered clear with a blue-rock bottom. Palm trees surrounded it, casting a perfect circle of shade. One tree grew figs.

"Wow," Cass breathed, unable to stop herself.

"Isn't it a true sight?" Imani asked, beaming as if she'd created the oasis with her own two hands. "My favorite place." She expertly skirted the pool to a tiny home on the left-hand side. She signaled the women to sit on a worn rug on the dirt while she gathered up bread, a strange white cheese, some dates, and apricots. She grabbed a gourd of water and four simple brown bowls. "We must find places like this when the world can be so very dark. Or when we have nothing else."

Cass glanced around. "You all live in voluntary poverty?"

Imani beamed. "Do we? I hadn't noticed. There is much poverty here. All over Egypt."

The image of the purple car she'd seen came back to her. "Not everyone lives like that."

Imani shook her head. "No. Not all. And those who do not would rather not see it. But we, the Madi Saghira, give what we can by serving those who have less than we."

"Who has less than people who live in houses made of sticks?" Vamshi asked with a little smile.

"Those who have no house," the old woman replied.

This cast a seriousness over the group. Cass took in the village one more time before focusing in what Imani laid before them.

Imani put the food down in the center of the half-moon shape they'd made and filled the bowls with water, giving each woman one.

"Thank you," Cass said, taking the offerings. She took a sip of the water and almost groaned with pleasure. It somehow tasted tropical and sweet and was soft on her tongue.

"It is my pleasure to bless others," Imani said, seating herself near the edge. She stuck her bare feet out and touched the top of the water with them. "So, American, you have come to hear about the dragon master, have you not?"

Cass froze, mid-bite of bread, her eyes snapping to Imani and her mischievous grin.

"How...?" Cass began, but stopped herself, quickly remembering Rana was there too.

"Smell," Imani said, tapping the side of her nose. "I can smell brimstone like a hound smells blood."

Cass quickly glanced at Rana to find the guide's face

expressionless, giving away nothing she might be thinking. If she thought this talk of brimstone was strange, she didn't say anything.

"And I see the fire," Imani went on. "I am blind, but spirits are not to be seen with the naked eye. Your soul is flame, child." She waved to Vamshi. "And yours is gold. It glitters quite nicely."

Vamshi met Cass's eyes and blushed. "Thanks," she said, a little proud. "I, uh, polished it myself."

Imani smiled and nodded. "You did. And you did a fine job."

Both girls looked at Rana, thinking she would be next. Cass wondered if it was some kind of parlor trick Imani did for visitors. But Imani's smiled faded when she looked at Rana.

"Some spirits are broken," she said seriously, the words ominous on her accented voice. "They need healing. And they can be healed, made whole again. But others have been bartered away."

Cass shifted uneasily. Rana's face remained impassive. "So," Cass said, picking up one of the soft, orange fruits. "What stories do you know?"

Imani smiled again, dropping her shawl onto the ground. "What do you want to hear? The Madi Saghira are an ancient people. The stories we keepers of lore we must learn are infinite."

"The dragon master?" she asked cautiously.

The old woman's face broke into a smile of wonder. "Ah, yes. Well, to tell you that tale, I must tell another."

Cass settled in to her spot of soft sand near the water.

Imani raised her head and took a deep breath. "The Madi Saghira believe the gods never left us. We keep them alive through prayer, honoring them, and keeping the fire lit. The sun rises simply because Ra wills it, often raising it into the sky on his own back."

Cass couldn't stop herself from looking up at the scorching sun.

"But it is a dangerous task," Imani went on. She reached up and moved her finger as if to stroke the sun affectionately. "All the sun touches is Ra's to protect. But once darkness falls..." She dropped her hand. "That is the realm of another."

Drawn in to the way the woman spoke, Cass sunk into a stupor, allowing herself to be entranced. "Whose?" she asked.

Imani took a deep breath, facing forward. "Apophis," she whispered. "I say his name softly because we believe in him. The serpent of the dark. The three-eyed devil."

"I don't remember him having three eyes," Cass said, thinking back to her ancient literature class.

"You wouldn't hear of it," Imani offered. "Do you know the story?"

Cass pressed her lips out to the side, thinking. "He's a snake. He attacks Ra on his way to raise the sun?"

The old woman nodded, closing her eyes like she prayed. "Every day, Ra boards the Mesektet and brings us the sun. And every day, Apophis tries to stop him." She reached down and folded the ends of a leaf up, placing it gently in the pool. It floated like a tiny ship. "But Ra is not the only one Apophis desires to entrap in his coils. No." She faced Cass. "We all have a heaven and a hell we strive to escape or reach once we die." She smiled, almost longingly. "The field of reeds for us. But first, one must weigh our hearts."

"Anubis!" Vamshi cried excitedly.

Imani smiled at her energy. "Yes, Anubis. Guardian of the afterlife."

"I've never heard of Apophis hunting Anubis," Cass added. But she knew Imani's answer before she said it.

"You wouldn't have heard it," the old woman said again.

She handed Cass the water gord and motioned for her to refill everyone's cups. As she did, Imani went on. "Apophis yearns to bring his darkness to the worshipers of Ra. Ra and his sun bring life. The lore says that if Apophis can cast the world into darkness again, he will have the moment he needs to bring up the dead."

Cass frowned and was surprised to find her mouth go dry. "The dead?"

Imani raised her head, brow furrowed. "Once, a darkness fell on Egypt and death took many lives. Apophis cannot retrieve the dead and raise them up if Anubis stands in his way. So even if Apophis overtook Ra, the guardian of the underworld would remain." She placed her hand on the earth as if feeling for its heart beat. "Words are powerful, are they not, Cassandra?"

Her eyes shot up, looking into Imani's blind ones. "Yes," she whispered.

"They can bind. Hide. Magic cannot be cast without incantation." Imani smiled. "The story of the dragon master starts during the ring of Ramses II—"

"Wait!" Cass cut in. "What about Anubis and Apophis?"

"We will return to them," the storyteller said, patting her knee gently. "As with most kings, the pharaohs sunk too deep into the sands of our land. Since the dawn of time, Egypt has used magic—the stars, prophets, the gods. It is our birthright. But Ramses had a secret cabal of priests who looked for...other magic." The woman reached behind her and, quick as lightning, dipped her hand into a bush. When she pulled it back out, she had a black asp clutched between her fingers.

Even Rana shrunk away a little.

"They called themselves some secret name that has been lost in time," she went on, holding the deadly snake close to her face. "They found an ancient serpent, sleeping deep under the earth. One of the priests, a follower of Thoth, discovered the power of words. They are so strong."

Imani dropped the asp and it slithered away, terrified of the fearless woman.

"This is why we write nothing down. Any longer."

Unable to take her eyes away from where the snake vanished, Cass asked, "Any longer? So you did at one point?"

The lore keeper nodded. "Ramses awakened the resting Coiled One—"

Cass sat upright. That was it! That was what the Script called the dragon she sought: Mehen, the Coiled One. Vamshi and Rana both noticed her sudden movement and her soft gasp.

"As with most beasts, the white serpent raged against Ramses for awakening it. Unable to be bound, it destroyed our people. Ramses didn't understand and the priest investigated for many years of his life. Until one day, they say the sun did not rise. Not the story you are thinking of," she added with a smile. "Another that is one you have not heard. A story of the Madi Saghira only. In Cairo, the sun still shone. But here? Darkness. Fearing something happened to Ra, the priest used the words to call to our gods."

She stopped.

Cass found herself leaning forward. "What happened to Ra?"

"Taken." Imani's face dropped and her shoulders slumped. "You see, the Coiled One guarded Ra on Mesektet. We didn't know. Understanding the words of the gods, the priest learned what had happened. And so he set about finding the words with which to speak to the Coiled One. To find her, control her. With Ra taken by Apophis, the world was dark and the black serpent was free to attack Anubis.

"So the priest made the words to speak to the Coiled One. She took him to the other world and there he found Apophis in deadly battle with the jackal god. Apophis had already released a few souls and hid them in the dark. Anubis was wounded and so the priest, astride the back of the Coiled One, did battle with the dark god."

At last, Imani sighed and smiled. "Triumphant, Anubis allowed him to live, though he had seen the faces of the gods. The priest made a temple in the place of the battle and together, he and Anubis freed Ra. With the gods restored, he let the Coiled One rest. She has slept for a long time. And the sun still rises."

Only the sound of the trickling water sounded for some time. Rana chewed a date quietly and Vamshi waited for Cass to speak.

Cass cleared her throat and asked, "Do they call him Vedic?"

"They say," the lore keeper answered, "that the priest wrote his words onto a tablet after the Coiled One returned to sleep. Yes, they called him Vedic."

"And he was the only one who could read them?" Cass asked. She couldn't keep her mind off the Dragon Script.

"He did what was needed to save his king, his people," Imani replied simply. "He did not intend to be the master of the Coiled One, but, yes. No one else could read the Script he inscribed onto the Tablet of Mehen. But he did not want to keep the power he had. Anubis offered him eternal life in exchange for protecting the underworld. Ra gifted him the power of the sun. But he refused. 'I am not that man,' he told the gods. 'I only said what was needed. No more. No less.'

"'But she is yours to command,' Ra replied, speaking of the Coiled One. 'What is your wish?'"

Cass smiled. She knew how the story ended.

"You know." Imani shared her smiled.

"My wish is my commandment," Cass recited. "He

commanded her to sleep, didn't he. To protect Ra in the other world."

Imani smiled and nodded.

Another moment of silence followed before Cass wondered, "What happened to the words the priest wrote? Did he destroy them?"

"No." The older woman shook her head. "No one can read them. The language is lost. Or never existed. When not even the priests of Thoth could translate the dragon master's words, they gave it up, locked away in Ramses' tomb. But sometime later, it vanished and was no doubt destroyed." She glanced out back towards the main city. "Only a few images of it remain, written on the walls of other tombs long since excavated. I suppose those pieces are in some museum now."

Lightning shot through Cass. "They're still around?"

Imani laughed. "Child, most of ancient Egypt is still around. You just have to find it."

Immediately, Cass knew what she had to do. She tried not to rush to standing. It seemed rude. She stammered and looked around, wondering how to make a quick exit.

"There's a museum in downtown Atminadab," Rana said, seeing Cass's urgency. "I bet you anything what you're looking for is there."

"What are you looking for?" Vamshi asked.

"Words," Cass said blankly, not sure what the ancient text might look like. It didn't matter. She was sure when she saw it, she'd know it. Or at least Pakhba would. And she had no doubt that she'd be able to read it.

The story had been fantastic. Part of her wondered if she'd have to do such a thing. Her stomach turned.

"Please," Imani said kindly. "Do not trouble yourself with civility. The fire in you is bright. It must be fed. Go."

The camel's slow gait infuriated Cass. The sun was already low and she knew the museum would be closed before they got back in to town. She'd have to go the next morning. But she might be able to get a head start. Especially if someone already knew their way around. Or had an idea what might lie in wait in the museum.

She dug in her pack for her phone. Eagerly, she typed a text. "Have a lead. Looking for ancient text. Something not translated. Thinking the museum downtown. Any thoughts?"

She hit send and curled her toes in the stirrups. A shiver vibrated her whole body. She didn't know if it was the chilling desert air or the thrill of texting someone she had a crush on.

Her phone buzzed and she read the reply: "Know the place. Think I know what you're talking about. If you're sure, meet me at the library across the street from there at 9AM tomorrow."

A genuine, blushing smile pulled her face. "Thanks, Charlie," she replied.

CHAPTER 13: CLUES AND LIBRARIES

"You told Charlie?" Vamshi hissed the next day as Rana led them down the cramped street into the historic district.

"Yes," Cass replied angrily, motioning for Vamshi to be quiet as curious heads popped out of the windows in the stacked houses that surrounded them. "He knows this place better than we do. With him and Rana helping us out, we're sure to find whatever we're looking for."

Vamshi massaged her temples hard, eyes squinted shut. "You are allowing yourself to be drawn into this guy."

"So?" Cass cut in. "Aren't I allowed to have feelings? To try to start some kind of..." Relationship? Curious-ship? She wasn't sure what she thought about Charlie. She just knew he intrigued her and could offer some insight. And had the cutest, saddest face she'd ever seen.

Vamshi opened her mouth to speak again, but Cass elbowed her hard to keep her quiet. Charlie leaned against a garden wall outside the library's grand facade. It was easily one of the nicer buildings in downtown Atminadab with its pristine white walls and red-brown accents, rivaled only by the museum across the street. He pushed himself up and approached the trio with a cautious look at Rana and Vamshi.

Cass greeted him a little over enthusiastically and awkwardly shoved her hands in her jacket pockets when she got the urge to touch his arm when introducing him. She briefly explained who Rana was and Charlie nodded to her. Vamshi crossed her arms and gave a soft death-stare, not shaking his proffered hand. Cass cringed on the inside.

"So," she said, moving past the formalities, "what came to mind last night?"

Charlie reached into his jacket and pulled out his phone. Turning it to Cass, he showed her a series of images. Vamshi and Rana crowded around to see as well. The screen showed a series and dark, glass cases. Inside, a yellow light shined dimly onto old parchment, folded like an accordion.

"These are the originals," Charlie said. "Or at least, what's left of them."

Cass frowned, confused. "That's not a tablet."

"They call them the Codex of Madi Saghira," he explained. "They were brought when South American explorers from what is now present day Mexico came, looking for hidden temples and stories of monsters."

Cass leaned forward, touching the screen of his phone gently to enlarge the images. "They're so blurry," she sighed. "Can we go in and see the originals?"

Charlie smiled and led them inside the museum. As they wound down dark, granite halls of statues, golden pottery, moth-eaten tapestries, and a few curiosities, he spoke.

"I've only been to Madi Saghira once," he explained. "A client some time ago asked to go there for research. But, as I'm sure you learned, they don't like researchers. Turns out, this client was a treasure hunter on a wild goose chase for the gold of some pharaoh, lost to the ages during a local war back in the 1800s."

"Cool," Cass breathe softly as they turned down a particularly dark corridor.

"Yeah." He nodded. He stopped in front of a long line of glass cases. "These are them. This technique of codex was actually used in South America long before the Egyptians were writing things down."

"South America?" Cass asked. "Like... Aztecs?"

He nodded. She took a deep breath and blew it out evenly. Listen, Pakhba, she thought, Things are getting out of control. I don't know what I am looking for. I'm here, help me out!

She peered into the darkness of the display. Even in person, the Codex was nearly impossible to read. The ink was faded and sparse. Leaning as close as she could, she pressed her nose up against the glass. A few lines stirred, but only just.

"It's too faded," she sighed, frustration mounting.

"Which is why," Charlie said to the other two as well, "we'll go across the street to the library. They have them on microfilm. A few years ago, a group of university students did a study on remote cultures and got them scanned and enhanced. But I thought you'd want to see the originals first."

"Yes!" Cass cried, this time allowing herself to grab his arm out of excitement. His lithe arms felt small under his jacket.

He gave a mild smile in reply, took her hand, and headed towards the front.

The vaulted, white ceiling of the library was just as impressive as the museum. Cass marveled, jaw dropping, at the interior design and ornate mouldings of the old building. The silence hissed, fueled by softly turning pages, gentle whispers, and the insect-like buzz of warm, yellow lights. Charlie led the trio to the back where Rana asked in Arabic to see the microfilm machines.

The librarian, a beautiful girl about Cass's age, looked at them kindly through gold-rimmed glasses. She whispered to Rana, who then turned to Charlie and held her hand out.

"Show me the pictures again," she said.

When he pulled his phone out, she snatched it and turned it to face the librarian. She squinted at it through her pretty glasses, then nodded, tapping her lip. She spoke rapidly to Rana and led them down a less elegant hallway. The librarian stopped and unlocked a door with a long chain of keys before motioning them to wait. Cass chanced a glance at Vamshi to find her friend cautiously watching Charlie. Cass elbowed her gently to get her attention. Frowning and shaking her head to ask why Vamshi was so untrusting, she nodded towards Charlie.

Vamshi shrugged and rolled her eyes.

A few minutes later, the four of them stood beside the microfilm machine, slowly scrolling through stark, black and white versions of the codex. Cass scanned them, her nose close to the screen. Would it work the same way as the Dragon Script? She had questions. As they all watched, she gently touched Pakhba on her wrist, wondering if she should summon him to have him look. After all, he could remain invisible.

With a cautious glance around, she whispered in her mind, Pakhba, come out. I need you to look at this. Stay invisible.

Knowing he would act as her familiar, Pakhba zipped out in a flash of blue and yellow light and smoke. Cass had to control herself from jumping at his sudden appearance.

"What is it?" Charlie asked, seeing her body jolt.

"Uh, got shocked," she lied quickly. Pakhba hung over her shoulder. Can you hear me? she asked.

Of course I can, the dragon replied. What have you found here?

Cass didn't realize how much she zoned out while filling Pakhba in until Charlie's bony hand touched her shoulder.

"Sorry," she murmured again, turning back to the screen. "I was just trying to put it together in my head."

"With what?" he asked, leaning closer. He leaned so close to her and the screen now that his gentle, blond curls tickled her cheek. Her skin burned where it touched her.

She bit her bottom lip. How much should she tell anyone? Vamshi had to know, but she'd fill her in later.

Cassandra, Pakhba whispered, who is this pouting boy you've picked up?

Rolling her eyes, she hissed, Help me read this or go back into the bracelet.

Pakhba drifted a bit closer. It is… incomplete. And this is not the Tablet of Mehen, as the woman said. Is this…? He didn't go on.

"Incomplete?" she said out loud before she could stop herself. "Is that why I can't read it?"

Rana frowned at the screen. "Really what?"

"Uh," Cass stammered. "I was just thinking, is it really some ancient language?"

All four of them leaned in close, eyes squinting. Cass felt squished between all the prying eyes. If she wasn't careful, her singular task would turn into a grand party of four traipsing across the globe. And something told her keeping it as secret as possible would be tantamount to success.

"Looks like Sanskrit?" Vamshi asked, finally joining the conversation.

Charlie shook his head. "No, maybe Aramaic?"

At last, Rana made a triumphant sound in her throat. "No. Neither. I've done some code cracking in my day." She pointed to a particular symbol on the screen, tapping it.

Then she scrolled back a few slides and pointed to the same one out again. "The lore keeper said this was a story. So we should see some repetition, but I wasn't at first. This repeats. I thought maybe it was a script used in Asia. It is based on an Arabic script that contained the original twenty-eight Arabic letters. But this..." She stepped back, smiling. Her brown eyes glowed with a golden light. "This is more like Pegon. A modified Arabic script used to write ancient, secret languages."

The glow, excitement, in Rana's eyes infected Cass in the best way. Genuine thrill and joy filled their guide's face. She couldn't help but share the smile. Cass suddenly realized in that moment that Rana, mysterious as she was, would be invaluable. She was street-smart, brave, totally engrossed in the quest, and hadn't asked a single intrusive question.

"What does that mean?" Cass asked, looking back at the screen.

Rana moved to the side and began to print the scans. "First, there are parts missing," she unknowingly confirmed what Pakhba had said. "But I have a theory." She stopped there, tapping her lip.

"Like what?" Charlie asked.

Rana smiled crookedly and shook her head, handing Cass the prints. "Look at these."

Once she held them in her hands, enhanced and edited by the previous team as they were, the letters finally moved for her. She gasped. It is Dragon Script, she mused to herself. Or something very much like it.

The more she looked, the more came into focus. A loop started around an existing symbol, inking itself in. Then it stopped. Cass frowned. She knew that symbol, but it didn't finish. "It's all incomplete," she moaned sadly. Curious, she pointed to the newly appeared script. "Can you see this?"

Rana, Charlie, and Vamshi leaned over to look. "No,"

Rana said simply. Vamshi didn't reply. Charlie shook his head, his shoulders sagging.

"You see something?" he asked, his face returning to its resting, sad pout.

Cass gave Vamshi a knowing look. Her friend's eyes widened, picking up the clue.

"Let's go somewhere to talk," Vamshi suggested, elbowing Charlie out of the way to stand next to Cass.

Ten minutes later, they sat in an open cafe on a dusty, windy street. The weather had turned from hot and dry to windy and cool in a matter of minutes.

"The weather changes fast near the shore," Rana said, setting down a tray of Turkish coffee served in beautiful, gem-colored glasses from a brass pot. She heaved her pack off her back and took out her brick-like laptop. She set a thick antenna on top of it and started to type madly on it.

"So, what are we looking for now?" Charlie asked.

"Somewhere old," Rana said slowly, eyes scanning her screen behind her dark sunglasses.

Sand and dust kicked up from a sudden gust of wind and swirled around inside the cafe. The brightly patterned curtains danced and snapped in the bright sun.

It would be old, Pakhba whispered from where he curled up in the seat next to Cass. There was a jungle. I remember it.

Cass frowned down at him, curious. "A jungle," she said out loud. "Look for a jungle."

Rana furrowed her brow, finally looking up. She took a sip from the jewel-colored coffee cup. "There are no jungles here. This is Egypt."

Feeling stuck, Cass sighed in frustration. The trip had

been long already. Only a few days, but for some reason, she'd expected to get in and out in a matter of forty-eight or so hours. A week at the most. She needed to get home. To a place she knew. But she hadn't even found the resting place of the damned dragon. She fell onto her elbows onto the rough wood of the table and rubbed the bridge of her nose.

It was here, Pakhba insisted. *Many years ago, but still. I recall the trees. The water. The temple.* His voice almost cracked, turning to what Cass thought might be sorrow.

"A temple," she murmured, thinking. The wind rustled the prints. The incomplete lettering was basically useless to her. Like the missing bits in the Dragon Script. "Oh, my god!" she said, sitting bolt upright.

The other three jumped.

"What?" Vamshi asked, grabbing her arm.

"I know where to look," Cass blurted, excitement shooting through her.

"Where?" Charlie asked, leaning in.

"No, not like that," Cass started. She began to gather the prints and packing her bag. She opened her mouth to explain as best she could when something outside the dust-filled window caught her sight. Two figures: one a woman with blonde hair tied up into a tight bun, her face hidden behind black sunglasses. And a man with shaggy hair wearing khaki cargo pants, boots, and a white t-shirt.

"Oh, shit," she whispered.

Charlie spun to look, seeing her face pale.

"Agreed," he whispered. He reached for Cass's hand but she lept up.

"We have to run," she said to Vamshi and Rana. They protested, but she growled at them. "Split up."

"Wait!" Rana shouted, but Cass dove under the table, grasping at the prints and tripping over her pack's straps.

"Go!" she urged them. She'd run. Hide. Then, when the

coast was clear, she'd head back to the hotel. Not sure where to go, Cass dashed toward the back to the kitchen area of the cafe. The workers shouted at her, cursing her for speeding through. Sliding under a prep table, she dove through the back, swinging doors into the alley behind the cafe. A dumpster hugged one wall, so she hid behind it to quickly catch her breath.

Shouting from the front told her the other three had dashed. Vamshi would be safe with Rana. And away from her. Clutching her pack to her chest, she opened the top flap and shoved the prints in. She had an idea of what they said and knew the Dragon Script would fill in the blanks. At last, she had something to work with.

Waiting a beat, she poked her head up over the dumpster to scan the streets. No sign of the woman or her crony showed. Cautiously, looking every which way, Cass hurried down another alley. Pakhba swished past her, leading the way.

"How did they know where you were?" he growled, flying at top speeds.

"I don't know," Cass panted. "But that was way too close. They're here, so I have to hurry."

"I could not agree more, Cassandra," the dragon said.

CHAPTER 14: GOLDEN SIGHT

Cass covered her mouth, panting into the dark public bathroom. She tried to press herself harder against the wall and its chipping green paint, but her pack prevented her. Pakhba floated up to the barred window and looked out, invisible to prying eyes outside.

"I do not see them," he whispered to her. "Where is the Script?"

Moving her hands just a few centimeters from her mouth, Cass whispered, "In the hotel. I thought... I thought it'd be safer there."

The dragon angled his body and stuck his head through the bars to see farther down the street. "Perhaps, Cassandra. If they know you are here, they may know where you are staying. One should never let the enemy know where one lays their head."

Cass rolled her eyes gently. "I didn't advertise it. They just figured it out." Somehow... It was too convenient that they knew where she was on the vast continent of Africa. Even if they had guessed Egypt, Atminadab was small, remote, and obscure.

She shoved herself up and walked quietly to the exit where the streets hummed noisily beyond. The blinding sun made her squint after just five minutes into the dark public toilet. She slipped out and almost ran into a huge stack of rolled up rugs outside a shop. Stopping to grab the tower of woven colors before it toppled over, she froze.

"I'm not a retired special agent," a deep, male voice snapped. "That bitch is slippery."

Hearing English is what held Cass in place. She'd heard a few other languages—French from some Haitians, even a group of Chinese businessmen—but not English. Holding still, hands sweating and clutching the pile of rolled rugs, she listened. Risking a glance, she pulled out her phone, turned on the camera, and slipped it around the rugs. She caught sight of a man in a white, cut-off shirt with a whole sleeve of tattoos, and shaggy brown hair, and another wearing a cheap suit, glossy sunglasses, bald, and the douchiest goatee she'd ever seen.

"I'm not either," the man in the glossy shades replied, "but I can keep track of a little girl."

"She's got company," the tattooed man replied. She recognized him now; he'd been the same one with the bald man and the blonde woman before. He'd forgone his suit in the hot, Egyptian weather. "Some woman who has a certain trained look about her is guiding her every move."

Shades tilted his head and raised a too-manicured brow at his colleague. He asked in a mocking tone, "Is Markus scared of a little girl?" Then, angrily, he shouted, "They're three women! Alone. In a foreign country. You're calling Meredith."

Meredith, Cass mouthed, frowning. That name was familiar.

"Where is she?" the one called Markus asked, dodging the order to call their boss.

"Looking for that temple," Shades replied, checking the

street before stepping out to cross. "There's nothing there, though. If there was a temple, it's buried deep under the sand. Or torn down."

"Nothing on the satellite images?" Markus asked.

Shades shook his head. Putting his head down, Shades led Markus across the street and into a dark parking garage where they flashed some kind of ID to get into.

Cass stood up, gasping for air. She didn't realize she'd been holding her breath. "Temple," she mused to Pakhba, who was still invisible to everyone else. "There's probably a bunch of them around here."

The hotel looked closed during the day. The doors were closed against the sandy wind and the vacant light was turned off. Cass guessed this had to do with the roaring nightlife of Atminadab being enough to sustain the hotel. The generators in the back didn't grind either, most likely recharging. Cass slipped into her room and closed the door, locking it. She folded the shutters on the window and locked those as well. They were thin, though, and she doubted they'd keep anyone out who really wanted to break in.

After texting Vamshi and hearing back that she and Rana were okay and would be headed back soon, Cass decided to go to work on the Script. With the door locked from the inside, Vamshi would have to knock before entering, giving her enough time to stow the book before Rana saw.

She sat on the floor, laying out the prints from the Codex before her and opening the Dragon Script to the page where the missing symbols were. For a brief minute, she wondered if she should light a candle, cast a circle, or close her eyes. She'd not done that before, but she also hadn't been this close (hopefully) to where one of the dragons lay sleeping.

When the thought hit her—that maybe only a few miles away—a real live dragon lay asleep, her heart skipped. She gripped the Script harder.

"Show me something, baby," she murmured. She closed her eyes, praying to anything that would listen for luck, then opened them. Her vision blued for a minute when she looked down, but it slowly came back into focus. As the room did, so did the symbols.

Something in her head clicked and started to churn. A warm, static-like fuzz consumed her brain. The edges of her vision turned gold, drowning out everything but the Script before her.

"I can't see," she whispered.

"It's all right," Pakhba said, his voice deep and echoing. "The golden sight is what you are seeing. When you understand a riddle, laid out in the Dragon Script, your eyes shine gold and you can see the answer."

Cass picked up one of the pages from the Codex. She blinked, and certain letters on the pages lit up. "Whoa," she breathed, looking up. When she did, the glowing letters followed as if attached to her eyes. "Oh, my god..." she whispered. Snapping her golden gaze back to the Script, the golden letters from the Codex landed, filling in the missing symbols. They seeped out in golden ink, touching the circles, lines, and dots that made up the Script. A thrill shot through her as the humming in her skull elevated to another note.

"It sounds like mediation bowls," she said out loud, realizing she couldn't hear her own voice.

"You're close, Vedic," Pakhba whispered. "Do not look down."

Cass glued her eyes to the Script, glad that the golden glow blinded her to her peripheral vision. She didn't know what

Pakhba didn't want her to see, but she was not about to spoil this amazing moment. "I see something," she said, studying the Codex pages again. A new set of letters stuck to her eyes, and she placed them on the Script. "It's almost words, but not. I recognize them, but they don't make sense." She stumbled through her brain to think if it was some kind of puzzle. Something else to be solved. Pakhba said she'd get this golden sight when on the trail of a riddle.

"Can you help me?" she asked, her head suddenly starting to hurt. The elevated humming and the fuzzy warmth turned to painful vibrations and stabbing torpidity.

"I should not lend you my power," Pakhba said cautiously.

"You're my familiar," Cass said with more of a pout than she meant to. "Help me, for crying out loud."

Reluctantly, Pakhba came into her view. He floated up, coiling around her head, turning to a sort of gold and blue circlet. When his head met his tail, completing the circle, the pain and vibration evened out.

"Thank you," she whispered, looking back down. Her mind must have been playing tricks on her because the wooden floor looked like it drifted several feet away, under her.

With Pakhba helping out, the magic redistributed between them. Cass focused harder, trying to read. The pages of the Codex filled in only two pages of the Script.

"It's still just jumbled symbols!" she cried, frustrated.

Then, the last line appeared, dancing on the page. She tried to read it but it shook, turning to vibrating smudges. She moaned in pain and her eyes watered, but it finally read a coherent thought: "The catalyst can be found in the claws of the motherless words." Beneath it, what she would have sworn was a hieroglyph appeared.

"What?" she cried, looking up. When she did, the room snapped back into view. The golden sight vanished, and she fell.

Cass screamed as she tipped backwards, falling three or so feet from midair. She landed hard on her backside, rolling to her back. The Script crashed down around her and a flurry that was the Codex snowed down, flipping and snapping like a torrential wind just whipped them around.

"I was floating!" she cried, remembering how the floor had looked far away.

The circlet that was Pakhba rolled off her head and then shot up, a flesh and blood dragon once again. "I should not have done that," Pakhba said sadly. "You are a Vedic, not meant for my powers."

"Well, we figured it out," Cass said with a huge grin as the Codex flitted down to the ground. "But my ass hurts."

Just then, the door tried to open. With a metallic clank and wooden thunk, the chain and bolt held it in place.

"Good god, girl, open up," Vamshi said, pressing her face hard into the tiny opening, comically bulging her eye.

Cass apologized, got up, and unshackled the door. Rana and Vamshi spilled in, dusty, panting, and sweating.

"What the hell happened in here?" Rana asked, scanning the mess. "Did they break in?"

"No," Cass quickly replied, putting out that fire before it erupted into more. "I was studying. And I think I have something to go on." She went to her pack and took out her journal and a pen. "I saw this symbol." She drew the square-like symbol that had appeared under the one coherent sentence she'd been able to read.

Vamshi peered at it, frowning. Rana, curious, frowned as well. Cass saw the millions of questions in her deep, dark brown eyes. She appreciated her respect for not asking.

"What is it?" Vamshi asked, wiping at her sweaty neck with her scarf and going for a glass of water.

"Naos," Rana said before Cass could answer. "It means temple."

That made sense, according to what she heard Markus and Shades talking about. Sort of.

"Did you find any temples around us?" Vamshi asked Rana.

Their guid pressed her red lips together in thought. "Nothing off the beaten path like you asked."

Cass absentmindedly rubbed her fingers together, repeating the line in her head. "The catalyst can be found in the claws of the motherless words."

Vamshi arched a confused brow. "Motherless words? The catalyst?"

Rana moved across the room to the bathroom and closed the door. Cass got the strange feeling she was giving them privacy. Rana didn't ask questions. That alone made her worth her fee.

"Motherless goat," Vamshi said flatly, reciting idioms that shared words with the phrase Cass has said. "Cataclysm sounds like catalyst. Words. Bird's the word—"

A sharp, high squeak burst from Cass as her heart raced. "It is the word! Vam, you're a genius!"

Her best friend stared in shock as Cass shook her with glee. "Stop and tell me what you mean."

"Thoth," Cass burst. "The god of words, poetry, magic. The master of scribes. Thoth, the bird god, wasn't born like other gods. He didn't have a mother. He was born from Ra's very lips. Spoken word, making him a motherless god."

The bathroom door burst open, and Rana stood in the portal, smiling. "There was a temple to Thoth in Atminadab."

"Yes," Cass said, still excited despite knowing the truth. "But I heard our mutual friends speaking. It was buried a long time ago. They couldn't find it."

Vamshi grabbed Cass's arm, her brown eyes wide. A wicked, gleeful grin spread over her face. "But where was it?"

Rana grabbed her pack and started to rummage through,

looking for a map and her tourism notes. Her movements were quick and Cass read excitement in her, too.

"Oh, no," Cass declared quickly, realizing why Vamshi smiled. "We can't dig. We don't have the means."

Rana stopped and looked up. Vamshi picked up Cass's hand, the one where Pakhba's bracelet form hung.

"But we can try a little magic, right?" Vamshi's smile never left. "I mean, a familiar is as a familiar does."

Pakhba had warned her against using his magic not minutes ago. But he'd given in. She was the Vedic, after all. And it was her task to find the dragons. Honestly, who could find dragons without a little magic?

"Okay," she sighed, making up her mind. Her blood raced as she did. She held her breath, then said, "To the temple of Thoth."

CHAPTER 15: NAOS ATMINADAB

Cass looked down at her phone. She'd texted Charlie the night before, saying they were going to sleep, buy supplies, and then head out to look for a buried temple. She'd asked if he was okay. Had the thugs found him when they split up?

The message waited on delivered. He'd not read it. She worried about him. If he'd gotten tangled up with the Future, it was her fault. If he got hurt, she'd be to blame. He was just here for work. She was here—apparently—to dig up a temple of god. After a night of not sleeping, she guessed a dragon might choose a god's temple to sleep in. Assuming Mehen got to choose.

What the hell was she supposed to do with the dragons once they were awake? Could they turn small and indiscreet like Pakhba? She sure hoped so or else she'd have a lot of explaining to do at customs. And to her parents if she brought a dragon home. She smiled a little at the thought and put her phone away. Rana kept reminding them to hurry. They needed to catch a tour bus that was heading in their general direction. She knew what temple Cass had mentioned and knew roughly where it might have been. That was all they had to go on.

Cass grabbed up her water bottle and slipped it into her now heavy pack. They didn't know how long they'd be gone.

"Holy shit, we're actually going to find an ancient temple," Vamshi whispered excitedly as she unplugged her hair straightener and turned off all the lights.

"Yeah," Cass breathed, puffing out her cheeks. "Things are... getting very real." The night before, she wondered if that golden sight could be called up on command. Could it show her Scripts in the temple? Would there be hidden messages she needed to read? Her stomach flipped and grew nauseous the more she thought about it. The golden sight had been cool, but it made her wonder what else she could do as Vedic.

Just as she reached for her hat, the thin wooden shutters over the window burst open. Cass screamed and flinched, using her arms to cover her face as splinters showered in.

"What the—" she started, but something she'd never heard in her life cut her words off.

Two gun shots went off and Vamshi screamed. Cass screamed and immediately hit the floor. A commotion erupted outside in the streets where the perpetrators broke in, and inside where Rana started to shout orders in rapid Arabic. Shouts from outside told Cass that the people in the street had heard the guns, too. Calls of "baltagiya!" filled the air. Somewhere down the street, another gun fired.

Cass looked up, spotted Vamshi belly-crawling towards the door, her pack shifting madly with each movement of her arms. In the window, framed by the sandstone walls, stood Markus and his gun-toting, tattooed arm.

"Get in there!" someone shouted from behind him, which Cass correctly assumed was Shades.

"They're running!" Markus growled. He gripped the windowsill and hoisted himself up.

"Yalla! Yalla!" Rana shouted, coming in to cover Cass. The woman stopped, drew a handgun from her hidden holster on her ribs, and fired at Markus.

The man shouted and fell backwards. Cass was sure Rana hadn't hit him, just scared him. Rana reached down and hauled Cass up, shoving her towards the door. "Do not go out the front," Rana commanded. "Kitchen."

"Markus!" Shades called from far away.

"I'm okay!" came the reply from the ground outside.

Confused, but in no mindset to argue, Cass bolted down the hall with Vamshi on her heels. Two more shots went off and shouts in Arabic snapped back and forth. The grubby housemaid appeared in the hallway, shouting at the girls as they ran past. Cass followed the tantalizing smell of tabouli to the kitchen. She burst through the stainless steel doors with little round windows in them and wove through the cabinets. Something boiled on the stove, giving them a little cover from the steam.

Would Shades think to come outback? Or would he run to the front like Rana warned them against? Cass froze in the middle of the dirty kitchen, the cooks shouting and cursing at them. She grabbed Vamshi's hand.

"Stay on me," she whispered. She raised her other arm, where Pakhba rested, and commanded him in her mind to come out. He appeared, glowering. "Go outside," she ordered. "Tell me if that tattoo guy is coming." Then she ran to the back of the kitchen. Pakhba zipped away.

Cass stuck her head out and looked into the alley. A dumpster and some overhanging sheets lined the brick way before dumping into the main street. It was just getting crowded as people went to work and tourist sites opened up. They might be able to blend in.

"He's coming," Pakhba said to her, zipping back to meet them. "The other has gone to the front gate."

Cass tossed her head down each exit of the alley. "Where's Rana?"

As if to answer her question, a motorcycle revved loudly to the end of the alley. Cass recognized the long legs on either side, and thick black braid sticking out from under the helmet.

"That's our ride," Cass breathed. Still holding Vamshi's hand tight, she dashed down the alley. The side car waited. It only had one seat, but Cass didn't care. She tipped herself in and pulled Vamshi on top of her.

"Stay down," Rana hissed, handing Vamshi a helmet. Cass didn't move.

"Go!" she hissed when Rana started a slow, meandering jaunt down the ever-filling road.

"No," their guid replied. "We go slow. Blend in. They will be looking for running."

Ten agonizing minutes of traversing the crowded streets of the dusty city drove Cass wild with nausea. She wanted to peek out from the floor of the sidecar where she huddled, but Vamshi kept her hand on Cass's head, pushing her down.

"Did you get shot?" Vamshi asked Rana.

The woman shook her head. "I got him, though. Just a nick, but it should give him pause."

This is insane, Cass thought. She'd thought getting to hunt down ancient dragons would be all magic, stars, and adventure. She'd expected danger. But nice, easy danger she could deal with. Not gun-toting madmen who actually tried to kill her.

Silently, she thanked every god of Egypt for sending her Rana.

The Mediterranean stretched out before them, blue and bright. It was close to noon when they finally lost their stalkers and made their way to a remote spot just on the shore. Resorts lined the shores so much Cass was shocked she could see the glittering blue from farther inland. She expected the shore to be empty, desolate even. Now she wasn't sure why. She couldn't even hear herself think over the ruckus that was peddlers, scammers, tourists, rich oil sheikhs, and an extra loud gaggle of social media influencers just off a boat from somewhere near Greece.

"What are we doing?" Cass shouted, wincing into the dust and sun.

"The temple you mentioned," Rana shouted back, pushing her way down a street towards a glossy marina. "It's on an island about two miles offshore."

The remote location put some pause in Cass. "How are we getting there?" Maybe Rana could swim two miles, but not her.

"Boat." Rana smiled and pointed down towards a set of piers and docks where an army of yachts, sailboats, and other aquatic vehicles bobbed in the bright water. "There are always people down here willing to take you out for a few bills."

Cass's eyes widened. "I don't have that much."

Rana waved her off. "I know a guy. Fortunately for us, he's a Bavarian scoundrel." Her twisted grin and the way she couldn't hide the sparkle in her eyes told Cass this guy owed her a favor. After seeing Rana out-gun the thugs and speed to their rescue on her motorcycle, Cass was not about to ask questions she didn't want answers to. She did glance at Vamshi, who shrugged warily.

Rana led them farther and farther down the shore until they got close to what Cass would call a more industrial looking set of docks and marina. Fishing boats, smaller barges, and even what looked like a government yacht dipped and swayed in these waters. She quickly deduced which boat Rana aimed for. A large, multipurpose offshore vessel was the only one dense and heavy enough to not be rocked by the light waves this close to shore. A few men and women moved around it, tossing equipment onboard just as the engine rattled and water shot out from the first start. The name *Phantom Ivory* splashed across the stern.

"Hurry," Rana hissed, grabbing the girls' hands and running to it.

As they clattered over the wooden pier, Cass squinted up at the thing. It had once been painted green and yellow, but the paint had long ago chipped away. A few rust spots showed where the ship needed tending. A giant, white crane arched out the open deck on the back along with a few hanging cables. Some yellow things that looked like rockets to Cass, and several other gizmos she had never seen before in her life, hung off the side. What looked like a cage hung off the port side.

"Ahoy!" Rana shouted, grinning broadly. She waved her arm up at the crew. She waited a moment when a man in scuba gear saw her, then disappeared over the side.

"What..." Cass started, but Rana held her hand up.

A minute later, a tall, broad man with dreaded blond hair and a sun-burnt face popped his head over the side into their line of sight. Cass could see the gruff man's face fall even under his long, tangled beard.

"Oh, it's you," he mumbled in a German accent, and then vanished.

Cass stopped herself from asking what again when a long, old and fraying rope ladder spilled over the side with a clunk. Still smiling, Rana galloped up the ladder onto the superyacht, hissing for them to follow.

Cass gripped the rungs tight, suddenly feeling the motion

of the ocean she couldn't see before. She moaned and clung on hard to get her bearings before ascending to join Rana.

Once on top in the open-air deck, she took in the salty wind and the rough company they'd found themselves in. Tall, muscled men worked the ship in various states of dress. Women just as toned and just as tall moved among them. The boat was dirty. Grime encrusted every flat surface, seaweed and other ocean flora dripped from something hanging above.

"What is this?" Cass whispered.

"It's a boat, *fräulein*."

Cass turned to see the blond and bearded man from before. He wore huge overalls over a thick sweater and was missing a front canine in his smile. "You, I am pleased to make the acquaintance of." He shook Cass's hand in his huge, calloused one, then did the same to Vamshi. "You, however," he said, pointing two fingers at Rana. "This is why I told Deston we should never come back here. She'd come to collect, I said."

Rana looked around, mock concern on her pretty face. "Where is your boy?"

"He's a man now, Rana. He's below, starting the engines," the German man sighed. He rubbed what smelled like fish guts into the front of his overalls and looked Rana square on. "What do you want, woman?"

"A ride," she quipped back. She pulled a now super-wrinkled map out of her back pocket. "To this island." She pointed to an empty spot on the map.

The German man picked up the map and squinted at it. "I see the coordinators. What's there?"

"An island," Cass repeated, half hoping it wasn't just a spot of ocean like on the map.

The man smiled at her. "And you're sure it's there?"

She dropped her jaw in uncertainty.

The man smiled and handed the map back to Rana. "You are lucky, woman. We are going that way."

Relief flooded Cass. "I'm Cass and this is Vamshi. How do you know Rana?"

The man tapped the bridge of his nose. "Rana Saad and Dietrich Van Volxem go deep. Deeper than any ocean trench, don't we, Saad."

"Van Volxem," Cass said, testing the exciting name. "Very cool."

"Very Bavarian," Dietrich agreed. "So, Saad. I assume you have come to collect on that favor from China?"

Rana hissed, waving away the story. "Yes. It's only two miles offshore. You will take us."

Dietrich smiled and shook his head, feigning defeat. "*Ja*, I will. This way, *fräuleins*."

Cass gripped the grimy, peeling rails of the strange boat. The wind bounced off the ocean, cool and salty against her skin. Vamshi stood next to her, holding onto her wrist with both hands.

"I can actually see the island," Cass mused. "I couldn't at first."

Vamshi nodded. "Is it weird that I'm nervous?"

"No," Cass quipped quickly. "I'm terrified. I didn't know what I was getting myself into. Don't know what I thought was going to happen. What did I think hunting down mythical creatures like dragons might mean?" She sniffled, her nose starting to run in the suddenly cool air.

Vamshi touched her forehead where a small, dried drop of blood showed under her black hair.

"What happened?" Cass asked.

"They shot at us and exploded that water pitcher on the shelf," Vamshi explained. "Glass hit me."

Overcome, Cass collapsed her face into her hands. "Damn, Vam, I'm sorry. This is... so much bigger than me." She looked up at the island slowly appearing on the horizon. It wavered in the heat lines from where the rays of the sun hit the cool water. She realized that must help keep the island hidden. From a distance, it looked like a mirage. Up close, it looked like an illusion.

Behind them, Dietrich called out to someone in German. Cass turned and froze. A tall, muscular frame emerged from the lower deck behind foggy windows. He strode up the steps two at a time with long, lean legs. He wore a wetsuit half rolled down to his waist. Shaggy, wet black hair clung to his neck. He strapped a tool belt around his slim hips and answered Dietrich in the same German dialect. He stopped, shook his head like a dog, spraying glittering droplets of seawater everywhere. Cass swore for a moment that a golden haze glowed around him like a soft light. He hiked up the steps towards the base of the giant white crane with the same graceful, long strides. The glow vanished and Cass realized it must have been a trick of the sun and the water droplets clinging to his skin.

"Deston," Dietrich said to the young man when he arrived on the top deck. "Don't use all the air diving into unplanned waters. We need that air for later. We're not making berth until after the Caribbean."

"Deston," Cass whispered. Someone touched her chin, dabbing at it as if wiping something away. "What the hell?" She looked over to see Vamshi grinning like a maniac.

"Down, girl, you're drooling on his wetsuit," Vamshi laughed. "But trust me, I am logging that ass away for later use in here." She tapped her temple, then glanced over her shoulder again at him. "Do they make them all like that in Bavaria?" she asked.

Cass blew a long breath out. "Can you imagine? I wish one of the dragons was hiding there."

Vamshi nodded. The girls looked ahead again and then felt the lurch of the ship. Rana appeared next to them.

"A man will take us out in the small motorboat," she said, handing them their packs. "Then it's down to us."

"Umm, Rana?" Cass asked, following her to the side where the smaller boat got lowered over the side. "How are we getting back?"

"Signal fire," she said easily.

"Signal fire?" Vamshi repeated, aghast.

"Your packs have flint and steel," Rana reasoned. "The government patrol will see it. We'll be back by morning if you want."

Unable to wrap her head around the logic and the absurdity, Cass just nodded and slid down the rope into the smaller boat. The bottom of the boat bumped and swayed against her knees until her legs buckled. Vamshi jumped down behind her, quickly followed by Rana. Within a matter of minutes, the girls sped off towards the island with a single crewman at the rudder.

The island spread out before them in a great gold and yellow arch. As they got closer, Cass realized it was a crescent-shaped island, and they were headed right towards the center between the two pointed ends. Dozens of tall hills covered in trees of every variety swayed in the wind. The golden sun bounced off the lush leaves, giving the approaching shore a kaleidoscopic emerald and gold design. The crewman stopped the motor several yards out and motion for them to get off. Rana led the way, splashing into the sapphire waves and marching inland.

The water soaked Cass's shoes, but she didn't care. Before them stretched an actual, wild, deserted island. She had barely set foot on the shore before Pakhba shot out, frightening her.

"I feel her," he whispered so only she could hear. Vamshi snapped her head over to look at Cass, realizing he must have come out but was invisible.

"Do you know the way?" Cass asked. Pakhba floated above her, eyes closed. He slowly rotated like the needle on a compass.

"I do," he whispered. "It is not far. This island used to be far larger. Follow me closely. I will move slowly for you."

Rana had been talking, but Cass hadn't heard her.

"This way," Cass said, interrupting her.

She took the lead. Nerves made her sweat more than she already was. Pakhba's soft, gold and blue glow hardly helped. Bugs zipped around them, curious about the new creatures tromping through the trees and over the patches of open dunes.

They came to a large sandy prairie after a little over an hour. The sun beat down from directly overhead, making it almost impossible to miss the landmark.

"Holy Krishna," Vamshi whispered.

"Yeah," Cass breathed, snapping a quick picture.

In the very center of the little, open desert rose a huge, black onyx obelisk.

"My god," Rana breathed.

The women were correct in their exclamations. The sand was more orange than yellow. It didn't glint like the inland sand. It was matte, dull. Almost like it absorbed the light from the sun. The light went down, touched the sand, but didn't come out.

"Like a black hole," Cass observed.

Pakhba hovered over the sand towards the obelisk. Unsure if touching the sand would curse her or not, Cass hesitated. But the dragon didn't stop. Cursing, she stepped out onto the shifting sands. The sand moved slow and dense under her feet.

Vamshi followed her, then Rana. The open desert gave them all pause.

The black obelisk appeared even blacker against the blue sky and orange desert. It looked solid and smooth until Cass was looking up at it. Ornate sigils, runes, and Script ran up the thing in such great detail it gave her a headache. The more she looked at them and studied them, the more of them appeared.

"It's Dragon Script," she breathed.

"Indeed," Pakhba breathed. "What you need is at the top."

Mouth popping open, Cass snapped her head up to the stop. "That's—that's," she stammered. "Thirty feet at least!"

Pakhba seemed unperturbed. "Read your way up, Vedic."

Cass stammered again, trapped between Rana seeing her and wondering what the hell that meant. Then it hit her. "The golden sight."

"Yes," the dragon hummed.

"But... Rana?"

"I know," was all he said.

He knew. Fine.

Cass dropped her pack and ignored Vamshi and Rana's questions as she dug the Dragon Script out. Vamshi protested and Rana grew quiet. Cass pulled her hat down on her head and opened the Script, feeling exactly what she needed to do. Opening the binding, she focused on the moving script of the obelisk and let go of the Dragon Script. It floated, untouched, before her.

Rana exclaimed something in Arabic and stutter-stepped back. Vamshi moaned and covered her face. Cass went deaf to them.

"Pakhba," she instructed as the golden haze overtook her vision, "keep Rana off me and Vamshi safe."

Giving the order in a flat, strong monotone sent a thrill through Cass. For the first time in her life, with her feet slowing ascending from the desert sand, the Script hovering with her, Cass felt in control. Strong. Sure.

"It's a story?" she said to Pakhba, who floated next to him. "About Apophis. Just like the one the lore master told us."

Someone grabbed her ankle. For one second, the golden sight wavered and Cass looked down. Pakhba shouted at her to focus or she'd fall. She felt it too. The moment she took her eyes off the script of the obelisk, she dipped and the sun blazed back into her black and gold vision.

"Rana sees," Cass whispered. Her voice sounded smooth, deep, like a huge brass bell echoing in a cave she couldn't see.

"As one does," the dragon replied, his voice dipping in melancholy. "Sometimes, people forget what one sees."

Cass frowned, but kept her eyes locked on the script to not fall again. She took in the story of Apophis, hearing it in the lore master's voice. Then she hovered over the top. The rest of the world had vanished into the golden haze, but the black obelisk stood out in stark contrast. At the top, a decorative ring was chiseled into the port of the onyx. Curious, Cass touched it, wondering if that would be enough to hold her in place. She had a weird feeling it would. Then she looked up.

Her breath flew from her lungs, snatched by the sight that greeted her. The hissing of gently shifting sand filled her ears. The dunes before her glowed just as golden as the sight. But nestled in the sand, a huge, ornate temple rose. Gorgeous, duo pylons rose to create the facade of the temple. They depicted a relief of Thoth facing front.

"Oh, how strange," Cass whispered, never once having seen an Egyptian image depicting a front-facing character. Thoth held his hand above his head, calling on something above she couldn't see. Around his feet, coiled up to his thighs, was a great serpent of some kind. On the other pylon, Ra and Anubis stood back to back, fending off a hooded serpent with three eyes.

Behind the pylons, Cass saw flashes of the hypostyle hall and the thick, golden enclosure walls. But the image slithered, made entirely out of moving sand. It glowed like a ghost. Behind the temple, a great, glittering pyramid jutted up, piercing the sky with its sharp edges.

"That's where we need to head to," she said to Pakhba. "The burial chamber will be right under the peak of the pyramid. If we can find the chapel and the offering hall, we'll be on the right track." She tried to recall the structure of such things from one of her classes. Her teacher then had driven home how the tombs were not like in the movies: they didn't have traps laid out, riddles to solve, sphinxes that needed answers or could see your true heart that you had to pass. But somehow, Cass doubted this temple-tomb would be so empty.

"Help me?" she asked Pakhba.

"It's what I'm here for," he whispered.

Finally, taking her eyes away from the ghost of the temple, the sands still shifting and hissing in her ears, Cass took the bracelet off her wrist, and slid it over the small point of the obelisk. It snapped into the indent there and clicked.

"Let's away," Pakhba said with some urgency. He touched Cass, and they quickly hovered towards the ground.

When they landed, the earth rumbled.

"Move, move!" Cass shouted, waving her arms for Vamshi and Rana to run even further back. The other two women turned and dashed. Cass looked back over her shoulder to see the obelisk turning like a screw. She cursed in fear and looked forward again to run faster.

Once Pakhba stopped, she did too, and spun around to watch. The onyx spire rotated slowly, steadily sinking into the sand. As it did, a familiar set of pylons rose behind it. Sand cascaded down the reliefs, rushing like a dusty waterfall. Then the ground split. An opening tore the desert wide, sinking in a perfect rectangle. The falling earth didn't stop though and rushed to meet Cass.

She cried out, but didn't move fast enough. Tumbling down, she rolled head over heels down a long set of golden steps, walls rising on either side of her. Pakhba called her name, but the roaring of the rising temple and the rushing of the sand cut out his words.

Wind rushed past her, blinding her with whipping granules. She covered her eyes with her arms, but peeked through them, forward. The door to the temple presented itself, farther down the ritualistic entrance hall. Above her, the towering walls cut off the sun directly, making a shadow cut a hard angle across the remainder of the steps. She realized that if the sun had been at exactly noon, it would have shone directly into the temple door.

In an instant, everything stilled and went quiet. Cass became very aware of her loud breathing. She even heard herself blink. The smooth sandstone amplified her fearful breaths.

Before her lay the dark, yawning entrance to the ancient temple of Thoth.

CHAPTER 16: THE DUAT

Cass squinted into the pitch blackness. The longer she looked at the dark entrance to the temple-tomb, the more she felt like a thousand eyes looked back. She got the distinct impression something moved under the sandy floors. *No, not moving,* she thought. *Flowing.*

A rushing didn't greet her ears, the muggy smell of underground water flowing didn't rise. Something else told her of movement beneath the surface.

Swallowing hard, she whispered, "Mehen?"

Nothing hissed back.

Now holding her breath, she breathed even more softly, "Apophis?"

The softest, most gentle rumble she'd ever heard in her life drifted up to her. The temperate rumble made every hair on her body stand up. Gasping, she turned to come face to face with Pakhba. The dragon's little face creased in determination.

"Well done, Cassandra," he hummed.

The shouting and running of Vamshi and Rana quickly dispelled the fear of the dark stillness. The other two women rushed down the steps, the sun on their backs.

"I knew you'd break your limbs," Vamshi cried, swatting Pakhba out of her way and hugging Cass tight.

"If I had, you'd be killing me," Cass grunted, gratefully prying Vamshi's arms off her. She faced Rana, ready to lie the little blue and gold hovering dragon away. Instead, the adventurous woman eyed him with a look that said, 'I knew it.'

"Pakhba, you know Rana," Cass said, waving her hand from one to the other. "Rana, this is Pakhba. My guardian, familiar, guid dragon-thing."

"He knows me?" Rana asked, pulling flashlights from her pack and handing them out.

Cass nodded, sheepishly taking the flashlight. "He's been with us the whole time." She scanned their guid. "You're taking this really well."

Rana smiled, upholstering her handgun from its hiding place on her side and moving to lead the way. "I've been well trained, American. I've seen things happen that shouldn't be allowed on this earth. Terrible and awful things. A little golden dragon is a nice change of pace."

Relief and a swirl of confusion splashed into Cass as she fell in step with Vamshi and entered the tomb's facade. She was glad Rana had reacted the way she did, but also felt sorry that whatever she had witnessed in her lifetime had made her so accepting and calm. Truth be told, that cool head of hers had saved Cass a lot of hassle so far.

The entry hall to the tomb angled down. The walls shimmered with faded paintings and shallow reliefs that had once been vibrant. Cass scanned it, looking for familiar scripts. To her surprise, some jumped out. She focused, willing the Script to grow and expand as it did when she read it. It did, but this time, as the golden sight overtook her, a voice whispered to her.

Her eyes watered and something hot and thick dripped down her face. The lights from the flashlights dissipated.

What am I reading? she wondered. *I need to find Thoth and get the catalyst.*

Someone called out behind her. She realized, but only vaguely, that she'd walked—or floated—ahead of the other two. She must be in complete darkness. The smell of the tomb suddenly hit her. Dust. Decay. And something that somehow smelled like cold, old, death.

For the first time, clear words came to Cass along the walls. The Script never came in full sentences except that one about the motherless words. This was just like that. The walls read, *Honor the gods, be humble of heart, carry Ra's light.*

"Enough with the riddles!" Cass shouted. Instantly, the golden sight vanished like a flash of lightning. Her stomach flipped as she fell.

And kept falling.

With a sudden scream, Cass realized she had floated into the labyrinth of the tomb while using the golden sight. She'd gone right out over a broken bridge, following the words on the walls. Just when she thought she'd not survive the fall, her body slapped hard against the cold water. The deep pool enveloped her, instantly chilling her. She panicked but realized no current ripped at her. No waves tried to tug her under.

Kicking madly, she broke the surface and gasped. Above her, Rana and Vamshi called down, blinding her with their lights.

"I'm fine," Cass called up, treading water successfully now. She looked around. The walls around her were perfectly circular.

"It's a well," Vamshi shouted down. "I can see the whole opening up here."

Cass spun in the surprisingly cold water to take in the pit. More hieroglyphs, runes, and Script covered every inch of the round walls. "There's writing down here," she called up. "I can try to read it."

A few moments of silence passed from above as she scanned the walls. Then Rana asked, "Can't you just float out? With that gold light?"

"I'm trying," Cass replied. But then she remembered: if she knew what she wanted, the magic didn't seem to work the same way. Being a Vedic meant doing what was required, not what one desired. So she emptied her mind and studied the wall. "It says..." she called up, frowning, wondering if she read it right. "It says that the tomb is a meeting place. Or..." She waited for the feeling of taking in the Script to fill her. It only did slightly. "A way between. The tomb is a passage between our mundane world..." She stopped, hoping she had misread the word. But the Script never lied.

"What?" Vamshi called down, finally taking a long coil of rope out of her pack. "A passage between our world and what?"

Cass gulped. "The Duat." She looked around, suddenly shivering. Normally, hearing about the Egyptian world of the dead wouldn't have put fear in her. It would have filled her with wonder. But this time, having seen the things she had, and having experienced the magic she had, she didn't doubt the validity of that sentence. "The river of souls," she whispered, suddenly looking down into the dark water. "Get me out!" she screamed up.

Above her, Vamshi and Rana scrambled to find something to tie the rope to.

"Just toss is," Vamshi called and the end of the rope launched into Cass's view.

She scrambled to the side of the well, not sure how deep it was, and reached up for the falling rope. It didn't reach her. Desperate, she dove under the water to check on the depth. The moment she did, she wished she hadn't. The dim light from above illuminated a black, smokey form. Cass screamed into the water and tried to back away. The thing turned and looked up. It was human-shaped, but lacked almost any discernible features. Still, she felt the things frighten at her exclamation. A sort of sorrow washed over her from it. This made her pause.

The black smoke figure didn't move, just floated. The longer she stared, the more she saw it had a physical form as well. Black wisps around it gave it that foggy quality.

What are you? she wondered.

As if hearing her, the thing held its hands out, spreading its fingers to show her it had once been human. Even as the water gently moved, the dead shadow did not. It was stuck right where she guessed it had died.

I'm sorry, she thought, realizing it meant her no harm and even if it did, it wouldn't move. *It's like you're between the Duat and the living world. I wish I could help you move on.*

The still quiet of the water helped her keep calm. She prepared to paddle back to the surface when the shadow person held its hand up again. Curious, she looked. It pointed further down. Cass nodded, went up for air and ignored Vamshi's shouts, and dove back down. She followed the thing's directions and found a discolored portion of the wall. A single, gray brick above a painted scene of a river of souls. Script wound around the hieroglyphs, hidden in the painting. One set wound up the body of a man with the head of a long-beaked bird. It told her to say a word. Frowning, she looked for it.

Akh.

The sound appeared in her mind. *The place between the Duat our world,* she thought. Opening her mouth, filling it with the cold, dead water, she choked, but got the world out.

Even under the water, she felt the temple rumble. It shook once, and a grinding started. The gray brick started to protrude further from the well wall. Cass grunted in shock and realized the water had begun to drain. Panicking, she swam to the moving brick that was now a beam sticking out of the wall and climbed on top before the water dropped too low. Looking back, she caught the shadow person fade as the water dropped. Knowing the soul most likely still remained, she wished she could help set it free. If only she'd run into Anubis, she'd tell him he missed one and he deserved to enter the field of reeds.

"How are you doing that?" Vamshi shouted, looking down, red-faced and out of breath.

"Look!" Cass pointed. More gray beams spun out of the wall, creating some dangerous, but obvious, steps all the way up to the top. Looking down, she saw another antechamber and a dark, blue paint lined door way. "I think I found the way we're supposed to go," she called up.

Vamshi took a lot of coaxing from Cass and Rana, but eventually climbed down the well and the stairs that Cass had discovered. Slightly cold, Cass moved forward with trepidation. Pakhba had returned to the golden bracelet before she could ask any questions. The image of the shadow soul loomed in the front of her mind.

Rana took the lead, carefully guiding them down dark corridors covered in sand and dust. "Did you know dust is man-made?" she asked as they passed an army of sandstone statues of ancient Egyptian soldiers. "It's human particles."

Cass and Vamshi shared a worried glance, taking in the dust-covered statues. Every one of them had a thick layer of soft, gray dust covering them.

They hiked for a few more minutes before Cass stopped and insisted on getting out the Dragon Script and reading to see if she could find a map. Rana agreed and found a closed off alcove for them to rest in. She ordered Vamshi to look around and find anything that might burn to make a small campfire. Vamshi didn't wander off far, but did come back with a few handfuls of what looked like old paper and a few tiny sticks. Rana used her skills and soon had a small, bright fire going in the alcove. That's when Cass looked up and took in the room.

She gulped. "It's a tomb." She pointed for the others to look around. "Vaulted roof. Guardian statues. And there." She pointed to the center, a few yards away. A long, low-rise sarcophagus rested on the ground.

"Is it a king?" Vamshi asked.

Cass shook her head, propping the Script up on her knees like she had before. "Pharaohs would be deeper into the tomb. This would have been a trusted friend, a warrior, or maybe a priest. There are probably more." She eyed the sarcophagus, half expecting the dead soul inside to hover out and greet her. Or worse.

Silence fell as she dried up a little thanks to the fire and tried to decipher some of the Script. She came to the part again that had been a combination of the Codex and the Script. It was still gibberish, but clear to see. She flipped a few pages further to where they were blank. She'd thought that once she was here, they'd fill out. But nothing. Nothing came into view like the words on the walls or the Script hidden in the painting of the well.

"Oh, my god!" she shouted into the darkness, making Vamshi and Rana jump. "It's Akh!"

Vamshi rolled to look over her shoulder at the words she couldn't see. "You mean Ankh? As in the cross of life?"

"No," Cass gasped, her heart thudding into her chest. "Akh was the word that made the steps appear. It was hidden in the robes of a figure I could hardly make out. It was a man with the head of a long-beaked bird."

"Thoth!" Vamshi exclaimed, rising up to stand on her knees. "The motherless god. With the catalyst!"

"Exactly," Cass said, joining her enthusiasm. She flipped back to the jumbled Script. "It's a cipher. Akh is the keyword for this part of the Script." She pointed to the symbol in the book she knew the other two could not see. "With the bits of the Codex that are not destroyed, the Script was incomplete. Together, and with the catalyst word we will read..." She trailed off, flipping back and forth between the encrypted passages and the one place Akh appeared.

Once she understood, the Script almost moved on the pages, becoming readable. But then, it shifted into an inking outline of squares, lines, and circles.

"It's a map!" she screeched in triumph. As the lines came into view, part of her excitement evaporated. The word, Akh, meant that place where their world and the world of the dead met. "We need to be careful," she said solemnly. She met Rana's and Vamshi's eyes over the fire. "You've seen what this place is like. We don't know what else might be waiting for us, the deeper we go." She swallowed. "I don't blame you if you want to turn back."

"Hell, no," Vamshi cut in. They both looked at Rana.

Their eccentric guid shrugged. "You know where I stand. Dragons and mummies are preferable. So..." She tossed a couple sticks into the fire. "Those people at the hotel?"

"Ah." Cass turned her face up from the Dragon Script and its slowly emerging map. "The Future."

Rana frowned. "Or you could tell me now so I can protect you."

"No," Cass laughed. "They're an organization called The Future." She touched the golden bracelet on her wrist. "They seem to be people who have hunted down the four dragons for centuries."

"*Four* dragons?" Rana asked, her brows raising.

Cass nodded, biting her lip. "Yeah. The one here is called Mehen. The Coiled One. She's one The Future hasn't been able to find—"

"In some time." Pakhba appeared in an elegant curl of smoke from the bracelet. He eyed Rana and then launched into telling her about his old master, the enchanter, who had scattered the dragons and their secrets to the four winds, hiding them. "The Future, and Meredith Navarre, have been underground for some time," he said in a deep, dramatic timber. "I don't know what made them resurface, coming after Mehen and Tianlong. Those were two they did not find last time. But they had half under their control. Using a young ward of the magisterium as their Vedic. But... he wasn't meant to be." Pakhba's face fell. "A Vedic cannot be trained. They are not chosen."

Rana's eyes flicked to Cass. "You?"

Cass nodded and laughed dryly. "That's me. Little Miss Not Chosen. Apparently, my confusion about my purpose in life was some magical calling to this thing." She tapped the Script. Even as she said it, she wondered if—during the adventures of seeking out the dragons—she decided it was her quest to find them. Would that make her no longer worthy?

"So," Rana asked, frowning, "if they're coming after you, chances are—" She stopped, eyes wide.

Cass heard it too. Someone—a lot of someones—were coming down the stairs to the tomb. Scooping up handfuls of sand, Cass and Rana doused the fire. Vamshi grabbed all three packs and scurried to the other side of the tomb and sarcophagus, where another archway led out. Cass didn't have to be told who those rushing footsteps belonged to.

"Hurry," she hissed, grabbing her pack from Vamshi and slinging it onto her back. "We need to get into the next section, and then I'll look at the map."

CHAPTER 17: RIVER OF SOULS

Cass spit venomously as she passed through thick, dusty cobwebs into an almost utterly dark section of the labyrinth. They trailed on her hands, getting in her eyes as she pushed through an archway. They'd ran in almost near pitch blackness to get away from the marching footsteps. Cass kept jogging until Rana grabbed her by the pack, jerking her back several feet.

"What the hell?" Cass hissed, falling onto the stone ground.

Rana held her finger to her lips, shushing her. Vamshi crouched down next to Cass and listened. The footfalls were far away, but the air was so dry and cold and the stone so still that the sound carried all the way to them.

"Maybe five of them," Rana whispered. "One is shuffling along."

"Hurt?" Cass asked, hoping the guy with the tattooed arms maybe stepped in a trap that snapped his ankle.

Rana shook her head. "Hesitating. Also." She pointed ahead to where she'd grabbed Cass back from. "Stairs."

Squinting, Cass rolled onto her knees and stretched her

neck out like a meerkat looking over the dunes. It was hard to see, but she spotted huge, wide-open stairs before her. Banisters made of stone or maybe granite arched off elegantly on either side into the dark. Cass looked back at the Script. A small image of a flickering fire appeared for a moment.

Cautiously, and without speaking, she got up and walked to the edge. She pulled her tiny survival pack off her belt and took out the flint and steel. Something in the air reeked the closer she got to the stairs. She inhaled deeply, then instantly regretted it. She coughed, but covered her mouth, trying to stifle the smell. Gasoline, or something like it, filled the air. She hesitated with the flint and steel.

Pakhba appeared by her right hand and stayed her as well. "Wait," he whispered. "I am not sure you will be able to bear what you might see."

"What's down there?" Cass asked, looking into the darkness. "Look." She pointed to the top of the banister. A huge basin hewn from the stone waited there. Something softly dripped into it. "I think it's a lighting system. The Script showed me fire."

"Cassandra," Pakhba said gravely, "you have passed beyond. These tombs are the Akh. The place between the Duat and the living world." He frowned, his little golden eyes turning darkly serious. "You may not have noticed. If you go forward and light the way, the way back will be shut."

With hesitation, Cass turned her head to look back at the archway they'd come through with the spider webs. It looked as though a black curtain had been laid over it.

She nodded and turned back to face it. When she approached it, no sound came from it. It reminded her of when she was a kid and would turn off the TV. Sudden darkness and soundlessness. She raised her hand and put it through. Her fingertips, then her hand up to her wrist, vanished into black.

"Holy shit," Vamshi whispered from behind her, watching. "What is that?"

"The way out," Pakhba whispered. He faced the other two. "You have come deep. I know what lies below in that darkness. Once the lights are lit," he waved his foreclaw to the basin of fluid, "there is only one way back."

Cass and Vamshi waited for him to go on, but he didn't.

"To have our hearts judged," Rana said solemnly. "Weighed on the scales against a feather." She looked away, face dark.

"So?" Cass asked, returning to the basin. "What does it mean exactly?"

Pakhba floated towards her. "It means, Cassandra, that should you be found unworthy..."

She understood. "Oh." She looked back to where the Script was propped open on the ground, the map held steady in a perpetual state of revealing. "I think," she started, frowning. Sure of herself, she said, "I think we can do it. If nothing else, I have faith that this Vedic magic will help. Plus, once we have Mehen, she can lead us out. As is her task."

Vamshi shuddered. "I can't wrap my head around it. It seems so unreal. I don't understand what it means, so... I guess I'm down with that."

They both turned to Rana.

Their mysterious guid fell into a gloom Cass had never seen the likes of before. Rana's normally sparkling brown eyes went dull. She was introspecting so hard that she almost sunk into the earth.

"I've done certain things," she whispered, her voice cracking and hoarse. "I don't see my heart being weightless."

Cass glanced one last time into the darkness. "I can't stop. I don't even know how great the stakes are, but I know I cannot stop."

"Wait. What if those thugs can get in, but don't get out?" Rana asked.

Cass'd thought of that. "That Navarre woman isn't here. Pakhba told me about a wizard who was part of their creed. They have magic I don't. Or don't know about. They're not just thugs in suits. I can't..." Her sister, Ella, and her mom and dad enjoying a day on the shore flashed into her mind. "I can't leave it up to chance; can't give up. I was chosen. But," she nodded to Rana, "I won't make anyone follow me."

The three women stood in silence for a moment. Thinking they'd made up their minds, Cass reached for the Script to pick it up. When she held her hand out to it, it slammed shut and zoomed into her hand with a hard thud. She gasped, half laughing, half freaking out. Vamshi smiled, eyes wide.

"Oh, what the hell," Rana grunted. She pushed past the other two with her own flint and steel in hand.

"Wait," Cass cried.

Rana struck the tools together hard above the fluid in the basin. Fire exploded into the air, blinding them all in a flash so bright Cass fell backwards. Vamshi screamed, and Rana cursed loudly. Pakhba tumbled over in the air, spinning madly. The fire died down, then flowed down the banister.

"I knew it," Cass mused, scooting to the edge of the stairs and watching the fire flow down the fluid in the crevices.

The light lit up the entire room. The ceiling loomed too far above to be more than an orange glow. The fluid flowed all throughout the room. Torches lit up and soon the whole, enormous cave-like room glowed hot with fire. When it reached further down, a loud hissing and groaning went up.

"My god," Vamshi whispered, pulling Cass up.

Below, a green river glowed, flowing like liquid emerald. It made no sound. Within its gentle waves and depths, white and black forms floated down. Cass recognized the smokey, ethereal forms.

"Souls," she whispered. "Ghosts. In the river. Can you see them?"

Vamshi nodded. "The water is so bright. Like a glow stick."

"Why are they here?" Cass asked. "If this is the other side, shouldn't they be where they belong?"

Pakhba landed softly on her shoulder. "They are lost." He sounded confused. The little dragon swung his head around as if looking for something.

"What is it?" Cass asked, gripping the straps of her pack. "What's wrong?"

"They shouldn't be here. You are correct," he mused. He looked across to the other side. "Where is Anubis? Why does he let them wonder?"

Cass's chest tightened. "Apophis. He's already awake. With Mehen asleep, he'd have free range." She glared into the bright river. "He might control them."

"Zombies?" Vamshi cried, fumbling on her belt for her bowie knife. "I did not sign up for zombies."

"Fear not," Pakhba whispered. "They may let us pass."

"They will or else," someone shouted from behind them.

The four of them spun around, completely taken off guard. There, just on the inside of the black archway, were the familiar blonde woman, the man with the tattoos called Markus, Shades, and a third Cass had never seen before. Between Markus and Shades was a slumped figure Cass had not expected to see.

"Charlie?" she gasped, taking an instinctive step towards them, hand out.

"Stay back," the woman snapped, pulling a revolver from her hip. She didn't cock the hammer.

Charlie leaned heavily on Shades. He had a bloody lip, a

dark purple bruise on his cheekbone, and a black eye. His usually lovely, wavy hair was matted with sweat.

"You hurt him?" Cass growled, gripping the Script so tight she wished the magic would seep into her.

The woman smirked. "We needed to know where you were going. You're not always hard to track down, but recently you've been very slippery. So we had to convince him a little."

"I'm fine, Cass," Charlie said, weakly pulling at Shade's grip. "But if it's all the same to you, I think you should tell them what they want to know."

Cass caught Rana move out of the corner of her eye.

"Don't," the blonde woman quipped, training her gun on Rana. "It's going to be very simple, Vedic." She turned back to Cass. She took a handful of Charlie's messy hair and yanked his head back hard, making him wince. She placed the barrel of her gun under his chin.

Tears brimmed in Cass's unblinking eyes against her will. She didn't feel like crying, her body just reacted with tears. Her face burned, though.

"Fine," she snapped. "You won't get out, anyway. The only way is to get past Anubis."

"Elena?" Shades asked softly, arching a quizzical brow.

The blonde woman, Elena, smirked. "We have our ways."

"Of course you do," Cass mocked. "But you need me to get there."

Elena nodded to Shades. "Jude, take the girl."

A sudden scurrying and scuffling broke out. Charlie pulled against Markus and Shades. The other man, Jude, dove at Vamshi. Rana shouted and she and Elena got into a stand-off, guns leveled at each other's faces. Vamshi screamed as Jude grappled her to the ground. Markus grappled both Charlie's arms behind his back and Shades came at Cass.

Cass took one step back, angling herself. She raised her right hand and a pulsing, orange light ignited in her palm.

Gasping, she turned to look. Tendrils of light whipped out from the golden bracelet and converged between her fingers, making what looked like a tiny sun in her palm.

"Elena!" Shades shouted, stopping his pursuit of Cass.

"Back off!" Cass roared. "You've nowhere to go but in." Everyone stopped struggling. "We can't go back out the way we came," she went on, gasping for breath as her chest tightened. "Follow me or you're trapped. I read the Script. I know you know how powerful it is, so I don't have to explain that to you." She scanned the Future thugs, the light in her hand wobbling as she shook. "You need me and you need the Script. So do as I say and we all get out. But we have bigger problems. Apophis is awake."

Markus, Jude, and the other Future members exchanged glances.

"I see you know what that means." She found herself whispering now. "I know I can't stop you from following me. I know you want Mehen for yourselves. So for now..." She swallowed hard. "For now, you follow me."

Elena shot her icy eyes at Rana's fiery ones. Then she met Cass's eyes across the room. "You are too right, Cass. Even if we knew where Mehen rested, we couldn't wake her." Her eyes shot a glare at Charlie, who hadn't moved yet. "But don't expect me to let you walk out of here."

Even though sweat drenched her body, Cass shivered. "I get it. But let Charlie go."

The woman smirked with her too-bright red lips and flicked her gun at Markus to signal him to let Charlie go. He did, shoving him towards Cass. She caught him and met his sad eyes to let him know she would find a way out. He looked down, defeated.

"I got this," she whispered, gently placing her hand on his bruised cheek.

He closed his eyes and rested his forehead against hers. "I know you do. I'm... I'm sorry."

She looked up, her eyes lingering too long on his lips as she did. Her face seared in embarrassment. "You didn't do anything wrong. I got you mixed up in this. So I'll get you out."

His blue eyes lit up. "Cass..." he murmured, placing his hand on the back of her neck.

Cass quickly looked away, sensing his intention. *Hell, no. Not here,* she thought. *Not with those dicks and Vamshi watching.*

But soon.

She smiled up at him and took a deep breath. To everyone else, she said, "We cannot cross the river. Something tells me our living souls wouldn't do well in there."

Opening the Script, she walked to the edge of the river, the glow almost blinding her. The Script told her the way out was on the other side.

"But there's no way over," she said to the book.

Vamshi stepped up beside her. "So let's go out the side door." She pointed.

Stammering, Cass looked to the side. Several yards down the bank, an orange archway opened into a darker room. "All right, smarty pants. Good job using your looking eyes."

"Better than using my kissing lips." Vamshi smiled and pulled ahead of Cass.

Feeling much lighter than just thirty seconds ago. Cass motioned for the others to follow her. She added up the troupe: four Future. Her, Vamshi, Charlie, and Rana. It was four on four. Only for them, Rana was the single person with any training. They couldn't take them. Someone would get hurt.

She looked down at her fingers where the light had glowed just minutes before. No, she wasn't supposed to use magic.

Pakhba had warned her. So for now, she had to lead the Future to Mehen.

A narrow, gold-encrusted hall filled with images of the gods led them to a room the size of a theater. Cass stopped and looked down at the Script. Tiny, circular Script scrawled over the bottom, underneath the map that showed the doorway they stood in.

"Why are you stopping?" Elena barked, regripping her gun threateningly.

Charlie gently nudged Cass, questioning her with his face.

"We're in their territory now," Cass announced, cautiously looking ahead. "I think we should proceed with caution. The way they'd want us to."

"What do you mean?" Charlie asked.

She pointed to the walls they past. "Notice anything about the way all the images are facing towards this room?"

The others looked at the walls in the beams of their flashlights and the flickering fire. "No," Elena snapped.

"Enough of this," the grunt called Jude snapped. He reached forward, grabbed Charlie hard by the scruff of his neck, and shoved him forward.

"Don't!" Cass screamed. She dropped the Script and lunged forward, hand out. She barely caught Charlie's right arm and pulled with all her might. The two of them jerked backwards, him falling onto her. Jude lost his grip.

"Move it," the thug growled back at them, taking out his own black handgun. "Elena, we don't have time for this."

Cass clutched Charlie hard, willing him to not get up and follow Jude. Rana and Vamshi stood back, bodies tense and watching. Jude scoffed and turned, entering the massive room. Guessing what would come next, Cass braced herself.

The temple rumbled and shook. Pieces of rubble fell onto the group. Jude froze. He turned around. His face turned ashen black, and soft wisps of smoke wafted up from his tall frame. His eyes turned orange and something akin to embers smoldered in his now-visible veins.

"This doesn't feel good," he coughed, black smoke belching out from his mouth.

"What the hell?" Elena gasped, running forward, hands outstretched to grab Jude.

"Don't!" Cass shouted again. "Don't touch him. He didn't enter the room right. It's a test. I told you." For some reason, seeing the man smolder before their eyes made tears come to hers.

Elena stopped but stuttered, terrified. She whipped around, looking for some way to help her comrade. Jude raised his leg to take a step, but it fell in two, soft cinders pouring out from the break below his knee.

"Elena?" he whispered. His body fell, landing in a pile of soft, warm ash.

Shades reached up, grabbing Markus by the back of his collar and yanking him back hard. Markus stumbled from the pull then gave Shades a "glad that wasn't us" look.

The blonde woman rounded on Cass, eyes red-rimed and glowering. "You knew!" she growled, raising her gun to aim at the couple tangled on the floor.

"Stay back," Rana growled, raising her own gun once again at the other woman.

"I tried to tell you!" Cass whispered, standing up and bringing Charlie with her. "You have to play by their rules." She pointed to the gods. She turned to pick up the Script, but it was gone. Shades held it.

"Get going," he ordered Cass easily, smirking. Markus coyly grinned next to his friend, looking smug.

Cass felt Charlie touch her hand behind her. Nodding, she faced the doorway where Jude's ashes had dissipated a little. "The images show that when approaching a god or a pharaoh, whom they believed were incarnations of the gods, they present their hearts."

"Oh," Vamshi whispered. "Enter the rooms with your left foot."

"Exactly," Cass confirmed. She took a deep breath. "Let me go first. Just to be sure."

Charlie grabbed her hand.

"I'm the Vedic," she said, pulling away and pushing past Elena. "They shouldn't harm me."

She toed the line between the hallway and the hidden room beyond. Despite the flashlight in her hand, she couldn't see further in. *They won't let me see until I make the choice,* she realized.

Vedics are meant to work on faith, Pakhba supplied in her mind. *To do as they are told.*

Cass bit her bottom lip, looked up from the floor into the darkness, and stepped in. The moment she did, the room burst into light. A domed, gray-stone chamber vaulted overhead by fifty feet. Green vines and bright-colored flowers growing from them cascaded in floral curtains. The rushing of a blue waterfall deafend her and filled the chamber with watery, humid air. The others stumbled in behind her, gasping at the sudden sight.

"Where's the exit?" Elena snapped.

Realizing she didn't see a door, Cass frowned and cautiously started a round of the chamber. The walls, floor, and ceiling were covered in Script and hieroglyphs. Reading the floor, she carefully followed a strain of Script that only made partial sense. Turning, she held her hand out to Shades.

"Give it to me. I need to read what's next," she pressed when he hesitated. Once she had it, she waited for the words to come. Her vision turned gold again. "It's about something buried?" she read out loud. "No, more like the earth. And something about the stars. Or sky." She looked up. Just more

Script waited above. The ceiling spoke of giving something up. Sacrifice.

Frowning, she looked back down. Now she saw them: across the chamber floor were pathways leading to four large, ornate tiles that had once been brightly colored. Faded chips of green, red, blue, and yellow hardly remained.

"Vam," she called. "Stand on that tile. The octagonal one." She moved to the yellow. "Charlie, green. Rana red."

Once they all stood on a tile, The Future looking in confusion, the waterfall gurgled and choked. It sputtered down to a mere trickle, revealing an opening behind it. A golden sandstone door with a hieroglyphic eye waited, dripping with water.

"Whoa," Vamshi smiled, looking back. "That's cool."

Elena, Shades, and Markus headed towards it.

"You won't find anything," Cass called. "The door's locked." She moved off her tile, and the water spilled down again in full force.

Elena jumped back, cursing. "Then what do we do?"

Cass thought. She wasn't sure. They needed four people to stand on the tiles to make the door accessible. There was no way they'd be able to walk under that many gallons of water falling fifty feet. They'd be crushed. If only Jude hadn't turned himself to smoldering ash minutes ago, she'd have The Future stand on them.

She spoke out loud to think. "Only I can see the rooms, I think. It's like they don't exist until I walk into them. They're emptiness, nothing, until I see them."

"So you have to go first?" Elena asked mockingly.

"Yeah," Cass answered, serious, moving back onto the tile to stop the water flow. "Once I'm inside, the room is real. But this one is closed off still." She looked back up at the Script on the ceiling. "Not stars," she whispered so just she and Pakhba could hear. "Sun. Light." She looked back down at her hand where she'd had that ball of magical light before. "But what does that have to do with…" She shook her head. "No, we have to invoke the god to open the door. That Script means to call to a god. From earth to sky. Calling to heaven, whatever."

"It's the eye of Horus," Markus shouted back to her. "What does that mean? We call to Horus?"

Cass turned back to the locked golden door. Squinting, she inspected it. Yes, a huge, hieroglyphic eye covered the middle third. The eye was a left eye, the looping accent hanging off to the left corner. Before she could speak, Markus faced the door.

"Horus," Markus shouted like an imbecile. "Open this door."

"That's not—" Cass started, but her voice was cut off by a loud, thunderous crack. A deep sound she could not describe boomed through the chamber, followed by a blinding flash of sunlight.

Markus screamed and fell out of the way, tackled by Shades. The two somersaulted one over the other from the sheer force of Shades' powerful reaction. Where Markus had been standing, a black scorch blasted out over the chamber floor. If Shades hadn't tackled Markus, he'd be less than the pile of ashes behind them.

"What the hell?" Markus shouted, shoving Shades off and bearing down on Cass. "You lied?"

"No," she snapped, slamming the Script close. She thrust a finger at the door. "That's *not* the eye of Horus."

"Then what is it?" Elena barked.

"It won't matter if I tell you," Cass replied, feeling more at ease and for once in control. "I have to enter the room. Someone has to stay back here and hold the water.

Elena suddenly smirked, and a look of overbearing confidence filled her frame suddenly. "I doubt it, Vedic. I know a thing or two about the Script as well. I've studied it all my life." She moved around the chamber towards Charlie. "I think once you enter that room, it will remain open. That's how this temple works, remember? Only forward. Never back."

Cass stammered, but the woman had a valid point. The temple would let anyone in once the Vedic crossed over. But it wouldn't let them out.

"I don't know," she sputtered.

"Let's try it." Elena smiled at Charlie, then kicked his leg with a savage cry.

Charlie screamed and fell over, hitting the stone ground hard. Cass gasped, but held her ground, unwilling to get closer. Elena grabbed Charlie by his hair and dragged him back onto the center of the tile. He clutched his leg, moaning loudly, curled over in pain.

"Now," Elena sighed, smoothing her hair back. "Open the door, Vedic."

"All right, all right!" Cass shouted, strapping the Script to her belt, letting it hang onto her hip. "Someone has to stand here."

Elena jerked her head towards Markus.

Unsure and still shaken from the god-like smite he'd almost caught with his face, Markus met Cass on her tile. They stepped off and on, one foot at a time, to not break any pressure. Cass made sure both Rana and Vamshi were sure before she walked away from them.

"We got this," Vamshi said stoutly, glaring at Elena. Rana nodded wordlessly.

Squaring up to the golden door, Cass marched up to it. She looked up into the huge, engraved eye. It somehow looked like it glared down at her.

"I'm not wrong," she whispered to herself and Pakhba. "The eye of Horus is on the right, the moon. This is the eye of Ra, the sun and left side of the face." She glanced back at

Charlie. Sweat trickled down from under his hair and his eyes locked on to her. She turned back to the door. "I invoke the god Ra," she said as loud as she dared. Nothing happened. She kicked the bottom of the door with her boot. "I'm the Vedic, damn it, open up!"

The sunlight suddenly got cut in half by a crescent-shaped shadow. The room began to darken to a dull gray instantly.

"What have you done?" Elena gasped. Markus began to babble with worry.

Cass squinted up through the round opening in the chamber ceiling. "A solar eclipse," she shouted so everyone could hear. "The sun is being hidden." Her eyes burned, and she looked down to see the circular shadow engulfing the sunlight on the gray stone. When it was halfway gone, the golden door rumbled and sank slowly into the ground, grinding and sending tremors all through the earth.

Unlike the other rooms, Cass could see into this one. It loomed dark, but just as wide open as the chamber she stood in. Inside, over a dozen statues stood along the walls, all facing the center. Each one represented an Egyptian god, their left feet stepping out into the center. Each god held a massive mirror in their hands. Ropes and chains fell behind the mirrors, attached to them, holding them steady. Cass stepped through, examining a single ray of sunlight hitting an altar near the back. A huge set of tarnished gold scales rested on the altar, catching the fading sunlight.

Behind this altar stood a tall, onyx-colored statue of Anubis. Cass froze, thinking she beheld a real being at first. The detail of the fur over his god-like chest looked too real. The striped gold of his nemes looked too clean. The cords of his flail were so detailed, she swore they were made of real leather. She approached, looking into his striking blue eyes shining out of his black-furred jackal face.

"Whoa," Cass breathed, coming closer to the scales. She

eyed them, taking in the ornate details and elegant metal work. She reached out to touch it, just out of curiosity, but stopped and looked up at the Anubis behind the altar. She met its eyes.

It blinked.

Cass screamed so shrill and loud that her throat stung. She stumbled back down the three stone steps that led to the altar and rolled head over heels backwards. Scrambling to her knees, she looked back into the waterfall chamber. The others were frozen. Vamshi was in mid-step, hand outstretched and mouth open to call.

"What...?" Cass looked back at Anubis and watched him slowly tilt his head to the side. "Are you...can you possibly be...?" She couldn't get a full sentence out.

"I am," Anubis murmured softly. His voice was so deep, Cass felt it reverberate in her chest.

Cass couldn't even swear. Her chest constricted so tightly she couldn't breathe to speak even if she wanted to. Anubis stepped out from behind the altar and walked towards where she lay. When he towered over her, she realized he easily stood seven feet tall. She recoiled, fear seeping from her pores.

The god held his hand out to her. "You said you are the Vedic," he said again in his soft, rumbling timber.

"Uh-hu," Cass managed to choke out. She eyed his huge, powerful hand. Making sure to use the hand with the golden bracelet on it, she grasped his. It was warm, soft, but hard with muscle. Yes, he was real. She gasped as he lifted her easily all the way to her feet.

"Then let us weigh your heart before you pass on, Vedic," he said. He led her back to the altar, pulling her along by her hand.

"I—I don't think, that is, I mean, I'm here for Mehen." She stopped when he let go and faced her.

"I know," he replied. "And I want you to pass on." He stood up tall, raising his canine head. He held his left arm out and she saw monstrous scars on his ribs. "Apophis saw you coming in a dream. He awoke and attacked immediately. I lost my cargo to the halls of this tomb."

"The river," Cass mused, finally meeting the god's eyes. "And the ghost in the well?"

"One not unlike you," Anubis replied. He motioned behind him. "Sometimes, when a Vedic is near, the echos of the past Vedic will arise, coming as guardian. a wayfinder."

Cass gulped. "A past Vedic. It came to help me? Will I see more?"

"Perhaps," the god sighed.

The scales had vanished from the altar. Now, a huge version of them loomed on the ground behind. Big enough for her to climb in. Her mouth went dry.

Anubis led her to the massive scales. "When you awakened, Apophis rose, guarding this temple from all who would come, seeking Mehen. The rising of the Vedic's spirit roused him."

"Damn," she mused, looking at the scales. "How do I know if I'm worthy? But, I am, right? I'm Vedic."

Anubis raised his head again, looking down at her with judgment. "Pride does not become a Vedic of the Dragon Script. Nor does channeling the magic of the sun." He gripped her hand and turned her palm over.

She realized he somehow knew she'd almost slung pure sunlight earlier. "But I didn't do that," she said in her own defense. "I don't know how that happened. It wasn't my fault. I know I'm not supposed to use magic."

Once again, the god's chest rose and fell with a patient breath. "Come, then. If you are so innocent."

Anubis gestured to the other side of the large scale, where a tiny, white feather moved in the sunlight. Then, he pointed to this side. Cass scoffed in doubt. Anubis knelt by the lip of the golden plate of the scale and held his hand out to her again. Understanding, Cass took his huge hand, put her foot onto his knee, and stepped up to ascend into the scale. She put her other foot onto the golden plate tentatively, expecting it to drop out suddenly from under her. It didn't. She reached up and grasped the massive chain that held the plate and hauled herself up onto the scale. Still, it didn't move.

The jackal god stepped away, eyeing her seriously. "Do you, Vedic, claim you have done no wrong? That you are worthy of passing through to the chambers of Mehen, waking her, and taking her power into your own?"

The loaded question took Cass by surprise. In the stories she'd read, these kinds of things were just tests, riddles. "Yeah," she said, thinking confidence would win over the god. "I'm here to stop someone terrible from getting the Coiled One."

The chains clinked. A groaning so loud Cass wanted to cover her ears screamed out from the scales. Her side dropped several inches. She cried out and grabbed the chains for support.

"What the hell?" she cried, seeing the feather side rise.

"Have you done no wrong?" Anubis asked again.

Afraid the scales would tilt even more against her favor if she gave the same answer, she said, "Maybe?"

"Such as?" Anubis asked, taking his flail up in his hand from the altar.

Panic surged through Cass. "Umm, I don't know. You mean like cheating on math tests?"

"As Vedic," the god supplied.

Cass sighed in frustration. "I don't know. Maybe? Isn't the point of being a Vedic not to know?"

Anubis shook his head. "It is about acceptance. Perhaps not believing in fate, but not fighting a task that has been presented to you. You were not chosen by any means. But it is you now, Vedic." His eyes softened just a little. "Are you worthy of passing through to the chambers of Mehen, waking her, and taking her power into your own?"

From where she sat, spotlighted in the eclipsing sun, alone on the scale plate, looking down at Anubis, she realized she had to be more honest than ever before. Even if she didn't know what she'd done wrong.

"I might not be," she started. "But I'm the one who can read the Script. There are two other women behind me who are great, though. I don't stand a chance alone. But with Vamshi? I can promise you, we'd try our damndest."

"It is best not to be alone in such a task," Anubis agreed. "But..." He looked away, almost disappointed.

"What do you want from me?" Cass cried, ringing the chains.

The god met her face again. "Perhaps, like the Vedics of old, you must prove yourself by actions. In battle, like a warrior."

Cass gulped, but listened.

"Vedic," Anubis said, making up his mind. "I am in need of aid. That much is obvious to even you. I want only the best to pass, but I have a duty. I cannot let the Duat remain open with Apophis's darkness growing ever stronger. Where there is darkness, the dead will walk. Already Ra is fleeing. Taking the sun with him. It is up to me to make the choice."

He ran his long fingers through the strands of his flail, considering her. "I must let you pass, but in return, I want a promise."

She shifted, a little cautious but curious too. "All right."

"They must all leave," Anubis said. "Take them all with you."

"What?" Cass cried, smirking. "The Future are horrid. Even if they never get their hands on the dragons, they've stalked me, kidnapped Charlie, hurt him to force to me to lead them here. And who knows what they'd do once they have the dragons."

"And what will you do?"

She shook her head. "I have to return them somewhere safe. Hide them. They're not for me to have."

"But they will be for a time." The god eyed her again. "What will you do then?"

Cass bit her lip, frowning. "Put Apophis away, first." She saw his face shift. "Listen, Anubis," she said, getting tired of the trial, "I need Mehen and whatever power she has to help shut Apophis up. I'll need it, as you say, for a time. But..." she growled. "If you let me pass, and don't hold it against me if I channel some dragon magic, I promise to make sure Apophis is gone. You'll be safe. And... I'll take those thugs with me."

Anubis narrowed his blue eyes and raised his head.

The gold plate she stood on shot up into her feet. Her knees buckled, and she fell hard, the scales tipping in her favor. With a loud clang, the plate with the feather hit the chamber grounds. Cass rolled over and looked over the edge. Anubis stood below, offering her his hand again. She took it and slid off the scale, landing hard.

"In that case, Vedic," Anubis said. I will let you pass into the innermost part of this temple. The place where she rests. Where you must speak the word to wake her."

Cass took up the Script in her hand. "I won't let you down."

CHAPTER 18: MEHEN THE COILED ONE

Where the scales had been, a huge sandstone archway rose. The ground rumbled and wind and grit flew into Cass's face. She winced and tried not to breathe in the flying particles. Behind her, a ruckus of voices went up, screaming, shouting, threatening, and calling to her. She turned, but Anubis leapt between her and the others. Vamshi screamed and someone fired a gun. Not to Cass's surprise, Anubis seemed unfazed.

"Go," he said to her. "They must stay behind."

Cass glanced back once more at Vamshi. Her huge brown eyes were locked onto Cass despite the towering canine god before her.

"You've got this, girl," Vamshi called. "Don't worry about us."

The Future thugs had been struck mute, mouths agape. Anubis, the god of the underworld, would be a match for them, right?

"Cassandra?" Pakhba whispered, appearing at her side. "We must away. Quickly. I can smell Apophis."

Facing the sandstone archway, nothing appeared to her. By

now, she knew she had to step through to see beyond. So she did, Pakhba on her shoulder. The moment she stepped through, all sound muffled, then faded away. Like a fire scratching away at wallpaper, the chamber vanished, to be replaced by a resplendent golden room. Perfectly even sand covered the ground and in the center rose the black obelisk from before. Only this time, it shone smooth and flawless. It didn't even reflect the golden hue around it. A single white marble cat statue stood guard near the base. Unsure, Cass stepped towards it, the Dragon Script in her hand.

She flipped it open, and the tome hovered in the air just before her at the perfect height for her read. "I couldn't have gotten here without Anubis," she mused to Pakhba. "I was meant to find him. I had to satisfy his riddle."

"And did you?" the dragon asked.

Cass shrugged. "He let me through. I have this feeling I've done something wrong. Something I'm not supposed to do. But he didn't say what. How am I supposed to know what will damage this quest to find the dragons if I can't find out?"

The little dragon hummed in thought. "Are you sure you don't know?"

Struck with another sense of infuriation, Cass nodded. "Yes. I swear I don't know." She flipped to the last page with visible Script and looked to the blank one across from it. She was perhaps one third of the way through the Script. "Mehen," she called. "I've come to wake you. To take you to safety. But first, the gods need you. Apophis has risen, and he's spreading a darkness. It's contained for now, but I'm afraid if we don't stop him, it will spread. My world can't handle ghosts and zombies, Mehen. I need your help."

Her voice echoed so loudly she almost winced. The Script told her to speak the words she read. "I have no idea how to read these," she told the pages as they blotched and inked in. "What sounds to even make."

"Faith," Pakhba whispered. She glanced over at him and saw he had his eyes closed.

A deep breath calmed her. Then she opened her mouth and whispered. Like before, with the golden sight, her throat filled with sound. It rose up melodious and lyrical from her lips. As she spoke, her body warmed and her heart calmed, as if the golden color filled her very insides. It made her feel invincible, and she swore bright, warm light flickered through her lips. When it hit the obelisk, the golden Script on it lit up once more.

At last, the script stopped, instructing her to call Mehen as the Vedic.

"Mehen!" she shouted in the full, lyrical tone. "I wish for you to arise. Wake and come to me. My wish is my commandment, Mehen!"

A thrill shot through her as the white marble cat leapt to life and paced protective circles around her. A single, molten gold strike of lightning cracked down the center of the obelisk. With a loud snap, it shattered, opening like two double doors. Inside the crackling portal, two golden, slitted eyes appeared. They drew closer and Cass was able to make out the shape of the creature and the face the eyes rested in.

Like a serpent, a white and gold scaled body moved out from the molten portal. A hood like a king cobra flared out from the dragon's head. First, her head slithered through the air and out. Then the heavy body of the serpentine dragon left the portal, waving and hovering in the air in bright, pearlescent coils. The golden highlights shined like pearls.

Once the entirety of the dragon's body left the portal, it snapped closed.

Silence filled the golden room, and Cass realized her mouth hung open. Mehen's lithe body filled with air and then hissed out in a sigh.

"Why have you awakened me?" she moaned in a deep,

feminine voice. Cass swore the dragon blinked lazily and looked a little irritated.

"Mehen?" she asked cautiously. The white cat still stood guard behind her.

"Indeed, that is I," the dragon replied, hovering a little closer to Cass. "I could swallow you whole for waking me, little woman."

Cass gulped and took a step back. The Script followed her, still floating before her. "I'm the Vedic," she tried. "I'm here to rescue you. To hide you."

Mehen arched a scaly brow and smirked, showing a long, silver fang. "I was hidden. I was safe." Her eyes flitted to Pakhba. "One so small follows you."

Cass reached up and touched Pakhba on her shoulder. "He came to me. Because the Dragon Script found me. Listen, ma'am..." She stuttered. Her eminence? Your dragoness-ness? How the hell did one address an all powerful dragon?

Mehen smiled, and something in her golden eye twinkled. She blinked lazily.

Cass went on. "Things have come into my life that are so much bigger than me. I don't know half of what is going on. I do know there are thugs with guns out there who stalked me halfway across the world. They want you."

"Mehen," Pakhba interrupted, floating gently off Cass's shoulder. "They have come. The ones from the tower."

Whatever this meant to the dragon, it wasn't good. The dragon's face twisted in horror, her slitted eyes widening. "Navarre?" she asked in a whisper.

"So we believe," Pakhba replied.

"And Catál?" she asked. "Tianlong? My brothers!" The dragon threw her hooded head back and roared. The ceiling of the obelisk room shook, pieces falling from above.

"Peace!" Pakhba shouted, rising above Cass's head. "They are safe. For now. Navarre never found you or Quezacotl.

Because of this, we believe she is closer to finding you and him."

Mehen calmed and a glittering dragon tear formed in the corner of her golden eye. "What happened, little one? What happened at the tower?"

Excitement rushed through Cass. Finally, she'd get some kind of history. Pakhba never spoke about it much after his first story. He'd refused, just wanting her to read the Script.

"It was Aiken," Pakhba started. "I didn't stop him from releasing Catál and Tianglong. In fact..." Pakhba's head dropped and his hovering catfish whiskers drooped. "By my undying regret, I aided him. Navarre had... grown too strong."

The larger dragon nodded, hissing. "She never knew when she'd reached beyond her place. But Aiken. He was not like her. Why did he waken my brothers?"

"He believed in The Future," Pakhba said. "That you— like me—were meant to be awakened, to have your power poured into them. Into their weapons of domination. They devised ways to take something as small as a scale, a claw, a tooth, and allocate it to their staves, swords, and even to imbue armies."

Something cold and large dropped into Cass's stomach. The blood drained from her face. She opened her mouth to ask for clarification, but the Script flipped its pages, pushing her hair back with the force of the movement. The words Pakhba spoke appeared there, and soon the golden sight took over. It blinded her. Then, in an eruption of fire and lightning, she saw an old stone castle atop a hill. A massive, black tower with cruel points sticking out the top.

A blonde woman in armor red with blood appeared before the castle. Cass felt more than saw that the woman raged at someone in the tower. Aiken. The name hissed through her mind. She held a massive blade that Cass couldn't fathom lifting. But when the woman raised it, she realized a green gem shone in the pommel.

"A dragon tear," she whispered. "Catál."

"Yes," Pakhba said from beyond the golden sight. "Meredith Navarre sought to become what we called an enchantress."

"Like a sorceress?" Cass asked, watching Aiken chase down someone through a dark cave.

"Worse," Pakhba replied. "An enchantress is more dangerous in that she possesses the powers of a siren. A silver tongue, a swayer of minds. Of hearts. She does not simply put a spell on you to do her bidding, but entices you, drawing you to her side by your own will, using the magic sourced from the dragons."

A vision of the medieval sky overwhelmed Cass. A huge, green European dragon with four legs and massive wings cut across the sky, quickly followed by a feathered serpent. They laid waste to the town below.

"Aiken was drawn in to her," Pakhba whispered. "As was I. We were enchanters! We deserved the powers of the dragons more than any humble Vedic. It was our right as those born to thread magic throughout reality. Enchanters had long been feared, hunted even, cast out from the cities. Then one of the lowly folk would crawl to us, begging for a cure for an illness. Asking for a blessing upon their crops."

Pakhba clenched his fists hard, gnashing his teeth and closing his eyes tight. "And we gave in. Again and again we bowed a knee to those not woven with our magic."

"It was ours to give," Mehen cut in, glaring, the single tear still and pearlescent in her eye. "You would not be able to weave magic were it not for us. We should have known our powers would be used to ensnare us. But we trusted mankind too much. Ever since, we have hidden, been subject to the protection of a Vedic. We did this to ourselves, but I can still hate those who take our source."

"But we repented," Pakhba reasoned. "Aiken saw the error of his ways. Knew that the dragons should not be used thusly. And for so long you have not."

"Not since the acolyte of the last pharaoh," Mehen offered.

Cass swallowed. "So the magic comes from you?" She looked up at Mehen and raised her hand, remembering where the light had shone.

"It does," Mehen raised a scaly brow. "Enchanters use our magic. Not Vedics."

"What if just temporarily?" Cass asked. "Like, if I needed to."

"It would taint your validity," Mehen explained. "Our power is not for a Vedic. A Vedic is to shun the power. To remain humble. To protect us from those who would take our power."

At that, another rumble softly rolled through the chamber. Mehen's golden eyes snapped up. A roar came muffled through the wall where Anubis had made the portal.

"I smell the dead," Mehen whispered. "Where is Anubis?"

"Oh, right!" Cass gasped. "That's what I'm talking about. We can't leave yet. Mehen, I ask that you grant me some of your power if I need it. We have to stop Apophis. He's risen and has attacked Anubis and taken Ra. Already the sun is hiding in the sky. This isn't about me having your power. It's about stopping him or we can't get out. And..." A sudden thought struck her. "I can't be trapped in here while that Navarre lady is out there."

"She may try to harness Apophis," Pakhba added. "And while Mehen is awake, she is vulnerable to the enchanters."

The gold and white dragon studied Cass hard, her hood spreading wide. "They were on their way to me," she reasoned.

"They must have thought they had a way to awaken me. Do they have a Vedic?"

Cass shrugged. "I don't know." Pakhba nodded, agreeing with her. She couldn't imagine any of those moronic thugs being a Vedic.

Mehen sighed, shaking her great head. "It is good you woke me. Anubis must be safe and Ra must be set free." She glared at Cass. "Vedic, you will be judged for taking a piece of my power, but I believe you to be right. I will bargain with Anubis when it comes to the scales and releasing you from the Duat. I will guid you through the journey back to your reality. As is my purpose." She blinked hard and the pearlescent tear slipped from her eyes, snaking down her smooth face. "This is a risk for me. I bow to no Vedic and I do not wish to create an enchantress. Do you understand?"

She did. As Cass reached up to catch the white tear, she realized this meant she could command Mehen. She was imbued with the powers of an enchanter. Mehen was worried it would go to her head and she wouldn't relinquish the power when she was done, enslaving her to Cass.

"I have a friend who will keep me honest," Cass said. The tear turned solid and attached to her bracelet like a charm. The moment it did, her heart stopped, then leapt, hammering against her chest. It beat so hard she cried out in pain, throwing her head back. From the tear, a white, searing light blasted through her. She thought she felt the roots of every tooth shatter. Every bone splintered inside. Her skull exploded.

Then it was over. She doubled over, gasping as the agony left as quickly as it had come.

"Rise, enchantress," Mehen whispered sadly. "Sit astride me and let us free the gods."

Cass couldn't imagine what it looked like from the other side. Mehen created a portal before them, a white and gold sparking circle, showing the room beyond. The dragon rose, ready to dive through. Cass sat astride the dragon at the base of her skull, the serpent's long body waving like a flag behind her. She raised her now glowing hand. The tear and bracelet shone with gold and white in intricate weaves and Script symbols hovering just over her skin. It vibrated with a warm buzz. Something like the golden sight encroached on Cass's vision, but she could see clearly through it.

Below her in the antechamber, all hell broke loose. Literally. The ground fractured, spewing hot ash and fire up, scattering the group inside. The vaulted roof cracked in puffs of stone and the waterfall splashed into the newly formed chasm. Rana was in the middle, hauling Vamshi towards the door they had entered from. The Future scattered, dodging falling rubble until Elena pointed and screamed.

Something shot up from the fiery sunders. At first, Cass thought it looked like Mehen, only black and red. It also had a hood like a cobra, but this one had three eyes. Like a dragon, it slithered up from the ground, barring sharp fangs dripping with yellow venom. Each hood had a wild, swiveling eye, taking in the group of fleeing humans. The head of the beast had one eye, huge and yellow, so bright it almost beamed light. Cruel spikes lined its back with a thick membrane in-between. Twisted horns protruded from its single-eyed head, pointed forward for goring beasts of its size. Apophis scanned the room before his three eyes lighted on Anubis, who stood his ground between the monster and the mortals.

"You stayed!" Apophis hissed. The viper's head lashed back as it laughed loud and cruelly. "Foolish guardian. Are there not other places where the Duat touches the world of the living that you must protect?"

"You pulled them from the Field," Anubis growled in reply. Cass knew he meant the Field of Reeds, the afterlife the ancient Egyptians craved. "I am here to return them."

Apophis opened his maw to reply, but then he spotted Mehen and Cass. "You," he seethed, glowering at the white and gold dragon.

Cass's blood froze when the beast's eyes flitted to her.

"And a Vedic." Apophis slithered slowly over the ground, sizing up his new opponent. "The dragons are awakening?" he mused. "What calls you? Why have you come, mortal girl?" He gnashed his jaws, spitting his words through them.

"It seems I've slept too long," Mehen replied in a steady tone. "Or was it fate that made the enchantress move to my resting place the same day you arise?"

Apophis gurgled a sardonic laugh. "Fate is the liquor of the fool. An excuse for actions he cannot justify." His head snapped to the Future where they had all amassed against a far wall. "Unlike you, Mehen, I am no servant of the enchantress."

"She's not!" Cass barked, feeling the power from what was now a gauntlet of light and magic on her right arm. "As if pulling souls from the Field isn't bad enough, I cannot risk the Future getting their hands on a creature like you."

The black viper gave another dark laugh. "Never would they. They could not cage me!" With that, Apophis swung his head back and struck.

Mehen dove quickly to the side, but the black viper went for Anubis. Seeing the dragon dive to protect the others, Cass thrust her glowing arm out towards Apophis. She missed slinging a beam of light by just an inch as the beast dove, bringing his jaws down over Anubis. The god growled and struggled against the fangs. Cass wondered if the venom would harm him. Surely not.

The white dragon's body landed hard against the ground as Mehen threw herself in front of the mortals. Cass caught Charlie's eyes just before Mehen swooped up again. His face glowed with sweat and worry. She tried to give him a reassuring look, but Mehen jerked her away before she could. The white dragon lunged at Apophis as Cass shot out another bolt of light from where Pakhba and the tear combined on her arm. Apophis lurched out of the way, but not before the bolt of light hit the eye in his left hood. He screeched, dropping the wounded god.

Mehen lunged again, engaging in a terrible striking dance with the beast. Cass held on with all her strength, aided by her temporary enchantress powers.

"Cass!" Charlie shouted from below. Vamshi had run to him and spoke rapidly, pointing at the seemingly useless mirrors around the chamber. "The mirrors!" he shouted.

Looking, Cass realized the eclipsed sun shone on just one perfectly. Like Ra had directed the sun just for this purpose. She couldn't calculate quick enough to know where it could hit if they angled them. Apophis didn't seem to like the light she slung at him, so surely the actual sun would do him harm. That had to be why he imprisoned Ra first.

Before Cass could instruct them, Mehen jerked her away. She flung more light at Apophis, making him enraged. Below, Vamshi and Charlie ran to two of the mirrors. Vamshi called to the others and Cass saw her eyes go wide and face scrunch like she did when doing algebra. Vamshi would figure it out. She could trust her.

"Mehen," Cass called over the bestial battle. "We have to direct Apophis to a specific point on the wall. I don't know where yet, but we have to get him there."

"How about the floor?" Mehen roared, snapping at Apophis.

Below, Anubis rose shakily to his feet.

"Damned dog," Apophis hissed, quickly slithering around Mehen and Cass.

"What's his problem?" Cass cried as she hurled another wave of light.

"He craves chaos," Mehen replied, following him. "He can only live in darkness. The more darkness that spreads, the greater his realm. But he will never match the dragons."

Cass swore she heard Mehen smile at this. The white dragon lunged again, blocking Apophis from clamping Anubis into his jaws again.

"Cass!" Vamshi shouted, waving madly.

Looking over her shoulder, she saw Vamshi and Charlie pointing madly to the place where the waterfall met the sundered ground.

"That's it," she called. "Mehen, take him down."

"What if we miss?" the dragon asked.

"I thought of that," Cass replied. She turned her glowing arm, inspecting the light. "You have to let me down so I can blast him, just in case."

She felt more than heard Mehen's pause. Then the dragon said, "Your wish is my command."

Mehen dived among the people on the ground. Rana dashed around the chamber madly, angling the mirrors and leaping over the volcanic cracks.

"Stupid mortals!" Apophis guffawed. "I see your weak plan."

The white dragon lurched up just as Cass cleared her neck and took the beats's throat in her maws. Apophis roared and reeled back, his long body writhing around the chamber. Cass dashed across the stone and leapt over a particularly mean looking crag of fire. Rana caught her hand and pulled her along.

"All we need is that one to turn," she panted, pointing to a mirror near the floor in front of Cass.

"Get clear," Cass said. She turned and faced Apophis and Mehen where they did battle. "Hey!" she shouted, waving to the beast and the dragon. At that, Mehen shrieked a roar. With all her strength, she slammed Apophis into the place Vamshi indicated the beam would hit.

Cass leapt to the last mirror and flipped it up to catch the crescent sun as it angled in perfectly through the singular hole above. She knew for a fact it was well past noon. The sun should have set. But it didn't, held in place by a hand she could not see.

The black and red beast thrashed, loosening Mehen's grip as the beam of light shot down. It ricocheted off the mirrors the others had angled and shot towards Apophis.

"Rana, fire when I say," Cass shouted, dashing to her right, several yards away from the mirror. Their guid looked confused, but pulled out her gun, anyway.

As the light blinked towards the monsters, Apophis bucked Mehen off and charged at Cass. Everyone screamed for her to run. Cass skidded to a halt, her heart in her throat, and faced the black beast.

"Rana!" she screamed and the crack of the gun cut through the other cacophony of sound. The bullet hit Apophis right in the side of his head where his cobra hood met his skull. It must have hit the joint to his jaw, because he hissed, maw flying open.

In the millisecond he turned to glare at Rana, Cass thrusted her arm forward, hurling a beam of light from her gauntlet. The deadly light cut through Apophis's large central eye, rupturing it. As he threw his head back to hiss in agony, Anubis leapt up over the beast's head, clutching his golden hammer, and brought it down hard onto Apophis's skull. With the beast rattled, Mehen went for his neck again, chomping down hard and pulling him into submission.

The black beast moaned, his wriggling body going still except for his heaving lungs. Cass couldn't take her eyes off the creatures before her. Slowly, she approached Apophis, her arm burning bright.

"I cannot see it, mortal," Apophis hissed in a guttural growl, "but feel it. The powers of an enchantress." He gave a horrid laugh that sounded like fluid filled his long throat.

"It shouldn't have come to that," Pakhba said, slipping out from the bracelet and the golden glow. He glared at Mehen.

"I asked her to," Cass said on the dragon's behalf. "She didn't want to. But I'm Vedic and so she did as I asked." She turned back to Apophis, hoping Mehen had a good grip on him. "This didn't have to happen to you. Why steal away the dead and put them here?"

The black beast grunted and tried to shift, but Mehen held him down. "To hide," he purred.

Cass clenched her light-slinging fist, making it pulse.

"That's the truth," Apophis replied, whinging away from the heat of the light. "We saw a Vedic coming," he indicated his head toward Anubis. "When they come, the dragons awake. When the four winds arise, we—the chthonian beasts —are weakest."

Confused, Cass looked up at Mehen. The golden eyes of the dragon slitted in confusion as well. *Chthonian beasts?* she wondered. Just something else she wouldn't know about, she guessed. But if they were anything like Apophis, she and the dragons could handle them. Unless maybe someone like the Future gathered them. She imagined a world-wide battle between the four dragons and what these chthonian beasts were. Surely that would be a war of apocalyptic proportions...

"Enough," Mehen said around Apophis's neck. She rose, dragging the beast with her. Cass watched in awe as Mehen's muscles flexed under her shining, white scales. With a quick snap of her head and a fighting growl from Apophis, she tossed him violently to a wide open, smoldering crag.

The black beast tumbled down into the fire. He roared once, then the ground snapped shut, taking him and his screams.

Cass limped back to the others. She looked down at her leg and saw a huge, bloody gash on her shin. She must have nicked it on the spines of the beast while she rode on the back of the dragon. She smiled at it, not even caring that it stung like hell. On one side of her stood Anubis, god of the underworld, and Mehen the Coiled One on the other. She smiled at Vamshi, whose black eyeliner had long since smeared all the way down her cheeks. Vamshi smiled and gave a weary thumbs up. Cass looked around for the Future thugs. They stood against the wall of the chamber.

"Thank you, Vedic," Anubis said, standing tall despite his wounds. He turned to Mehen. "I know you cannot stay. Apophis has been stopped for a time, perhaps."

"He has," Mehen said, taking a deep breath and relaxing against the earth. "I will give you my blessing so that you may sail the Mesektet and take those souls back to where they belong."

Anubis bowed his jackal head to the dragon, hand over his heart. "Go in safety."

The scene vanished. Cass jumped as it did and Anubis melted into the shadows. Everything went entirely black.

"What's going on?" she cried.

She spun around and suddenly a sky of stars came into view. She slipped on the sand under her feet. Looking around, she realized they suddenly stood on the dunes, surrounded by the roaring of the ocean. They were so near the shore, a boat— no doubt the one the Future used to get to the island— bobbed just a few yards offshore. The temple was gone. The walls, Anubis, the scales, the ghosts—all gone. Her bracelet returned to normal, gold and simple. Pakhba still floated above her, though.

"What happened?" she asked.

"She released us from the Duat," he replied simply, yet gravely. "Look." He pointed to her bracelet.

Hanging from the golden dragon bracelet was a simple, opalescent charm in the shape of a wild, coiled dragon.

"It's her," Cass mused, gently touching it. "Holy shit," she gasped, turning to face the others. A sensation the likes of which she had never felt in her life coursed through her. Her heart lightened, and she laughed hysterically.

Vamshi ran to her, hugging her tight and joining in the hysteria. She screamed "Oh, my god!" fifteen times, jumping with Cass.

Cass turned from Vamshi and grabbed Charlie's face in her hands. Giving a wild smile, she pulled his lips to hers and kissed him hard. A shock shot through her face down to her toes, melting her feet to the sand. She kissed him again, parting her lips to pull him deeper.

At last, his hands went to her face as well and reciprocated.

CHAPTER 19: THE MEMORIES

Charlie's fingers tangled in her hair until he grasped ahold of her, holding her tightly to him. Cass panted into their kiss, her mind spinning. When she finally broke the kiss, she looked into his eyes. She smiled so hard her cheeks hurt. But Charlie's gloomy eyes didn't meet hers. He looked away, blinked to release a tear, and sniffled.

"Sorry," Cass smiled weakly. "I just... I've been wanting to do that for a while." She bit her bottom lip. "Was it okay to do that?"

Charlie gasped a sob back and shook his head.

Confused, frightened that she'd done something wrong, and getting annoyed, Cass stepped back from him. "I'm sorry, I thought..." What? That he felt the same way?

His hand shot up and cupped her chin. His blue eyes swam in unshed tears. "It was okay," he whispered, pulling her closer. "I'm... I'm so sorry."

Fear overcame her giddiness. "What?" She pulled away.

"Let's go, Charlie," Elena shouted from behind them. Vamshi and Rana spun around to face the trio. "Get the damned thing."

A freezing wind rushed in over the ocean, chilling Cass to her bones. Or was it the sudden confusion? "Charlie?" she asked, her eyes darting to Elena.

The woman stood still, gun pointed at them. In her other hand, she held Cass's pack with the Script in it. Charlie's hand trailed down her arm to the bracelet. He gently picked her wrist up by the bracelet. Confused, Cass froze stiff. She didn't know what was happening.

"Give me the dragons, Cass," Charlie whispered. "Just do it so she doesn't hurt anyone."

Vamshi cursed somewhere behind her. Cass couldn't even swallow to stutter. Her body rebelled in its shock. Two seconds before, she had kissed him hard and deep, thinking she had an ally like never before. Someone not only to support her but to be there for her like a best friend. Someone who could be so much more. She imagined them going on the next dragon hunt together.

"It was supposed to be like *Romancing the Stone*," she whispered, dazed and hurt.

"Drop it," Rana called to Elena, pulling out her own gun.

Elena smirked. "I counted your shots. You have four left. Do you really want to risk reloading while you're outnumbered?"

At that, Shades and Markus both pulled their handguns from their holsters behind their backs. None of them moved.

"Wait," Cass choked, feeling at least coming back to her lips. "Charlie, what the hell?"

"He's with us," Shades gloated, smirking.

Vamshi gave a high-pitched gasp.

"How?" Cass cried, almost begging. Hot tears flooded the corners of her eyes.

Beside her, Pakhba gave a deep growl. "The Future has always taken a few children under their wing. To train them. Elena," he said directly to the woman, "Meredith Navarre knows better. She's done this before. Choosing a Vedic does not make them one. I was there when Edward fell under her spell. This is not how the Script chooses those who can read it. It will not take an offering."

"We just need one," Charlie said, still holding Cass's wrist. "If I had Mehen, we think the others will come. Quetzalcoatl is wild, untamed. We couldn't find him first. Fortunately, neither did Cass." He met her eyes.

When he did, rage boiled up in her cheeks. She tried to jerk away, but he held her hard. "You lied to me," she spat. "You used me. Followed me. I told you everything! And you were one of them?" She gasped, choking to keep her sobs down. "Damn it, Charlie, why?"

"He didn't have a choice," Elena cut in. "He was raised in the shadow of the Future. His purpose is to wake the dragons. To be Vedic."

"I told you!" Pakhba rumbled, his eyes narrowing into dangerous slits. "The Script will not take one such as him as Vedic."

"We've never had one dragon in our possession," Elena countered. "With our magic, we will pull Mehen from the charm. Charlie has been prepared. She will bend to his wishes. All we needed was one."

"Did you not have two when Edward was sacrificed?" Pakhba gnarled dangerously.

Cass realized what her familiar spoke of. She'd seen it in a vision. "Aiken," she said out loud, wondering if she had it right. "He had an apprentice named Edward that they raised for the sole purpose of being Vedic." She frowned. "I saw it in a vision. There were two dragons. What stopped you then?"

Elena raised her head, teeth gnashing. "Aiken. He was an enchanter, gifted the magic of the dragons not unlike his master Meredith Navarre."

Even the ocean seemed too quiet.

"There is less magic in the world now than there was then," Elena went on. "Aiken was strong. Perhaps his locking the dragons away then is what made the magic weaker. No longer do they grant that gift to mortals. It's too dangerous. With the Vedic, one who was willing to learn and protect the dragons, they would be safe from other enchanters."

Vedics are protectors, Cass realized. *That's why we're not meant to wield their magic. So that way we rely on the dragons. And being bound to a Vedic makes them safe from those who already have their magic.*

And Apophis? she wondered. He'd said that the dragons could tether him into submission. "Those who control the dragons control the..." She frowned. What had he called them? "The chthonian beasts."

The magic she had been tasked with protecting ran deeper —was bigger—than she had originally thought.

"Could Charlie be Vedic?" Cass asked Pakhba. "Have I ruined my place as Vedic by taking up the tear from Mehen?" Would another Vedic be chosen?

Elena sighed, frustrated. "If he's not, then he's useless to us. So he better try."

Cass saw Charlie swallow hard, his sad face making her heart almost hurt for him again.

"I'm tired of this, Charlie," Markus shouted, aiming his gun at Vamshi. "Get the dragon and let's go."

Charlie rubbed his thumb over Cass's skin gently, begging her with his eyes.

"No," she cried, trying to jerk away again. "Charlie, please."

Elena cursed and finally drew back the hammer to her gun and aimed at Vamshi, too. "I've run out of patience. Take it, Charlie!" She flicked her head towards the boat just yards away on the shore.

With all her strength, Cass jerked her hand out of Charlie's grasp and shoved him. Just as she did, Rana fired a shot towards the thuggish trio. She caught Markus in his shoulder and he spun, dropping his gun. Shades dashed to his colleague's aid, firing at Vamshi as he ran. The shifting sand he dashed on made his aim terrible and he missed Vamshi by a mile. Chaos erupted as Elena and Rana fired again at one another and charged.

Cass dodged past where Charlie fell and also sprinted to the boat. Someone, she guessed Shades, fired toward her and a strange buzzing whizzed past her ear. She dropped to the sand and rolled to avoid another shot. A flurry of bodies and feet charged past her. A final shot rang out and Vamshi cried out behind her. The engine to the boat kicked on and the ocean gurgled into the motor.

Panting, Cass pushed herself up, sand and dirt in her eyes. The boat sped off towards shore. She shoved herself up and ran back to Vamshi and Rana. Vamshi clutched her arm, blood seeping from between her fingers.

"They shot you," Cass cried, a new round of tears cutting tracks through the dirt on her face.

"Just clipped me," Vamshi gasped, but her face glowed red in the starlight and sweat trickled down her jaw.

"I'm so sorry," Rana whispered, shaking her head.

Cass breathed a few times to calm her heart. "You were amazing." She looked up at Pakhba, who zipped back to her after giving chase to the boat before it out ran him. She wanted to ask him something, but didn't know where to start. And Charlie...

"Fishing boats will come in the morning," Rana said, standing up and holstering her gun. "Let's make a camp and try to rest until dawn."

No sleep came to Cass at all. The sand fleas crawled over her arms and she worried they'd hop inside her ears. Vamshi fell asleep after Rana stitched her arm by the firelight. Pakhba hovered close by, half curled like a cat. He hadn't gone back into the bracelet. Anxious, Cass checked her watch: four in the morning. That's when Pakhba finally broke the silence.

"You have witnessed great things, Rana Saad," he said suddenly into the night.

Rana and Cass looked up at him.

"And you have born it bravely." He uncurled. "You beheld the sun, held in the sky by the very hands of Ra. Laid eyes on Anubis. Witnessed the awakening of one of the four dragons who command the very magic that holds our world in place."

Cass didn't like where this sounded like it was going. "I couldn't have done it without her, Pakhba. She's brave and good."

"You misunderstand," the dragon sighed, but his head turned down sadly.

Vamshi stirred and opened her eyes. She sat up, rubbing the sleep away.

"She is the kind of warrior they sing about in the ballads," he agreed. "If there were more like her on the side of the Vedics, we might have far less to fear."

"What do you mean?" Cass asked, emotion filling her again. "Pakhba, I won't let you harm her."

Rana adjusted herself on the sand near the fire. "I won't give away any secrets," she bargained. "It would do me more harm than good. They'd think I was crazy." She almost smiled, but caution lingered in her brown eyes.

"I have no doubt," the dragon said. "But these things have a way of driving one mad despite their silence. You will want to know more. You will crave the answers. There are beasts, dragons, magics in this world you cannot see or control. You will hunt them down. At best, you will live in utter fear of what is to come."

"I won't let you hurt her," Cass shot, sitting up squarely on her hips.

"Nor do I wish to," Pakhba whispered. "Rana Saad, I must take what you know from you. Return you to your life. Set you free of this quest. It is not your burden to bear."

Now she understood. "Take her memory?" Cass cried. Vamshi protested too, joining Cass and Rana by the fire. "No, Pakhba," Cass said. "How is that better?"

"Without temptation," he said solemnly, "she will be safe. She will return as if this trip had been a failure. You didn't find the ancient site you sought. She will doubt it ever existed in the first place and return home to her next adventure."

For some reason, losing Rana like that hurt just as much as Charlie's betrayal. Cass blinked and hot tears fell. "But I don't want her to forget it," she begged, her voice cracking.

"She swore to not tell," Vamshi bargained. They both looked at Rana over the fire.

The fearless woman simply frowned in thought, eyes boring into the center of the flames. She took a long and steady breath. "I understand." She nodded, sure of herself. "I do understand. I've done deployments where I've been sworn to secrecy. Missions I couldn't talk about. If I had had this option," she nodded to Pakhba, "I would have taken it. There are other things I'd rather not remember. I wish I could hold on to this."

"You can!" Cass cried, moving to take Rana's hand. "I don't know why, but I don't want you to forget."

Vamshi nodded, eyes sparkling with tears too. "We've been through so much together. You never asked questions. You were ready when those thugs came into the hotel. You were just so..." She shrugged sadly. "Amazing."

Pakhba hovered closer to Rana. "As is the way with great warriors of the past, they fade into memory. If you remember her, it will be as if she does. I cannot turn back time. What happened, happened. I can never change that. Cassandra, this is for the best."

"It is," Rana agreed. She sat up, crossing her legs and facing Pakhba straight on. "Whenever you are ready."

A slight glow emanated from Pakhba. He reached out his little foreclaw to Rana's forehead. Gently, he dug his talons into her skin.

"Rana," Cass said, kneeling before her. "Thank you. Thank you for everything. For saving me and protecting us."

Rana smiled.

CHAPTER 20: VEDIC'S DUTY

Cass couldn't bring herself to look Rana in the eyes the last day in Egypt. When they got back to the shore, even Atminadab felt normal compared to the day they spent in the temple. The buzz of the people simply going about their lives puzzled her. They had no idea what had just happened off their shores. The city felt vacant, small. Colorless.

Vamshi took control of their trip to the airport and then called a rideshare to take them back to campus once they were home. Cass was grateful, pretty sure she wouldn't have been able to get home without her best friend. Her mind felt numb and dizzy at the same time. She spaced out for most of the trip and jolted back to reality when Vamshi swiped her student ID to get into their dorm.

"I'm sorry," Cass sighed, climbing the stairs to their floor and lugging their packs. "I feel so weird. So out of touch now."

Vamshi faced her, hair matted and face grimy. They hadn't showered or even cleaned up before the sixteen hour flight home. She felt bad for anyone they sat next to on the plane.

"Don't be sorry," Vamshi said, taking her pack too. "This was easily the craziest two weeks of my life. I don't even care how much calculus homework I have to catch up on."

"Homework," Cass mumbled, ascending the last of the steps like a zombie. "Please don't let me zone out. I don't want to... sink into whatever is eating me up inside."

"You need time to process," Vamshi offered kindly.

They reached their apartment-style dorm and Vamshi immediately went to work with the electric kettle and making tea. The plant on the coffee table hung dead and crispy. Cass had forgotten about it before they left. The tiny living room felt cold. The quiet was loud. Her bed waited, half made as she'd left it. Her crowded desk had one spot empty where she'd shoved everything aside to place the Script down.

A sob rose in Cass's throat. "Pakhba," she called, sitting on her bed despite being dirty. The blue and yellow dragon didn't appear in a sliver of smoke. "Hey?" she said, rubbing the bracelet to try to wake him up.

Not now, Cassandra, the dragon's voice said. *Give yourself time. Give* me *time.*

"Vam?" she called, desperate for someone to talk to. Vamshi appeared in a second, a steaming cup of tea in her hand. She gave it to Cass before joining her on the bed. "Did I seriously mess up?" she asked, letting the tears come. "I lost the Script. They have it. I don't know how to even begin to get it back." A tear plunked into her tea.

Vamshi laid her head on Cass's shoulder gently. "You were asked to do something no one in five hundred years has done. And, honestly, probably only like three people in the history of mankind have ever done. And..." She scoffed darkly. "That damned bastard tricked you. I should have warned you that he felt off."

"Don't pretend I'm not pathetic and desperate," Cass interrupted. "I wanted something between me and Charlie so bad that I might not have believed it if you weren't there. It's like he sensed my stupid-ass desire to dig into his mysterious melancholy and used that against me. But..."

"What but?" Vamshi asked, still fuming.

"They used him too."

"No," Vamshi moaned. "I knew you'd try to justify it. Don't, Cass. He may have been brainwashed or whatever by them, but he chose how he manipulated you. He studied you and figured out what would worm into your heart strongest." She embraced Cass and sighed. "You're kind. He turned that against you." She waited a minute before asking, "What did your little dragon say?"

Cass sniffled and took a drink of the tea. "He won't talk to me. I think he's pissed I lost the Script."

Vamshi reached down and tweaked the golden bracelet hard. "We can get it back."

"How?" Cass asked.

Her friend stood up and went to the living room. "We know where they are going. They said it themselves. They needed Mehen before getting that other one with the weird name."

"Quezacotl?" Cass asked, following Vamshi out cautiously.

"That one!" Vamshi turned her pack over and shook out the contents. About a pound of fine sand and dirt came out with it, covering the carpet. She shifted through the items until she found a plastic zip bag. She pulled it up triumphantly. "We have a bit of a map to follow. And we know where to look for clues."

"What is that?" Cass reached for the bag and opened it. Inside was the Codex. "I forgot about this!" she gasped, opening the accordion folds.

"Well, I ran some searches on the one image I can see,"

Vamshi explained, grabbing up her tablet and turning it on. "I swear to God, that's a map on that middle one."

Cass scanned the third square of the Codex and nodded. "It's not even Script. It's just ink."

"Yup," Vamshi agreed happily. She spun her tablet around for Cass to see. A map of Mexico and the surrounding islands glowed on it. "I know that long land mass. And that," she pointed to the end on the Codex, "is Havana."

Cass's heart leapt in her chest. "Yes," she breathed, squinting at the faded map. "That makes this," she pointed, "Mexico. And this," she traced the arch of the land down, "is Cuba." She frowned, thinking. "Quezacotl. Mexico. Aztec people. They had to be Aztecs."

"Yes," Vamshi crowed, pumping her fist. "My father's boss has a timeshare in Mexico City. We've also been to Havana twice, but who's counting? I'm betting there are some great remote places in the Gulf of Mexico that would be a great place to start. Probably places that aren't even on the map, like that temple of Thoth."

Cass dove for her laptop and impatiently waited for it to turn on. Once it did, she opened the maps to join Vamshi in scanning the Gulf of Mexico. "Somewhere remote," Cass mumbled. She flicked her finger over the blue ocean. "There are small islands off the coast of Tampico here. And a few near Ferric Veracruz."

Vamshi frowned, using her fingers to pinch in on her map. "I bet you anything related to these dragons and your Script doesn't show up on these satellite images. We'd need old maps."

Cass thought, but her brain was dark as her anthropology class room. Then, a light turned on. "Like Cortés's maps." She looked up. "He had hundreds made, but these days everyone thinks they're inaccurate. What if..." She thought. "What if they were super accurate? But the places he found have vanished since then. Even just years after him."

"Those kinds of maps have to be replicated in any book about Cortés," Vamshi agreed. "I'll hit up the library."

Cass nodded, grateful to her best friend. "Thank you. I couldn't do this without you. And I'm sorry I put you in danger."

"Be more sorry I have a calculus exam tomorrow," Vamshi sighed, putting away their treasure hunting materials and pulling out a fat textbook and calculator. "We have a lot of work to make up."

And she didn't have the Script. She couldn't work on finding the next dragon if she wanted to.

Overwhelmed with excitement and relief, Cass began to cry fresh tears. "At least we know where to start." She took a deep breath. "I don't want to, but we have to get our normal lives back in order before we disappear again. We were lucky to come back this time. But I don't know what to expect now."

Ms. Dawnstride was pleased to see Cass back alive and well. Midterms were at the end of the week and she offered her any help she could give to help her catch up on homework and study materials for the test.

Cass sat mostly numb in the class in the dark now as Ms. Dawnstride whipped through slides. At first, her body tensed at the mention of a test, simply out of habit. Then it passed, replaced by the overwhelming memory of speaking to actual Anubis. She looked down at the golden bracelet where Pakhba slept. Mehen's pearly teardrop-shaped gem glittered in the warm light. She touched it gently. The dragon had saved her life, lent her power to Cass. She wanted to bring her out again and get to know her. She felt something of a kindred spirit with Mehen.

"These digs and opportunities are really only for graduate students," Ms. Dawnstride was saying. "But I think it would be a great experience for everyone to at least take a look at them and see what the process is like."

Cass whipped her eyes up to the projector screen. "Digs?"

Ms. Dawnstride nodded, smiling. "You have enough on your plate, though, Cass. You don't have to look into these."

"Where are they?" she asked.

Ms. Dawnstride smiled kindly. "Only graduate students can apply. They're all over the globe, sponsored by everything and everyone from private investors and collectors to full-blown fortune five hundred companies. It would take forever to go through the list, but if you go to the website," she turned and wrote it on the whiteboard, "you can search by region, culture, or time of year the dig is."

Cass scribbled the website down. No, she wouldn't apply, but if it could cover her next excursion, she wanted to at least look into it.

The rest of the day and week melded together in a surreal, note-taking blur. Cass made herself swear that Thursday would be a rest day. She left her homework, backpack, and even laptop in her dorm when she went to work that evening. Felicity and Everly were thrilled she was back and gave her long hugs, asking about her trip, did she learn anything, and "please never be gone for that long again."

Opening boxes of Mayan and Aztec gods made her ill to her stomach. She placed them on the glass shelves, glaring at each scolding Aztec deity. A nice shipment of Buddhas and witchy pentagrams soothed her in the next box. She inhaled deeply, holding her breath, then letting it out as she placed the ornaments in perfect rows. Felicity smiled at her through the glass shelving and mimicked her breath.

Cass grinned at the eccentric lady and picked up a mirror for a far wall that needed to be displayed. She had to move several hooks of bracelets and earrings to make a space for it but eventually, stood on tiptoe to hang it. The thin leather strap on the back was soft between her fingers. She reached to hang it and caught a reflection in the mirror. Behind her, a pair of sad blue eyes under waves of blond hair caught her attention.

She gasped, dropping the mirror and spun around. She half caught the thing in her hands, preventing a crash. Charlie looked back at her from only about two yards away.

"Hey," he whispered, hands in his hoodie pockets.

"What the hell?" Cass hissed. Her body began to shake. "What do you want? There are cameras in this store."

Charlie's icy blue eyes flicked from one camera to the next. He nodded and slowly moved through the maze of shelves and tables towards her.

"Cass, listen," he said softly. "You have every right to be mad at me for keeping The Future a secret."

"No shit!" she snapped. She looked around. Felicity had vanished. All she had to do was let the mirror drop and then scream. They'd come running.

"But we're very similar," he went on. She gaped at him in disbelief. He nodded. "We're both Vedics."

"Are you?" she asked. That weird, jealous fear rose up in her. Wasn't she the only Vedic?

He didn't answer directly. "Cass, they raised me from a kid. They took me out of the system and trained me. Showed me how I could be an enchanter."

Her eyes flicked to his fingers. She wasn't sure what she looked for. Glittering smoke? Crackling lightning between his evil, long fingers that had been entangled in her hair?

"Finding the Script, reading it, and waking the dragons is the point to my entire existence," he went on. He sounded like he tried to reason with her. She narrowed her eyes. "But that's not true with you," he said. "You have a life. A purpose outside of the Script. I don't. Let me have it. Let me fulfill my destiny."

She scoffed so hard, spit flew from her lips. Her eyes rolled before pinning him again with her gaze. "That's not how it works, Charlie."

"How do you know?" he countered. He was close now. Only feet from her. His small nose, sharp cheekbones, and melancholy gaze lured her in just like before. "Meredith Navarre has lived thousands of lifetimes," he said. "She was there when Aiken hid them. She's told me more about the Script and the ways of enchanters than you might ever know."

His condescension made her cheeks burn. "Pakhba is a dragon. He told me," she tried, but even to her, the words sounded unsure.

Charlie nodded. "I'm sure he did. Maybe he just didn't want to wait for another Vedic to be chosen. He waited nearly four hundred years for you. He does things the old way. Meredith has shown that I can be Vedic." He held his hand out like he expected her to take it. "Just say that it's me."

"No!" Cass spun away from him, clutching the mirror. "You used me, Charlie. Made me have feelings for you. I thought you were in need of a friend, but it was all a ruse. God!" she swore, laughing sadly. "Vamshi was right. I let myself be drawn in too easily. Screw you."

"Cass, wait." He trotted after her. She put a table between them. "You felt that power, right? Mehen gave you just a taste of that power. Who wouldn't want that?" He finally stood next to her. He placed his hand on the side of her face and leaned in close. "Cass," he whispered. "You'd make a great enchantress. Strong. Sure of yourself. Commanding." His heavy-lidded eyes looked up at her through a soft, blond fore-lock that fell in front of his gaze. He leaned in close.

Her feet froze to the ground as he had her trapped between shelves and a table. His hand on her back and cheek burned to her very core where their skin touched. She swallowed hard, mind reeling. His nose touched a tender spot she didn't know she had between her jaw and neck. She gasped and dropped her hands; the mirror hanging limp in her fingers.

"We are Vedics, Cass," he whispered, his breath tickling her neck. "That power is for us to take. It's our destiny to control the dragons. We are the only ones who can. Doesn't that mean it's our right?"

His petal-soft lips touched her then, landing soft kisses up her neck, to her cheek until they finally landed on her lips. No scent came from him. The only sensation was his kiss. He kissed her once softly, then again, more urgently. Suddenly, his hands cupped her face, and he took her mouth in his.

The jolt that shot through Cass brought her back to life. She grunted, pulling away and shoving him hard. As she did, he tripped, knocking over a whole tower of wooden incense burners. She also dropped the mirror, and it crashed to the floor, glittering glass shattering all over between them.

"No one should have that kind of power," she growled. "I don't want it. I want to make my own destiny. We're guardians, Charlie. We're the ones who are supposed to make sure the dragons don't fall into anyone's hands like that again. Look what it did to Meredith Navarre. Immortality? What?" She stopped. Saying it out loud, she realized what that means. "Holy shit," she whispered. "Immortality."

"But I want it!" Charlie snarled back. His crystal blue eyes turned to sharp shards of ice. "It's rightfully mine. I didn't waste my whole life to be stopped now."

Charlie took two dangerous steps towards Cass. She

gasped and backed up. Just then. Felicity came around the corner, shawl and long hair flying.

"What happened?" she asked, eyes wide. "Are you all right, Cass?"

Cass nodded mutely. When she looked back, Charlie had booked it across the store and vanished out the front glass doors. Cass sighed and dropped her face into her hands. As soon as she could, she wanted to have a word with the dragons on her wrist.

CHAPTER 21: DRAGON COUNCIL

That weekend, after her shift at Witch's Bones, Cass packed up some snacks, a hoodie, tied on her hiking boots and went for a long walk down a nature trail in the northern part of the state. Away from Rookwind, Wheathermoore University, and away from any distractions. She wanted solitude and safety to bring out Mehen and Pakhba and tell them her next steps. She didn't have many, but maybe the dragons had advice.

Vamshi begged to go, but Cass pleaded to have time alone. Vamshi thought The Future might be tracking her and maybe attack when she was alone, but Cass doubted it. She got the feeling they wouldn't act rashly in public. Not so close to her home. They had been bold in Atminadab, but there, they might have had more freedom. More anonymity. No one would care about the set of foreigners chasing one another down.

Despite it being early November, Connecticut hung on to its warm weather and humidity. The cold air fluctuated too much for Cass's liking. So by the time she reached the summit of the hill she climbed, following the trail, sweat dripped through her shirt and made a halo around her face. She'd gone out late, hoping the early setting sun and the gray clouds would give her and the huge body of Mehen coverage.

She moved into a copse of trees and took in the area. A few brambles offered thicker walls. Most of the leaves had fallen, opening the sylvan canopy above to the sky. To the west, the hill spilled down into a more rocky side that led into a clearing with a river that eventually fed into a huge lake. Bugs sung, and a few landed on her humid skin, biting her.

"Just you wait," she threatened the bugs, slinging her pack off her back and moving to one of the abandoned fire rings. "My dragon will burn you with hellfire."

She waited until the fire crackled and she'd toweled off a little and taken several drinks of water before lifting the bracelet to examine it in the firelight. "Pakhba," she said softly. "Come out a minute, please."

A soft hiss preceded a puff of blue and gold smoke as the smaller dragon appeared. "I can hear you, you know," he whispered. "You don't have to summon me like a genie."

"Sorry," she grunted, pulling out a pint of ice cream from her backpack. She opened the top and set it down, knowing he liked the cold dairy snack. "Got a minute to chat?"

Pakhba eyed her condescendingly, but floated down to stand near the carton all the same. "For now, I have all the time in the world."

"Yeah," Cass sighed. "I need to talk about that." An overwhelming rush of guilt swamped her. "I'm so sorry I lost the Script."

"As am I," Pakhba whispered. He turned his golden eyes up to the sky above, where a single star appeared. "But you have done well, Cassandra. Though, I worry."

She wondered if they feared the same thing. "Charlie came to see me the other day."

He nodded, stabbing a claw into the ice cream.

"Right," she sighed, remembering that he most likely spied on her all day, every day. "He made it sound like he could be Vedic. That Meredith had found a way around it."

A deep, smooth voice joined them. "I say he lied." A white slipstream of smoke shot out from the bracelet. The white gem that was Mehen turned clear as the dragon appeared before them. Her lengthy, lithe body filled the copse. Her moon-like scales glittered and Cass swore she heard them tinkling like tiny crystals or gems. Her golden eyes almost beamed light down on Cass in the growing darkness.

Pakhba put his fore claw over his chest and gave Mehen a gentle bow with his head. "I would say the same," he agreed. "But the boy spoke of things I have never heard before."

Mehen yawned and stretched like a cat, her serpentine hood shivering with the sensation. She coiled her body up and laid her head on it. "Enchanters are deceivers, little brother," she sighed.

"If Charlie was an enchanter," Cass wondered, "why didn't he just use his magic on me or something? Why the long con?"

"Because of that, I do not believe he is an enchanter," Pakhba said. "Though he betrayed your trust, Cassandra, I believed him when he said the Future used him. He is not innocent. He is perhaps even wicked."

Mehen blanched, lifting her head. "He *is* wicked."

Cass nodded, thanking the great white dragon for being on her side.

Mehen went on, "He used her love, her affection against her. Like the damned tricksters they are, he found her weakness and exposed it. Cassandra just happens to be a caring heart."

"A lonely one," Pakhba slipped in, taking a bite of the ice cream.

"Hey," Cass exclaimed. "I am not lonely."

Pakhba froze, claw in the ice cream, and looked up at her.

"Attraction is perfectly normal," she mumbled.

"Have no guilt," Mehen said kindly. "His treachery was by design. However, we must move forward, Vedic."

Cass nodded. "So, is what he said possible? Could he be Vedic?"

The dragons looked at one another in silence. Mehen turned her head to the sky and closed her eyes like she made a wish on a shooting star Cass couldn't see.

"Guys," she said, pressing her palms into her knees. "I've..." She suddenly choked on what she was about to say. Tears burned her eyes. "I've been pretty brave up until now, I think. I put myself at risk. I left my life to travel halfway across the globe on a hunch." Her nose prickled as the emotion rose. "I'm not doing this in the dark anymore. Either tell me every-thing you can, as simply as you can, or... Or I quit!"

Mehen cocked her head, looking back down at Cass. "Vedics do not abandon their destiny."

"Why not?" she shot back.

Pakhba hummed next to her. "They die before they can. But..."

"But?" Cass pressed, crossing her arms.

"You are the first to read the Script as it is," he said steadily. "Aiken made the Script when Meredith tried to use Edward to control the dragons. Never had it been written down like that."

"Then what's this?" Cass dug in her pack. "This Codex is much older than your Script." She brought it out for the dragons to see. "It's how we know where to go next. This is Mexico. It's where I think Quezacotl waits."

"Ah, my brother, who is quick to anger," Mehen said softly. "Thunder and lightning, gale force winds—destruction is his power. He has slept for some time. He will be anxious to awaken."

"I fear that," Pakhba agreed. "You are correct, Cassandra, that this Codex is old. But the magic has gone from it. Look."

Focusing on the Codex, Cass tried to read any Script that might appear. A few smudges moved and stirred, but nothing came to light. "It's like it got erased," she said.

"Yes," Pakhba agreed. "When Aiken made the Script as we know it, he took the powers from the Codex of Quezacotl, the Tablet of Mehen, the Tome of Catál, and the Scroll of Tian-long. Four pieces of writing belonging to the part of the world the dragon rested in. They were rendered useless, partially or completely destroyed. The Script is all that's left. One place for all the magic to reside, to keep them safe. One Vedic at a time."

"Before," Mehen added, "four guardians watched over us. Protected us from the dark ambition of the The Future. It was their job to make sure no enchanter bound us."

Cass looked dolefully down at the blank Codex. "Damn," she whispered. "I thought I had something. That must be why part of the Script was able to finish what is written here."

"You do have something," Pakhba said. "You know... generally where to start. But I fear this quest might be harder than the last. I understand what I am asking you to give up."

Cass laughed dryly. "Yeah, I bet the last Vedics didn't have to worry about final exams. Or family."

Mehen closed her eyes and bowed her head. Cass spotted glittering, diamond-like tears gathered in the corners of her scaly eyes. "Sacrifice is always made. Especially when it is forgotten that we are dragons."

"Hu?" Cass arched her brow. "What does that mean? How could anyone forget you are dragons?"

"Mankind becomes complacent," Pakhba said, reading Mehen's face. "Sometimes your people treat great and powerful magic like a trick to be bandied about. They lose respect for the ferocity that lies beneath."

"Jatziri did not lose respect," Mehen cut in, glaring down at Pakhba.

"She did not," he agreed quickly. "But the people of her village did. Treated Quezacotl like a wish machine. Forgot the ferocity under his green skin. Jatziri was ignorant, though. And she had greater faults."

"She was kind," Mehen argued back.

"Yes," Pakhba sighed. "Perhaps too kind. Too eager to love." His eyes bored into her.

Mehen uncoiled herself and slithered through the air, encircling Cass and the little campfire. "Let me show you through dragon fire." She clenched her body, pushing Cass close to the flames. "Do not fear the tongue of heat. For now, they will not harm you. Stand in side."

Cautiously, Cass reached her hand out to the fire. The closer she got, the less heat she felt. Curious, she put her hand into the center of the fire. Only the gentle licking of flames touched her skin. It didn't burn. Convinced, she stepped into the fire pit. For some reason, she held her breath until she realized no smoke rose. Then she looked at the walls of flame that sprung up around her.

"Look with the eyes of the Vedic," Mehen instructed.

"I thought I couldn't read with the sight unless I had the Script," she said.

"The Script is only to be read by a Vedic," Pakhba answered. "The power does not come from it. It comes from you."

"Whoa," Cass exhaled, understanding. The entire time she thought the Script had given her the powers. Could she just activate the sight any time she wanted? She made a mental note to try it later.

Concentrating on the highlights and shadows of the fire, she looked for images, words—anything that she might read. One tongue of flame flickered and snapped. She thought for one second that it took on the shape of a tree. Then a hill. A river.

"I see it!" she gasped. Tall grass waved in oranges and yellows, slowly taking form. "There's a girl. Running."

"Jatziri," Mehen said sadly.

Concentrating, Cass brought the moving images to life. Green hills, silver buildings, and lush forests burst to life before her eyes.

*J*atziri, *black hair tangled and dark skin shining with sweat, ran down the hill from a temple made of gold. A priest of the temple ran after her, calling her name.*

I can't understand, Cass thought. What are they saying?

As she listened, the words morphed. Like the Script, she didn't hear the words, she simply understood. The ancient language of the Aztecs landed in her ears, but she understood.

"No!" Jatziri screamed, flailing her arms at the young man. "Get back, Xoco. He wants me."

"I won't let that monster take you," the priest, Xoco, growled. He caught up and grabbed Jatziri by her arm.

Jatziri cried, pulling against his iron grip. "He's taken the village. He'll kill you. Hide everyone in the temple and let me go, Xoco." Tears blinded her, making the fire of the burning village blur in her sight.

Xoco held her tight, forcing her to face him. His brown eyes rounded in fear and love. "I will not lose you. Not to him."

She glanced over his lean, tanned shoulder to the temple in the trees. "It is a good hiding place. The enchanters will hide it. You will be safe. But you have to help the people flee the village. Let me go to Quezacotl alone. It is I who has upset him."

"Are you not his master?" Xoco growled, scanning the skies for the rampaging dragon above. Lightning flashed, quickly followed by a wind so strong it shoved the fire deeper into the forest, consuming the trees.

Jatziri blinked the tears out of her eyes. "I am not. I am his guardian and I failed him. I let the enchanters near."

"It wasn't your fault," Xoco urged. "Come with me to the temple. Hide. I am not your enemy. You know I love you."

"I know this. He does not." Jatziri shook her head. "He won't stop. He wants me. Is sacrifice not something we know?"

Now Xoco's eyes shone with tears. "But I love you, Jatziri. I defied the gods and my people for you. Does that mean nothing?"

Smiling sadly, Jatziri shook her head. "A Vedic should be alone. I told you that. But you would not listen. You brought this pain onto yourself."

The priest finally dropped his hands, stepping back. "You do not love me." He didn't say it like a question.

Fresh tears burned Jatziri's eyes. "I want to. My heart aches with it, but—"

Behind them, one of the palace's collapsed, the sound of falling, smoldering timber mixing with the cry a dozen souls burning alive in the dragon fire. Jatziri cringed, knowing all those lives rested on her shoulders.

"No, Xoco," she shouted, shoving the priest hard. "I do not love you. I hate your controlling ways. How you grovel to the temple." Her heart burned hotter than the fire of Quezacotl that drew ever closer. Never had she loved a man more. They'd had to do it in secret as well. At first, this sent a thrill through her. But loving an enchanter had been her undoing. Now she had to save him.

"I curse you," she hissed. She narrowed her eyes, unable to stop the waterfall of tears burning her cheeks.

Xoco swallowed hard and stepped back. She saw the moment

his heart broke in his eyes. Without another word, he turned and walked, wounded, back towards the temple.

Jatziri watched until she knew he wouldn't stop. Then, she turned and galloped towards the burning village where Quezacotl ravaged her people, looking for her. She spotted the enchanter who had betrayed Xoco dashing into the village on the main path. Good, she thought. He needed to be taken care of as well.

The village burned so hot, Jatziri felt her skin burn just from the proximity. She ran to the one place she could see her dragon: the star tower. From there, she could call for him. When she reached the top, overlooking the tall, swaying trees and carnage below, she found the enchanter there as well. His red and green robes and gold adornments made his rank known to her.

"Leave!" she cried, shoving him back towards the spiral stairs they both had just ascended. He held a long, twisted branch in his hand with a green gem on the end, clutched in wooden tendrils.

"Vedic, you do not command me," he spat, standing his ground. She was surprised to find him near her in age. "This is your doing," he went on. "You have failed at your task, failed your people, failed the dragons. And my brother in the magic has betrayed us all by giving you his heart. Was your love worth this?"

Jatziri ground her teeth, pushing his words away. The truth in them pierced her. As did the realization she needed his help. She pointed to the wand. "I need you. We cannot fight now." She took his hand, putting aside their rivalry, and ran to the top of the tower onto the balcony where just hours ago the priests had been reading the stars.

She scanned the skies, coughing as the smoke filled her lungs. "Quezacotl!" she shouted, hands cupping around her mouth. "Your Vedic calls you!"

The enchanter clutched his wand, shrinking a little. "If you cannot control the dragon, what hope have I?"

"You wield their power," Jatziri reminded him. "What sway I have over him is waning. I need you. He will come to me. When he does, bind him with your magic and I will put him to rest in a safe place. A monument to himself."

The enchanter glared at her, his long hair whipping over his sharp eyes in the fiery wind. "Why did you not let Xoco follow you?"

She unflinchingly met his gaze. She didn't need to tell him. He understood: they were not going to get out alive.

"No!" the enchanter snarled. "Their power belongs to us."

Just then, lightning struck across the sky, hitting the top of the tower, then bouncing back to a huge, leathery beast in the sky. Quezacotl flapped his wings, hovering and glaring down at her.

"You want me to sleep!" he boomed into the night sky. "To be no more than a monument to our power, buried in your earth."

"To be safe!" Jatziri cried.

"From them?" the dragon sneered, his green eyes glaring down at the enchanter next to her. "I cannot be safe while mortals who hold my power walk free. And you, Vedic. You have betrayed me. The lips with which you have called me have touched the lips of those who would enslave me."

"I haven't betrayed you," she called, motioning for the enchanter to bind the dragon while it spoke. "My task is to protect you and keep you safe from them. I woke you to hide you."

"Yet here one stands," Quezacotl growled. "I can protect myself, Vedic."

With that, Quezacotl threw his head back. A ball of torrential wind and yellow lightning gathered around his open maw.

"No, wait!" Jatziri screamed.

The deadly orb of power shot from Quezacotl at the enchanter. The man screamed, but only for a moment. Jatziri *covered her face and turned away to avoid being blinded by the dragon's light. When she looked back, only a black, ashen outline of the enchanter remained on the gourd. As did his wand. Jatziri eyed it as Quezacotl laughed to the skies above.*

Kneeling, she picked up the wand. Without thinking or the slightest hesitation, she roared and thrust the wand towards Quezacotl. She wept at what she had to do. A green bolt shot from the gem, tethering the dragon with powerful chains. He roared and thrashed, but the magic held fast.

"I did not give you my blessing," the dragon growled. "You have taken the power for yourself."

"I've always had it," Jatziri said, sweet beading on her brow. "We're just not supposed to use it." She gripped the wand with both hands. "Quezacotl," she commanded. "Sleep and be hidden!"

Her command shot from the wand and hit the dragon's chest as he shot one last orb of wind and lightning. The breath devoured her just as he vanished from the sky.

Cass stumbled backward as if the blast had hit her in the chest and not the other Vedic. She panted, catching her breath as the vision left her mind. She imagined Jatziri and Xoco running amidst the beautiful Aztec forest. She tried to solidify it in her mind, to remember for later.

"There was a wand," she said, hoisting herself up and dusting off her backside.

"To channel the power," Mehen said through a yawn. "Raw power might tear a body apart. The enchanters learned this. And so a Vedic must never make such a weapon."

Cass nodded. "That would look suspicious, huh? So..."

She held her hands up, remembering the ball of white light she'd used to defeat Apophis. "I used your power."

Mehen nodded. "By my blessing, channeling through the tear. But I won't do it again. It is not for you."

Pakhba added, "A Vedic is one who abstains. Who denies themselves the power to keep the dragons safe. This is why it is a heavy burden to bear. Knowing what you *could* do. What you *could* control. But we respect the will power of Vedics who do not touch the power. That is why we obey."

The bond between dragon and Vedic seemed unbalance to Cass. "I have dragon magic in me?" she asked, aghast. "But I can't use it?"

The dragons nodded.

"Damn," she whispered, turning to grab her pack.

"Yes," Pakhba confirmed. "It is a cursed role. Do not let the temptation take you over, Cassandra. Not now."

She slung her pack on and prepared to hike back in the dark. "But what if Quezacotl attacks me? He seems a little hotheaded. He killed his own Vedic."

"I will protect you," Mehen said, raising her head up.

"As will I," Pakhba offered. "So long as you remain Vedic, we will guard you with our lives."

Remain Vedic, Cass thought. *He means not becoming an enchantress.* But she could. Charlie had been on to something. "All right," she said out loud. "I'll find a way. I can't stop halfway. Besides, the Future probably knows at least where to start. And they have the Script. They might get lucky and stumble onto whatever monument Quezacotl is buried under." She bit her lip, holding her arm up for the dragons to return to their talismans. "And if Charlie wasn't lying, they might be able to read it and find out how to release him." She sighed. "I guess I have to hurry."

CHAPTER 22: TREASURE HUNTERS

"Ms. Dawnstride?" Cass asked timidly, peeking into the office space.

The faculty offices nestled in the center of Weathermoore University in a building they called Old Main. Unlike some of the buildings on the outside of the campus, the center of Rookwind's oldest institution boasted old academic buildings. Red brick, white siding, towers and turrets, enough to satisfy even Cass's thirst for mystery. Ancient trees spread a colorful canopy over the walkways now. October had been and gone and November was in full swing with cooling winds and bright red and gold leaves.

Ms. Dawnstride looked up from her antique roll-top desk. Her Black skin and dark brown eyes glowed behind gold-rimmed glasses. Behind her, three Gothic cathedral windows spilled the sun over stacks of globes, old maps, dusty books, and other odd things gathered from all over the world.

"Cass, I expected you to be out with a significant other this time of day." She smiled and closed her laptop.

"If only," Cass laughed darkly. She rolled her eyes. "Not in the mood for any more of that right now."

"I'm sorry." Ms. Dawnstride steepled her fingers. "What can I do for you?"

Cass took an old, red wingback chair on the other side of the desk and faced her mentor. "Could you read my essay?"

Her eyes narrowed in curiosity, but she took the proffered pages stapled together. She ran her eyes over the cover. Sighing, she removed her gold and jeweled glasses. "Cass, this dig is for seniors. Grad students mostly. There is no way you'll get accepted." She picked up a brochure next to her. It was about the dig in Mexico. She scanned it quickly.

"I think I make a good case," Cass argued. "I learned a lot in Egypt."

Dawnstride eyed her over the essay. Cass realized she hadn't told her teacher anything about the trip. She no doubt was curious.

"I'll read it," she said steadily. "But please don't get your hopes up."

"Thanks." Cass stood up, smiled confidently, and ran out to catch Vamshi between classes. Yes, she knew there was no way she would get accepted by the committee gathering people for the dig. But she didn't exactly have to. She just needed the story.

The girls met up, but didn't talk much. It wasn't until the next morning that Cass put her plan into action. Dawnstride emailed her, said the essay was exceptional, but far too vague. "You should have taken pictures," she wrote. "Otherwise, a lot of this cannot be corroborated. Remember, you need that in our line of work."

It didn't matter. Cass opened her laptop in Algebra and sent the essay to the committee. By lunch, she had a reply.

Dear Miss Warren,

We received your essay and thoroughly enjoy it. We see great potential in you. However, our dig and the accompany opportu-

nities are solely for graduate students who need to fill their field-work and have specific research in mind. We are sorry to tell you this. However, we do not want to discourage you as you clearly...

She didn't read the rest.

"Whatever," she sighed, closing her email and opening a web browser. "I just thought I'd give it a shot."

"Perhaps it's better this way," Pakhba said, slithering out of the bracelet to sit on her desk.

"What do you mean?" she asked. She typed in random words that might turn up freelance sailors heading to the Gulf of Mexico. She ended up on strange, poorly maintained treasure hunter websites. "They have a community for this kind of thing?" she mumbled, scrolling through some of the oddest pictures and blogs she'd ever seen.

"If you go with a group," Pakhba said, "they will watch over you. You will be 'missing' if you wander off for more than a few hours. They will see what you are doing. It is better this way. The fewer people know, the simpler it is."

Her heart sank. He was talking about Rana. For some reason, having her memory taken hurt Cass. Nearly broke her heart. Rana had been brave, smart, and accepted the world of dragons with ease. And even some excitement. It was a true shame to have had to lose her.

"Wait a minute!" Cass gasped, sitting up straight suddenly. Pakhba blinked up at her, frowning slightly. "What was the name of that ship?"

"Oh, no," the dragon said quickly. "Cassandra, no. I didn't like that one man. His eyes took you in too much. They are men of ill repute, they are modern day pirates!"

"Exactly," Cass smiled. She typed in the name of the boat, the *Phantom Ivory*, to a search engine on one of the treasure hunting websites. "They won't ask questions."

"And how will you pay them?" Pakhba crossed his arms.

"I hope I find something along the way," she sighed. "Something they might want. Surely anything in an ancient, long-lost temple will be worth a few thousand."

"Cassandra!" Pakhba bulked. "Those artifacts are sacred. They could hold any key—"

"That can only be read by a Vedic," she cut him off. "And right now, that's me. As you said, since there is only one Script, there is only one Vedic." She froze, the gravity of what she'd just said hitting her. "Oh, God, Pakhba."

The dragon looked up at her, still scowling.

"If they wanted Charlie to be Vedic, they could have killed me at any time." She paled. "I was acting like I was indispensable."

"You are," he corrected, laying his fore claw on her wrist. "They do not know what he could be. Remember, the Vedic is *not* chosen."

She shivered. "Still. I'm sure if Charlie tried, he could be." She shook her head. No, she wasn't *sure* sure. But it was still a risk. "First, treasure hunters."

"Pirates," Pakhba scoffed.

In only a few more clicks, Cass found the man she'd been looking for. Dietrich Van Volxem was not a hard man to find. She hadn't remembered his last name, but when she saw it on a few sites and some profiles, she remembered. She found him on a few old school message boards and found out he was going to an expo in Houston, Texas. From there, his latest activity said he and his crew were "heading for Aztec treasure."

"There must be something going on in Mexico," she mused, tapping her lip. "Welcome to the world of archeology and anthropology, I guess."

She typed up a message, imploring Dietrich Van Volxem to take her along, that she'd find her own way to Houston, and that he could have a share of anything she found on her humble expedition. She sent it, hoping he'd remember her and see how serious she was.

"I don't like them," Pakhba mumbled for what was surely not to be the last time.

The next day, a message came back from the treasure hunter with little to no punctuation, asking her to hop onto a video call to discuss a few things that might be better not written in an email. Cass had to skip algebra to make sure Vamshi was out of the room when they called.

"Why are you hiding this from her?" Pakhba asked softly as she came back from shutting the door, drawing the curtains, and holding a bottle of orange juice.

Cass sat down, tucked her red hair behind her ears and squared up to her laptop, turning on the video camera. "Because, Pakh, she got *shot* in Egypt. She was lucky this time. What if that luck runs out?" She shook her head. "I am not involving my family or her any more than I have. And by the grace of Anubis, no one else either."

"Well." Pakhba smiled wickedly. "The world would be better off without pirates such as these."

The clock ticked slowly. Eleven in the morning couldn't come quick enough. "They're treasure hunters, Pakh. Not pirates."

"They steal from cultures off their shores," he growled gently. "Sell them at a profit. How is that not deplorable?"

She was about to answer, arching a skeptical brow, when the video call rang on her monitor. "Hush," she ordered him. Taking a breath, she turned on the call.

A Bavarian accent rumbled annoyances loudly as the man's screen flashed and smudged as he moved rapidly. "How do I make it look at my face?" the man rumbled. "I can't see anything."

"Dad," another, unaccented voice sighed, "put the computer down. It's not like your phone."

An alabaster face with stunning emerald eyes and silky black fringe came into view as the picture steadied and finally settled as the laptop was set against a solid surface. The familiar, bearded face of Captain Dietrich glowed white from a single hanging light above him. Beside him, a handsome man closer to Cass in age frowned into the camera, adjusting it. The green eyes and beautiful black hair belonged to him. Cass's throat ran dry.

"Ah, there you are!" Dietrich boomed, smiling suddenly through his golden mustache. "Well done, Deston."

The handsome man, who Cass now remembered from her brief stint on the boat, nodded and turned to leave.

"Don't go!" Dietrich called, grabbing his lithe arm and pulling him back. "What if it does something *unheimlich* again?"

Deston shook his head, sighed and resigned himself to babysitting his father through their video call. Cass waited awkwardly for the men to get situated.

"Sorry." Deston smiled at her. His eyes peered into the camera when he spoke, making his emerald gems stare right into her soul. "Dad can find a fork made of gold at the bottom of the South China Sea, but doesn't know the first thing about video calls."

"I won't very well be calling Poseidon to ask about his trident, will I?" Dietrich mumbled. He folded his hands and looked at Cass on the screen. "I wanted to see you again, to remember who you were," he began. "I recall now. You were with Rana Saad. A dear friend and I'd do most anything for her."

Cass sensed the "but" coming before the large Bavarian man said it. She deflated a little.

"Captain," she said, "I know it's a lot to ask. And I know I'm not guaranteed to find anything. Or even come back."

Dietrich nodded. "I cannot be responsible for you, *fräulein*. I am not a pleasure yacht. We go to rough waters. There is also the matter of security."

Cass tilted her head. "Trust me, I know how to keep a secret."

Deston leaned forward here. "What my father won't tell you is that what we do—where we do it—is often frowned upon by customs and other water-ish police."

"No." Dietrich shook his head. "It's not that."

"Also," Deston added, his full lips turning to a serious line. "Treasure hunters guard their leads very carefully. We cannot have others learning about our destination. It becomes a race then. We want finder's rights. Doesn't always hold sway, but sometimes..."

"Oh!" Cass laughed, relief filling her. "Trust me, I'm not after what you're after. I'm self-sufficient. After my jaunt in Egypt, I can handle more than you think."

Deston smiled, and her toes curled. "I don't see how she'd be any more of an issue than your little runt."

"Eugene is a scientist!" Dietrich hissed back. "He's invaluable to the crew and me."

"*Vater, bitte,*" Deston tried again in German, tilting his head towards Cass.

"*Nein,* Deston," Dietrich warned, glaring at his son. As if reading a hidden message in Deston's eyes, Dietrich turned back to Cass. "I am sorry. But it's still no."

"I'm going to the expo in Houston," she tried, gripping

the sides of her laptop. "I can meet you there. I'll cook or something. Anything."

She looked at Deston. His eyes showed sympathy. He lightly nudged his dad.

Dietrich exhaled and closed his eyes. "Still, no."

The video went blank. Screaming, Cass pushed back from her desk. She seethed for just a moment, realizing she over-reacted.

"Well?" Pakhba asked, appearing from the smoke.

"I'll find a way," she hissed through gritted teeth. She pulled back to her computer and opened the site for the expo. There was a page announcing important people who were showing at the expo, speakers, and important guests who were "due to appear." She scanned the profiles of all the different people: anthropologists, paleontologists, writers, museum curators. Near the bottom, the cold, empty gray eyes of a woman caught her attention. Bright red lips in a pale face surrounded by sheets of strawberry blonde hair.

"Meredith Navarre?" Cass gasped, reading the name. "Oh, shit, Pakhba. She'll be there." She leaned in, reading the small blurb next to her photo. Besides some sentences describing her excursions, the blurb mentioned she was presenting a tome at the expo and looking for a linguist.

"She's looking for a Vedic." Cass's heart dropped into her stomach. "Shit, Pakh, I have to go now." Lightning struck her brain. "Oh, my god. I can take it back."

"Cassandra," Pakhba said warningly. "Do not do anything rash. You have Mehen. I need you to finish the job."

"This is the way, Pakh," she said with finality. "She'll have it. She'll be showing it off. She'll invite people to look at it. All I have to do is find an opening."

"And if she kills you?"

Cass gulped. "Will she? I don't know." She glared lightly at the little dragon now. "There's a lot I don't know, huh? But that's why I'm Vedic. Because I do things when the path isn't always clear. I just *know* I have to keep moving."

"You are just going to leave?"

"I'll ride Mehen if I have to."

In her head, the white dragon yawned. "Oh, that sounds exhausting."

CHAPTER 23: THE HOMEFRONT

"What do you mean you don't have a lead?" Vamshi asked, black-rimmed eyes wide. Her fork hovered halfway to her mouth. They sat together in the coffee shop she worked in on the weekends. She was on break and "taking care of out-of-date scones."

Cass shrugged. It hurt lying to her friend. "We have a vague outline on an old codex. That's it. I'm not about to drive a million miles down to Mexico and just look around. I don't have the Script."

Vamshi narrowed her eyes at Cass, slowly chewing the strawberry pastry. "You're fibbing," she quipped, taking a long drink of black coffee. She didn't even confirm, looking at Cass as she said it.

"I am not!" Cass lied. "I just don't know what to do right now. When I find something, I'll tell you." Her eyes drifted to the scar on Vamshi's shoulder and the remnants of the terrible stitches Rana had administered in the field. "Look, Vam," she started again, but her phone vibrated.

A text from her sister Ella glowed: *Hey duh-face, not to alarm you or anything, but a black Chevy has been parking outside our house for like two days now. Comes around five. Wanted to let you know since it's the weekend and maybe you want to come home.*

"Oh, shit," Cass gasped. Her heart skipped a beat. "A black car has been parking outside my parents' house."

Vamshi froze mid swallow. "Do you think it's those thugs?"

Cass nodded, frowning. She tried to harness her breathing and slow it down. "But why? They have the Script." She stood up, her body on autopilot. "What more do they want?"

Vamshi swallowed the too-big bite in her mouth, cringing in pain. "They can't read it. He…" She checked Cass's reaction. "He couldn't read it."

She had no feelings left for Charlie. What did it matter if he couldn't read the Script? What would they do about it? Her heart sank. What would they do to him?

To her utmost disappointment, her breath shuddered as she took a deep one. "Maybe not. Maybe they're going to threaten my family. Oh! Sheriff Reece!" She picked up her phone and called Ella.

Vamshi looked up. "That guy you had a crush on when we were like five?" She giggled. "Our little Cass had a crush on an older man."

Cass rolled her eyes as the phone rang. Sheriff Reece lived next door. He had been a senior in high school, going into the police academy, when Cass was five years old. Yeah, she had thought he was cute and made any excuse to go and talk to him. Her parents had thought it was adorable to have their pigtailed daughter smitten by a young man. He'd moved into his parents' house, the one next to hers on the water, when they retired to Florida.

"Ella!" Cass gasped in relief when her sister finally answered her phone.

"Call me on SnapChat me like a normal person," Ella

quipped. Her adorable round face had taken a much more angled, mature look in the last few months.

"What'd you do to your face?" Cass asked, jibing her like a good older sister should. "And why is your hair neon pink?"

Ella smiled proudly. "A gold medalist can do as she pleases, in the words of mom."

"You got gold!" Cass cheered for her sword-wielding sister. "I bet mom ate those words when she saw what you did to your hair."

"It was dad's idea," Ella laughed. "And those were *his* exact words."

Cass shook her head and smiled. Their parents loved each other, but had this weird, almost friend-like rivalry when it came to having her and Ella do things that would rub the other the wrong way. The girls never minded, though. It had made for some amazing family memories.

"Well, congrats," Cass said, still smiling. "But your text kinda freaked me out. Black Chevy?"

Ella's face went slack and her eyes ran over the horizon Cass couldn't see. "Yeah," she said flatly. "It's almost three. Why don't you drive up here?"

It might be a good idea. Or a bad one. She could be placing herself in harm's way. But her family...

"You know what?" she said, making up her mind. "I think I will. It's close to the end of the semester and I need a break. And I haven't seen you guys since—" She stopped herself. *Since before Egypt. Damn,* she thought. *I should have gone home sooner.*

Ella arched a pale, blond brow, glaring too close to the lens, making her face distort. "What's that, sistah?"

"Ugh, nothing. You're so annoying," Cass moaned. "Keep me posted. I'm on my way."

"On your way?" Vamshi asked, gathering her trash.

Cass nodded. "I want to go see my family. Haven't been home in a while. You know."

Vamshi eyed her as she tossed her refuse. "Yeah," she said, a little too stiffly. "Be back Sunday night?"

"Yeah."

As she left, Cass felt Vamshi's eyes burning into her back. She hated to lie to her best friend. To leave her behind. But she couldn't risk her safety any more than she already had. Not for some wild, unbelievable, dragon quest. Vamshi didn't need that in her life.

Cass drove as slowly as she dared to her parents' house on the coast near Mystic, looking everywhere for dangers or signs that someone followed her.

"Why did I think they'd leave me alone after Egypt?" she asked the dragons in her head as she turned into her family's neighborhood.

"They took the Script," Mehen answered drowsily. "They had that little rat boy tell you they didn't need you. I see why you came to that conclusion."

"Almost like they planned it," Pakhba agreed.

Cass glared ahead, down the seaside road to the big white house at the end of the street. "Yeah, they wanted me to think they were off my back. Damn. They must have a plan. They're trying to get me to slip up."

A black Chevy had parked outside her driveway. She slammed on the brakes, making her backpack go flying into the passenger seat footwell. Three figures sat inside.

"Did I just walk into a trap?" she whispered, palms sweating on the steering wheel, despite the cold weather. She spotted Shades in the driver's seat, Markus next to him, and Elena's blond head in the back. "Do I run inside?" she asked the dragons. "Or will running trigger them to—"

She jerked the door open. Shades had opened his door, and he and Markus began to march towards her house. Cass threw her seatbelt off and dashed up the sidewalk, leaving the door open, the car running, and her pack inside.

"Hey!" she screamed on instinct. Markus turned and his hand hovered over his hip. "Don't even think about it," Cass warned, holding her right hand up. No magic light appeared in her palm this time, but they didn't need to know that she no longer had the powers of an enchantress.

"Well, look who it is," Shades drawled, smirking towards her. They had stopped walking, but Cass kept circling around them towards her front door.

"Get out of here," Cass shouted, glaring at them. "You have what you want."

Back at the Chevy, Elena opened the back door and stood up, sporting sunglasses herself. "Cass, don't make a scene," she said, stepping onto the pavement. "Why don't you come here and have a chat with us?" She stepped aside as if to usher Cass into the car.

"Like hell I will," Cass shot back. She was maybe twenty feet from her house. "What more do you want? You have everything." Her eyes darted to the Chevy.

"It's not here if that's what you're thinking," Shades said. "And neither is your little boyfriend."

Not that she cared, but... "Where is Charlie?" she asked.

"Not here," Markus shot back, coming up alongside his thuggish cohort. "We don't have to get nasty if you just come with us." He tilted his head towards the house, grinning deviously up through his chestnut fringe.

"Cass?" a voice called from the house next door.

Cass spun to see Sheriff Reece walking to get his mail. She

waved to him. He had his uniform on, apparently just getting off his shift.

"Hey, Sheriff," she called, pausing her primal stalk towards her house. "Just visiting."

He smiled and waved, continuing on his way to his mailbox on the other side of the street.

She caught Shades and Markus exchange quick glances. Markus looked back to Elena, who shook her head, looking annoyed. Cass glanced back to Sheriff Reece. He sifted through his mail, standing in the street. They wouldn't move while he was there. Something about real world authority kept the thugs from moving in.

They don't want to draw attention to themselves, she realized. *Like they only operate in this secret, magical world. The real world stops them. They have no power here. Yet.*

"Right," Shades sighed. "Sorry, wrong house." He grabbed Markus by his arm and pulled him back to the car quickly. In a matter of minutes, they covertly cruised down the street and turned out of the neighborhood.

Cass's head exploded in relief and pain as she realized she'd been holding her breath. She took a deep gasp and ran inside the house.

"About time," Ella shouted, trotting down the stairs. "I saw you standing out there forever." She punched Cass playfully in the arm as she walked past her. Ella squinted down the street. "Did I miss the creeps leaving?"

Cass sighed gratefully. "You didn't seem them down the street?"

Ella shook her head.

"Yeah, they left," Cass said, relieved she wouldn't have to explain. "Probably just casing houses. Sherriff will see to them." She smiled.

"Staying for dinner?" Ella asked. "I made sushi."

"*You* made sushi?"

Within the hour, Cass sat around the table out in the sunroom with her sister, mother, and father.

"I can't believe you got in," Mom said, smiling and taking a sip of white wine.

"I never doubted her," Dad smiled, winking at Cass across the table.

Around them, the waves crashed gently against the piers and the sides of the boats along the shore. The dim yellow light glowed above, making everything outside the circle of her family dark and invisible.

"Yeah," Cass said slowly, measuring her every tone. "Ms. Dawnstride didn't think an undergrad could get it, but I did." She smiled at each parent in turn. When her eyes landed on Ella, she faltered.

Ella narrowed her eyes at Cass over the uneaten sushi. Her little sister was a bloodhound when it came to lies. And to Cass in general. Her stomach flipped gently when she caught Ella sussing her out with her eyes. She thankfully kept her mouth closed.

"Well, that's..." Mom stabbed at her rice with chopsticks gently. "That's good, but. What about school? All these travel plans you've had this semester have taken away so much time."

"It's okay," Cass smiled. It felt fake. It felt wrong. "Since it's for school, I get excused absences and can catch up before the semester ends. I have As in all my classes right now. And it will only be for a couple of weeks."

Mom and Dad quickly exchanged glances. "But Thanksgiving break?"

Immediate relief flooded Cass. "Yeah, see? That week is

Fall Break. I don't even have school then." She smiled nervously.

Ella dropped her sushi roll and flat out glared at Cass now. Cass smiled at her, begging her to keep her mouth shut. Ella had spotted the lie, the flaw. Why hadn't Cass thought of that?

The rest of dinner passed with her parents wishing her good luck, to stay in contact, and to please be safe. After more light conversation, Ella stood up and said, "Hey, Cass, come down to the pier with me." Not waiting, she grabbed Cass by her arm and pulled her up and out of the house.

The evening grew chilly quickly, so Cass shivered as Ella marched her down the street and onto the docks.

"Ella, the ocean wind is biting my literal bones," she said through chattering teeth.

"Good," Ella snapped. "It will put out the fire on your pants, you liar."

Her body stopped shaking for just a moment. "What makes you think I'm lying?"

"Oh, yeah, haha, Fall Break," Ella said in a mocking tone, rolling her eyes. "Really? What are you up to? Why are you lying?" Her eyes suddenly bulged. "Oh, no. You're pregnant."

Cass burst out laughing, genuinely smiling. "Holy shit, no!" She dropped her arms, but then quickly crossed them again. The wind puffed in her ears and the waves sounded more intense than soothing now. The pier was dark except for a few lights on every other post. The boats were almost invisible in the surrounding darkness. She took in her sister's face. Ella looked hurt, but also angry.

"Look," Cass sighed. "Okay, you're right, I lied. But only partly. I am going to Mexico. But not with the dig team."

"Alone?" Ella asked, miraculously steady. Cass never gave her little sister enough credit. She acted far more mature than she was.

Cass nodded.

Ella sighed and looked out into the water. Her eyes caught the lamp lights and glittered a little. "Well, remember everything I taught you. Angle up to make your body smaller. Step with your leading hand."

"Ella!" Cass smiled. "I'm not going to get into combat. Relax."

"You're not?" Ella's brows went up. It was like she knew. Damn, Ella's intuition was too strong.

Cass mutely shook her head.

"Whatever," Ella sighed again. She crossed her arms now. "Just don't get into trouble. And be stupid." She met Cass's eyes. "Let me know you're safe every now and then, okay?"

Cass smiled. "Deal."

CHAPTER 24: I KNOW

"What do you plan to do?" Mehen asked. She had turned herself to about the size of Pakhba and curled up on Vamshi's beanbag chair. Her golden eyes watched Cass dart around the room, packing fiercely while Vamshi was at work.

"I'm going to buy a bus ticket," Cass said, running out of breath. Packing in a flurry took more effort than she had anticipated. "I couldn't do it before, but I'm going to print directions so I at least know what times are at what stops."

Pakhba sat on top of the mini fridge with a pint of vanilla ice cream. "You are going to show up at the expo and just blindside the pirates?"

"Treasure hunters," Cass corrected. "And yes. I'm running out of time, Pakhba."

"How will you convince them?" he asked.

Mehen arched a pearly scaly brow. "I think she has a good chance if she speaks with that younger man." She smiled and Cass caught it, blushing. "He seems... interested."

"Can't imagine why." Cass took a deep breath to bring the blood out of her cheeks that had rushed there.

Yes, Deston was... something. She couldn't put her finger on it. He had a kind side—she saw that when he tried to convince his father to let her come along. He was adventurous; no person in their right mind would be a treasure hunter on a ship, constantly chased by international governments and maybe even some mobsters who were avid collectors. That meant he had to be brave, smart, and strong. He also had the deepest blue-green eyes she had ever seen. And she loved how, in their brief video call, he had that cute lock of hair that fell in front of them. He also had the most perfect scruff around his full lips...

She stood still in the middle of her room, holding a red hoodie to her chest.

"Ahem," Pakhba said politely, clearing his long throat. "What is your plan, Cassandra?"

Cass snapped back to her dorm room, shoving Deston's alabaster face into her mind for later. "Right. Let me go print my directions."

She threw her adventure pack closed and tossed it on top of her little piece of luggage and ran into the common area one floor down. The T.V. blared some adult cartoon and a pair of boys played noisily on the ping-pong table near a row of vending machines. Cass slipped into one of the study rooms and hooked her laptop up to the school printer. She found the bus route for the next few days, heading south, and printed them out. The printer ran low on ink, making ugly yellow stripes streak across every page. Shrugging it off, she ran back up to her room.

The gear Rana gave her still needed to be packed. Cass dug around the floor of her bedroom until she found it. The rope was still wound tightly and the climbing gear unused. She wouldn't take any chances though and brought it out to shove into her adventure pack.

Vamshi sauntered out of her side of the dorm. Cass froze,

hand on the zipper of her luggage. Vamshi held two dresses up to herself. One had red, glossy fabric and yards' worth of a skirt. The neck cut deep with a single shoulder strap. The other was a more modest emerald dress with an elegant halter top.

"Which one?" Vamshi asked, looking at herself in their floor-length mirror.

Mehen and Pakhba had vanished.

"W-which one?" Cass stammered, moving to cover her luggage.

"Mhm," Vamshi replied. "Which one would be good for an exhibit on ancient artifacts, also featuring speakers, expos, and an auction?"

Cass stammered, mouth going dry. How did she know?

"Actually..." Vamshi walked up to Cass, tossing the hanger with the red dress on it over her head. She situated it over her body, flaring the skirt out. A slit ran to the hip with elegant lacing pulling it together just enough. "Yes," Vamshi said with a grin. "A thick, gold necklace, I think. Red gem earrings. And a thin bracelet."

"What are you—" Cass started, but Vamshi let go of the dress, taking the green one for herself.

"Did you think you were going to walk into that swanky expo in jeans and a hoodie?" Vamshi asked, trading her green dress for a black one.

"Well... yeah. Wait, how did you know I was going?"

Her best friend turned around to face her, lips pursed. "I'm a little insulted, Cass. I knew you were trying to hide it. At first, I thought you were doing it out of annoyance. Like, was I that bad in Egypt?"

"Vam, no!" Cass cried, fighting to get the hanger off from around her neck. It got stuck in her red hair and pulled several hairs out painfully by the roots. "I just can't let you get hurt."

Vamshi came out of her room, her luggage already packed,

and opened it to fold her black dress in, along with a pair of black stilettos. "Do you think there will be hot guys there?" she asked.

"Vam!" Cass cried, grabbing her friend's arm to make her stop packing. "I can't let you come with me this time. It's too dangerous. I don't even know what to do if The Future unleash their enchanter powers. Or get another dragon before I can. Or what Quezacotl will do once he's awakened. There's just too much that can go wrong. Too much I don't know."

"Oh, like what if they turn me into a frog?" Vamshi laughed dryly. A forced laugh. "Or do you mean this?" She yanked her sleeve up, showing Cass the ugly scar on her shoulder. "You think I don't know?"

Mutely, Cass shook her head. "I know you know."

"Ignorance is not protection," Vamshi went on. "Keeping me in the dark is not protecting me. It's making me ill prepared. Leaving me behind is not keeping me safe; it's abandoning me. You think I don't know that I am powerless in this whole dragon thing?"

The words hit Cass hard. Her heart immediately ached. "Oh, Vam, I'm so sorry. I didn't know you felt that way. You're not powerless. I couldn't have gotten Mehen without you. Couldn't have navigated university without you."

Vamshi waved her hand. "I know that. But I'm not useless. I'm no Vedic, but just because I'm not doesn't mean I can't help."

"I don't think that—"

"I know!" Vamshi shouted back. "Just let me prove it so that way *I* know that."

Tears pricked at Cass's eyes, and her nose tingled. "Okay," she whispered, willing the tears not to blur her vision. She stood stiffly, wanting to hug Vamshi but not sure she should. Vamshi went back to packing, tossing in a few other essentials she had forgotten, like a hairbrush.

"I bought us plane tickets," Vamshi said, almost sounding like her old self.

"Really?" Cass asked, rubbing her eyes dry.

"I am not about to spend over thirty hours on a nasty bus." She pulled out a printed boarding pass from her own adventure pack and handed it to Cass. "We fly to George Bush International airport tomorrow night. We need to leave early, though. It's a fourteen hour flight. That will give us time to get there, rest, and get hella sexy for that expo."

Immense gratitude filled Cass. "Thanks, Vam. People have been telling me to grow a spine and say no. To stand my ground. But, sometimes I think it's okay to cave."

"Caving isn't the same as seeing a good argument and accepting it. So," she turned to face her. "What's the plan?"

Pakhba kept asking, too. She wasn't sure. "All I know is the Script will be there," she began, moving over to her laptop to show Vamshi the speakers and events for that day. "And Meredith will be there."

"Holy shit," Vamshi breathed, looking the ageless woman in the eyes. "Are you going to confront her?"

"Hell no," Cass said. "I have noticed that in places with a crowd, especially on our home turf, The Future seem reluctant to act rashly and in the open. Like they don't have the power here they do in this other world the dragons and I inhabit. Like they're not ready to be blasting themselves into the public eye. Alone, out in the Egyptian temple, magic was the only law. They want to lie low, so I don't think they'll do anything to attract attention at the expo. But I still need to be stealthy. Need to get the Script and get to the captain of the *Phantom Ivory* before the night is out." She sighed. "I have a lot to do. I think most of it will be on the fly, while we're there."

"I'll help." Vamshi grinned and rubbed her hands

together. "This is like a heist, right? Should I bring my lock picking kit?"

"I forgot you had that," Cass laughed. "I thought the principal confiscated it after you broke into the computer lab."

"Nope," Vamshi beamed. "And the cops didn't take it when I got into that warehouse, either. I'm a master of my trade."

Cass leaned over and finally hugged Vamshi. "I'm glad you convinced me."

Vamshi returned the hug. "Me too. Besides, if you think I am letting you weasel your way onto that big Bavarian guy's boat without letting me watch his fine ass while you do, you are insane."

CHAPTER 25: THE EXPO

"I look like a gilded strawberry," Cass mumbled to Vamshi as they clambered out of the rideshare car.

Vamshi spared no expense in getting Cass ready for the expo after they landed in Houston. She brought ample amounts of hair product to combat the humidity and more shades of lipstick and false eyelashes than Cass even knew she owned. She'd let her best friend do her hair and makeup after Vamshi took too long to reply after Cass did her own. Vamshi curled Cass's red hair, piled it up on her head and let a few long spirals fall over her exposed shoulders. The red dress left Cass feeling naked. The neckline plunged down to her bottom rib, exposing her pale cleavage and the glittering gold and ruby chunk of a necklace Vamshi lent her. It matched the dangling chandelier earrings that brushed her neck with even the slightest movement. Cass continuously fidgeted with the slit in the dress, worried it would flash her matching red thong.

"They are going to see my ass," Cass grunted, holding Vamshi's black-nailed hand as they walked down the sidewalk. "This dress is flipping open with every step."

"Mhm," Vamshi said through a smile frozen on her face.

She flashed her pearly teeth and sparkling eyes at anyone who looked their way. "To show that hunky Bavarian your creamy gams."

Cass almost vomited at Vamshi's wording. "I'm here to convince him to boat me to Mexico, not bang him."

"Eh." Vamshi shrugged, still grinning.

The night cooled a little, but the humid, warm southern air made Cass's cheeks flush red under her caked on makeup. Vamshi had a talent for making a regular face look like a rockstar. Underneath all the strange sensations, Cass knew she should be grateful. It had been the right call: everyone attending the expo was decked out to the nines. Cass realized some of the people presenting were famous in the artifact world when a few reporters and photographers appeared, asking questions and taking interviews. Besides, with this much makeup and under the false lashes, maybe The Future thugs wouldn't recognize her if they were here.

The museum the expo took place in was called The Museum of International Treasure and boasted a facade that would make the buildings in places like Washington and New York blush. A man at the entrance offered to check their purses and shawls. Cass insisted on keeping hers and had Vamshi do the same. They didn't carry so much as their IDs in their purses, though. Vamshi's held her lock picking kit, some latex gloves, an earbud, and a cheap bug finder she bought from an army surplus store. Or at least something like one. Cass's purse had her phone, a tiny bluetooth earbud connected to Vamshi's, and a weird, little round mirror on a stick that Vamshi insisted she bring for checking around corners.

"This feels insane," Cass whispered as they entered the main area. Waiters in starched vests handed out champaign, security men in dark sunglasses stood on every corner, and each display shined behind a glass and gold frame.

Vamshi made Cass follow her around the displays in a clockwork pattern, searching the faces of the attendees, finding each room where a session would be taking place, and getting a feel for the grounds. Cass noted the red exit signs and the ones that warned to only be opened in an emergency because an alarm would sound. She took in a few of the artifacts and posters, realizing this treasure hunting world was far bigger than she realized.

"Maybe I should get into this," she whispered to Vamshi as they looked at a sarcophagus freshly rescued from the depths of the ocean.

"You will," Vamshi promised around a mouthful of fresh strawberry. "Your anthropology degree makes you more qualified than these seafaring rednecks."

"These seafaring rednecks don't need degrees," a deep, accented voice said.

Cass whirled around to find Dieterich standing just behind them. She met his eyes and his lit up with recognition.

"Ah, so it is you, *wilde kind*." His eyes, which happened to be the same color and brightness as Deston's, smiled at her. "He told me you would show up here, despite my persistence."

"Oh?" Cass asked, holding her ground and making herself stare the man down. "Who said I'd be here?"

"I did." Deston appeared behind his father. His black hair had been brushed and doused in product, but the rebellious fringe still fell in front of his green eyes. His alabaster face had a playful grin masked over it. "I knew you wouldn't take no for an answer."

A young man about Deston's age accompanied them. He had a sprite-like quality to his face and messy, dirty blond hair. Vamshi smiled lustily at him, which he answered with his own sensual look. He didn't wear a suit, opting to wear a silky vest with the sleeves of his dress shirt rolled up.

Feeling a little proud, Cass smiled but blushed when Deston saw her do it. "I have something I have to get done," she said, focusing on her shoes. This only brought her eyes to her very bare leg. She shot her head up just in time to notice Deston following her gaze. Her knees went weak, and she clutched Vamshi hard to keep from falling. Vamshi's eyes still glued to the new young man.

"Klaus," he said to Vamshi, taking her hand. "Fellow friend and treasure hunter from the Father Land."

Cass rolled her eyes inwardly at Vamshi's stunned silence. But she did take in Deston's outfit as well. Deston wore a black silk suit that had obviously been tailored to cling to his body's every angle and curve. His narrow waist tapered underneath the formfitting pants to show off his shiny leather shoes. He caught her staring, and she died a little more inside.

God, focus! she chided herself.

"And I'm going to see it through," she said, finishing her previous thought.

"I admire that," Dietrich said, nodding. He took a quick drink of the champagne flute he held delicately in his thick fingers. "I am just sorry you came all this way. The answer is still no." He raised the flute to her and turned to leave.

"He's stubborn," Deston offered. "And perhaps a little too superstitious for a modern man."

A bit of Cass's enthusiasm melted. But she had more to do than just convince the wild treasure hunter to let her board his boat. Maybe she could find it in the harbor. There were no docks in Galveston, but she could take a raft out. Even a boogie board would work for her needs. She just needed to know which one was his from a distance. Several of the strange-looking treasure hunting boats bobbed among the yachts and other pleasure vessels in the Gulf.

She turned to Deston, feeling guilty about how she was

about to flirt with him to learn where the *Phantom Ivory* was anchored.

"I'd love to show you the vessel," Deston said suddenly. His deep green eyes smiled, but he tried to hide it.

That was easy, Cass thought. Why was he offering the information? "I'd like that," she said to him. She immediately sensed the power shift. He had offered to take her. She didn't have to manipulate him. He wanted her to spend time with him this evening.

He liked her.

"Uh," Cass stammered as the realization hit her. "But not yet."

"What?" Vamshi hissed, digging her nails into Cass's arm. "Why not? Let the nice man show us his boat." She glared into Cass's eyes.

"I have to look around first," Cass whispered. Besides, she knew now that Deston would take her whenever she deemed it time. "I have a, uh, book I want to look into."

Deston watched her as she steered away, but didn't look hurt. He gave a cocky half-grin to her and said, "I'll be waiting."

"Oh, my god, girl!" Vamshi hissed as they ducked into a hallway to read the order of ceremonies. "He's so hot, and you said no."

"Ugh, Vam, I'm not here for that," she said, scanning the glossy paper. "Tell you what." She dug in her purse and pulled out the tiny ear bug. "Put in yours and we'll be in contact."

"Oh, like a James Bond movie." Vamshi excitedly pulled out hers and turned it on. "Testing, one, two, three?"

"Copy loud and clear," Cass confirmed. "Keep your eyes on Deston, so when I'm ready we can hurry."

"Eyes on that fine Bavarian ass, got it." Vamshi marched back into the main room to hobnob and spy.

Shaking her head, Cass slipped out to the garden square

between the four main buildings. She glanced around to get the layout as fast as she could. This green square sat in the middle of the four buildings. A green house, some maintenance buildings and a few large bins were the only things in the garden, aside from the garden walls and trees. The main buildings had the names of them above the double glass doors. Checking the pamphlet, she found that Meredith Navarre would be speaking in the one called the Jay and Daisy Memorial Center. She looked up. It glowed on the other side of the square.

She took one sure step in that direction when she spotted two people standing too still a few yards in front of her. A woman with a short blond bob and a bald man in a well-tailored suit. She recognized Elena, despite her glossy purple dress and makeup. Cass spotted a black band around her thigh where she knew Elena must be concealing her firearm. Squinting, she realized the man was Shades. Without his Shades, which is why she didn't recognize him at first. She thought his eyes were small for his face and that must be why he hid them all the time.

Ducking under the shade of a tree, she peeked out to watch them. Shades had vanished in the two seconds she took to hide.

"Shit," she murmured.

"What is it?" Vamshi's voice whispered.

"Shut up," Cass hissed. "I need to hear."

"Oh, damn, Cass!"

Annoyed, Cass pulled the bug out of her ear. She glared down at the bracelet. "Pakhba," she whispered, "get out here."

The dragon silently slinked out of the bracelet in a ghostly, blue smoke form. "I see," he murmured silently. He glanced around her. "There are too many people. They won't draw attention to themselves."

"Good," Cass nodded. "I need you to go into the opposite

building. Let them see you, just for a second. So they run over there. The fewer people around Meredith Navarre and the Script, the better."

Pakhba streaked off in the opposite direction. When Cass looked back out around the tree, the two thugs were gone. She should have known Meredith Navarre wouldn't go anywhere without her entourage. Surely an eight-hundred-year-old woman needed security.

Cass ran low through the garden towards the Memorial Center. She stopped when she spotted Markus exit the building. He scanned the area, then took the sidewalk that led to where Pakhba had baited them. Thinking she was in the clear, Cass stood up and started a brisk trot through the dewy grass.

She hadn't gotten two steps when a soft hissing rose behind her. Something cold, solid, and flexible slipped around her neck, instantly cutting off her air. She choked and tugged on the thing. Flailing around, she caught sight of a nice suit and black tie: Shades.

Gathering her wits, she elbowed him with all her might. Shades grunted but didn't let go. He was tall and strong. He pulled her backwards towards the maintenance building, throttling her the whole way. She kicked and one of her shoes flew off into the center of the garden.

"Your time as Vedic is over," he hissed into her ear. "You have to be removed for another to—"

With a shout, Cass flexed her right hand and blasted a beam of light into Shades' face. The man grunted and let go, falling backwards. Cass stumbled forward, gasping and taking in her once again glowing right hand.

Don't do this! Mehen called in her head. *Stop pulling on my magic.*

"I'm not," Cass gagged in her defense. "It just happened."

She turned when the sound of more scuffling drew her

attention back. Deston had Shades in a powerful grapple and had given Shades a black eye.

"Security!" Deston shouted. He kicked Shades' ankles, making him fall into a submissive pose. Cass watched with unabashed admiration as Deston wrestled the man to the ground.

Two security guards showed up and, after a quick glance at Cass in her disheveled state, locked Shades in handcuffs and escorted him off the grounds. Cass watched them go, wondering if she should tell them he attacked her. *No*, she decided. It wouldn't matter. Surely an age-old society like The Future could spring one of their thugs from a holding cell.

"Are you all right?" Deston asked, coming to her side and taking her hand. He handed her back her missing shawl. His thumb rubbed gently over her neck where no doubt a wire-shaped bruise blossomed.

She nodded. "Thanks, too. I mean, I had him, but thanks."

"I saw," Deston said, arching a single brow and looking down at her.

Cass paled. "You saw?"

"Well," he replied, shyly looking away. "I mean, I saw something."

He tried to laugh it off, but Cass knew better. Her shoulders dropped, and she looked away.

"I need to find an event," she said, rubbing the bridge of her nose and holding up the glossy pamphlet. "Any idea what room?"

She pointed to Meredith Navarre's face.

"The linguist?" he asked. He pointed to the Memorial Center. "Happening right now. Dad's in there."

The bug in her ear had fallen out. She glanced around the grass for a moment but realized in the dark, she wouldn't find it. "Deston," she said, grabbing his arms. "Come with me inside. Please."

His deep green eyes shot around the garden area. "Fixing to get attacked again?"

She swallowed. "Yeah, actually."

CHAPTER 26: MEREDITH NAVARRE

Cass jogged as well as she could into the Memorial Center, her high heels clopping on the hard marble as they entered. The room was mostly swathed in darkness. A few a-frames showed images of past explorations, digs, and other things Navarre had most likely done. Dim lights shined down on them, making the room look surround in torches. A stage with a black skirt waited at the back of the room before a wall of ornate windows. On it, a digital screen showed some now very familiar pages to Cass. A podium stood to the side of the temporary stage. The single lamp on it barely illuminated the woman's face. Cass stopped at the back of the room, Deston right behind her, and looked at the woman who had been hunting her all semester.

Meredith Navarre stood easily, almost six feet tall. She had the angled cheeks and sharp chin of a Grecian statue. Her hair was a golden-strawberry color, thick, and glossy enough to be silk. She didn't wear it up, but instead let it fall down her back. Somehow, the long hair was more impressive than if she'd piled it up in an elaborate do. Her strikingly gray eyes flashed like a storm at sea. She wore lipstick redder than Elena's. Cass got the innate feeling this woman had seen more ages of the earth than even Merlin.

Before Cass could speak, Deston took her hand and led her a little closer. As they approached—Navarre speaking in a gentle, deep tone—something appeared around her. Cass froze, blinking. The light around the woman twinkled just above her skin. A golden haze wavered in and out of sight as Cass tried to focus on it. Locking in on the aura, Cass squinted. Sound faded just enough for her to concentrate.

Meredith Navarre had a golden aura around her. As she moved, it wafted up like disturbed dust, trailing behind her hand as she waved it and sprinkling off her hair as she moved. Within the golden sight, Navarre's eyes turned to pure, golden, smoldering coals.

A shadow, made of the smokey gold glitter, stopped moving with Navarre's physical body. Cass gasped as the formless face of it turned and looked at her. Cass shrank a little, feeling someone clasping her shoulders from behind, bracing her. The golden shadow of Navarre blinked, focusing in on Cass like it couldn't see her well. Then it turned and melded once again into the physical woman.

"What was that?" Deston whispered softly. He'd been the one behind her, bracing her.

Comforted by the solid feel of him behind her, Cass shook her head. She looked back up at the slides on the screen. They showed towering Aztec pyramids, thick jungles, and a map of Mexico.

"I have the best," Navarre was saying when Cass listened again. "Our investors are not to be doubted. Money is no object. What we seek is so much greater. This will be the find of a lifetime." She smiled at the people listening to her. "For those interested, I will be on my yacht this evening after the events of the night. But be warned." She scanned the crowd. "This exposition is not for the faint of heart. What I disclose is of the utmost secrecy. Please understand that as we conduct our interviews." She turned to the side to motion to a man waiting in the darkness. "Dr. Edwin Charles is the head archeologist on this expedition."

The man came forward. He had a neatly trimmed black beard and combed hair tucked behind his ears, touching his shoulders.

"No way," Deston moaned behind Cass. "Dad's going to be mad."

"Why?" Cass asked, watching the man begin his own slides. "Who is he?"

"He used to work for a big corporation," Deston informed her. "They were privately owned and dealt in all kinds of antiques and artifacts. They have a private collection up in the city. Then, when they screwed him over, he went freelance as a consultant. Worked for dad for years. He was supposed to come with us. Guess he's going to renege on his deal with dad. I have to tell him we needed him."

Cass shrunk into the shadows of half a dozen potted palm trees when Meredith Navarre scanned the audience again as a few linguists came forward to speak with her. She felt oddly under surveillance. Like Navarre knew she was there.

"She said her boat was off shore?"

Deston nodded. "Don't do it, Cass."

She glared up at him, half sarcastic, half impressed. "How do you know what I'm going to do?"

He looked at her knowingly. "You made it pretty clear the kind of crazy you were when you begged complete strangers to take you thousands of miles away in their boat. And when you traveled just as far to show up here at the convention. Am I wrong?" He smiled crookedly.

"You're not," she said, turning and jogging back out of the room. If Meredith Navarre was going to spend a few minutes working the audience, looking for someone who could read the Script, Cass wanted to find it first.

"Mehen, can you hear me?" Cass whispered. She took her shoes off and ran down the street to the beach. The warm, Galveston air made her forget it was halfway through November.

Of course, the dragon replied in her mind. *I can see your thoughts now, too. You are thinking that you can find the Script tonight?*

"Yeah," Cass said. She came to a running stop to take in the piers farther down the shore and the few people milling about the beach. A small private boat slowly drifted towards her. It moved into the marina, where a familiar, tall figure disembarked.

Dietrich, Mehen said. *Are you still planning on trying to convince them to take us south?*

"Yeah," Cass repeated. She jogged to the marina. "I don't know what to tell him. How to convince him. I can't promise him money. I can't even tell him what I'm looking for."

The dragon hummed in her head. *Go to him anyway. Ask once more.*

Cass debated, watching the huge Bavarian man pace the deck of his tiny, yet luxurious, boat. He spoke on the phone. Trusting the dragon in her head, she clenched the straps of her shoes tightly and marched down to the marina. Knowing it was rude to board someone's boat without asking, her heart skipped a beat as she stretched her leg out to hop across. The slit in the dress made her blush as Dietrich's eyes moved to her. He spoke in quick German before facing Cass.

"Ah, our little would-be-stow-away," he said, hands

hanging at his sides. His face turned down and his eyes had lost some of their sparkle. "My son has just informed me that a man vital to our excursion has left us."

"Dr. Charles?" she asked. "I just saw him speaking with a woman named Meredith Navarre. Mr. Van Volxem, she's also heading south to Mexico. I don't know what you and your crew were after down there, but she's got to be competition, right?"

The captain eyed her, crossing his thick arms. "What makes you say that?"

Cass to a deep breath and gulped. "I read about how treasure hunters are very secretive of their plans. Everyone wants discovery rights, right? Well, she stole a map from me."

At this, Dietrich sat up, but he didn't drop his arms. "You had a map? To what?"

Now Cass smiled. "I can't tell you. You know that."

He nodded, half sharing her grin. "But she stole it from you?"

"Yeah. While I was in Egypt, following another lead." Telling the treasure hunter this much was risky, but it had the desired effect.

"*Mein Gott*, you are ambitious." He eyed her now with a kind of admiration. She could tell from how his eyes narrowed that he wondered what in Egypt had led her down to Mexico. "Quite the adventurer. Well." He dropped his hands, slipped his phone into his suit pocket and moved around her to disembark. "I will be on shore tonight. I hope nothing questionable happens with my boat while I'm gone. Or *The Andsaca* moored just there." He pointed with his finger. "It'd be a shame if something went missing from it while the lady was distracted inside."

Cass glanced over Dietrich's shoulder to where he pointed. A large party yacht bobbed off shore, dim and showing no signs of anyone being on board. "What if something were to go missing?" Cass asked. She enjoyed the older seaman's artful hint.

"Well," Dietrich said. "That'd be a tragedy. But you know what treasure hunters do best?"

Cass shook her head.

"Capitalize on tragedy."

When Deston showed up to sail Cass out to *The Andsaca*, she protested at first, but then realized she wasn't the best at the smaller vessels. She and her family had only ever sailed her dad's boat, and they did it as a team. Nerves ate away at Cass as Deston shut the motor off and drifted closer to the larger ship's side.

"Won't they see us coming?" she whispered, tossing her heels aside. "I should have called Vamshi to come with us. She's good when it comes to locked doors."

Deston smiled. "She was quite enraptured by my friend Klaus. I think she's busy."

Cass smiled, gripping the metal ladder down the side of *The Andsaca*. "The tall guy? Dirty blond hair and a sharp vest?"

"That's him," Deston smiled back. He helped her up from the bobbing of the small boat to the more steady big one. "I don't see any lights on. Do you know if she travels with security?"

"Ugh," Cass moaned, vaulting onto the deck. "I know a few of them. They stalked me all the way to Egypt."

"Damn," Deston mused. "But one got taken away by security?"

She nodded. "But there are at least two others I know of."

She scanned the deck and upper section. Deston was right; it was dark on the yacht. "Is the captain's quarters below deck?" she asked him.

Crouching, Deston tiptoed to the white door below the upper deck. The round window was just as dark as the rest of the boat. "Should be down here." He jiggled the handle, but it didn't move.

"This is why I need Vam," Cass sighed.

"I got you covered," Deston smirked. He reached into his inner suit pocket and pulled out the same pick kit Vamshi had. Only his was older, the leather case was faded, and one pick was missing.

Cass scoffed. "You guys really are pirates. Pakhba was right, I guess."

The handle clicked, and the white door swung inwards. They both waited a moment. Not sure what she expected to rise up out of the dark lower deck, Cass craned her neck to look as far down as she could. She took a lighter out of her thigh pouch, noticing Deston's eyes going to her exposed leg, flicked it to life, and walked down quietly. The narrow hall of the ship pressed her into Deston's warm body as they both covertly fought to take the lead. The hall ended in a T-intersection, branching off to two doors.

"I'm left," Cass said, flicking her head for Deston to go right.

She held her breath as she opened the door. It brought a study of some kind into view. A desk bolted to the floor was covered in maps, charts, long reports, and a bottle of red wine. A golden globe stood off to the right, lit up by the moonlight shining in through the wall of windows. Book shelves stood under the windows, locked with small chains over glass doors. To the left, in the corner, a black safe waited, nearly camouflaged in the shadows.

"Hello," Cass murmured, running to it and kneeling

down. Again, she needed Vamshi. She scanned the safe. It was old. Maybe she could listen and crack it like Vamshi taught her.

Mimicking what she'd seen Vamshi do, Cass held her breath and pressed her ear to the safe. The dial was a rusted silver. She hoped the inside was just as rusted. Closing her eyes, she started to turn it. The gears ground faintly in the thick safe door. Cass turned until she felt mild resistance, heard a moment of silence, then felt something click ever so lightly under her fingers.

"I'm amazing," she whispered, spinning the dial in the opposite direction now.

"You are fantastic," a deep, feminine voice snapped in the dark like lightning.

Gasping a high-pitched note, Cass spun around from where she sat on the floor. The lights to the cabin flared on with a hiss. Old oil lamps, linked up by small copper piping along the walls flickered into life. Two familiar thugs stood on either side of the doorway, smirking at her: Markus and Elena. Between them stood Meredith Navarre, clutching Deston. His arms were twisted sharply behind his back like she'd magically bound them. She was so tall that she matched him in height, easily holding him. He looked more pissed than anything else.

Meredith Shoved him off to the side, and Cass saw actual, magical binding on his forearms. It glowed gold and looked like neon. She moved to stand up, but Elena drew a small black handgun and pointed it at her.

"I didn't believe Samuel when he told me about you," Navarre said, her lids heavy as she looked down at Cass. "Where is he?" she asked Elena.

"Taken by security," the thug replied.

Cass made a face. Shades' name was Samuel? She blinked.

"How do you know who I am?" Cass asked.

Elena and Markus shared a glance. Cass kicked herself

internally. She raised her hand where the bracelet adorned her wrist.

"You won't," Navarre sneered. "To use the powers of the dragons is to be an enchantress. That is not who you are, Vedic."

"If you knew who I was all night," Cass spat, "why wait for me to make a move?"

"Solitary," Navarre answered, waving her hands to her elaborate cabin. "Away from the prying eyes of those who do not know what power holds their pathetic worlds in balance." She smiled at Cass. "I'm not going to harm you. We want the same thing."

"You need me to read the Script."

Navarre's brows went up. "Of course. That's a given." She held her hand out to the side and Deston jerked back into her claws by an unseen force.

Cass took a shuddering breath. *How the hell is a Vedic supposed to stand up to an enchantress?* she wondered. Her fingers twitched, considering asking the dragons to lend their power again.

Navarre ran her hand down the side of Deston's face. He grunted into his gag and struggled against the bonds. "I also need a more seaworthy vessel," she said.

"Don't you have millions?" Cass spat. "What's the point in living as long as you have if you haven't gathered limitless wealth?"

The tall woman smiled. "We think alike, Cassandra. I did once. But times have changed. This world changes too much for an old creature like me."

Deston frowned and Cass caught his eyes darting around the room, taking in what he was hearing.

"I prefer to remain hidden," she went on. "At least, until I can rise, unstoppable. That's where you come in, sweet Vedic.

We've already had one failure. But you, you have found Mehen. You can find Quezacotl as well."

"I don't get it," Cass interjected. "You're an enchantress. You already have their power."

Navarre raised her free hand, fingers flexing. Something materialized in her palm. A long, thin, knotted wand nearly a yard long appeared in her hand in a swirl of crackling light and smoke. A rough, pink gem topped it, clutched in the gnarled fingers of the staff. Cass couldn't stop her mouth from popping open. Navarre pointed the wand at Cass. Before she could move, a hot, searing pain shot through Cass from her skull to her toes. She couldn't stop the scream that the spell pulled from her, like being shocked.

Her back arched painfully, her head tossed back as the pain writhed through her. Just as quickly as it came, it vanished. She cried out again and fell to the floor of the cabin. Deston growled behind his gag and struggled away until Markus tackled him once again.

Cass panted, clutching her skull.

"A fraction of the power I could have. That I deserve." Navarre whispered. "I want to move under the surface. I want his boat." She pointed the wand at Deston.

"Don't!" Cass shouted, crawling to her knees. Tears blurred her vision.

But Navarre didn't heed her words. Deston's body snapped back in the same agony she'd felt. He grunted into the gag and fell, writhing.

"Stop!" Cass screamed, running towards Navarre.

The woman used her other hand to thrust out at Cass. Something like an invisible claw grasped Cass's head, holding her in place. She growled against the magic, begging Mehen and Pakhba to come out. They didn't answer her. Deston gave a fresh wave of cries, his body contorting in pain.

"Fine, fine!" Cass shouted, backing away from the invisible hand. "I'll take you there."

Navarre eyed her for two seconds more before releasing Deston. He gasped, completely exhausted on the floor. Cass faced Navarre. "Whatever you want. I'll read the Script and I'll take you there."

The woman smiled and sighed joyfully. "I knew you would. Elena!" she snapped.

The other blonde woman approached her boss, a curious look on her face.

"Markus, get the Script," Navarre ordered. The man moved to the safe and opened it. "Elena, you will be my eyes on this venture."

Cass scoffed darkly. "You're not coming with us?"

The enchantress smiled. "When you get to be as powerful as me, you will understand." She reached out, seizing Elena with that invisible hand. The woman made a soft exclamation but didn't fight. Navarre held up the wand, touching Elena's forehead.

Elena screamed and her eyes burned pink. The veins on the side of her head pulsed. In a flash, everything went back to normal. When Navarre let go, Elena whimpered and rubbed her eyes, which streamed with painful tears.

"You could be this strong, Cassandra," Navarre whispered. She held her hand out to Markus, who handed her the Script. Navarre offered it in turn to Cass, who swiped it. "Perhaps once you have seen the feathered dragon, you will consider my power for yourself."

"Hell no," Cass shot back. "You're crazy, you old hag."

Navarre smiled joyfully and laughed behind closed lips. "I am. But what do you expect from one who has touched the power of the universe? Who has ridden on the backs of dragons and locked away the magic that weaves together our power? Cassandra, look at the dragons. Know their power.

They hide it from you. They always hide the true strength from their Vedics. You are nothing more than a guardian. A puppet they use to hide away. I understand this too well, pet." She shook her head. "They made their magic to be harnessed and then deny you and condemn those who would use it."

The gentle, soft tone of the woman helped calm Cass. It was true: the dragons were secretive. Perhaps too secretive. She'd risked her life, her future, for them, but they hardly shared anything with her. Not what might happen or could happen. Not what she could do. Only what she could not do.

"With all of them in an enchantress' grip," Navarre went on, "reality can be anything I want. Didn't you feel that power? Don't you want it again? To feel that? To have more? To possess the meaning of your own life in the palm of your hand."

In the moment, face to face with a literal Egyptian god with a mythical monster trying to eat her, yes, it had seemed the only way to get out. But Mehen had told her there would be consequences for using the dragon's magic.

"Shut up," Cass snapped. She clutched the Script to her chest. "Let me prepare, and we'll leave when I'm ready."

"You will be ready by sunrise," Navarre said easily. She swiped her wrist and the bonds on Deston vanished. He groaned and rolled over onto his side. "You may go."

CHAPTER 27: SET SAIL

After Meredith Navarre left the cabin, Markus, Elena, and two other Future thugs Cass hadn't seen grappled her and Deston, taking them abroad Dietrich's boat. There, they found that Navarre had seen to it already. The crew was gone. The thugs had removed all the radios and disabled the Wi-Fi. Even Shades had made his reappearance on the upper deck, looking disgruntled much to Cass's pleasure.

Maruks shoved Cass hard down the stairs of the treasure hunter's boat. Deston came behind, held between two others.

"Where's my dad?" he grunted, tripping on the way down.

"Inside," Elena replied, her eyes red. "We need him to sail us there."

"This is my fault," Cass moaned. "I'm so sorry, Deston, you don't deserve this." She glanced to the side of the tight hallway and saw Dietrich pacing in his cabin. He looked alright in that he was walking. A huge black and yellow bruise took up the entirety of the left side of his face. He hadn't gone down without a fight. He crackled his knuckles as he walked.

When they passed, Dietrich looked up and met Deston's eyes sadly.

"We'll be fine," Deston said as Shades unlocked a second door that led to the small, tight quarters. "We've been in situations like this before."

Cass doubted that. Maybe they got in trouble with customs or Coast Guard. But most likely never encountered ancient enchantresses wielding dragon magic. But she appreciated his bravery.

"Hey," Cass snipped when Elena shoved her into the room. "Where's Vamshi?"

Elena made a groan that told Cass she remembered how fiercely Vamshi had fought in Egypt. "She's fine. But Meredith is keeping her."

Then she was not fine. Cass swallowed hard, hoping Vamshi would not try to escape and just stay safe until she came back. She couldn't imagine her fiery friend tethered to a desk or locked in a dark basement. She hoped Meredith Navarre didn't hurt her. Or worse.

Markus tossed the Script into the room where it thudded loudly onto the metal ground. "Read that. In the morning, we're out of here. If you don't have coordinates for us..." He pointed to Deston. "We'll find ways of making you read."

Cass knelt and quickly snatched up the Script. "It doesn't always work like that, you bastard," she hissed.

He glared at her. "Make it work like that."

Elena nodded, slamming the door seconds later. A clattering of keys told Cass that she had locked it. Cass glanced around at the tiny porthole windows.

"I don't suppose these open?" she asked.

"Into the ocean?" Deston asked, half smiling, but also looking beat. "We're below the waterline down here. The ship is deeper than you think. Need it to be for when we haul things up from deep down."

"With that crane on the upper deck," Cass said. She hadn't seen it just now, but remembered it from when Rana had introduced them. "One day, you'll have to tell me about your treasure hunting adventures."

Deston let his face relax into a real smile now. "Dad tells them better than I do. He makes them sound so exciting." He leaned up against a metal pole at the end of a bunk. "But your story is looking far more interesting."

"You just had to ask," she sighed, sitting on the floor and opening the Script.

He shrugged. "Kind of hard not to when my bones are being set on fire by a magical-looking stick." He nodded to the Script. "So what is that? Some kind of code book?"

Cass ran her hands over a blank page, just after the last one that had revealed itself to her. "They call it the Dragon Script. I'm the only one who can read it. It's a long story. But right now, I need to read it to figure out where this temple or sacred ground might be where Quezacotl is sleeping. I have to go there and awaken him to protect him." She held her bracelet. She touched the golden one, tapping Pakhba on his golden nose. "Pakhba, my familiar kind of guardian thing. He loves vanilla ice cream." She gently lifted the white, tear-shaped gem with one finger. "Mehen. She's the one I found in Egypt."

"You have dragons with you now?" he asked, joining her on the ground. His deep green eyes looked honest. He didn't make fun of her behind his cute forelock over his eyes. This made her melt a little. "Why not use them to blast these sons of bitches out of the Gulf?" he asked.

With a sigh, she flipped another page. "It doesn't work like that. Taking their power, using it to my own advantage, is wrong or something. The ones who do that are called enchanters. I'm a Vedic. I'm just supposed to guard them. Not use them. It's like a betrayal if I do."

"And the enchanters, like that psycho lady, are bad?" he asked.

Cass thought about this, looking up from the Script. "I'm

not sure. There was a story where one enchanter kind of had a thing for the Vedic. I don't see why you couldn't use the dragon magic for good. But I also see how using it at all might be cause for worry."

She looked back down. Deston's knee was awfully close to her bare one. She half hoped they'd fetch her pack and bring her her clothes. No way in hell was she going to traipse around Mexico in this red dress with her cleavage out. She wondered, since he was so tall, if Deston was looking at her chest. She didn't look up.

The Script glowed. Deston flinched, but didn't say anything.

"It's okay," Cass said, relieved it finally came to her. "This is good." She scanned the pages. The blotting leaked over the page, the spidering Script appearing in sharp shapes this time. They seemed to be telling her numbers. "I don't get it," she whispered.

"Do you see something?" Deston asked. His voice came distant.

"Numbers?" she whispered. "I don't understand. I've never gotten numbers before."

"What are they?" he asked, suddenly calm and interested.

"22.182925," Cass blurted, the numbers coming and going quickly in puffs of gold and black ink. "93.748326."

"Coordinates!" Deston crowed.

Cass blinked, and they were gone. "Shit! I don't remember them," she cried, shaking the Script like that might bring them back.

Deston smiled. "I do. Dad had me memorize those kinds of numbers all the time." He repeated them back to her perfectly.

"You sure?" she asked. The room felt darker now that the golden glow of the Script had vanished.

He nodded, a cocky smirk making its way over his handsome face.

With his reassurance, her body collapsed. Her spine arched, and she dropped her elbows onto her knees and her face into her hands. The night's events broke what little resolve she had left. Deston scooted closer to her. When he put his arm around her, she first wanted to push him away. Not because she didn't like it. Quite the opposite. She wanted to throw herself at him. It just felt wrong. She had gotten him into this. They'd finally witnessed a tiny fraction of Meredith Navarre's power and she knew there was more. And the wand...

"I'm really sorry," she said, not letting herself collapse on to him. "This should have never happened to you and your dad. And Vamshi. It shouldn't have happened to me!" Never did she imagine she'd be kidnapped on a boat heading out into foreign waters. This was so much bigger than Egypt.

Deston pulled her closer, wrapping his other arm around her. She thought he'd let go sooner or later, but the way he repositioned himself, she realized he was in for the night. Sighing in resignation, she let herself lean against him. His heart thudded in her ear as she rested her head against his chest.

"Thank you," she whispered.

"Are you kidding?" Deston said gently, but she heard his stupid smirk on his lips. "I get to hang out with a sexy magic dragon girl. I feel pretty lucky, all things considered."

"Oh, my god," she moaned, but grinned.

The next morning, Shades threw open the door without so much as knocking. He, Markus, and one other goon marched in to yank Cass off the lower bunk. She'd never really fallen asleep but had drifted in and out, unused to the swaying and bobbing of the *Phantom Ivory*. They grappled Deston and hauled them both up into the navigation cabin where they had paper maps laying out over the normal instruments. Elena waited there, arms crossed and glaring. Outside, the sun blazed bright, shining off the gentle waves of the Gulf. Outside the dipping horizon, Cass couldn't see the shore any more. They must have moved out overnight.

Elena handed her a lukewarm plastic cup of coffee. "Show us," she snapped. Her eyes were still rimmed red and looked irritated.

Cass clasped the cup of coffee and looked down at the map. It was all squiggles and grids to her. She gulped and looked up nervously. "I-I don't know."

Markus balled his fists, but Shades held him back with a tap to his shoulder.

"Listen," Elena sighed, one hand on her hip, the other on the table as she leaned over it. "We don't have a lot of time, Vedic. Any of us."

This last statement made Cass inspect the thugs. All three of them looked more tense, worn out, and anxious than before. Suddenly, Cass understood. "Meredith Navarre has all the time in the world," she said steadily. "But we—you— don't. She has Vamshi and knows where my family lives. We're replaceable." She made sure to look Elena in the eyes. "Another Vedic could come a hundred years from now. Doesn't make any difference to her. Deston?" She looked up at him. "You remember the numbers." She pointed to the map.

Deston jerked away from Shades, ran his hand through his black hair, and looked over the map. He mumbled as he scanned one, then moved it aside for another. On the second map, Cass recognized the horn-shape of Mexico. Deston ran a long finger down the map. "Here," he said, finally pointing. Cass sighed in relief that he remembered the numbers.

Markus tilted his head, frowning and leaning in close to the map. "That's literally the middle of oceanic nowhere."

"That's what I read," Cass said as bravely as she could. "I swear. Everything I have is at stake. I have no reason to lie."

"True," Shades mumbled, rubbing his chin. He glanced up at Elena. "We'll head there. Get the captain."

They herded her and Deston to the side and put under Markus and one other goon's watchful eye as they fetched Dietrich from the captain's quarters.

"Dad, are you okay?" Deston asked anxiously.

The big Bavarian man waved his worried son off with a tired gesture before being taken to the helm. Markus shoved Cass out of the navigation room, followed her out, and locked the door. She stumbled onto the huge open deck of the treasure hunting ship and instantly felt the salty, cool wind cut her skin. She crossed her arms, fully aware of Markus eyeing her cleavage.

She glared at him, but didn't turn away, realizing the game of chicken she'd just gotten herself into. Her red hair whipped into her face, but she didn't blink.

"Hey," Elena called, coming up from the lower deck. She held Cass's adventure pack. She tossed it to her. "Put some clothes on and don't even think about wandering off."

"To freaking where?" Cass mumbled, marching down to the room she'd slept in. After she changed into jeans, her Converses, and had an army green jacket over her arms, she came above deck again. Aside from the huge crane hanging off the back of the boat, dozens of other oddities caught her attention as she waited for the Future thugs to release Deston. Once they did, she went to his side. Mostly so his massive frame could block the wind.

"We have a few days off of sailing to go," he informed her. "We're already far out or I'd recommend going over the side."

Cass squinted into the wind, taking in the blue horizon and how it stretched out into eternity. A feeling of fear and being trapped like never before consumed her. "We have to try to not piss them off," she sighed. "Keep me busy with all your big gadgets, will you?"

Deston shot her a curious, but playful, look.

"The stuff you used to find treasure, perv," she laughed.

That day and the next, Deston explained the things she found on the boat. A large yellow cylinder of metal that looked like a tiny submarine or some kind of bomb turned out to be a thing called a boat-towed side scan sonar system.

"Helps us see the bottom of the ocean floor," Deston explained while they stood on the side. "For the deep, hard to reach treasure."

The one tool that caught Cass's attention more was a remotely operated underwater vehicle that had a light and camera on the front. "Don't suppose you have a manned one?" she asked Deston as Shades and Markus watched closely on the third day of sailing.

"No," he said. "But we do have a set of scuba diving propellers. You hold them in your hand and they drag you through the water. You can get going pretty fast with them."

Cass made a note of it. She had no intention of jumping ship, especially out in the middle of nowhere. But she wanted options.

The next day, Cass woke up to the *Phantom Ivory*'s engines quieting. She sat up in her bunk, heart racing.

"It's okay," Deston said as he stared. "Just means we've reached our destination." He rubbed his eyes. "They have to be planning to hit land in Mexico, though. We really only have about a thousand miles of fuel on this thing."

Cass grabbed up the Script, wrapped it in her's and Deston's belts and hung it from her hip. She slung her pack onto her back. "Great. Which means they might drop us off and leave."

Deston wrinkled his face, unsure. "I doubt it. Stealing a ship like the *Phantom Ivory* sounds too high profile for these guys. They like to lie low, I gather."

He was right. She'd seen them back off when her neighbor looked over into their yard. They wanted to be stealthy, stay a secret. She vaguely wondered if she could use that to her advantage when Shades yelled out from above for them to come up.

Taking her hand, Deston led Cass up. A loud clang told them they'd dropped a massive anchor she'd not seen. The chain on it rattled loudly for a dozen minutes as she, Deston, Elena, and the others approached the side of the massive open deck.

"Well?" Elena asked, glaring at Cass.

Cass took a deep breath and looked over the vast, endless blue. Taking in the wide open nothingness filled her with that terrible, trapped dread again. Not a single ship, sandy coast, or odd rock formation came into view.

"See how there're no birds?" Markus said snidely. "They can't come out this far. Nothing to land on. That's how isolated we are."

She understood better than the thug knew. Licking her wind-dried lips, Cass looked out. She rubbed the bracelet, silently begging for help.

I know this wind, Mehen said solemnly. *We were here once.*

Long ago. She paused and Cass thought she heard the dragon take a breath. *He is here.*

"Where?" Cass mumbled, fear starting to mount. Did she need to read the Script again? She glanced over at Deston, who waited for her. She gulped again and looked out over the emptiness.

Look as a Vedic, Pakhba suggested. *Then, you will need to call to him. There will be words in the Script.*

Her breath speeding up, Cass took the Script from her hip and opened it to a blank page. Her hands shook. Looking out into the blue ocean, she willed the golden sight to help her. She unfocused her eyes until the glittering, snapping golden hue appeared in her peripheral vision. As it did, the ocean water turned more and more clear. The blue of it never vanished, but she could see through it.

"Holy shit," she murmured as a single sandstone structure came into view below the surface. The more she looked, as always, the more came into her sight.

The structure was clearly an Aztec pyramid below the ocean. Hundreds of gold stairs stepped out into the deeper blue, but she could see a dirt path coming out from the base. Behind the pyramid, an ever-green jungle sprawled out, rolling over hills and into an ancient village made of stone. It was like looking down over an Aztec city with the view of a bird. Suddenly, she recognized the pyramid.

"This is where Jatziri tried to stop Quezacotl," she breathed in utter awe. "Xoco ran to her here. He was an enchanter and a priest. She was a Vedic. He loved her, but she stayed to save the city from the wrath of Quezacotl."

"I thought enchanters were the bad guys," Deston mumbled, flicking his head towards Elena.

"I don't get it either," Cass said, scanning the ocean-dwelling city. She held the Script up, ready for the next step.

The pages flipped of their own accord until the massive tome hovered before her without her holding it. At this, a few gasps went up and everyone stepped back from her. Even Deston.

Cass glared down at the Script and felt a hot wind pick up the long, red strands of her hair and toss them around her. Her feet left the deck. Looking down, she saw she rose several yards above the boat. Ignoring the cries, she focused on the city below the waves. The higher she ascended, the more she saw the underwater jungle and city spanned far out underneath the *Phantom Ivory.*

The Script drew her attention back down as words appeared. Instinctually, she knew she had to read them out loud. She didn't understand the sounds or words she made or how she made some of them, as they sounded only like the gentle, throaty roar of a dragon. After each word was spoken, it vanished off the Script. Instantly, she felt compelled to raise her arms. Letting the magic tell her what to do, she slowly lifted her arms over her head.

As she did, the crashing of waves and rushing of water deafened her. The city rose. Water poured out from the windows of stone homes and the temple. The trees bent and bowed from the weight of the ocean, then sprang back as they were freed of its embrace. The jungle rose with the pyramid and the city until it hit the bottom of the boat. She heard everyone below cry out, but couldn't stop. She held her hands high, fingers flexed until the deck of the ship met her dangling feet, making her knees buckle.

She gasped and fell, the golden sight vanishing. She slipped backwards on the slanted deck, but Deston caught her. Curious and terrified, Cass scrambled to her feet and ran to the edge of the ship. The slight angle made sense as she looked over to see the poor *Phantom Ivory* now perched on a huge, jungle-spotted rocky cliff. The metal groaned as it settled into the earth and held the ship fast.

A burst of colorful birds crying and fluttering out of the now top-side jungle canopy drew Cass's eyes to the expansive city and temple before her. The top of the pyramid poked out of the trees and looked to be a mile away.

"Get a ladder," Elena snapped. "We go now."

CHAPTER 28: FIVE SUNS

The Future thugs made Cass go down first, weary after the danger they put themselves in while traversing the temple in Egypt. Once on the ground, Cass looked back up at the *Phantom Ivory*. It looked ridiculous perched on the hill. Elena finally came down after all the others. She checked her phone and looked surprised.

"Excellent service," she mused. "Vedic, if you try anything, I give the word and your accomplices start to drop."

They had Vamshi somewhere, kept Dietrich hostage on the ship with two other members of the Future, and the trio, plus their newcomer, outnumbered her and Deston.

"We're going to need people," Cass grumbled, leading the way into the jungle. "The Aztecs believed the only way to keep existing was blood sacrifice."

She smiled lightly when she caught Markus give Shades a quick glance. Tightening the straps on her pack, she put her head down and entered the ancient jungle. Insects and creatures buzzed all around them, making a constant strain of noise.

If a jaguar jumps out to kill me, you better have my back, she thought to Pakhba. *That shouldn't count as using your magic. You have to protect me, too.*

Of course, the dragon whispered back. *You will need us before your little jaunt is over. Quezacotl is not a gentle dragon.*

Deston nudged her. "What were you doing just there? You made a face."

Cass held up her golden bracelet. "Telling my dragon sidekick he better have my back."

"Remind me again why we can't use the two all-powerful dragons on your wrist to wipe these jerks off the face of the earth?" he asked.

"Not my power," she reminded him. She looked up, taking in the slowly approaching pyramid where she'd seen Jatziri sacrifice herself for her people. "Pakhba," she asked out loud, swatting at a mosquito, "what do you mean I'll need your help before the end?"

The dragon slithered out of the bracelet in a transparent sheen. Deston stumbled and stopped walking, eyes locked on the dragon. Cass grabbed his arm and marched him on, knowing that they couldn't stop or the Future would get suspicious.

"Since the age of the fifth sun, he has been enraged with your world," Pakhba said. "I fear a part of him wants to destroy it."

This was news to Cass. "I thought you guys were... I don't know, good?"

"It wants to destroy our world and we're going to wake it up?" Deston hissed.

"Ah, the pirate," Pakhba moaned, glaring at Deston. "I'll deal with you later."

The reminder that Pakhba should erase Deston's memory made Cass's heart heavy. He'd been brave, advocated for her to join them on the treasure hunt, and stuck around when she revealed her quest. Losing Rana had broken her heart. She couldn't imagine what losing Deston would feel like after they had this adventure together. He already made her toes curl in the best way. She didn't want to imagine it. Assuming they made it out alive.

He may show mercy, Mehen said to only Cass. *Your pirate has shown valor beyond what we expected. Your heart chose well, young Vedic.*

Don't get my hopes up, Cass replied sadly.

The thick trunks of the trees, curtains of vines, and long, rubbery leaves of the undergrowth made it hard to see where they were going. A parrot screamed, fleeing from a branch Deston cut down with a machete Shades brought. Cass jumped, the sudden noise frightening her.

Once they reached the city, they slowed to a trudge, taking in the architecture. Not a sign of overgrowth, neglect or age showed in the city. In fact, Cass wondered if villagers would pop out at any moment. The pyramid was in the center of the village. Cass blinked. A flash of gold-glowing people milling about the streets appeared, then vanished in the space of the blink.

What she called the golden sight seemed to be the one piece of magic she possessed. She blinked again and witnessed a packed village square: women carrying baskets on their heads, men bringing in the prizes from their hunts, and children playing a game in the duty streets. When she blinked and saw the golden ghosts, she heard them too. The sound snapped into her ears, making her jump. She led the group onward, every once in a while stopping to look upon the past. Curious statues poked out of a copse of trees to her right, somewhere a river ran pleasantly, and now and then, a slight breeze stirred her sweaty hair.

She took out her phone and snapped a few pictures, saving them to her cloud drive for later. Then, she went back to looking for the ghosts.

"This is incredible," she whispered. "I can see them. It's almost like—ah!" She screamed, reeling backward.

She'd blinked and a young man appeared directly before her, glaring into her face. He'd shouted at her, nearly bursting her ear drums. Deston caught her, asking her what happened.

"Just..." She swallowed. "Just seeing things." Had that been the enchanter? Remembering how she saw the ghost of the Vedic in Egypt, she wondered if all of them—Vedic and enchanter alike—could come into her sight. *Great,* she thought. *The last thing I need is the supernatural world working against me, too.*

Starting again, she stopped looking for the golden sight. Instead, she wound her way through the city towards the temple in silence. But she still felt the eyes on her. Many eyes. Like she walked in that world, too.

She stood at the base of the pyramid, looking up at the hundreds, or maybe thousands, of stairs before her.

"Look," Deston gasped, pointing to the ground.

Cass looked down and saw she had two shadows. "What the hell?" she mumbled and looked up at the sky. "What. The. Hell?" she repeated, slower this time.

The whole party looked up. The sun set in the west, visible through the gaps in the city's structures. But to the east, painting the sky a bright pink and splashing light over the jungle they'd just come through, rose another sun. The dual light source made her cast two shadows onto the steps.

"What does that mean?" Elena asked, marching up to Cass. "You know all the histories of these places. What is that?"

"Uh," Cass stammered, not sure. She racked her brain. It

could be something based in the rich and expansive myths the Aztecs had, or it could be something to do with Script. "I don't know," she began, but then it hit her. Pakhba had said something about Quezacotl and the fifth age. "The suns," she whispered. "The creation story," she said when Elena looked about to lose her patience. "But there was something about time in the Script." She spun to face the west and the sun that set there. "We have five suns to figure this out."

The others exclaimed, spinning on the spot to look around. "What does that mean?" Markus asked.

"The Aztec gods made five suns," Cass explained. "Each one got destroyed or fell from the sky until they made the fifth sun. Our sun. That one is said to be destroyed by a great earthquake, sinking the land into the ocean."

Deston faced the east where the sun rose. "That's the second sun. The first is about to go down. What do we have to do before the first sun sets?"

"I don't know!" Cass cried, pulling the Script up. "But we might only have this one chance."

"Just raise the city again," Elena said harshly, hand on her hip.

"Oh, yeah, of course," Cass growled sarcastically. "Right after the city gets sunk by a huge earthquake in a few suns."

That shut The Future up. Elena dropped her hand and looked around, nervous. "Whatever it is, it's going to be in that temple."

She hadn't even finished her sentence before Shades and Markus started to gallop up the stairs. Deston sprinted after them. Elena and Cass shared a glance, knowing full well whatever did wait at the top wouldn't be accessible without her. And it was thousands of years old; it wasn't going anywhere. The two women took their time, saving their breath as they ascended the stairs.

Cass had to stop halfway up and chug from her water

bottle. The two suns made her sweat profusely until the front of her shirt was soaked through. Once at the top, she stopped to take in the dark stone doorway before them.

"It's so much bigger than I thought it'd be," she panted. She peered into the doorway, but nothing broke through the solid blackness. "I have a weird feeling that once we get in there, it will be like the scale room in Egypt. Basically, on a totally different plane of reality. The inside will be bigger, not laid out like a traditional Aztec pyramid."

"What do you mean?" Deston asked, slowly creeping towards the doorway. "I can't see beyond it."

Cass nodded. "Because it's like it doesn't exist until we enter. Must be some kind of magic to keep it safe." Taking a deep breath, she crossed under the stone lintel. As she expected, the moment her foot crossed the threshold and landed inside the main temple, the room expanded in size. The others gasped silently as they passed in. But it wasn't as grand as she had expected. The sun shot through from two windows, one on the east, the other on the west and crossed on the floor where a stone altar waited. The large rectangle altar was ornate, decorated in the angled features of creatures Cass didn't know right away.

She squatted down to examine the beings, frowning. Before admitting she didn't know who or what they were, she flipped open the Script. The first thing that appeared was a blotching animal print with claws.

"Oh, jaguar!" Cass cried. Her voice echoed five times before it dissipated. "So it is the five suns." She looked up at the altar. Five figures danced across the front.

"There are five basins up here," Deston said.

Writing appeared under the jaguar paw. "Nahui Ocelotl," she read slowly, not sure she pronounced it correctly.

"Sun of the Jaguar," Elena confirmed.

"Then," Cass said, her legs starting to cramp after all the stairs and now the squatting. "Nahui Ehecatl?"

"Sun of the wind," Elena confirmed. She squatted next to Cass.

"Oh, I know that story!" Deston interrupted. "Third was rain, fourth was water, and then—Cass was right—the earthquake. But before that, Nanahuatzin became the moon." He pointed to the fourth deity on the altar. "But he only did it because there were two suns in the sky and they were killing the people the gods had made. He sacrificed himself when none of the other gods would."

Cass stood up. "I still don't get it." She scanned the basins. Yes, there were five. And five deities. "Do we need to gather something?"

Silence fell as the shadow from the western sunk lower and lower.

"We need to make a choice," Elena said, shifting her feet nervously. "We need to leave now if we cannot solve the riddle."

Cass put the Script down onto the altar and leaned hard onto her palms, looking over it. As she looked, the stone scraped, little puffs of dust flecking off as words chiseled into the stone before her very eyes. She pushed back, gasping.

"Script is appearing," she told the others, remembering they couldn't see it. She traced it slowly, reading as the words appeared. "It says I can call out a name for help."

"Like a god?" Shades mumbled, scratching his head.

That was an idea, but not something that sounded like a good one. The Aztec gods wanted blood. She couldn't blame them; they sacrificed themselves to make the earth. A sudden idea hit Cass.

She cleared her throat and looked around the room. "Umm," she called loudly. "Jatziri? I'm sorry to call you up, but you're a Vedic, I'm a Vedic. I need help. I don't understand."

She heard the others whispering behind her. No doubt thinking she was crazy. But she'd seen ghosts in the Egyptian temple. Surely something of Jatziri's spirit remained. Would calling up the dead go against her role as a Vedic? She waited, listening, but neither Mehen nor Pakhba spoke. Just as she was about to call again, a shadow appeared on the floor. The others behind her gasped and turned to the east.

Cass squinted up into the rising sun coming in the long window and saw what cast the shadow. Wreathed in golden sunlight, spikes of it flashing through a palm crown around her head, Jatziri descended the beam of light as if it were a simple set of stairs. Beside her, which she held on to, a near horse-sized jaguar came with her. Its green eyes pierced into Cass.

Jatziri wore the robes of an Aztec priestess and colorful stones, gems, and gold hung from her neck, ears, and arms. Bright flowers and rubbery leaves wreathed her head. She looked stoic as she bowed her head to Cass.

Before Cass could speak, the Aztec Vedic said, "Five offerings you must find. Bring them here, and each god they're due."

"What's she saying?" Deston whispered to Cass. She realized only she could understand Jatziri.

"But," Jatziri went on, her voice fading in and out. "You must give an offering for each sun." She pointed behind Cass to the west. "See how the sun dips? You have very little time. Find the offering."

"Deston!" Cass shouted, whirling around to face them. "What's the story of the first sun?"

Shaken at her sudden urgency, he stammered. "The jaguar sun," he began.

Cass glared in thought at the jaguar beside Jatziri. "What happened?"

"It was the god Tezcatlipoca," he said, running his hands quickly through his hair. This made his forelock fringe attractively over his eyes and made Cass distracted for just a moment. He was so cute when he thought and was frazzled, she decided.

"He was the sun, but he was weak. So our friend Quezacotl was angry with him."

Cass shook her head. "That's not all. Something we can offer."

"Acorns!" he suddenly shouted, his green eyes widening. "The people were giants, so the small sun couldn't keep them warm. The gods gave them acorns to eat, but when Tezcatlipoca fell out of the sky, enraged, he sent jaguars to kill the giants."

Even without asking, Cass knew the spirit jaguar was out of the question. She guessed it had to stay with Jatziri while she sojourned in the world of the living.

"I saw them!" Cass cried suddenly. "When we were coming through the jungle. There were three huge statues of warriors or something poking out of the trees." She glanced at her bracelet. "I can get them before the sun sets." She turned to Jatziri. "Are the others having to do with the story?"

Jatziri smiled, not giving an answer.

"Deston," Cass said, "what might the others be? We split up, each get an offering. That way, we have them all as the suns set."

Elena looked between Shades and Markus nervously. "Can we do that?"

"You're as good as enchanters," Cass grumbled. "I'm sure you count. Deston," she snapped again. She took the white dragon tear off her bracelet, ready to summon Mehen. "The story?"

"Okay," he said, calming himself. His eyes shot to the western window. The sun had dipped below the tree line now. "The people became corrupt and Quezacotl sent a hurricane to wipe them out, but not before turning them into monkeys."

Cass blanched. The last thing she wanted to do was catch a monkey, kill it, and offer it up to the gods. She looked over to Shades.

"Fine," he acquiesced. He unholstered his gun and ran back out the door.

"Then," Deston went on, "the third sun? That was the rain. But it's not rain like you think. It was fire. There was a creature the gods had made—I can't think of its name—and Tezcatlipoca stole his wife. But the creature was the sun. So he made it rain fire from the sky, destroying everything."

At this, Markus made a noise that sounded oddly guilty and said, "That sounds about right." Cass glanced at him to find him turning away, rubbing his chin.

"Find us fire, Markus," Elena snapped. "I have a feeling the lighter won't work. Gather supplies to make it with your hands."

Grumbling, Markus followed Shades out.

"Okay, fourth?" Cass asked.

"Water sun," Deston said. He looked a little calmer now. "The creature's sister was chosen to be the sun, but by now, Quezacotl was jealous of the suns. So he struck her down, and she tore open the sky, flooding the world. But that's where it gets interesting," he said.

"We don't have time for interesting," Cass cut in. "Elena, water. A sacred spring or somewhere that would be special to the people."

Nodding, Elena ran out.

"And me?" Deston asked.

"With me," Cass breathed, running out to the top of the pyramid. "We have to fight giants."

Cass loved the feeling of flying on Mehen's back. She'd called up the dragon, asked for her help, and then she and Deston had mounted her. More than the flips her stomach did from flying on the back of a dragon, she loved Deston's arms clamped tightly around her middle. His panting breath came in hot puffs against her neck as he pulled them together tightly.

Thrilling isn't it? Mehen asked and Cass heard her smiling.

Remind me to fly on you more when we have a spare moment, Cass replied.

Mehen gave a chuckle. *I'm not talking about the flying.*

Pakhba made a strange sound somewhere between a snort and growl at this. Cass blushed and couldn't stop her toes from curling up in her boots.

"There!" Cass pointed to the grove she'd seen before. A giant made of stone stood in the clearing. It looked fierce, wearing a feathered headdress and holding a spear.

Mehen circled from above. "Be careful, Cassandra," she called. "Remember: in this story, you are the jaguar."

She and Deston dismounted a good distance off and slowly approached the clearing. "It looks like a sparring circle," Cass noted. Mehen vanished into the bracelet.

As they neared, they spotted a rack, ornate and made of stone, holding a variety of weapons. Deston reached for the obsidian spear, but Cass grabbed his wrist.

"Wait. I feel like if we grab it, that warrior comes to life." She scanned the area. Behind the warrior, a thick oak tree grew, looking strongly out of place. "That's what we need." She pointed to the large, golden acorns growing on it. And they had to hurry.

She scanned the weapons and also grabbed a long, obsidian spear, hoping to the keep the warrior at a distance.

Channeling her younger sister Ella and all the sparing she'd made her endure over the years, she removed the spear from the wrack. Deston took one at the same time. When they did, they heard the soft thud of bare feet against the soil.

Cass bent her knees like Ella taught her and held the spear out in front of her. Spinning around, she saw the warrior had vanished. "Watch my back," she ordered Deston as she slinked towards the oak. When she felt him turn back to back with her, some kind of connection hooked her to him. Almost like she could sense his movements and read his thoughts.

She lunged towards the tree, but a sudden, terrifying war cry froze her to the spot. Feeling Deston move as if in slow motion, she ducked. The warrior leapt from the jungle bushes and landed in front of her, cutting her off. She sank to her knees just as Deston's spear helicoptered over her head. The warrior leaned far back, dodging the spear. She thrust hers up, stepping with her lead leg for power. She grazed the warrior's side.

Deston rolled over her to face the warrior and entered a kind of back-and-forth combat that sent a thrill through Cass. The spears clacked loudly against one another as Deston drove the warrior back. Cass took the opportunity to run at the oak again. Behind her, Deston grunted, and she heard his body hit the f. She spun to see the warrior raise his club up with a victorious shriek, ready to bring it down on Deston's head.

Cass screamed, lunging with the spear. Knowing the warrior would tilt back again, away from her thrust, she didn't put all her weight into it. This time, when the warrior dodged backwards, she jerked the spear back, quick as lightning, and thrust again in an upward motion. The warrior had to take an extra step back he hadn't anticipated, and stumbled. As he did, Deston spun his spear at the warrior's feet from the ground. The sweeping motion took the warrior down long enough for Cass to help Deston up.

Together, they circled the warrior. His mask-covered face danced quickly between the two of them, the feathers snapping back and forth on his headdress. Finally, he began a deep, guttural chant.

"That's not good," Deston guessed. "Get the acorns, I'll distract him."

Cass sensed before she turned that Deston wouldn't move fast enough to take the warrior on by himself. But maybe she was fast enough? She dropped the spear to run faster and dashed to the oak. Behind, the warrior gave a great cry. Cass sensed Deston's movements. He dodged left, ducked, struck out with the spear. Even before the warrior moved, she knew Deston had put too much force into his leading leg. Just like Ella had always told her not to do. She spun, terrified he'd be killed.

The flat side of the warrior's obsidian-lined club struck Deston in the side so hard she swore she heard his ribs break. He crumpled to the ground, moaning and holding his side. Sweat and tears of pain ran down his temples. The warrior turned on Cass, realizing she was closer to the goal than before. Chanting again, he ran towards her. With every step, he grew in size. Cass dashed towards the oak, screaming. The shadow of the warrior turned giant as it returned to its stone size. She had no hope of defeating that.

Turning, she faced it and screamed for Mehen. The white dragon exploded from the bracelet, roaring, teeth bared. The force of Mehen's appearance shot Cass backward as if she had a cannon strapped to her arm. She soared backwards, ramming into the oak so hard, all the breath got knocked out of her. Her head thudded against the trunk and a red light blinded her with a shot of pain.

When she blinked the light away, she beheld Mehen grappling with the giant, her huge serpentine body wrapped around it like a rope. Deston had rolled onto his side and panted, still clutching his wound. Looking up, Cass grabbed a golden acorn. The thing was the size of both her fists and heavy.

"I got it!" she cried.

Mehen gave the giant a final shove with her sharp head and turned. With her fore claw, she scooped Deston up and shot towards Cass. Cass vaulted onto her dragon's back and the three of them shot into the reddening sky. She clasped the acorn to her chest and turned back around. The warrior watched them go, his face turned up to them, and then turned back to stone.

"Holy shit," Cass gasped. Her ribs hurt too from the blast from Mehen.

"Well done, Vedic," Mehen called to her. "Many forget that a Vedic is a warrior as well as a scholar. You did well."

She didn't feel like a warrior or a fighter. Her entire body trembled in left over adrenaline and pure fear. "Thanks," she replied anyway. "Is he all right?" She leaned out to the side of Mehen's neck to take in Deston. His eyes were closed.

"He is strong," Mehen said, a praising smile turning her tone. "Pakhba was right in saying he has courage. For a pirate," she added with a smirk.

When they landed on the pyramid, Mehen returned to the bracelet after gently setting Deston down. Cass took one step towards him, but stopped. The first sun hardly peaked over the horizon. She turned and ran into the temple, shouting an apology to him.

Inside, she found Elena and Shades waiting. "I have it!"

she shouted. She dashed to the altar and dropped the acorn into the first basin. When nothing happened, she pulled out the Script. The ghost of the dead Vedic and the jaguar were gone. "That's right, right?" Cass asked, panic making her shake all over again.

The earth shook in a galloping rhythm. The Future thugs' eyes widened and Cass met them, also terrified. It felt like a giant horse ran across the horizon.

"Where's Markus?" Shades shouted in panic.

Cass ran outside, having a weird feeling. She stopped where Deston lay and looked out. Her heart leapt into her mouth. Galloping over the horizon towards them came the huge, spotted form of a massive jaguar. One so large it could have swallowed a semi-truck. It dashed right for them.

"Get inside!" Cass screamed as Shades ran past her in the opposite direction. She grunted, heaving Deston's half conscious body up. She tracked Shades and saw him run halfway down the temple stairs to a fleeing Markus, heading in their direction. He held an armful of kindling and branches. "Hurry!" Cass shouted.

A golden light burst out from above. She looked up to see a glittering, golden bubble appear above the temple and start to trickle down over just the part of the pyramid they stood on. Protection, she realized. She looked back; the jaguar gained on them. "Hurry!" she screamed again.

Shades had grabbed Markus and leapt up the steps two or three at a time. She took Deston inside and told Elena to get down, just in case. The whole room shook madly with the beat of the jaguar's paws. Cass looked out and saw the golden barrier trickle down. Elena stood up, shouting the guys' names. Just as the barrier passed over the door, Shades and Markus dove in, landing hard in a mess of branches and dry leaves.

Something slammed into the temple, rocking them all like

a head-on car collision. Cass grunted, clutching Deston tight. Through the western window, she watched as the jaguar leapt off the barrier and tackled the sun, both cascading down the horizon. Utter darkness filled the temple room for a moment until the second sun glowed again, halfway up the sky.

Cass looked out the western window. "Good thing we got all the offerings." She looked over at Shades, a little grossed out.

He pulled a dead monkey off the back of his pack and tossed it into the second basin.

"You probably could have just caught one and brought it in live," Cass growled. "Monster."

Shades shrugged. "Couldn't catch it. Could shoot it, though." He laughed to himself.

Cass was preparing a retort when movement caught her eyes. Her shadow slid across the floor so quickly, she could see it happening.

"The sun!" Elena cried. "It moved when Samuel put the offering on the altar."

She was right. The sun tracked across the sky. Not lightning fast, but quick enough to be noticed. Soon, it peeked over the top of the tall western window.

"Brace yourselves," Cass cried, realizing what was about to happen.

"What?" Markus asked.

"Well, considering a giant jaguar just tackled the shit out of the first sun," she said, laying Deston down. "I assume we're about to be hit with a hurricane."

"We're too far inland," Shades reasoned, looking condescendingly down at Cass.

"No, we're not," she snapped back. "We're on an island, you idiot."

As if remembering for the first time that they were in fact on a magically ascended floating island, Shade's face paled.

Cass stood up and walked to the doorway, looking out. No sooner had she stepped outside than the sky turned gray, than black. Wind, cold and harsh, picked up. Elena joined her at the doorway, looking out.

"Will the barrier come back?" she asked.

"I hope so," Cass said. "Unless the offering wasn't meant to be monkey blood." She looked up. Lightning cracked across the sky and rain poured down. Cass flinched at the freezing rain but waited to see if the barrier came back. "If not, I hope this structure is strong."

Elena scanned the horizon as the wind whipped the jungle canopy. "Next is fire? We should get started. We might have to go out and get more kindling. Could take a while to start a fire by rubbing sticks."

"Do you have to do it that way?" Cass asked, wondering.

"Do you want to risk a hail of fire?" Elena shot back.

No, she didn't. She shook her head. "Get started. I need to see to..." She trailed off. Her breath stopped. A wave the height of a skyscraper roiled towards them from the ocean. Both she and Elena spun to look up. To Cass's relief, the golden barrier ignited and trickled down again.

"Inside!" she shouted, dragging Elena with her. "Hold on," she said to the others. She crouched next to Deston, who had come to and who moaned in pain, holding his ribs. "It's okay," she whispered to him, leaning close to his face. She glared out the doorway, watching the hideous wave get closer. The barrier trickled down just as the wave crashed into the temple. The sight of the white and blue water crashing into a clear barrier just yards from her shot a thrill through Cass she never wanted to feel again. The roaring deafened her and struck so much fear into her, tears welled up in her eyes.

The wave crashed for several minutes, water whipping up and around. The temple shook and Cass feared it would drop out from under them any minute. In the time the hurricane raged around them, she didn't notice Deston sit up. But did notice when his arms went around her and held her close to his chest. She realized then how much she shook. His warm hand petted her cold, soaked hair. She couldn't believe how steady his hand was.

The storm rage for an hour more, water lapping up and over the temple. They watched it through the doorway. Lightning struck the water, sending flashes over the horizon that were now only a flood. Gale winds and maelstroms swept over the water's surface and the temple groaned. Cass wrapped her arms around Deston and waited.

"Do you have water?" Cass asked Elena once the wind quieted, and the water began to recede. It was dark out, the hurricane having dosed the sun.

Elena just nodded, holding up her water bottle. "There was a place of worship inside the village square. A fountain decorated the middle. So I took some."

Cass silently wished she'd given herself one of these easier tasks.

The third sun rose and Markus and Shades went to work on making fire. Cass sat Deston up against the altar and dug in her pack for her first aid kit. Inside, she found some pain killers, an ice pack she could break, and yards of elastic bandages. She moved to put the ice over Deston's shirt, but he lifted it over his shoulders before she could. Her mouth went dry as she came face to face with his bare chest and muscled stomach. She sucked her lips in so hard, her front teeth hurt. Looking up at him, she was glad to see he didn't notice. He leaned his head back and groaned, face twisting in pain as he lifted his arm over his head to remove his shirt.

Her face blazed so hot, Cass thought she might catch even the ice on fire. She opened the pain killers and pulled his water bottle out of his pack.

"Hey," she said, tapping his face. "Take these before I start wrapping you up."

He took them and swallowed several mouthfuls of water. "Thanks," he mumbled, tilting his head back again. He closed his eyes.

Cass watched his throat as he swallowed. His veins stood out just under his alabaster skin. Her eyes trailed down his sharp shoulders to the bruise on his ribs. His entire left side was purple and yellow. Gingerly, she touched his side, and he hissed.

"Probably broken, maybe just fractured," she said gently. She held the ice pack to his ribs and started to wrap the bandage. "It has to be tight," she said when he groaned again. "Sorry."

She leaned close to him, and he rested his arms on her shoulders to give her easy access to his middle. They'd been hiking all day, fighting warriors, dodging earthly destruction, and he still smelled amazing. Her face came close to his chest each time she wrapped the bandage.

"Your hair smells great," he mumbled from above her.

"Thanks," she whispered, blushing so hard she thought her eyeballs would boil. "It's this coconut stuff I found at the dollar store."

"Amazing," he whispered.

Once he was all wrapped up, she handed his shirt to him.

"No," he grumbled. "Don't want to raise my arms again if I don't have to."

So he was just going to sit here, sweating and all chiseled, with his shirt off? Cass turned away, blowing her cheeks out. What was it about him that made her all crazy? Something beyond reason made her head spin about him.

"We got it!" Markus crowed excitedly.

Cass spun to see the man run towards the altar, a flaming

coconut husk in his hands. Exclaiming in pain, he dropped it into the third basin.

They all froze, waiting. The sun moved like a hand on a clock. Cass tracked it until it vanished into the top of the eastern window and then fell down the western.

"Is it moving faster to anyone else?" she asked. "I mean, faster than even the second."

"You're not wrong," Elena murmured, slowly walking to the doorway again.

A silence fell.

Something like a distant crackling started to fall towards them. Cass frowned, looking out. The sky was clear. The crackling grew louder. Before Cass could call Elena back, a fiery asteroid the size of a minivan smashed into the temple stairs. As if held by magic, the stairs didn't collapse. The fire spewed out, shooting little flaming rocks towards Elena. She screamed and dove back into the temple.

The golden barrier covered them once again. Cass watched in horror as fiery hail rained from the sky. So much smoke came down with them that the horizon turned black. The orange embers ingested the world outside in flashes of red and yellow as they made impact with the earth. Each one shook the temple. Hearing the fire rain on top of the barrier made Cass tense up. Her body shook with exhaustion and fright. She wasn't sure how much of this she could take.

They waited in silence; the hail cutting out any conversation they could have had. Several hours went by until the fire grew smaller and less frequent.

"One last flood," Elena mumbled. She walked towards the altar. Cass wasn't sure what it would mean if they started another destruction so soon. But she didn't have the remaining courage to wait much longer, either. The waiting was just as bad as the actual catastrophe. So she didn't stop Elena.

Elena dumped the water into the basin. Another roaring came up as the rivers flooded. Cass sat down, drawing her knees into herself. The barrier didn't vanish as the rivers doused the flames, making mist rise. The barrier fogged over so they couldn't see out. They had to wait blind.

Darkness encroached on the windows, plunging them into a total blackout. No one spoke for almost an hour. Cass watched the doorway, wondering when the last sun would rise. Instead, the more she looked, the more she saw a white-blue light come out. It lit up the jungle canopy, outlining it in white light.

"The fourth sun turned into the moon," Deston said, looking out with Cass. As they watched, it dipped below the horizon and the final sun rose behind them.

Cass stood up, opened the Script and placed it on the altar. "What's the fifth offering, then?" She looked at Deston as he stood up.

"Not sure," he said, frowning. "During the fifth sun, our sun supposedly, Quezacotl made human kind. He made them with bones and blood mixed in a bowl."

Cass's stomach dropped out. "I am not asking anyone, even those clowns, to put their bones in here."

No sooner had she said it, than writing appeared in the Script. It caught her eye, and she read it. The sloping lines and sharp angles told her to speak a phrase.

"It says only the Vedic can say the phrase that will bring the resting place of the feathered dragon to light," she read.

"So say it," Elena pressed.

Smoothing out the pages, Cass read the Script out loud. It sounded like nothing to her, confusing sounds, and looping enunciation. When she spoke the last word, the temple shook.

"Did I do it wrong?" she gasped.

With a cry, Deston pulled her back. She stumbled back as the altar dropped out from under her, sinking into the floor, taking the offerings with it. As it slowly moved down, stone steps appeared behind it, leading down into another pit of darkness. She waited until the grinding and shaking stopped to descend.

Below, the Script glowed in the darkness.

"One last offering," she mumbled and went down into the opening.

CHAPTER 29: QUEZACOTL THE LIGHTNING BEARER

Cass got down first, the others slowly slinking down the long stairway after her. When she reached the bottom and the lower level came into focus, she gasped. The altar stood in the center of a jungle grove. Tall trees with long palms, rubbery succulents, and curtains of dripping vines surrounded the area. Moonlight cut through the canopy above, making white spots of light on the jungle floor. The soft singing of night bugs filled the air, interrupted only now and then by mysterious sounds from other animals she could not see.

Behind the altar, the ghost of Jatziri stood with her jaguar guid. When Cass caught sight of her, the Vedic turned and walked into the darkness, vanishing before a large stone platform with stairs on all four sides, making something of a small pyramid. Atop it laid the ornate stone form of a sarcophagus. Cautiously, slinking into the contained jungle and moonlight, Cass approached the coffin. The image on top was primitive, but showed what could only be Jatziri. The image faced away, holding a radiant codex in her hand. Suddenly, Cass understood.

"You two," she barked at Markus and Shades. "Come help me." She set her palms hard against the top of the sarcophagus. "Sorry, Jatziri," she murmured. "But I need bones."

Bones of a Vedic, a soft voice echoed to Cass.

She looked up to see Jatziri still standing there. "Bones of a Vedic? That's how we summon this dragon?"

Jatziri didn't reply, eyes glassy.

Markus and Shades positioned themselves on either side of her. Shades counted to three, and the trio grunted, growled, and huffed. The lid slid with a loud grinding, making Elena and Deston cover their ears. The night bugs went silent at the screaming stone.

"A little more," Cass huffed, counting again and shoving with all her might.

This time, the lid moved enough for her to see inside. The moonlight touched the wrapped bones of the Vedic. The ornaments of respectful death arrayed the woman inside. What had once been colorful dressings were rotten and gray. Markus gagged when Cass reached in and pulled out an arm bone. She turned back to the altar and the last basin. Elena handed her a round stone from the ground to break the bone up with.

"Thanks, Jatziri," Cass sighed. She looked up at the ghost only she could see. The Vedic waited. Cass hammered on the bone, breaking it up as much as she could. It was brittle and turned to powder quickly. She stared down at it, waiting.

"Blood," Deston reminded her.

"I thought maybe that was figurative," Cass sighed, looking at the four of them.

"One of you," Elena snapped, crossing her arms.

Cass figured as much. She took out her switch blade from her pack and rolled up her sleeve.

"Hold on," Deston said, grabbing the knife from her. "Let me."

"Why?" Cass hissed. "You're already banged up."

No sooner had she asked, than Jatziri raised her hand, staying Cass. *Him,* she confirmed.

Deston pushed past Cass, distracted by Jatziri's order, to stand in front of the basin of bones. "I have a weird feeling. Get your first aid kit out again, though."

Cass wanted to stop him, but also knew they had limited time. She didn't want to argue. And the ghost of the past Vedic had said it was to be him. Cass sighed, stepping away to let him closer. Jatziri smiled.

Watching him cut his forearm, she winced and moved to stand beside him, gauze in hand. He squeezed his fist over the basin, covering the broken and powdered bone. The redness glittered in the moonlight from above. The silence hung so dense that every drop sounded loud.

Bones of a Vedic, Jatziri said flatly. *Blood of an Enchanter. So the dragon is called.*

"What?" Cass shouted, her heart stuttering.

Before she could ask herself if she heard the dead Vedic correctly, a roar rattled the trees. The party looked up. The walls of the underground tomb had vanished, and they stood in an actual jungle space. Lightning leapt up from the canopy some yards away and struck the moon. The party scattered, panicking. Cass grabbed Deston by his arm, pressing gauze to his wound, and ran into the denser part of the jungle. The trio of the Future came close behind them.

A bright light, part fire and part lightning, sprang up again from where Quezacotl had no doubt awakened. The earth rumbled, followed by high, ear-splitting roars. A wave of wind and lightning washed over the treetops, igniting a few of them. The wind pushed the smoldering palms, catching more on fire. Cass looked around, wondering if the dragon would swoop down on them from above. When she turned to face forward again, she froze.

A pair of yellow, crackling eyes glared back at her. The fire from the trees licked a long, green neck that curved down into a main of brightly colored feathers. Two twisted horns arched over the glowering brows. Quezacotl coiled along the ground, green and feathered body slowly moving through the fire. A line of bright feathers tracked down his spine to the end of his tasseled tail. A pair of massive wings flared out to his sides. He looked directly at Cass.

"Another Vedic!" he roared. Quick as the lighting crackling between his wings, he dove towards Cass.

She scrambled, nearly slipping on the jungle floor. She wouldn't get out of the way nearly fast enough. Another body galloped before her, holding their hand aloft. A pink glow pulsed in their hand like the gold and white had done in hers when she was gifted a bit of Mehen's power. It was Elena.

Elena turned to glare at Cass. Her eye, the one Meredith Navarre had imbued with her essence, bled and had turned a vibrant pink.

"Go!" Elena shouted. "This one is ours."

"No," Cass growled. She scrambled to get to the bracelet.

Elena shot a crackling orb towards Quezacotl, hitting him square in the face. He reeled back, laughing until the fiery jungle rang. Turning his head to the side, he spotted Markus and Shades. Licking his lips with a long, red tongue, he dove after them.

"I'm sorry," Cass panted to Deston, letting go of him. He leaned against a tree, waving her off. She grabbed up the white gem and shouted for Mehen to come out. The white dragon leapt out of the gem, growing in size instantly. "Mehen," Cass panted, tears spilling from her eyes, drawn out by the smoke, "he's crazy. How am I supposed to catch him?"

"A binding," Mehen said, eyes tracking her wild brother. "I can help you."

To their right, deep into the smoke and fire, a man

screamed. Another shouted in terror and Elena cried out a string of words before a bright pink light cut through the darkness.

"Hurry!" Mehen shouted, dipping so Cass could mount her neck. "She is binding him!"

Cass flattened herself against the white dragon's neck. Roars, cries, lightning strikes, and utter chaos rang from where Quezacotl fought the Future. Mehen cut through the trees with quick, sharp movements.

"Get off," Mehen instructed. "I have to subdue him. It will be too dangerous for you."

Preparing herself, Cass rolled off, crashing to the jungle floor. She rolled a few feet before stopping, running into Markus. He fell over, but didn't get up, eyes huge, tears spilling out from them. "Sam!" he screamed into the tumult that was now the battlegrounds.

Cass scrambled to her feet and looked around. Elena was locked in combat with Quezacotl, pink tendrils whipping out at him.

"It'll kill her," Markus whispered. He scampered backward, putting his back against a tree. "It killed him! We can't fight it."

Cass spotted a bloody streak over the earth where it looked like someone got dragged a few yards, bleeding out. Quezacotl must have devoured Shades. She felt a drop of pity, but all that went away in the next second.

Elena stumbled backward, screaming that she couldn't do it. Cass charged towards her but in a flash of bright, neon light, Elena vanished with a shriek of pain, and Meredith

Navarre stood in her place. She wore a long black coat over tight boots and her hair was down, whipping madly in a wind only she could feel. In her left hand, she clutched the long wand with the gem on top.

"Weak bitch," Navarre hissed. She marched towards the grappling dragons. "Dragons! Meet your rightful master." She held the wand up, the gem sparking.

"Pakhba," Cass cried. "Help me!"

The golden bracelet glowed, and the little dragons shot out, rushing towards Quezacotl and Mehen. Navarre spun, hearing Cass.

"They let you live?" she growled. "My followers are all weak. Pathetic!" She shot the wand towards Cass. A string of lightning leapt towards her, crackling madly among the flames.

Cass ducked, holding her arm over her face. The lightning struck the bracelet, absorbing the magic attack. Unsatisfied, Navarre thrust her claw-like hand out toward Cass and used her invisible hand to toss her far to the left. Cass hit the ground with a thud, cutting her side on a branch she landed on. Navarre went back to the dragons, her pink tendrils snaking around Mehen and Quezacotl, binding them.

Pakhba shot back to Cass, holding a bright rainbow feather in his hand. "I took it from him. Use it. You have to fight her."

"But you said dragon power wasn't for a Vedic," she panted, holding her side. Blood trickled through her fingers.

"I cannot argue now, Cassandra," Pakhba said, shoving Quezacotl's feather into her palm. "We will address it later. But," he looked very serious, the flames shining off his blue scales, "his power is madness. You will feel it inside you like a hurricane. His gale force winds will spin your mind. Try to hold on to yourself."

"This sounds so much more dangerous than Mehen's

light," Cass said. Her fingers shook as she clamped them down over the feather.

From between her fingers, bright multi-colored light erupted, blinding her. At the same time, her body shook. What felt like tornadoes pulsed through her blood. A rushing like she'd never felt before surged through her. She couldn't stop the scream that burst from her lungs as the torrents of wind exploded from her. The bushes and flexible trees around her were pushed nearly flat from the explosion. Navarre fell forward, shouting.

Cass ran towards the struggle. The ground smoothed out as she ran, every dip and rise gone. She ran on the wind. Her lungs panted, overrun by the pulsing air inside her. As Pakhba had warned, her brain began to spin. A strange, unbridled wildness filled her. She wanted to laugh and scream all at once. She shot past Navarre and put herself between the enchantress and the dragons.

Wildly swinging her hands over her head, a wall of wind appeared before her, rising and out. She shoved her right hand forward, bursting a windy force towards Navarre who fell backwards. She dropped the wand on Cass's side of the wind wall. Cass dove for it, taking it up into her own palm. When she did, the tendrils and lightning flashing from it turned to a rippling green and yellow, like the scales on Quezacotl's body. The golden sight had been activated at some point and she saw the ghostly, gold smoke that had appeared around Navarre before, now around her. But it flowed from her body, into the wand. The more it flowed, the wilder she felt. And weaker, like she had to give in to the dragon magic to stay conscious.

Behind her, Mehen burst out of the binding tendrils and wrestled a still screaming Quezacotl to the ground. The fire raged into the trees, smoldering branches falling from the canopy.

Navarre looked up at Cass, eyes wide in wonder. "You

see?" she said, smiling darkly. "That's how much power you could wield. You could be master of the dragons, but they hold you back. Cassandra, we could destroy anything we wish and build a new world from the ashes of our conquest. You will bend a knee to no one. Free to use the power that should be yours. But you need me."

She got up onto her knees and slowly reached for the wand. Cass hardly understood what Navarre said. She just wanted to scream, to tear something apart. And she was angry. This magic was hers. Only hers! No one else should have it. The powerlessness she felt in her everyday life was perfectly insignificant now. She could destroy any of the annoying customers who came in to bug her. Anyone who made her feel small. She didn't need a purpose in life. *This* was her purpose.

"Cassandra!" Pakhba shouted to her left. "Take her down."

She looked back at Navarre who had come so close, her hand rested on Cass's wrist where she held the wand. She screamed and shot wind and lightning from the wand. As she did, her skin burned. Starting from her palm where the wand rested, crackles of cinders and lightning spread over her arm. The pain made her wild with rage. Her golden aura had dimmed significantly since wielding the wand. It was taking her essence, and the evidence showed on her body.

"I can't hold him!" Mehen cried as a fresh wave of fire and lightning burst from the brawling dragons.

But Cass couldn't give up the magic. She wanted it so badly.

Another form ran up behind Navarre where she still spouted her promises of power. The person ran right up to Cass and pulled the wand from her hand. It was Deston. He spun and blasted Meredith Navarre into a roaring pillar of fire. The woman screamed. Her hair on fire, she thrust her hand to Deston, and the wand jerked from his grasp.

Just as she caught it, Quezacotl broke from Mehen and dove at Navarre. The woman shrieked and, with a crackle of pink lightning, vanished just as she'd appeared. Elena stumbled down, groaning in pain, reappearing where Navarre had vanished. It seemed Navarre used her thugs like anchors to teleport.

Cass wanted to scream. They took her wand, her power! She growled and flexed her fingers, ready to shoot every bolt of lightning she could muster into Deston for taking her wand.

Deston faced her.

"Let it go, Cass," he said. He walked to her, hand out to hers where she held Quezacotl's feather.

"No," she spat, her voice crackling and howling like wind. "It's mine. I gave up everything to find the dragons."

Deston lunged at her as she raised her arm to smite him. He snagged her wrist and pulled her to the ground. She fought, kicking and screaming, until he pried her fingers open. He ripped the feather from her grasp and held it away from her. It burst into flames in his hand as his eyes flashed orange.

Everything went quiet for a moment. The air left Cass's lungs, and she panicked, unable to breathe. Her mind stopped spinning and became clear. She looked up into Deston's eyes and knew instantly she'd done something wrong. She'd almost hurt him, but he'd stopped her. Ran to her when she could have incinerated him. And he'd held her. All at once, she gasped and cried.

CHAPTER 30: RIDDLE OF THE VEDIC

"Be still!" Mehen roared, clamping her jaws down onto Quezacotl's neck. Pakhba zoomed towards the yellow dragon's forehead and touched him between his horns.

Cass, gasping and shaking in Deston's arms, watched as the furious dragon calmed, his hot breath shooting out between clenched fangs. His snapping, yellow eyes bored into her with a hate she could not see the depth of. Then they flashed to Deston.

"How low you have fallen, Mehen," Quezacotl growled in a voice that sounded like static. "To bow a wing to such as these." He gave another jerk, but a blue pulse from Pakhba subdued him again. "Perhaps I have slumbered too long. Why have you awoken me now, if only to smother my power?" His voice rose with each word until he roared, matching the crackling of the fire.

Cass grunted, rising to her feet and leaned heavily on Deston. "Are you okay?" she asked him, looking him up and down. "How did you use that wand? That was insane." She looked at the three dragons. "I thought only enchanters could use magic like that."

Pakhba looked at her sadly, then at Mehen. "Brother," he said to Quezacotl, "be still or your sister will rend your wings from your spine."

The yellow dragon growled submissively. Slowly, Mehen unclamped her jaw from around his long, thin neck. Quezacotl raised himself up onto his legs and shook, his bright feathers rustling like leaves. He spread his wings once, stretching to their full length, then folded them calmly. "But what of them?" he asked, tilting his great horns towards where Elena and Markus sat.

The pair of them looked beat. Elena's right eye had swollen shut, blood crusted down her cheek and neck. Her hair no longer had that golden, glossy shine. Markus' eyes were empty as they hovered on the bloody spot where Shades must have been killed.

"Sh-she knows about you now," Elena stammered, more from pain and exhaustion than fear.

"About who?" Cass snapped. "She's been chasing me for months. Or have you forgotten what you've been doing all year?"

Elena stood up, pulling Markus with her. She wrapped her arms tightly around one of his. "No. Not you, Vedic. The enchanter." She pointed to Deston.

Quezacotl growled, his feathers bristling up and down his spine. "I knew I smelled stolen magic!"

"Peace!" Pakhba snarled, preparing to touch Quezacotl again with his calming, blue light.

Cass couldn't look at Deston. She had felt something strange from him when he took up the wand. But she couldn't let herself believe it. Not again. Not another betrayal. Her heart swelled with hurt.

"Even we don't have the ability to wield the wands of

enchanters," Elena said, looking aggravated at having to admit that. "We could learn, but it takes more time than we have in our lives. Others..." She looked at the three dragons. "Others are born to it. Source-born, we call them. Birthed with the Source of the dragon power already in them."

"Why are you telling me this?" Deston asked. "I didn't do anything. I didn't feel anything."

Elena took a deep breath. "But you will. Especially now. Perhaps being so close to a Vedic, the dragons awakened the Source in you." She looked earnestly at Cass. "Natural born enemies."

Confused, she finally faced Deston and his damned beautiful emerald eyes. "You didn't know?" *Please,* she begged with her eyes. *Don't lie to me.*

He seemed to read the plea on her face and shook his head. "I don't believe it even now."

She looked to Mehen. "Will the Future come for him?"

The white dragon shared a glance with Pakhba before nodding. "A Source-born is not something the Future will give up."

For the first time since she'd met him, Cass saw Deston show a little fear. "I won't go with them," he said aggressively.

"It would be folly to turn over the Source-born," Quezacotl growled. "He is too strong a weapon to hand to Meredith Navarre. And too dangerous to be left alive."

"Wait, no," Cass begged, moving to Deston's side. She took his hand timidly. "I won't let you have him," she shot at Elena. To Quezacotl she said, "And we will not get rid of him or whatever you had in mind. He didn't know. He's not our enemy. Not my enemy. We only have one enemy." She glared at Elena and Markus as they gripped one another.

Elena's shoulders fell, her one eye showing her courage fade to bargaining. "We've lost our comrade," she started, and Markus tried and failed to hide a sob, turning his face away.

"We are not equal to Meredith Navarre. We are... disposable. Vedic, show pity. Let us leave in peace and we will do all in our power to hinder Navarre's hunt for you and your enchanter."

"Ha!" Quezacotl barked in his sparking tone. "The plea of vermin. Let me devour them like I did their companion."

"We are at your mercy," Elena said, still holding her head high, knuckles turning white as she gripped Markus's arm.

Cass realized Elena didn't hold her colleague out of fear. Elena gripped Markus to comfort him. She was the brave one. Something in Cass softened, bringing repulsion with it.

"But I do not ask for mercy," Elena went on. "I ask for pity. Let us go."

Cass cringed away from the begging. She looked up at Deston. Slowly, she put her hand on his chest and said, "What should I do?"

Gently, he tucked her dark red hair behind one ear. But his face fell. "I don't know. I know you'll choose whatever is right, though."

Pakhba floated gently to her. "This is part of the riddle of the Vedic. What must you do to keep your world safe? But what must be done to keep your goodness intact; the thing which guides your heart and your passion? That which fortifies your role as Vedic?"

Cass groaned, not liking the riddle-like dragon talk. Couldn't someone just tell her what to do? She dropped her head against Deston's chest, closing her eyes. He wrapped his long arms around her, pulling her close.

"If I let them go," she said, "it's only a matter of time before Meredith comes looking for you. But I'm afraid if I make this one choice, to have them..." she gulped. "To have them 'taken care of', then I might make other choices later that turn me into something I don't want to be."

She'd felt it a little when Quezacotl's power surged in her. She had a hunger there, a potential to want more. To do something dark. She trusted herself to try not to, but there was no telling what kind of pull magic would have. She didn't have the power to stop it. That wasn't her role. Her job was to make sure someone else didn't get that power. To take charge.

She turned to face Elena and Markus. "We'll let them go," she said to the dragons. She looked up at the setting sun. "The fifth sun. It will be up to you to get off the island before it sinks, taken in to the ocean by the earthquake."

Elena's lips turned down in disgust. "How diplomatic of you."

Cass raised her brows. "I suggest you hurry. I'm riding a dragon out of here."

She turned, taking Deston's hand and marched to Mehen. Firing at Quezacotl, she said, "As Vedic, I command you to submit to me. Got it?"

The yellow dragon's lips twitched in a soundless snarl. When Mehen replied with an audible warning growl, he bowed his head. With a crackle of yellow lighting and a gust of harsh wind, he vanished. Cass checked the bracelet to see a brightly colored feather charm hanging near the opal tear.

Looking up at Mehen, she smiled in relief. "Thank you."

The white dragon smiled and started to reply, but Cass threw her arms around her long neck as best she could, hugging her. Mehen closed her eyes and sighed. Over the top of the dragon's head, she saw Elena hauling ass through the trees, gripping Markus's hand hard. They fled like the hounds of hell were right on their heels.

"Let's depart. I am weary," Mehen said.

ehen flew them out until they spotted the *Phantom Ivory*. She carefully slid into the water until both her riders slipped into the ocean, then, she vanished into the bracelet. Cass paddled hard to reach the bottom of the boat and shout up for someone to hear. The sound of one of the smaller speed boats ripping into the ocean and fleeing made her worry.

"That was the mosquito," Deston panted, treading water. "Someone ran."

Cass floated under a ladder several feet above her and hammered on the hull of the boat. "Hey! Vamshi? You there?" She glanced back at the island. The sun had sunk beneath it, turning the ocean blood red. "We have to get out of the water or the island will suck us down," she gasped. She prepared to shout again when a head popped over the side, looking down.

A man shouted in German and a few gears started to grind. Deston shouted up, answering in German. A few choice curses and cries of thanks came down after that. The silver ladder cranked down slowly until Cass could reach it. She slipped once on the way up, the rungs being made of metal, but Deston caught her. When they finally made it over the side onto the big, open deck, Dietrich was still cursing.

"Dad, what happened?" Deston asked, grabbing his hysterical father by his shoulder. Dietrich went off in German.

Before he could calm down enough to speak English, a crack split the air. A crack so loud Cass thought the sky had burst open. They all spun to look at the island. The trees shivered and a flock of birds evacuated the canopy.

"Go, go!" Cass cried. The ship jerked as the helmsman thrust it into gear.

A wave boiled up from the island, smashing out, then racing towards them. From here, she couldn't see the details, but knew beyond a shadow of a doubt that the island was sinking. A second wave burst out just as the first hit their stern. The *Phantom Ivory* bucked, shoved by the wave and launched itself over the ocean. Cass screamed and fell. The wave splashed up onto the deck, washing her to the starboard side. She cried out as the railing drew closer, knowing she'd slip under. She tried to dig her heels in, but to no avail.

A strong hand grabbed her by her pack and she jerked to a stop just as the second wave hit. She flung herself around to grab onto Deston, who held her. She clung on hard for what felt like hours until the ocean calmed. Deston picked her up, and she looked back. The island was gone, and the sun was below the horizon. She panted, wet and cold, leaning into Deston.

Dietrich swore a few more times in German, eyes locked on the horizon. "Too many damned storms," he growled in English finally. "Swept us out to sea."

Cass looked around, scared and worried. She worried about Vamshi. "Where are the other thugs who had you guys under lock and key?" she asked.

"They ran!" Dietrich cried, throwing his arms into the air. "Took the mosquito."

"Why?" Deston asked.

Dietrich pointed just off the port bow. Slowly coming their way was a government ship with a few smaller boats surrounding it. The Mexican flag and emblem flashed on the side in bright green, white, and red.

"Good riddance," Cass spat.

"No, not good!" Dietrich cried. "They will take anything they find on our boat. Even if it's not from their waters. They will take our find from China. All of it!" He wailed loudly.

A smaller police boat drifted up along the side of the *Phantom Ivory* and five officers in uniforms boarded the boat.

"Captain Dietrich?" one asked in a thick Mexican accent, hands in his belt arrogantly. "This is your boat?"

The large man shrunk sadly and nodded. The man in the uniform began to talk to Dietrich, pulling out official papers to help him translate.

"Cass!" a high voice squealed from the edge.

Cass spun and received an affectionate tackle from a black blur. Vamshi hugged her so tight, every bruise and wound ached all over again.

"You look beat up," Vamshi cried. She grabbed Cass's arm and turned it over, taking in the damage. "I got away, oh, my god, girl, it was insane! I called the coast guard, or whoever these guys are. Got them to take me out here."

"This was your doing?" Dietrich cried.

"Dad," Deston snapped, pulling him back to the angry man in uniform.

Cass didn't care. She didn't know what this meant for them, but did it really matter in the grand scheme? She fell against Vamshi, hugging her tight. Hot tears filled her eyes as she realized, for now, she was safe.

"What happened out there?" Vamshi asked, sensing the change in Cass.

She sniffed, and her eyes fell on Deston. His alabaster skin turned a warm color in the setting sun. His wet shirt clung to every muscle on his torso. Pakhba had been right: he had great courage. And he had a wild, adventurous life. The kind perfect for her and her studies. *He* was perfect. And yet, he may as well be forbidden fruit.

"I'll tell you when we're safe on land," she mumbled sadly.

CHAPTER 31:
UNCERTAIN

Cass shoved her water bottle into her pack and yelled for Vamshi to hurry up. "We have one day left in Mexico, and I want to see Mexico!" Cass shouted into the bathroom door where Vamshi had been locked for five minutes.

"You saved the world from an evil enchantress, isn't that enough?" Vamshi called back.

Groaning, Cass pounded on the door one last time and marched back to her hotel bed. Outside, the sun glowed warm and bright, hanging still just as it should. She wasn't sure, to be honest. Meredith Navarre had vanished, and she was hurt, but how much would that slow her down?

"She could lie low for the rest of your lifetime," Pakhba said, curled around a pint of vanilla ice cream, cooling himself.

Cass lightly touched the charms on her bracelet, letting the tear, then the feather, fall from her hands. "Do you think she will? She can outlive me, easy. Maybe that's what she'll do." A sudden thought made her heart sink. "I have to keep you guys safe. But I don't know what to do with you."

"Your family's safe," Vamshi said, finally emerging from

the hotel bathroom. She threw her pack up onto her back and slammed her hat on to her head. "Take them back to Connecticut and lock them up. Your house has cameras on it. Your mom is often at home. They'd be safe."

It was a good idea. She'd have eyes on the safe all the time if she wanted to, using her phone and the security app. But then why did she feel sad?

"I guess I just don't want to give you guys up," she sighed, petting Pakhba's silky mane and scaly head. He glared up at her, insulted by the gesture. "But I can't hold on to you forever. I'll miss asking you questions and talking to you. I also can't have you in there forever. Is there some magical sanctuary where I can hide you away?"

"Actually," Pakhba said, rubbing his bearded chin with a claw, "there is. Perhaps. If it's still there."

"What place?" Cass asked, excited.

The dragon looked around. "I don't trust these walls. Summon me when you are alone in the wilderness." He crawled over the top of the table and turned to a wisp, vanishing into Cass's bracelet.

Vamshi raised her brows. "Cryptic. So, hiking?"

"To the volcano!" Cass cheered.

The girls met Deston at the trailhead after an hour's drive out in public transportation. Cass thought he looked cute in his hiking gear. She hadn't thought about asking him to join them, but Vamshi insisted on it right before she showed Cass that she had added his number to her phone and added him on all her accounts while she had been in the shower.

They climbed up the stunningly green path until it sloped

up above the timber line, turning to a strange, black gravel. A few people passed them on horses before they reached an overlook a couple of hours later.

"Whoa," Cass sighed, taking in the horizon. "You can see so many mountain ranges from up here. And... is that a lake?"

Deston nodded. "If you have time, we should hit that trail. It's beautiful."

Cass crumbled a little, slinging her pack off to sit on the wooden bench just off the trail. "I can't. We have to get back. We're in school. I'm getting an anthropology degree, actually. Maybe I can come on one of your treasure hunting adventures." She smiled and her cheeks flared up.

"Dad might not like that," Deston laughed, wiping his lips after taking a drink. "He's still upset about the customs fine. And they did end up taking that set of armor we found in China. So now he wants to go back. He thinks you're bad luck."

"Well," Cass mumbled playfully, "that's fair."

An awkward silence followed. How could she bring up the whole enchanter thing? What did it mean? As far as she knew, those people were bad news. But if Deston didn't know he was whatever Elena had called it, did that spare him from turning into the power-hungry maniac he could be?

Before she worked herself up too much, Pakhba slithered out and hovered before the three of them. His face slackened with the weight of what he was about to say.

"We have much to decide, young Vedic," he said to Cass. "We have been gracious in letting your companion know of us and walk this road with you." He gestured to Vamshi. "With Rana Saad, perhaps you could have made a case. But with this man," his yellow eyes narrowed at Deston, "he is your enemy. What he knows, and being who he is, makes him more dangerous than any of the Future. Especially since you have certain thoughts about him."

Cass almost vomited on the spot from embarrassment, knowing she must have let slip a few thoughts about Deston.

"You're not going to let me have a say?" Deston cut in. "I don't know what you think I am, but I'm not. And I'm not going to hurt Cass. I helped her fight those crazy witches."

"Pakhba," Cass begged, "please don't wipe his memory. When we fought the giant, I felt something with him. A connection or something. Like I knew how he would plan his movements. We were so fluid. He didn't have to come with me onto the island, but he did. He poured his blood onto that altar." She found herself taking his hand and clasping it in both of hers, holding them to her chest. "Please, Pakhba. We shared something together and I... I don't want to lose that."

The dragon raised his head, narrowing his eyes once again. "I was not merely speaking of taking his memories, Cassandra. Such as that would not last on a Source-born."

"You want to kill me?" Deston growled.

"It is the most efficient way."

Deston stood up, pulling his hand out of Cass's. "You brought me up here to kill me?"

"No!" she and Vamshi cried together. Cass rounded on Pakhba. "I won't let you."

"He's an enchanter, Cassandra," Pakhba bellowed. "Your enemy. Descended of the ones who took our power for themselves. Those who have hunted down Vedics for millennia. Whether he means to or not, some time he will find out his task is to stop you."

"What about Jatziri?" she shot back. "Xoco was an enchanter, but she loved him. It was part of her spell to keep Quezacotl safe. A Vedic and an enchanter had to be there to open his cage. She knew there could be a bond between the two. I couldn't have gotten Quezacotl without Deston. Just because he was born this way doesn't mean he's going to turn against me. He doesn't even know how to use the magic you think is in his blood."

Pakhba shifted back in the air a few inches, listening to her words. Only the wind whispered in the silence that followed.

Don't lie to her, minion, Quezacotl's voice rumbled in their minds. The feather charm on her bracelet glowed gently. *Remember the caveat. Such a bond is real.*

"But dangerous!" Pakhba barked.

The bracelet began to vibrate as Quezacotl's rage built up.

"Stay calm, please," Cass hissed, gently touching the rattling feather charm. The last thing she wanted was the enraged dragon bursting out and doing something rash. "What's the caveat, Pakhba?"

"A warning," he replied, defeated. "Long ago, a Vedic from what you now call China built a secret place. She bonded with an enchanter who aided her, hiding it away from the then grand enchantress. They hid Tianlong there for one hundred years before moving him to another location when Mehen first awakened. But that place has never been discovered. Ever since, the enchanters and the Vedics have been at odds with one another. Sometimes, like my master Aiken, an enchanter will change and choose to protect the dragons. Other times, like Navarre did with Edward and now with the boy Charlie, she will try to raise a Vedic up within the Future. Vedics and enchanters have been bonded forever. But they are two sides of the same coin, forever warring. I do not see how they could work alongside one another. Ever."

"But they've tried," Cass put in. "Is this secret place somewhere safe?"

Pakhba nodded. He sighed deeply, lowering his eyes. "If you insist on remaining close with this enemy, I will insist you let us go. Take us there and find one who guards it. They call it the Caveat. It is hidden deep inside that country."

Cass groaned. "I can't right now. Pakh, I have a life to live. I have to go back to it."

"Do so," the dragon said. "But leave him behind." He pointed his claw at Deston.

"He doesn't even live near me, Pakhba," she groaned.

"Well," Deston cut in, tilting his head so his black forelock drifted in front of his left eye. "I was thinking it might not be bad to take some time off from treasure hunting and maybe see New England?"

Pakhba exclaimed and launched into a growling tirade Cass couldn't understand.

"Hey," Deston cut in. Cass loved how his dark green eyes flashed. "You're acting like me turning into an enchanter and using that for nefarious purposes is my destiny, dragon. Like I don't have a choice."

Cass expected Pakhba to snap back, but he didn't. He floated quietly for a moment. "The Source is within you, enchanter. It is written into your very being. You cannot change that."

"You said that old master of yours chose to stand up to the Future," Deston said. "He was an enchanter and changed sides."

"Yeah," Cass added. "The Script is his. He wrote it. Taking all those other things—the Codex and the Tablet and the others—was his doing. Just because Deston was born a certain way doesn't mean he has to live a certain life. He's not helpless."

"I'm not a victim of your Source," Deston added severely.

"Just like you and Aiken weren't," Cass added.

Deston scoffed and grinned at this. "Wait. This whole thing was his doing?" He cocked a brow at Pakhba. "Kind of an important detail, dragon."

"Not something you needed to know, pirate," Pakhba said dangerously softly. "What you think you are choosing to do—

walk with a Vedic—is a dangerous path. Not just for you and all the danger she will put you in, but for her." His orb like eyes snapped to Cass. "Do you understand? The Vedics job is to guard, to protect. Can you watch over this enchanter?"

She nodded mutely.

"Cass said she became Vedic because she didn't know what to do," Deston went on, speaking more confidently now that he had some ground in the conversation. "Isn't the point not to know? To take a chance and trust in your own choices?"

"It is indeed," Pakhba murmured.

Cass waited, but neither of them spoke.

"I'd feel safe with him," Cass said in finality. "And..." she thought back to the bloody streak that had been Shades. And the way Elena and Markus had run for their lives. "I'd rather not have any more lives lost. No matter whose they are." She started and looked up at Pakhba. She set her face in determination. "My wish is my commandment," she said, invoking the words to command the dragons.

Pakhba nodded gravely. "As you wish."

CHAPTER 32: DESTINY

The end of November left Cass in the autumn dust. Her mind melted the last few weeks of school with catching up was near impossible and she ended with one D and Cs in the rest of her classes. She made herself not touch the Script or her pack of proof that the adventures had happened for two weeks after the semester ended. She moved back in to her parents' house for the holidays, but didn't have the courage to tell them about Deston yet. He kept his distance, which at first made her sad. The more he stayed away, the less she thought about him. He didn't even show up in Connecticut like he'd said he might. They only spoke through text and the occasional video chat.

Cass threw herself into working at Witch's Bones to take her mind off of everything. Everly and Felicity stared at her too much, showing they saw the change in her, but she ignored them. Thankfully, they didn't harass her. The more she ignored people, the more she numbed herself until finally, she had no thoughts going through her head. This is when Vamshi stepped in.

One late Friday night, the old woman who always gave

Cass a hard time came in to the store looking for some obscure statuette of a certain deity. The woman kept changing her story for why she needed it until she finally blurted out, "Where is that bracelet you were wearing earlier this year?"

"What?" Cass asked, having to focus in on a conversation for the first time in weeks. "Oh." She looked down where Pakhba had hung around her wrist. She'd stopped wearing it the moment she got back into Mystic. "I don't wear it anymore," she said flatly.

The woman pressed her purple-lined lips together, raised her penciled in brow, and smirked so hard she smoothed out every wrinkle in her leathery cheek. "So. How much do you want for it?"

Cass blinked blankly at the lady. "It's not for sale."

For the first time, the woman held her tongue. Her lips fell, and she opened and closed her mouth like a fish. Cass realized she'd never been forthright to this woman before. She always caved or ran to Felicity for help.

"Try me?" the woman countered. "Name a price."

She'd had enough. She'd faced monsters, crossed rivers of souls, battled powerful enchanters, and tamed a wild dragon. "Listen, lady," she growled. "It's not for sale. And you see this statue? It's priced as marked. We don't bargain. This isn't a pawnshop. And yeah, I may be a shop girl, but you can't treat me like I'm stupid because I'm younger than you. I know who the Beatles are *and* how to connect to my Wi-Fi on the first try. If you're not going to buy something, leave."

Cass had started to lean forward at the woman, making her back up. She did until she was pressed against a life-size statue of Boudica. The woman quelled.

"Well, I never—" she began.

"I bet you never," Cass shot back. The bell rang, announcing a new customer. Cass looked up to see Vamshi frozen in the door, holding two coffees. "Anything else I can help you with?" she said politely to the lady.

The woman shook her head soundlessly and slipped out, away from Cass. She shoved past Vamshi who exclaimed, raising the coffees over her head to save them. Cass followed the woman, locking the door once she was out. Vamshi moved to the back where Felicity did card readings, calling for Cass to follow her. Cass loved the back. Bejeweled veils hung from the rafters, making it feel like a fortune teller's tent. Oil lamps sat in the middle of the mandala-covered tables and incense permeated the air.

"Sit," Vamshi said, pointing to a chair across the round table from her.

"What's going on?" Cass asked, cautiously sitting down. "Why do you have my pack with you?" She noticed as she sat.

"Because I'm tired of the moping, Cass." Vamshi shoved the coffee at her and slung her pack up onto the table.

"Vam," Cass sighed, "it's almost ten at night. I'm not drinking coffee now. I have to open in the morning."

"You aren't sleeping," Vamshi chirped, pulling out her laptop. She logged in.

"How do you know my password? Never mind," she cut herself off. "What are you doing?"

Vamshi dug in the pack and pulled out the locked box of prints Cass had made from the pictures on her phone before she deleted them. It was also open. Vamshi had a way with any lock, it seemed. Then she took out the bracelet. Making eye contact, Vamshi slowly slid it across the table to Cass.

"Put it on," Vamshi ordered. "I'm not going to soften anything I'm going to say to you, got it?"

"Do you ever?" Cass asked, allowing herself a small smile.

"Okay, then I'm going to be a bitch." She picked up Cass's hand and forced the bracelet on. "I know why you're acting this way."

"Tell me, then."

Vamshi took a drink of the coffee and made the kind of pleasant face that only comes from being burned by the life-giving roast. "You were a big part of something huge. Life changing. You know now that there is more out there than you ever thought. Your little anthropology degree will never scratch the surface. And that bugs you. You've done something great and you can't tell anyone. Yes, I saw you looking at that internship in China. You want to show them these."

Vamshi pulled the pictures out and fanned them out like a tarot deck on the table. "But you know you can't."

Cass glanced at the bracelet, remembering Pakhba's many warnings about keeping everything a secret. Vamshi was right. She was saying what Cass couldn't. She waited for her to go on and lessen the tension in her heart some more.

"Cass," Vamshi said, struggling to find words. "Go. Find the other two dragons. You and I both know that that witch is not going to stop in your lifetime. Something tells me she may have a personal vendetta against you now, too. You're in this thing. And you have to finish it. You can't hide it away, mope around, and ignore that super hot Bavarian piece of ass who is now texting me because he can't get a hold of you."

She looked up, a weird drop of hope falling into the pit of her stomach. "He texted you?"

Vamshi nodded.

"But, Vam, I can't just leave my life. I have a family. My sister. School, work." She shrugged helplessly, a tear coming to her eye. "I can't leave them. This dragon stuff puts them in danger. I'd have to do it alone and I don't know if I could handle that."

"So live a double life," Vamshi said, as if suggesting the easiest thing in the world. "I'm not saying it will be easy. I just know that you're suffering. You don't even see value in the life you did have before. That's what's eating you. You've had a taste of something fantastic and you aren't letting it go."

"I'm trying to!" Cass shouted suddenly. "I put this all away. The bracelet, the Script—everything. To get it out of my line of sight. I finally reached a place inside where I don't care about it."

"Yeah, but you don't care about anything else either," Vamshi added. "And you won't be a lone. He wants to be with you. Why won't you let him?" She held up her phone to show a picture of Deston. In it, he perched at the prow of the *Phantom Ivory*. The wind tossed his shaggy black hair into his deep green eyes. He smiled genuinely, his white teeth glinting in the sun. God, if only he wasn't so cute.

Cass moaned and dropped her face into her hands. "I can't, Vam. I don't know what it means for him to be Source-born. I don't know what it could mean."

"You sound like Pakhba now," Vamshi grumbled. "Let him make his own choices. Just because the stories say he might be an evil wizard someday doesn't mean he is now. Or will ever be! And remember that story you told? About the Vedic and the enchanter who were together? They were stronger together, right?"

Cass nodded. She shut her eyes tight, making the tears fall. She pounded her chest. "It hurts right here, though. I don't even think I love him. How could I? I've not known him long enough. But it feels like heartbreak to push him away."

Vamshi took her hands and gently held them. "You had a choice to follow the Script. Let him have a choice to follow the magic or not. If you do, he'll help you find your back to being Vedic."

Cass forced herself to look into Vamshi's eyes, to watch her expression as she said the next words. "That's not comforting at all. If I think about it, Deston and I have these abilities if we choose to. I did what probably all Vedics before me have done: protected the dragons. Even if Deston was given a choice, he will inevitably choose magic. Right?"

Vamshi tilted her head and her shoulders slumped sadly. "You really think he would? Out of malice? Lust for power, what?"

When she said it, conviction took Cass. "I don't. At least, I hope he wouldn't. But it's innate in him. How can he refuse it?"

"God, Cass, give him the chance!"

Vamshi's raised voice shot Cass through her heart. She took a shuddering breath, looking into Vamshi's dark brown eyes. They glowed in earnest.

"I'll call him," Cass whispered.

Making the decision was all it took. A blanket-like weight lifted from Cass and she was able to hold her head up higher. She felt lighter and even the bags under her eyes disappeared. Mostly. Ella gave her weird looks when she woke up early, made fresh orange juice, and even dropped her phone in shock when Cass woke up before the rest of the family and made them breakfast.

"Have you finally given in to your natural urges and taken a lover, sister?" Ella asked, moving around Cass and her new energy to make toast.

Cass smiled, blushing. If only. Deston hadn't come to Connecticut yet, but had promised to that weekend now that she opened up communication again. Unabashedly, Cass opened her phone and showed Ella a picture of Deston. Ella spit her juice into an orange cloud, coughing.

"Gross," Cass moaned, wiping her phone on her pants. "But, I know, right?"

"Where? How?" Ella stammered. "You're so stupid and nerdy."

"If it makes you feel better," she went on, grabbing butter from the fridge, "I have not followed my natural urges."

"Oh," Ella moaned empathetically. "Because you don't have the drive? Don't worry, sis, it happens to the best of us."

"Shut up!" Cass yelled, punching her sister hard in the arm, which was a mistake.

Ella grabbed her wrist, pulled her through the motion, and pinned her to the counter. "Fencing wasn't enough for me," she hissed. "I took up Tai Kwon Do to release my anxiety."

"How much anxiety do you have?" Cass grunted into the countertop, her arm screaming. "Let me go, Luna Vachon."

Ella released, but not before snatching her phone. "Sorry, it's all in good fun." She zoomed in on Deston's eyes.

"If only everyone else's sister was a combat maniac," Cass moaned, rubbing her shoulder. "You have to teach me that, by the way." It would be useful later. She held her hand out for her phone, but Ella didn't hand it over.

Her little sister went still, gazing deeply into Deston's eyes. "Hey," Cass said, nudging her. "Give."

Ella grudgingly handed over the phone. "I tell you what, Cass," she sighed, going back to her toast. "He's... he's something else. Something about his eyes is... enchanting."

Cass cast a quick glance at Ella. If only she knew how ironic that was to say about him. "For sure. It was so weird, it was like infatuation at first sight with him. Even Vamshi was into him. She was mad how not into him I was at first."

"How *not*?" Ella asked, aghast.

She wasn't sure. He'd been a means to an end at first. But then, being near him had driven her wild. She'd never had those thoughts before. And so quickly. The squirming in her stomach made it all too real. She couldn't get enough of his black hair, ocean-green eyes, his long legs in jeans.

Cass took a deep breath, putting out the fire in her gut and grabbed a smoothie in a to-go bottle. "I'm off to meet him and discuss our spring plans. Don't let mom and dad freak out."

"But I'm going to tell them," Ella quipped back.

Cass didn't mind. They'd probably be too shocked to think Ella was telling the truth. It had been too long since the last one. And that had ended so messily. And it had been the first. Like her, her parents thought she'd never find love again.

Only the magic of all-powerful dragons could make her think twice about a man.

She spied Deston in the window of a bookstore. His head turned down to something he was reading, making his amazing hair swoop in front of his eyes. She waited several minutes, just watching him. Pakhba almost squirmed around her wrist.

"I know you don't like him," Cass mumbled, crossing the street, "but this isn't your choice. This is the Vedic's decision."

So proud now, Pakhba moaned into her head. *Such a Vedic now.*

Cass smiled. "Yep, I know what I want to do. And I'm going to do it."

When she opened the door, Deston looked up. He smiled, making her knees almost buckle. She sat down quickly; her pack thudding to the ground with the weight of the Script.

Her mouth went dry, but she mustered up her newly found courage and said, "I'm glad you actually came."

"Took me a while to get up the nerve to come this far north," he joked. "New England is... not the south."

She giggled and shook her head. "The East Coast is for sure not the Gulf."

He nodded, taking a drink of his tea. "I don't think I've seen a single black-cast grill since Kansas. Do you people even grill?"

She nodded. "We barbecue all the time."

He hissed, wincing at her use of the word. "Just because it's a grill doesn't make it barbecue. We'll fix that, don't worry." He crossed his arms and looked down before saying, "Look, Cass..."

"Wait a minute," she interrupted. She reached across the table and took his hand, watching his face for his reaction. "I don't want to make our friendship anymore complicated than it has to be. Ancient dragon magic be damned. I don't want you to think you have to stay away from me. I also don't want you to think that we're more than we are."

He looked pensive, gem-like eyes showing hesitation. "What are we then? Two enemies, doomed by fate to fight?"

Holding her breath to stop the shaking, she turned his hand over and opened his fingers with hers. She gently ran her finger down his lifeline in his palm. "I think there is deeper magic and history between Vedica and enchanters than we know." She watched the hairs on his arm stand up at her tingly touches. This made her smile. "I think maybe at one time they were not different, but that history has been burned out by the fighting in recent... centuries."

He laughed gently, not taking his eyes off their hands.

"I think keeping us apart will make us weaker," she went on. "I have this feeling inside me. Deep down. I felt it when we fought the giant. Some kind of connection. I don't know if that was the magic or the past of Vedics and enchanters. But it didn't feel bad. But," she said with a sigh, finally closing his fingers into a fist, hers on the outside. She forced herself to meet his eyes. "I also don't want you thinking you have to hang around me because of some magical bond. Because you don't. We met because I was trying to force you to sail me around. You don't have to stay in my life."

But please do, she begged. *I want to do this with you.* She couldn't explain why. It just felt right.

Deston sat back and shoved the book he'd been reading towards her. Frowning, she looked down at it. It was some sort of photography book, filled with full-color pictures from around Asia. It clicked.

"China?" she asked.

Deston nodded. "Cass, I'm a treasure hunter. Adventurer. Hell yeah, I want to do this with you."

Cautious optimism filled her, making her face warm as she smiled.

"But after the holidays," he added. "Christmas is big in the Van Volxem house."

Cass's eyes watered with joy. "I can do that. We'll wait."

"Are you sure?" he asked.

She nodded. "I've done my part for now."

ABOUT THE AUTHOR

K.N. Nguyen is a fantasy author and founder of DragonScript. Growing up, she often found herself immersed in some imaginary world, conquering enemy nations, and saving the day. As time went on, her love for horrible puns and nerd culture pulled her out of these worlds and brought her back to reality.

It wasn't until she started working at her office job that she felt the itch to begin writing. Since 2015, she's been bringing her stories to life, one-by-one, and following her passion by delving into new mythologies.

A native of Sacramento, California, K.N. Nguyen spends her time singing karaoke, playing taiko, enjoying rhythm dancing games, and travelling with her friends and family when she isn't writing.

ALSO BY K.N. NGUYEN

THE FALLEN SERIES

King's Blood

Oath Blood

God's Blood

Nightmare Blood

OTHER BOOKS

A Song of Strength

The Easter Egg Hunt

ANTHOLOGIES K.N. NGUYEN HAS APPEARED IN:

New Beginnings: Science Fiction/Fantasy Anthology by DragonScript

New Adventures: Science Fiction/Fantasy Anthology by DragonScript

Coffins & Dragons by Dragon Soul Press

The Once and Future Kingdom by Irish Horse Productions

Towards the Sun by DragonScript

First Stain by Inked in Grey

Another World by SummerStorm Press

Wicked West by SummerStorm Press